WHEN THE DEVIL IS OWED

Vengeance versus Justice

Chrissie Yates

WandS Books

To Jan,
Thank you for
your support.
Chrissie Yates

ISBN-13: 9781914243110

Cover design by: More Visual

For my husband Nick,
who has always been my super hero
from the moment we met.

PROLOGUE

How it continued...

Carnage.

That's the word many used days, weeks, months, years later.

The school car park now represented a typical war zone, a newsreel filmed in a far distant land.

Smoke billowed from what was left of the burning car, its metal shards now scattered across the burning asphalt.

A cacophony of screams and distress echoed as if on a stereophonic sound system, its volume seemingly at full pelt.

Chaos.

People running in all directions.

Bodies lying unmoving on the ground.

He was now searching for her.

He couldn't see her.

People were shouting words at him, asking him questions he was not able to understand or compute.

Where was she?

Christ, but if anything's happened to her...was all he could think...

CHAPTER 1

Standing alone and unprotected in the local corner shop that was both his pride and joy, Noor Acharya was recognising with growing alarm, that he was in the unwelcome presence of pure psychopathic hatred which had an insatiable need to make him pay for who he was. Nothing he had personally done, but simply because of who he was born, how he looked and the place he chose to pray in. He was now wishing he had taken the protection that had been offered to him but had understandably refused because he hated what the 'protection' stood for and the 'strings' that would be undeniably attached. He'd been warned by the offered 'help' that there was a chance he could be the next target and he was now realising how naïve his refusal of help had been, foolishly arrogant even.

As the first bottle smashed to the floor, followed quickly by the hyena type squeals of those now prepared to do more smashing, Noor had attempted to plea for calm hoping that perhaps decency could possibly make an appearance. "Please, I don't want trouble. Just take what you

want and..."
The strutting young men continued as if he hadn't spoken, emptying packets, throwing food with abandon, smashing eggs, emptying milk. Chuckling now, the shaven haired leader of the pack spat on the floor suggesting to the frightened man, "Why not try to stop us?" before adding, "because you've got no guts have you? Just another fucking Paki low-life and a fucking coward to boot too!"
"Boot eh? Good one," chuckled one of his foot soldiers and Noor knew with dreaded certainty, then that there was no chance of this ending well and was mentally preparing himself for the kicking he knew was coming, hoping he wouldn't be out of action for long. When the shop door buzzer indicated someone else was entering the shop, Noor's heart had plummeted at the sight of his favourite customer, the diminutive Mrs Yara Abrahms, nearly ninety-years young who was stood almost transfixed, as if the scene before her was beyond her comprehension but feeling herself being tugged back to a past she believed had been buried long ago, buried with so many she had loved and lost.
"What on earth is happening? Noor?"
"Get lost Grandma if you know what's good for you," swaggered a particularly acne scarred vandal as he approached the octogenarian who looked at him with something akin to pity before her outrage took over.

In her thick eastern European accent, she replied without fear, "How dare you?! I am not your grandma young man and I thank God for it!"
Turning from Noor, the obvious leader of the pack now turned his attention to the tiny bundle of fury. "So what have we got here then? Another fucking foreigner who has no business being in our country!?"
Noor now no longer afraid for himself, rushed from behind the counter to wedge himself between him and Yara saying, "Mrs Abrahms, don't worry about me, I'll be alright, but you must leave," as he gently tried to move her back to the door and away from any harm, which now seemed like a palpable inevitability, as if it had a life of its own.
"No Noor I won't leave you to this! These ridiculous boys must leave and then we must tell the police!" The gang was now focusing solely on the two figures huddled together, circling them like wolves circling their prey. Noor was now shaking with terror, not for himself but for the frail old lady here beside him, knowing that he would never forgive himself if she were to get hurt.
Looking closely at the clear leader of the wolf-pack Yara saw the tell-tale signs, the shaven skin head, the large boots that could easily kick someone to death and then the obligatory tattoos. She knew instinctively that there would be a swastika on his person, if she was to look

closely enough. "So you think you can make me afraid? You think thugs like you haven't tried to hurt me before?" Shaking her head with a look of profound sadness on her face she continued. "Real Nazis have tried and they failed, not silly little boys who think they are tough men if they shave their heads, have tattoos, wear big boots, destroy food and try to make good men and old women afraid."

Suddenly the sneers and swagger stilled as if all the air had been sucked out of the shop. The vandals now stood and looked, waiting to hear at what their undisputed leader would now command them to do. Noor now braced himself, clenching his fists, preparing himself to take what was to come but knowing he would do what he had to do, would take what was coming, as long as he could protect his aging friend.

The leader of the pack seeing her anger knew, almost instinctively the history within her, making his lip curl with cruelty and complete disdain. "Real Nazis you say? Well they didn't do a good enough job then did they? The ovens should have burned until the very last of you lot were fucking ashes!"

Eyes blazing with fury Yara swung her aging arm only for it to be easily caught, exposing the now faded tattoo on her wrist. Noor now sprung forward pushing Yara's tormentor away from her, wrapping her tightly in his arms, desperate to protect her but knowing with a growing horror and certainty what was to come. And come it did.

*

There were times when Barnsley born Detective Sergeant Eddie Sinclair thought he had seen it all but today this crime scene was now making him think seriously for the first time in over thirty years, about actual retirement. As part of Sheffield Central's Serious and Organised Crime Squad the team had been alerted to the incident that had taken place just off City Road's terraced back streets, a predominantly Asian area that had settled and lived there for generations but were currently experiencing an upsurge in reported incidents of violence which were now being viewed as an escalation of perceived 'hate' crimes.

Donning the required white plastic decontamination suit, Eddie approached the Medical Examiner Mike Gates, who was already processing the prone, still, very dead bodies of Noor Acharya and Yara Abrahms. Looking up, Mike shook his head saying, "Bloody hell Eddie, but for Christ's sake! How bloody senseless is this?!"

"Aye, you're not wrong Mike lad. So cause of death as if I can't guess?"

"Blunt force trauma. From the marks forming I would suggest by a series of kicks by heavy boots to the head and torso. They were bloody kicked to death by several boots." He then reached for

Yara's arm and indicated the faded tattoo that could still identify the number she had been given as a child when the monsters of the past had taken her prisoner, killing all she loved, nearly eighty years earlier. "To have survived that then to die like this is just..." lost for words, unable to finish, Eddie merely nodded, squeezing the ME's shoulder as he turned to greet his colleague Detective Constable Isiah Hanson. "Bad business but no one saw anything or at least aren't telling us if they did."

Sighing Eddie ordered, "Someone will know or have seen something so house to house ok?"

The crowd outside the police taped premises was now growing and the questions hurled at the police presence becoming more and more vociferous and angry. Pushing through the growing crowd, a police officer, clearly off duty came rushing through the police cordoned tape. "Whoa sonny! Where do you think you're going?" this from Eddie.

"My cousin! What's happened to him?"

"And you are?"

"Police Constable Asif Khan Sir. I've just heard over the radio. Is Noor ok? Has he been hurt?"

"May I ask what your relationship is with Mr Acharya?"

"He's my cousin Sarge but we're more like brothers." Now looking scared, Asif swallowed hard saying, "What aren't you telling me?" Shaking his head Eddie just looked at the young officer and the look told it all. Staring into Eddie's eyes, as if willing him to say something he could begin to make sense of, Asif now looked towards the shop entrance. "I need to see him."

"For a start you're not suited up and you know better than to contaminate a crime scene," then more gently adding, "and it isn't pretty lad and I'm not sure it will do you any good."

Just then, both turned to see the stretcher containing the covered body, now being taken to a place where more strangers would examine and pry in order to make sense of the senseless.

"Thanks but I need to see him. I need to see for myself," as he pushed past his superior officer who now allowed him to go unimpeded.

Acknowledging a silent signal from Eddie, the Forensic team lowered the stretcher allowing Asif to kneel beside it as he unzipped the plastic coverall which contained his blood relative.

Following him Eddie and Isiah stood at a respectful distance as Asif looked at what was left of his cousin's face. Lifting him up by his shoulders Eddie eased him away from the remains of his cousin, walking him to a quiet corner as Asif struggled to compose himself.

"I'm right sorry for your loss lad. Terrible business, but we're going to catch the animals that did this, on that you can be certain." Asif turned his face towards Eddie, a man he knew by sight, a man he had tremendous respect for. With eyes burning with shock, grief and unshed tears he nodded before informing Eddie of a fact he had yet to learn but which would fill him with real fear and concern. "They will be caught Sarge but not by us unless they're very lucky."

"What are you talking about?"

"Noor and I were brought up together to protect Noor from his father, to stop him becoming like him. It was his mother's dying wish".

Swallowing hard, Eddie asked, "Who are we talking about?"

Closing his eyes and sighing heavily, "Who do you think? Who would be the last family in this city you'd want to cross?"

CHAPTER 2

"I wanted to be transferred here Sir because I want to learn from the best and after your personal take down of Sheldon well… it's become the stuff of legends even over the Pennines in Manchester." Max was carefully scrutinising the newly transferred Detective Constable Richard Braxton as he sat opposite him, taking in the carefully coiffed, expensively cut, blonde streaked hair, the lean physique that clearly had a daily gym workout and the immaculate clothes, including very shiny shoes. He was a handsome chap alright in that Jack Grealish sort of way and absolutely knew it, giving him that air of confidence that only the truly pretty have.
"So it was your idea to transfer here from Belle Vue then?"
Seeing the young officer's confident smile now begin to slip slightly, Max pressed on. "Let me make this clear DC Braxton. Your transfer here is due to a personal favour I have done for your Area Commander who seems to think you are worth giving another chance to. I personally have no time for any officer who cuts corners

then tries to blame another for it." He allowed his words to hang in the air before he continued, "There is no defence for the inappropriate collection of key evidence that ultimately leads to a clear cut conviction not being upheld. It means victims go without justice and criminals are allowed to reoffend and produce more victims. This has happened more than once, right?" As the young officer nodded, not meeting his superior officer's eyes but instead looking at the floor with a very red face.

"We run a very tight ship here, so be warned. This is your last chance. Do you understand?"

As Richard Braxton nodded his assent, Max reached for his internal phone then spoke into its handset, "Dan, my office please. Thanks."

Both men sat in silence with Richard being the only one feeling uncomfortable, as Max was actually enjoying the young officer's discomfort. He hated those who cut corners, but more than that, hated the ones who had a 'teflon' approach to the job, passing blame, making sure that mistakes made did not 'stick' to them. Dan now appeared at Max's door much to Richard's relief.

"Dan this is..."

"Richard Braxton. Not seen your ugly mug since Hendon."

Glad to see a friendly face Richard stood up to shake the hand Dan now offered. "Been a while mate. How you've been?"

"Great, couldn't be better thanks."

"Ah, well its good you two know each other. Dan, Richard is joining the team and I'd like you to show him around and help him settle in."

Nodding Dan replied. "No problem Sir." As both men left the office, Max called Dan back quietly saying, "And Dan? Watch him okay?"

Dan smiled knowingly, "Absolutely Sir."

Being practically tied to a desk was not Max Stainmore's idea of being a police officer albeit the newly appointed Detective Chief Superintendent in charge of Sheffield's Serious & Organised Crimes Division but he had only been allowed to return to the job he loved on certain conditions, the main one being... practically tied to a desk.

Recovering as he had from two gunshot wounds had been nothing short of miraculous but it had been a long process. It had happened nearly two years ago in the picturesque market town of Penton. The shots had come from out of nowhere and still the perpetrator had yet to be caught, no clues to be found so obviously a professional hit. Max knew he had made many enemies because he was very good at catching very bad people and now he had the bullet hole scars to prove it.

He was now looking out onto the open-planned bustle that was Sheffield's Serious and Organised Crime Division and was suddenly nostalgic for the 'good old days' when Police Stations were cold damp places, with poor heating, permanent clouds of cigarette smoke and even worse ventilation. He was remembering his first station in London's Upper Norwood region, with its peeling paint and ancient plumbing combined with that distinct odour of despair that seemed to permeate every nook and cranny. All this glass and shiny stainless steel which were constantly being cleaned, were making him positively homesick.

The plushness of the new build however, did not mitigate what the officers he was observing were involved in. He knew with a fatigued kind of certainty what each desk was currently dealing with, each desk being almost a microcosm of life's worse kind of human behaviour. Actions generally driven by greed, perpetrated by someone onto someone else, destroying individuals, often whole families and always tiny pieces of the victims and perpetrators' souls in equal measure. It was enough to make a person almost give up on humanity, almost. There was still enough good in the world to get up for and he reminded himself and his teams of that often.

Looking towards his opened door, Max now saw a very grim faced Eddie enter his office. "So... how bad is it?"

"They don't come much worse. A young Asian shopkeeper, well liked and respected from all accounts and a very old lady, a holocaust survivor from the looks of it who was in the wrong place at the wrong time. We're trying to contact her family that is if she has any and some poor lass has become a widow way before her time."

"Cause of death?"

"Blunt force trauma. Kicked to death in real terms."

"Jesus," muttered Max.

"There was no God of any description there today Chief, just pure unadulterated senseless brutality!" Eddie was now slumped in the chair, shaking his head with a look on his face Max had never seen before. Looking up he added, "There are times when I think I'm just getting too old to deal with this sort of lunacy. I mean where does this kind of hate come from?"

Nodding his understanding Max rose from his seat and said, "Right assemble all teams in the Major Incident Room, we need to nip this in the bud fast!"

Shaking his head Eddie replied, "May be already too late because Noor Acharya was connected, albeit reluctantly.

*

Entering the Major Incident Room of the Serious and Organised Crime Division, Max was greeted by nods and smiles of all assembled there. Deployed by the National Crime Agency to pursue hardened criminal Cameron Sheldon, he had arrived in Sheffield two years earlier like the proverbial whirlwind. Sheldon had previously avoided incarceration, despite being the perpetrator of an array of criminal activities, including murder, human & drug trafficking as well as money-laundering. His grisly demise had put an end to countless misery but Max had paid a heavy price too and in more ways than one, was still paying. He had also been the catalyst that had not only destroyed Sheldon's criminal empire but had wheedled out Sheffield police corruption at the highest level. For this alone, he had gained immense respect and loyalty from all who worked with him but particularly the core of his team who had worked with him from his arrival and the ones he now subtly acknowledged as he walked to the front of the room, namely Detectives Lydia Smith, Dan Devon, Beth Fairchild and Isiah Hanson.

Nodding to the assembled detectives Max began as he stood before the Major Incident Board which already displayed the photographs of Noor Acharya and Yara Abrahms.

"Ok! This is a bad one, make no mistake. Recently there have been a number of attacks on various premises within the city's Asian community, so far seven, but this is the first that has resulted in two fatalities," as he pointed to the board. "More than that, if that hadn't been enough, Noor Acharya's death could cause us even more problems." He now nodded to the uniformed officer who had discreetly entered the room. "Constable Khan, would you join me? That is if you feel up to it?"

Asif nodded then threaded his way past the

desks, placing his hand on the shoulder of his former partner Beth Fairchild as he passed her to join Max at the front, before nervously facing the room. "Over to you Constable."

"Noor Acharya is the estranged son of Omar Mirza, the main Asian Organised Crime Warlord in this area. Noor refused to be part of his father's criminal activities from a young age but that won't mean that Mirza won't exact revenge. He will denounce it as a direct challenge to his authority so will do everything he can to find the perps and he won't care who gets in his way."

"How do you know this?" asked Beth who was clearly taken aback by Asif's obvious authority on the subject.

Smiling sadly at his former partner but still good friend he replied, "Noor and I were brought up together after his mother's death. We're first cousins and yes I'm unfortunately part of Omar Mirza's bloodline too although I wish to God I wasn't. My mother is his estranged sister and Noor took his mother's name so no one connected him to that side of the family."

"Bloody hell mate, but you kept that quiet."

"Well it's not something you advertise in our line of work mate and I've been considered dead by him and his head case son Mohammed from the day I put on this uniform." Max moved over to where Asif stood and put his hand on his shoulder saying, "Thanks Asif. We may need your input on this case so I've requested you be transferred to the team, okay?"

"Anything I can do sir."

"And also on behalf of us all here Asif, we're very sorry for your loss."

Max now looked at the assembled men and women before him as he now solemnly pointed to the first picture. "This is Yara Abrahms who was eighty-nine years old. Her body was found in the arms of Noor and we can only surmise he was trying to shield her from the animals who did this to them." The Interactive Whiteboard came alive behind him as he pressed the remote to show the team a blown up image of the faded tattoo that was found on Yara's wrist. "Yes people this is what you think. She was a Holocaust survivor." Those last two words had the effect Max had anticipated. Silence, the shaking of heads and a profound sadness that a life which had already survived such horror, had ended so violently was now permeating the room.

At this point Asif interrupted Max, "Sir if I may? Noor and I met Yara years ago when we were kids. She lived round corner from us and one day we saw her struggling to move a garden bench so we went to give a hand like. I remember her insisting on giving us biscuits and lemonade for helping and that's when we first saw the tattoo. We asked her straight out about it, thinking she must be a really cool old girl to have a tattoo," this now bringing a ripple of smiles from the others listening intently. "She told us she came from a little village called Opusztaser in Hungary. I remember how Noor and I found the name of the place hilarious but how we both always remembered it." Asif's voice broke slightly at this point, taking a moment to compose himself before continuing, "We became regular visitors for years, helping her when we could, listening to her stories. She told us how the Nazis came for her and her family late 1944. They'd manage to avoid deportation for years as they were hidden by many non- Jewish families but eventually they were found and sent to Auschwitz where she was tattooed. She was only eleven years old and the only member of her immediate family to survive, which included her twin sister." Sighing heavily, he added, "She deserved to die peacefully, not like this."

Nodding Max now looked at the collective faces of the professionals gathered and he saw sadness and dismay but also for some a disgusted determination to do their upmost to bring those responsible to justice. But not all and this made him uneasy.

"We need to know where to start looking because someone will know so we go back to the other six premises that have been attacked and as reluctant as they may be to help us, you must try to get any snippet of information possible. Retrieve any wiped CCTV and bring it in for the techs to look at but we need to know where to start. CHIS's the lot. Ok? I'll be taking the lead on this one and whilst I want everyone on the lookout for any information I'm aware you all have large case- loads too. So Lydia, Isiah, Beth and Eddie, will work closely with me on this so you may have to off load anything imminent. Right, get to it people."

Asif had more to say at this point. "Sir there is something else I really need to say, so with your permission...?"

Nodding Max gestured for Asif to continue. "I love being a copper and I believe I work with the best people, made some friends for life," as he nodded to Beth who was now sitting forward, hanging onto his every word. "But it's taken a while hasn't it? I mean it's not that long ago when I kept finding bacon stuffed inside my locker and the 'Paki' jokes eh? I had to find them funny or I couldn't take a joke. There's still not enough coppers who look like me on the force..."

"Or me mate," interrupted Detective Isaiah Hanson, "but in my case it was bananas. I mean you'd think the idiots would try to be a bit more imaginative wouldn't you?"

This brought about smiles and chuckles, a warranted relief from the tension now evident in the room. Max scanned the faces and saw anger, some shame faced but also from some, a defiance and it was this that worried him. So his next words brokered no argument but made his position and the position of the investigation, crystal clear. "There has never ever been room

for this sort of racist crap in the police or anywhere else so if anyone here needs to
excuse themselves from this investigation make sure you see me before I need to see you. Now let's get out there and find the scum, because make no mistake, that's what they are and before they hurt anyone else."

"I may have something of interest boss?" this again from Beth Fairchild who was now being subtly nudged by her partner Lydia Smith who was also discreetly shaking her head. Ignoring her Beth continued. "The Head of Grove South, my good friend Imogen Holt, who has just returned from an extended sabbatical, is having problems with racist literature being found on premises and fights between various gangs within the school breaking out. She's found weapons such as knives on school's premises too so I think a visit to her in school by someone on the team with rank could be helpful Sir."

Eddie was now openly grinning, with Dan and Isiah trying really hard not to as they all avoided looking a Max who was now looking very stony faced at an innocent looking 'butter wouldn't melt' Beth before eventually saying, "Thank you Detective Constable Fairchild, I shall bear that in mind. Right everyone, get to it."

Walking back to their designated desks Lydia looked at her partner with raised eyebrows. "You really know how to sail close to the wind. I actually was in fear for your life there for a few seconds!"

"Sometimes people need a push in the right direction for their own good," replied Beth smiling smugly.

"If Imogen decides to kill you and bury your body on the Trans Pennine Trail, don't expect me to come and dig you up. Ok?"

"Sometimes my mate Imogen doesn't know what's good for her and Max Stainmore is." Shaking her head Lydia turned towards the screen on her desk, leaving Beth with her thoughts and to be honest, her fears.

Beth and Imogen, along with their friends Sarah and Harriet, aka Harry, had been joined at the hip since they had been five years sold. They had been through so much together, including the murder of Sarah's husband Grant Downs, a violent, vicious gangster who had physically and emotionally abused their friend until he was found stabbed to death two years earlier. Closing her eyes, Beth was momentarily taken back to that awful time when her own sanity and actions had been questionable, remembering how close she had come to losing everyone and everything she loved. Getting Max and Imogen back together was the least she could do.

Her thoughts from the past were interrupted as Dan came over to introduce the new addition to the squad room. Beth recognised his type before he opened his mouth.

"Lydia, Beth, this is Richard Braxton who is

joining us from Manchester. Richard, this is my fiancé Lydia."

"Fiancé? Congratulations, just a pity I didn't get to meet you first."

Rolling his eyes Dan moved on to Isiah, Dan's partner and best friend, "Isiah, Richard," as both men shook hands, "and this here is Lydia's partner Beth Fairchild."

Richard took one look at the blonde Amazonian that epitomised Beth and automatically began his charm offensive, "Well, very pleased to meet you Beth," as he held onto her hand just that bit longer than necessary, making sure that their eye contact suggested from him that he was very impressed with what he was seeing with a clear intent on getting to know her better.

Smiling Isiah said, "Oh good timing. Hey Brad," as he gestured to the uniformed officer who had just walked onto their floor, "over here. A new addition to the team."

Sergeant Brad Fairchild, a huge 'bear' of a man walked over to greet the new member of the squad who had to look up considerably to make eye contact. Brad extended his hand saying, "Brad Fairchild, pleased to meet you."

Richard looked from Brad to Beth who just smiled knowingly back as her husband turned to her saying, "I may be late clocking off love, so can you rescue the oldies from our Terror Tot later?"

Beth nodded as her internal phone on her desk rang. As she spoke into the receiver saying,

“Right Sir, straight away. Looks like the Chief wants to have a word.” Lydia shook her head throwing her a look which conveyed “I told you so!”

Isiah grinned saying, “You do love living on the edge Beth.”

“What has she been up to now?” grimaced Brad.

“Just passing on intel husband of mine.”

“Yeah right,” he replied, as he waved his goodbyes leaving Beth to whatever scrape she had got herself into.

Walking into Max’s office with its glass walls, separating it from the open planned spaces of the rest of the unit, Beth stood almost to attention as she faced her superior officer. Max looked at Beth then surprised her by saying, “What the bloody hell was that about?”

Sighing heavily Beth opted for honesty asking, “May I speak frankly Sir? Perhaps without our respective ranks for this conversation?”

As Max nodded he also indicated for Beth to sit as she began, “She’s back now from...”

“I know where she’s been.”

“You knew? So why didn’t you go and get her? I mean you came back from London for her! Whitby is hardly the other side of the planet!”

“Only the fact that she changed her phone so that none of you, not even her mother knew where she was for a while or could contact her and the Trust wouldn’t give out the information, making me feel like a bloody stalker and ...”

"And what?"
"Perhaps some things need to be left alone."
Sitting back in her chair Beth, clearly surprised, remarked, "Well I didn't see that coming?"
"What?"
"You could have brought her back and didn't bother?"
"I had been shot... twice!"
"Are you blaming Imogen for that?"
"Course not!"
"So why...?" then pausing continued, "oh I get it. You're basically scared! Scared that she'd keep turning you down. Well I really gave you more credit!"
Narrowing his eyes Max's voice was now ominously quiet, "Watch yourself Constable!"
"Oh back to ranks now are we? Always a sign that the argument is lost isn't it Sir?" the emphasis on 'Sir' now dripping with sarcasm. "So if that's all Sir and if you clearly can't see sense, then I'd like to continue trying to nail a few racist killers if it's all the same to you? But before I do, tell me honestly one thing. Why are you still here in Sheffield? Why are you not back in London and the NCA?"
Looking defeated, Max merely shrugged and avoided answering the question. "So anything else Detective Constable?"
"No Sir," as Beth angrily stomped out of his office, shaking her head in disgust as she went.
Looking at her partner's face Lydia asked, "No

progress then?"
Shaking her head Beth muttered, "Sometimes I despair!" Then changing the subject, "What do you think of the 'newbie' then?"
"Fancies himself nearly as much as he fancies you," was her friend's pointed reply adding, "just love the effect Brad has on those who cast an interested glance your way."
"Oh yes, my 'bear' is one of a kind and thankfully he's all mine," smiled Beth, remembering again how close she had been to losing him too.

CHAPTER 3

"Suicide? Are they sure there's no other explanation?" Imogen, sitting across from her distraught colleague, was trying to make sense of what she was hearing.

"His brother found him in the garden shed. There was an empty bottle of vodka and... and ..." unable to continue Janet Downing appeared to implode with grief. Imogen now held the sobbing woman, gently stroking her back as she cried the tears of the broken hearted. Janet Downing had worked for over thirty years with children who had Special Needs and was well loved and respected within the school and its wider community, having never taught anywhere else but Grove South. Now Assistant Head for Safeguarding and Raising Aspiration she was at the forefront, daily supporting struggling pupils and their families. Pulling herself together, Janet now extricated herself from Imogen's embrace continuing, "My apologies Imogen..."

"Nothing to apologise for Janet but I need to know the full facts."

"Of course." Breathing deeply, she began. "It would appear Ollie had gone out to his den, a shed at the bottom of the garden, where he would spend hours or so I'm told. He'd been gone some time but again, according to his mum that was nothing out of the ordinary. When his brother got in from work he went to find him only to discover... he found him..."

"Go on."

"He had stabbed himself with the bread knife... through his stomach."

"Oh my God," gasped Imogen, "that's...oh my God".

Nodding at Imogen's horror Janet continued, "The police found an empty vodka bottle and a book from the school library on the Japanese Samurai and the ritual of 'hara-kiri', which is suicide by self- disembowelment on a sword." Imogen was now completely stunned, looking at her colleague with bewildered horror. After minutes of both women digesting what had happened Imogen was the first to speak. "We need to keep as many details as possible from the rest of the school population although it will only be a matter of time before it gets out. I'll access the Grief Councillors who will need to work closely with Ollie's small group of peers before anything else and I'll go to see his mother today to see what the family need but bloody hell, what could have possessed him? Were there any signs that his mental health was so bad?"

"He was very upset when his friend Samuel passed, I mean that's been bad enough for the school to deal with but now this..." as Janet's tears began again.

"Okay Janet, you need to go home, no," as Janet began to protest, "you're not in any fit state to be here so I'm officially sending you home and I don't want to see you back until you can be of use to me Janet because you clearly aren't at the moment if I'm being brutally honest." Janet nodded her understanding as she stood up to leave. "I can't believe it. That poor boy, his poor mum."

"I know, now go and get some rest."

"I should have seen it coming, should have done more to stop him..."

"Stop it. If you could have you would have, now go home." Smiling sadly Janet walked with Imogen to her office door, where they embraced before Janet left, leaving Imogen sagging at the closed door, still in shock at what she had just learnt about poor little Ollie Manderson, a sweet boy whose Asperger condition had made it impossible for him to function in the mainstream.

Moving to the window which overlooked the school fields and paved social areas, she now looked down on the melee of young people as they were going about their daily school lives. She saw the shoving and pushing, the laughter and banter, the tears and the arguments, all the norms of school life. She was now also seeing tiny, individual worlds each child represented. What did each one fear? Who was feeling despair, even hopelessness? It felt like only yesterday when she and her 'three closer than most sisters' friends were sitting on Penton Grammar's school field. The laughs, the tears, the hopes and fears all shared as they huddled together, shutting everyone else out and if you hurt one, then you had all four to contend with, a fact that was as true now as it was then. They had endured and despite the events during Covid, were still loyal, still closely bound together even more now because sometimes secrets have to be kept; sometimes love requiring not doing everything that is perceived as 'right'.

Imogen's desk telephone interrupted her thoughts. "There's a Detective Chief Superintendent Stainmore wanting to see you Ms Holt," said the clear tones of Imogen's PA Agnes Mane. Completely stunned Imogen found herself just looking at the device which was informing her that the one person she wanted to avoid most in the world was asking to see her. "Ms Holt? Apparently it's urgent police business that can't wait." Hearing the concern in Agnes' voice, Imogen now pulled herself together saying, "Well then you'd better show him in." Imogen smoothed down her dress and stood facing her door whilst staying barricaded behind her desk. The longest seconds passed as the door opened and Max was ushered in by Agnes Mane who was smiling broadly, enquiring how he'd like his coffee. "That's very kind. Strong and black please, if it's no trouble."

"Oh not at all," simpered the normally very composed to the point of stern Agnes, whom Imogen actually thought was now fluttering her eyelashes at the tall handsome man that epitomised Detective Superintendent Max Stainmore, a man who turned heads wherever he went. Smiling at her departure Max was now looking directly at Imogen who now found herself needing to sit down. Pointing to a chair across her desk, she said, "Please take a seat Chief Superintendent."

Smiling wryly as he crossed the room, his eyes never leaving her face, Max replied, "Really? Formality? After all the times we've shared bodily fluids we're back to using titles?"

Imogen remained silent, with only the tell-tale signs of an embarrassed flush creeping up her neck that would give a clue how his words had affected her. The awkward silence was interrupted by Agnes and the coffee which Imogen was grateful for. "Thanks Agnes and hold any calls until the Chief Superintendent leaves please." Nodding Agnes moved to leave but not before beaming her smile in Max's direction once again which Max politely returned.

Alone again, Max now no longer smiling began

with, “Sorry, that was way out of order”.
Imogen’s smile was sad as she replied, “Certainly an ice- breaker, that’s for sure,” then added, “but it is good to see you looking so well after what you’ve been through.”
“Not going to pretend it hasn’t been tough but I’m doing okay.”
Nodding her understanding Imogen opted for professionalism, hoping to get this encounter over as soon as painlessly possible. “So what is it you think I can be of help with?” Max didn’t respond but looked at her with those ice blue probing eyes as if trying to read her mind. Ignoring her question Max instead asked, “So are you happy to be back or missing the sea air?” Acknowledging her look of surprise, he now added, “I know where you’ve been all this time.”
Registering the sub text that he could have tracked her down if he had chosen to do so and trying to ignore the unexpected stab of hurt that he hadn’t tried, Imogen merely shrugged saying, “Well you are an exceptionally gifted detective aren’t you. So how can I assist you?”
“Before I get to that there’s something I need to get off my chest, have needed to for a while.” Imogen now waited for what she knew would be coming.
“How come you stayed by my bedside for the five straight days and nights I was in a medically induced coma, despite the medics trying to insist you leave? Then when told I was going to actually

live, you decide to take a job, miles away from all you know and care about. Explain?"

Shaking her head Imogen now looked for words that would explain without revealing her truth. "Once you were out of danger I felt it better we stayed apart for all the same reasons you left. Those reasons are still there and will never not be."

"Perhaps the reasons I came back outweighed the reasons I left? Perhaps I've come to believe the future is not the past!"

"The past and the present aren't as neatly divided as we'd like them to be Max and for some of us, the past is a dangerous place." A silence of unspoken pain was now evident only broken when Imogen asked, "So may I ask again, what the 'urgent police business' is?"

Looking stonily at her he said, "Detective Constable Fairchild alerted the squad that you may have information that is linked to an ongoing investigation."

Narrowing her eyes Imogen merely nodded and Max found himself actually feeling sorry for Beth when next in Imogen's orbit not needing to be a 'fly on the wall' when that conversation happened. "I'm told racist literature has been found in school and also weapons?"

Reaching into her desk drawer Imogen withdrew a sheaf of papers, handing them over explaining, "These were found in the lockers of the Cowden boys, Paul and Joe, who I believe have been the main instigators of a series of fights that have occurred between groups of pupils, namely white kids against Asian ones. Found this rubbish littered around school and traced it back to them." Max looked at the A5 sheet, reading its far right view of the world and what needed to be done to ensure the survival of the 'white race'. Shaking his head Max, now all police business, asked, "Wow, this is pretty hard core stuff. Would they have the means to produce this alone?"

"No and it's not just here either. I was at a Head's meeting earlier today and it's in nearly every secondary school in the city. Real racial tension too, between groups of children that have lived and played happily together since they were toddlers. Something or someone is creating some serious mischief and I'm scared where it's going Max. Behaviour has never been so bad and my exclusions are going through the roof. I'm worried they may trigger an early Ofsted visit and I'm not alone in this either."

Nodding his understanding Max added, "You've heard what happened yesterday?"

"The awful murders just off City Road?" Max nodded, "and you think this could all be connected?"

Shrugging Max replied, "I don't know as yet but a good start will be interviewing these boys. Where will I find them?"

"I've had no choice but to suspend them and to be honest it will most likely lead to permanent exclusions despite this being their exams year. We have zero policy on racist behaviour and carrying weapons here so I suspect they'll be at their home, but I warn you, the father is a particularly difficult man to deal with."

Max now flashed his most unnerving smile, nailing her with 'the look', the one guaranteed to make her heart beat faster saying, "Used to dealing with difficult individuals, I mean I managed to deal with you… eventually. Did you actually lodge any of those Official complaints you threatened me with?"

"I remember you worked on being charming so no I didn't," as she now tried not to smile, feeling his pull and again found herself wishing, if only.

Just then there was a loud knock on the door followed by Agnes Mane popping her head round saying, "So sorry Ms Holt but we have a situation in Reception. George Cowden is there screaming blue murder. We've sent for the SSO who tells us he's on his way."

Max and Imogen both rose from their seats and made their way towards the large Mezzanine Reception area just across from Imogen's office where in all of his beer bellied glory was the belligerent form of George Cowden. "Where is she then? Where is that glorified, stuck up pencil-pusher who thinks she can treat my sons like they're shit on the bottom of her fucking shoes?"

"Mr Cowden." George Cowden swung round

and nailed Imogen with a look of total fury, marching towards her whilst pointing his finger at her, shouting, “You have some fucking nerve! How fucking dare you?!” Max at this point moved Imogen behind him standing squarely in front of the oncoming man who abruptly stopped just short of his target shouting, “Get out of my way before I cave your fucking head in!”

“I’d really like to see you try!” Unlike the man confronting him Max delivered these words calmly, without raising his voice but with real menace which stopped Cowden abruptly in his tracks. At this point they were joined by SSO Constable Rob Tyler who came upon the scene of two men squaring up to each other on school premises. “Ok you two, that’s enough.” At this point, Max flashed open his warrant card, which Constable Tyler read, gulped and said, "Wow," then, “sorry Sir, didn’t recognise you.”

Looking confused Cowden blustered, “Recognise who?”

Max acted as if he hadn’t spoken but merely said, “No problem Constable. Are you doing the honours or shall I?”

“What honours? What’s happening?”

“I’ll tell you what’s happening. George Cowden, I am arresting you for Disturbing the Peace and for threatening behaviour in a public place. You do not have to…”

“You can’t do that!”

“Just watch me. Constable?” The star struck

young constable now roughly handcuffed the reason he had been sent for and continued saying the obligatory words, "You do not have to say anything. But it may harm your defence if you do not mention..." as he escorted the now shocked to the core lump of belligerence that was George Cowden, to the waiting police squad car.

Turning to Imogen Max looked at her with worried concern asking, "And what would have happened if I hadn't been here?"

"I deal with Mr Cowden and many like him on a daily basis and they're really mostly all talk and you know I don't scare easily," shaking her head, "but thank you. It won't have done him or any of that lot any harm seeing what can happen to threatening bullies," indicating the gallery of young people who had gathered on the balconies above, all with their phones, all filming the incident. Nodding, Max turned to leave as Imogen touching his arm whispered,

"Stay safe Max."

Looking at her Max felt he had never wanted to hold her more but instead he curtly nodded and walked away.

Watching his retreating back Imogen was joined by a sighing Agnes Mane. "If only I was a few decades younger." Imogen merely smiled and reminded herself again why she couldn't have him back in her life.

CHAPTER 4

Looking at the men gathered, Gareth Jackson saw the 'cannon fodder' required when waging 'a war'. What was really exciting him though was the potential he saw in the young man, barely out of his twenties sitting at the front, instinctively knowing he had just what he was looking for. He could see the lack of empathy in his eyes, the permanent arrogant sneer, the disdainful slouch of his body language, the hard to impress veneer. Here was a man whose need to be a 'someone' would enhance his already evident psychopathy that was required if they were to win 'the war' but more importantly, to make him very rich.

"Good to meet you all finally and to thank you for the solid work you've already begun," referencing the 'hate' crime attacks on the Asian community and the distribution of the far right literature that was causing so much trouble in the city's schools. "But let's applaud with all we have for what our brother here has achieved," as Gareth now pointed to Brandon Cowden, urging him to stand to accept the plaudits now being offered. "Without hesitation he showed what the sub-humans amongst us can expect from now on. No mercy!" as the cheers, and stomping of their feet rang out from those assembled in the small back room of the public house in the city centre, whose landlord shared their views and thoughts.

No one was openly saying that Brandon and his team were responsible for the recent murders on City Road. However, hushed whispers and furtive glances were abundant and the young psychopath was treated with awed respect and unease in equal measure. No one there would risk getting on the wrong side of him, that was a given.

Flushed with pride and pleasure Brandon faced his audience and as Gareth suspected, loved being singled out, loved the positive affirmation and would want it again and again. "And make no mistake my brothers," continued Gareth, "this is only the start of things to come. This country belongs to us and we're here to take it back! Back from those multicultural, diversity obsessed bleeding hearts that run our councils, our schools, our hospitals allowing the Jews, the Pakis, the blacks free run of our institutions, re-writing our white history and abusing our women! Their time is now no more. Our time is the future!" Looking at the rapture on the faces of those he was addressing, whilst loud applause was ringing in his ears, Gareth Jackson could only reflect how easy it was to manipulate a mob. All you needed were words that an audience wanted to hear.

Later that evening Gareth took Brandon to one side and began his offensive. "You have a very bright future with us Brandon, I hope you know this. Wallace told me you were special, but we didn't know how special."

Still preening Brandon Cowden puffed out his chest, saying, "I only did what any decent white man should do when taking back what rightly belongs to us. I'm just grateful I met Wallace when I did, worth being nicked for and spending time inside to just be in his presence." Wallace Senior being the former leader of Sheffield's White Supremacists group until convicted of murder over a decade earlier. Whilst in Armley Prison Leeds, he systematically sought out and radicalised the lost young men who had been failed by everyone and everything from birth, being easy pickings to pursue his white supremacist agenda on his behalf when released. Brandon Cowden was an excellent case in point.

"Wallace told me you had what it takes and you've shown this already but there's so much to be done and we need the funds to do it with too. Weapons aren't cheap or is getting our message out either." Gareth paused at this point then leaning more closely continued with, "I'm told your dad is a small time drug dealer."

Bristling at the term 'small time' Brandon

replied, "What of it?"
"It sounds to me like he's missing a trick that's all. I mean, you do know who controls most of the drugs in this city don't you?" Seeing Brandon's non response he ploughed on, "the Mirza family. The fucking Pakis! I mean how fucking dare they sell our drugs?"
"That's not right."
"No son it isn't. I think perhaps your dad, with our help should develop his business interests further, what do you think? Give you and your family the life-style you deserve whilst allowing our cause to have the funds it needs and send those towel heads back to where they belong, in the bloody gutter! What do you say?"
Nodding his assent, Brandon replied, "When do we start?" Smiling Gareth leaned back thinking to himself, "Job done Gareth, job well done indeed."

*

Brandon and his crew were high on the adrenalin of the meeting. They had all met in prison, watched each other's backs and had made plans for when they were released which as luck would have it was within days and weeks of each other. They consisted of the much older Brandon, Mark Frith, Luke Eden, Finn Raithes and Carl Smith with Brandon as their undisputed leader, the brains, the decision maker which up to this point in their association they were all happy to go along with. Brandon had watched their backs, protected them whilst in prison and now enjoyed their blind obedience. Now walking back to their respective homes the young men were keen to know what Brandon had planned next.

"I've got something epic planned and this city won't know what's hit it," Brandon was stating proudly adding, "no one will dare treat us like scum again. In fact, just let anyone fucking try! We begin our planning tomorrow, got it! Bright and early."

"But they don't know for certain it was us on City Road do they?" asked Finn who was obviously worried but trying hard not to show it.

Narrowing his eyes, Brandon turned to his friend. "They know although they don't know for sure. Only us five do. You're not scared are you?"

Swallowing the lump of fear that was forming Finn was now shaking his head saying," Going down for murder won't be like the last time we were all banged up that's all."

"Not going to happen! As long as we all keep schtum! Including you!" The menace and threat were evident, all laughter now gone as the four now looked at the one.

"I wain't say owt. Why would I? I'm in it with you it's just... I don't like the thought of others knowing that's all. That's how the cops will find out."

"You're worrying too much mate, always have," said Mark. "Come on, let's get you home and back to your Nan."

Now laughing the young men carried on their journey going their separate ways as they approached the City Road intersection. Mark now turned to Finn. "You alright mate?"

Shaking his head Finn now struggled to find the words. "I didn't expect the other day to go that far. I mean I wanted to give the Paki a good kicking but… as for that old woman? She looked just like… my Nan." Shaking his head, his shoulders hunched, Finn now seemed lost in his own thoughts.

"Promise me you'll never let Brandon hear you talk like this. You know what he'll do don't you," Mark now visibly afraid for his friend adding, "what's done is done now. Forget it. I have!"

Nodding his agreement Finn now looked at his friend and wondered how it was even possible to properly sleep again, never mind forget.

CHAPTER 5

"Not like her to be late," mused Sarah, referring to Imogen. Thursday night was 'the girls' night', with all four friends gathering in their favourite wine bar in Penton to have their weekly catch up. With Imogen's absence from the area, it hadn't felt the same so their meet ups now were particularly looked forward to, like old times. They'd been hurt when Imogen had taken the secondment to troubleshoot in another school in the Trust she worked for and had missed her terribly, but understood her need for distance and anonymity. Now they were pleased that the four were back together and getting on with their lives.

Always the perceptive one Harry was now eyeing Beth, who was looking shifty, before asking, "Ok Beth, spill it?"

Sighing heavily and looking worried too, Beth came clean. "I may have suggested that the boss pay Imogen a visit at work and I think he might have." The others were now looking at her with something akin to consternation.

"She could not have been clearer. She went to

bloody Whitby for God's sake and wouldn't even tell us where she was," this from a normally very mild, slow to anger Sarah. "I mean I would have probably been married by now if she hadn't left!" Sarah was relatively newly engaged to her childhood sweetheart who was now back in her life after they had been apart for many years.

"I did it for all the right reasons... oh bloody hell! She's here." They all turned as one to see their friend walking towards their table, without her customary smile, her expression serious.

"You are so dead," muttered Harry.

"Imogen," gushed Beth, "just wondering where you were. Let me get you a drink..." Imogen sat down, looked at the assembled bunch then nailed Beth with the look.

"Really?"

Swallowing Beth spread out her arms whilst shrugging saying, "You had information I deemed..." seeing Imogen's raised eyebrows, Beth now opted for honesty, "I thought it was an opportunity to get you guys together, okay! So shoot me now!"

"Don't bloody tempt me," muttered Imogen as she reached for the bottle of wine, pouring herself a large measure.

"And?" asked Harry. Taking a large sip of the much needed alcohol, Imogen looked at her friends. They'd been friends for as long as they could remember and had been through so much, particularly two years earlier when the murder of Sarah's husband had plunged them into the terrifying world of organised crime.

Sighing heavily Imogen shrugged saying, "Nothing to report." Looking at her friends who she knew only had her best interests at heart she now added, "We can never go back, so let's all move on. Ok?" Now changing the subject she asked, "So how are things? How's my gorgeous Lola?" making a reference to Beth's eighteen-month old daughter whom all the friends adored like no other and to whom all three were Godmothers to.

"Running us all ragged now she's found her legs," laughed Beth, "and the words are also coming so watch out world. Thank God for your mum and my dad Gen because Brad and I wouldn't have a hope if they weren't able to child care despite them both completely spoiling her something rotten." Imogen's widowed mum Arlette and Beth's widower dad Terry, had become a couple after years of being alone and in Imogen's mother's case, finally having a partner whom she could love and trust. Imogen's father Jake Taylor had been a vicious, violent man who had met a grisly end many years earlier, allowing Imogen and her mother to finally live a life without fear or violence. The love Arlette and Terry had now found together was wonderful to see and Imogen was particularly grateful that her mother was allowed the status of Granny to Lola, something Imogen could never give her.

"Bumped into your Olivia the other day," said Sarah to Harry, "my word but she's beautiful Harry and so tall, I mean, her legs go on forever! Towered over me although, let's face it, that's not hard is it," she laughed, "and the young man with her? Gorgeousness personified."

"What did he look like?"

"Very tall, dark and very, very, very handsome," purred Sarah.

"That will be Riz, Alan's partner's son," answered Harry whose husband was the local GP. "He walked in the other day and I had to remind myself that I use to change his nappy when a baby," laughed Harry as she pretended to fan herself. "Alan can't cope that his little girl is now turning heads and having boys calling, even the ones we've known since they were babies. He even mentioned the length of her skirt the other day, I mean he's turning into my dad before our very eyes."

Imogen looked at her friends and not for the first time felt blessed to have them in her life, despite what they had all endured and the ill- judged decisions they had all made with the exception of Sarah. Only Sarah had no idea of the secrets being kept.

"So Gen, tough day?" asked Sarah.

Glancing around her, to ensure they weren't overheard, Imogen relayed the awful news delivered by her colleague earlier that day. "Lost a child to suicide." The gasps from her friends said it all.

"Oh honey," said Harry, "how bloody awful. What's happened?"

"Not sure, if I'm honest and no doubt the police will investigate as it was particularly gruesome. The thing is, it's the second death from that Unit of kids in the last six weeks."

"Another suicide?"

"No," Imogen now shaking her head, "a sudden unexplained death whilst the child slept." Harry took her hand, instinctively knowing how her friend would be blaming herself for not being aware one of her pupils needed mental health support.

"Don't do it Imogen. You are not at fault and can't save everyone, despite trying."

"I know, but... he was the sweetest boy. Can't imagine what could have been so bad or why he didn't know we were there for him, particularly Janet Downing. She runs her blood to water for those kids."

"Mental health issues can never be underestimated," said Beth, "and thank God that we are at least aware of them these days. Come on enough of this now. Let's leave the 'doom and gloom' where it belongs for a few hours."

Later after much gossip and laughter, they said their goodnights and went their separate ways, leaving Beth and Imogen finally alone. "Sure we're okay?"

Imogen knew why Beth would be insecure about

her response as it wasn't that long ago they had been very much estranged, both so damaged and hurt, that for a brief time, there was a possibility that a friendship that meant so much would be beyond repair. "I know you meant well but some things are best left alone for all our sakes. Anyway Max is clearly past caring or he'd have found me sooner."

"I was surprised he knew you'd gone to Whitby," then sighing with obvious frustration Beth continued, "but the guilt isn't yours and you and Max shouldn't be the ones paying the price."

"No," now shaking her head, "that's not it".

Puzzled Beth shook her head saying, "I don't get it."

"Since Max walked into my life and in my presence, he has been hit by a car and shot... twice. Don't you see? The pattern? My husband Neil, my unborn baby boy and now Max? I'm cursed and I suspect Max knows I am too."

CHAPTER 6

Without a doubt Denise Cowden hated her life and sitting here in her home, if that's what you could call it these days, she was asking herself when and how her life had come to this.

She and her husband George had met at school, had been in the same form group and fell into going out from there. George in those days was always the 'cheeky chap' spending more time in Isolation than in main stream which had made him perversely popular with everyone with the obvious exception of his teachers. His 'bad boy' swagger and good looks made him a magnet for the girls too and Denise had felt special when he had singled her out at the tender age of fifteen.

Her parents had hated George from the start, doing all they could to dissuade her from being involved with him which, as is often the case, made him even more attractive. Pregnant at seventeen with their first son Brandon sealed her fate and now she realised she only had herself to blame. She used to ask herself when had George changed? Now she knew he hadn't changed, had never wanted to work, but had always looked for the easy way to do anything. Her sons Brandon, Paul and Joe were following his lead and it made her beyond sad.

So she endured being a social pariah, constantly defending her three sons' antics but thanking God she had her Katie. Her daughter was her pride and sanctuary who despite having Dyspraxia was doing really well at school and was basically everything her brothers weren't; clever, kind, thoughtful and honest.

Now listening to her eldest son's outrage, Denise realised that things were going from bad to worse. Since Brandon had been released from prison he had returned home a very different person. Always cruel and thoughtless he was now filled with something else, something which filled her with a real sense of foreboding. He was talking about a 'new order' and what the new future would bring. It was beyond her except that it made her uneasy and it made her afraid, fearful almost.

"They did what?" Brandon was now screaming, his outrage bouncing off the four small walls of their tiny living area.

"Look! It's all over Facebook!" this from Paul one of his younger siblings. Peering into the phone's screen the brothers were now witnessing the unceremonious arrest of their father at Grove School and also reading some of the comments being written too, many texting how hilarious many thought the incident to be.

"How fucking dare they?" screamed Brandon adding, "and that fucking bitch! She's gone too far this time!"
Trying to calm the situation Denise was now putting on her coat saying, "I'll go and see if I can get him home. They're probably just letting him cool down..."
Brandon sprang forward pinning her against the wall, "He did nothing wrong and they put handcuffs on him!"
Looking into his hate filled eyes Denise pushed back shouting, "He went into school with all guns blazing and he made a show of himself and this family and remember who you're bloody well talking to my lad?!"
Brandon was momentarily surprised but then the sneer returned as he replied, "I bloody well know who I'm talking to and I don't give a shit what you think. They are going to pay because there's a new order coming whether you or they like it or not!" Shaking her head Denise pushed passed him, grateful Katie was safe at school and away from harm because Denise now acknowledged that her home had become a very dangerous place.
A knock on the front door startled them all and Denise knew it was the police before she opened the door. Recognising Beth and Lydia on her doorstep, she summoned up what she knew was expected of her as she began with, "What do you want because I can tell you now it's not my lads?"

Smiling Beth replied, "Hello Denise. We'd like to ask your sons Joe and Paul a couple of questions if that's ok?"

"Whatever it is it can't be them because they've been here and grounded since that bloody cow excluded them ... again!"

"And it's about that exclusion and its reasons we are here, so may we?" asked Lydia. Allowing them to enter Denise looked at Brandon, silently begging him to not make matters worse so it was a surprise when Brandon came forward, all smiles and charm asking, "So to what do we owe the pleasure ladies?"

"We'd like a word with your brothers here. Paul, Joe, are you up to us having word about what was found in your lockers at school which has resulted in you both being excluded?" Both boys looked as if they were frozen to the spot, terror now taking root. They were used to being in trouble at school but up to now had avoided the police. This was an all-together new ball game for them.

Brandon replied for his brothers, "Do you mean those daft leaflets they found down at the Skate Park?"

Lydia showed Brandon the offensive literature. Barely looking he continued, "Yeah that's one of them. My fault really, told them to gather them up and tell the school about it, but Ms Holt jumped the gun, as usual and blamed them instead. I mean they were trying to do a public service weren't you lads? But you know when your name is Cowden Ms Holt just sees an easy scapegoat, always has."

"So all this is a complete misunderstanding then lads?"

Brandon nudging Paul to respond now, cleared his throat before replying, "Meant to hand it in but didn't get the chance."

"So," asked Lydia, "how did it get distributed around the school then, if safely in your locker?"

Joe, feeling newly empowered, "No idea, but it wasn't us and you can't prove it!"

"No we can't. Not yet and to be honest we're more interested in finding the organ grinder behind this not his or hers' little monkeys," Lydia now smiling as she said this and looking at them with a certain satisfaction at the flush of anger now on the boys' faces.

Denise now had had enough and summoned up the usual belligerence expected of her in these instances. "So if that's all may I ask you both to bugger off? I have a husband to try and get home if it's all the same to you. Pity you lot haven't got enough to do than persecute my family!"

Nodding Beth replied, "Ok, we'll see ourselves out."

Closing the door after the retreating officers Denise now turned to glare at her sons. "So again I have the police on my doorstep," then addressing Brandon only added, "and if it's not enough that you are known to them you drag these two bloody numpties into whatever rubbish you've got yourself into as well."

"Like I said, a new order is coming and they will pay and you, mummy dearest, had better choose a side."

Muttering, "God help us," Denise got her coat and left to visit Sheffield Central and hopefully find George. She couldn't cope with this on her own and hoped to God George would for once take her side. Brandon now seriously scared her and she was at loss what to do.

Paul and Joe had been standing stock still as they listened to the exchange. Joe was the first to speak saying, "So what are we going to do Brandon? How do we make them pay?"

Chuckling Brandon turned to his young siblings, recognising the gleam in their eyes, the thirst for revenge and adventure. "With fire and brimstone lads. With fire and brimstone!"

*

Around the same time Denise was dealing with the police on her doorstep, George was in Interview Room three facing Eddie and Max. The belligerence was gone now being replaced with confusion and an urgent need to leave this place as soon as possible. Staring at the men opposite he was now waiting, for what he did not know but he sensed he was in trouble.

Eddie began, "Well George, dropped a bit of a bollock today wouldn't you say?"

"I didn't do anything any other father wouldn't

do!"

"Oh George really? Threatening the Head, then the Super here? Disturbing the peace?"

"She had it coming. She's always picking on my lads who never..." Max silenced him with a look. He now pushed forward the racist literature Imogen had given him.

"So what can you tell us about this?"

Not even looking at the pamphlet before him George gave the predictable response, "Never seen it."

"Well it was found in your sons' possession. So are you behind this garbage?"

"Just because you don't like it doesn't make it garbage."

"So you have seen it, know what's written? Know that it's designed to create hate and division which George, happens to be a crime." Max was now leaning back in his chair, watching the man's discomfort and seeing that he did indeed know more than he was saying. "What about that lad of yours George?" asked Eddie, "how's he doing now he's out? Got a job? Do you think he might have an idea where this, shall we call it literature, came from?"

"Leave our Brandon out of this. He's done his time!"

Shaking his head, Eddie replied, "Lad he beat with a crowbar for spilling his drink, will be doing 'time' for the rest of his life."

George was now sweating profusely. Max was

staring at him, now sensing he knew a lot more than he was saying and he also sensed that he was afraid, very afraid and Max was determined to find what or whom he was afraid of.

"We're not really interested in what your lads are up to, but someone is stirring up a lot of trouble in this city. It's already resulted in two deaths so it would be in your interests, if you want to protect your lads, that you help us find out who's behind this."

Pregnant seconds ticked by until George asked, "Do I need my Solicitor?"

Shaking his head Max replied, "No, neither Ms Holt or myself are pressing any charges."

"Well then no comment and can I go now?"

*

Chief Constable Jim Haggerty was also having a difficult meeting. Looking at the assembled body he knew that he needed to find the words that would give the city and the police a temporary reprieve from what he feared was on the horizon. Round the table the community leaders representing the diverse communities Sheffield, as a sanctuary city, prided itself to have welcomed many generations ago, were demanding answers. Answers Jim Haggerty and his team could not as yet give.

"Our people are rightly concerned Chief Constable."

"Our children are afraid to go to school, go out to play."

"Our businesses are suffering."
"And as far as we know not one arrest has been made," said Salim Shah, South Yorkshire's representative on the Muslin Council, a man known to be fair, moderate in his outlook and a believer in all communities working together in harmony but it was clear to see that even he was struggling for composure.
"We really do understand your frustration but please be assured that this is our top priority, with our best people on the..." Jim Haggerty was stopped mid flow by the sound of quiet chuckling coming from the silent man seated at the far end of the conference table.
"Something to add Mr Mirza?"
Omar Mirza, the undisputed warlord of his area was now smiling and shaking his head before his public school modulated voice began with, "I am in no doubt that this is your top priority Chief Constable yet..."
"We really are putting every resource available in trying to ascertain information that will lead to at least one arrest," interrupted the newly appointed Assistant Chief Constable Zoe Yale.
Omar, nailing the Deputy Chief Constable with a look of pure venom continued as if she hadn't spoken, "But I would like you, Chief Constable," pointedly looking at his Assistant, "to tell me what sort of 'justice' we can expect those responsible for the brutal murder of my son to face?"

Rabbi Soloman Kaufman now spoke up saying, "It wasn't only your son who died so pointlessly Omar, don't forget that. Yara Abrahms was a good woman who had already survived the worse that men can do to each other."

The palpable silence echoed around the room as all were remembering the senseless brutality, broken now by Jim Haggerty saying, "I had hoped we would never have to deal with such senseless, abhorrent behaviour again, that we had become better than our past, that the deaths of Stephen Lawrence and others had been our 'watershed' moment," now shaking his head, "sadly this is not so but I implore you all to allow us to do our jobs unheeded and we will bring those responsible to justice. You have my word."

"Ah, that word again. Justice!" and with that Omar Miraz got up from his chair, fastened the button at the waist of his over-priced Armani jacket, stared at each person present one by one then left the room without speaking another word.

Soloman was the first to speak, "Come my friends, I believe all has been said." Rising from their seats all now moved to leave the room.

"We will find them!" stated Zoe. The nodding, silent heads showed they had heard her words, her silent plea for calm as the door closed behind them.

Outside Salim and Soloman joined Omar as he puffed angrily on his cigarette. "What a fucking

waste of breath that was!"
"They're doing their best Omar. We need patience and we need calm," implored Salim.
Shaking his head Omar was emphatic. "No Salim. I am proposing that we release our police friends from the task of finding the scum who did this. We have our own intelligence, our own foot soldiers."
"And when you find them?" asked Soloman, fearing the answer.
"With respect," this from Salim, "I don't think the rest us would want your brand of Sharia as much as I personally respect our Elders tradition of settling disputes, this must be done as befitting the laws of this country which is now our home. Your son wouldn't want it either. And Soloman, we have prayed for Yara in our mosques and mourn her passing. She was a good woman who only cared for the quality of one's soul, not their creed."
Omar looked at the men who both visibly shrank under his gaze. They knew and feared what Omar would now do, as they knew what he was capable of, knew what he and his son Mohammed did on a daily basis. Omar could sense their fear and it made him smile.
"Keep on praying old men, and leave the rest to me."

CHAPTER 7

"So can you help me? I'm been told on very good authority that you are the man to approach to 'fix' any situation one may need fixing here in Sheffield."

"What is it you need fixing?"

"I want the scum who kicked to death my great aunt Yara Abrams."

"I'm told the police are doing all they can..."

"Oh please spare me. We know what that means and quite frankly even if they managed to find the scum what will they do?"

Malcolm Speight looked at the man sitting across from him, took in the expensive suit and air of entitlement as Jakob Abrams was indeed a wealthy man and also a man who had no time for prevarication. He wanted answers and he also wanted revenge. "Sorry for your loss. Were you close?"

"Most Jewish families are close Mr Speight, because let's be honest, we have to be what with our history." Shaking his head, he continued, "We wanted... no begged Aunt Yara to come and live in our family home in Golders Green but she didn't like London. Didn't feel safe there. Felt she had a community here who cared for her. What a joke eh?"

"She wasn't the only victim that day…"

Cutting him off, Jakob continued, "I know and we're saddened for his loss too but he is not my problem. You will be able to get answers, go where the police can't or daren't."

"And if I find the scum responsible?"

Shrugging now, "They will be dealt with as appropriate."

Malcolm Speight was indeed a man who could and would go where others feared to tread and after his boxing career days, had made a successful career out of 'fixing problems' in a certain manner. Although his methods were never remotely legal, he did pride himself that those he dealt with had it coming, had done unconscionable things to the innocents. It's how he had come to be known to Imogen and her friends during the Covid year and who was the principle reason Imogen and Max were estranged from each other.

Nodding he stood and stretched out his hand. "I'm more than happy to do what I can but it won't be cheap."

"Money is not a problem," as he took the proffered hand, "just find the scum or at least… bring me their heads!" As his visitor got up to leave Malcolm was struck by the manner he carried himself.

"So you're heading back to London?"
"No. I will expect imminent results so I will remain in Sheffield."
Malcolm was now intrigued stating not asking, "When you say 'Jump' you expect the response to be 'How high?' don't you Mr Abrahms? So what exactly is the business you're in down in the Capital?"
Smiling with a certain confidence that only the very rich possess he replied, "Gold Mr Speight! And lots of it!"
Watching the man's retreating back Malcolm turned to his trusted henchmen, Ed and Albert, huge, physically intimidating men who had been at Malcolm's side for more years than anyone cared to remember. "Well lads. Thoughts?"
"Looks like a big pay day coming our way," smiled Ed.
"It appears that way but you know lads? I'd do it for nowt to get the scum that would kick to death an old lady. But we needn't tell Mr Abrahms that eh?"

*

Across the city Max was having his own meeting with an old school friend. Benny Reynolds former Military Intelligence and now NPSA, the National Protective Security Authority better known as Counter Terrorism, was regaling Max with his latest gripes regarding working for His Majesty's security services. Benny had been the biggest rogue in their South London comprehensive, barely escaping permanent exclusion on more than one occasion, that it was with a bemused astonishment for Max when he discovered his old mate was also working in a version of law enforcement too.

"Talk about being the 'Accidental Diplomat!' I mean it was bad enough being stuck in bloody Washington, with the bloody Americans, during bloody Covid but to have to spend twenty-four hours in a Jakarta prison, to make sure certain people didn't lose face, was just taking the mick. And how was I rewarded? A fifty quid Amazon voucher!"

"Good to know that some things can always be relied upon Benny boy. So? The powers that be think what's happening here is a Counter Terrorism issue?"

"No not really. Hate crimes are on the increase all over, here and in Europe but I thought it would be good to come up here and see what's keeping my old mate from returning to the 'smoke' and I bet she's a looker eh?"

Smiling Max merely shrugged replying, "I've found 'God's Own Country', that's all mate."

"Yeah course you have," then leaning forward, "and what about the bastard that put two bullet holes in you? Any leads yet?"

"None. Definitely a professional hit."

Shaking his head, Benny now was all seriousness. "We'll bide our time but we will get the bastard, on that you can rely on but since

I'm here how about I give a hand with what's happening?"

"Great. Come and meet some of the team."

Heads turned as Max entered the main open plan area of the Serious and Organised Crime Unit, obviously interested in seeing who the stranger with their boss was. Benny Reynolds was the antithesis of Max to look at. He was around five feet ten inches but carried a good deal of weight around his middle area which made him look squat and unfit which in reality was furthest from the truth. His balding ginger hair and freckled complexion, revealed how easy his skin would burn in the sun but he carried himself well, with confidence and an assurance that he would handle himself well in a crisis; that you would want to be on his side in a fight.

"Heads up people, I'd like you all to meet an old school mate of mine, Benny Reynolds who believe it or not works for Counter Terrorism, although back in the day, trust me when I tell you that Benny boy here terrorised plenty."

"Yeah mate but only the bloody teachers and they had it coming," as all now turned to look and grin at the exchange.

"So we're looking at possible Terrorists boss? Here?" asked Isaiah.

Max saw worried looks exchanged across the desks as Benny now took over. "No... well not yet but I thought I'd cast an informal eye that's all, mainly because I wanted to see what was keeping

my old mate from returning to the 'Smoke'. Apparently he's found 'God's Own Country'?"
Joining in the chuckles Max added, "So everyone, share what you think Benny might have some insight or thoughts into. Whilst he's here he may as well make himself useful. Isiah, look after him for me and try and keep him out of trouble."
"You'll be the first mate," mocked Benny, shrugging his shoulders whilst Isiah merely grinned back.

CHAPTER 8

Unable to look, Sarah thrust the white plastic stick at Harry. Now pacing around her large kitchen come living room, Sara was trying for calm but failing miserably. "It's probably negative, I mean my period can be late for all sorts of reasons can't it?"

Harry merely smiled back at her whilst scrutinising the tiny object that would give her friend the news she so desperately craved or would temporarily consume her with the bitterest of disappointments. "Well it would appear that you'll be alcohol free for a while and I must insist that you now begin a course of folic acid and zinc supplements..." now smiling at her dear friend, who had dealt with the worst of times, "because my friend you are going to be a mummy and a very yummy one at that!"

"Oh my God! Really? John and I are going to have a baby?" snatching the stick to look at the very clear blue line for herself. "Oh Harry, can I be so lucky? After everything? After the wickedness I've done?"

Harry now drew her friend into her arms and

held her tight. Harry knew that Sarah had nothing to blame herself for, had not been the one who had ended the life of her late husband, Grant Downs. The real perpetrator had to be protected by the three remaining friends but Harry was now disputing the decision to keep this fact from Sarah. At the time it seemed the right course of action. The irony was that Sarah was the only one of the four who didn't have blood on her hands and now, seeing how tortured this most innocent of them all was, didn't seem just or fair.

"Sarah, this is your chance to have the happiness and life you and John were always destined to have. Leave the past behind you now honey, where it belongs; where it can't hurt you anymore."

Smiling through her tears, Sarah nodded saying, "I know you're right. Oh wow, a baby, our baby. I can't wait to tell John and the others. Gosh, Godmothers again!"

"So when can you let John know?"

"He contacts me when he can but it's not always possible and I can't get in touch so... just have to wait. He'll be so thrilled. He never wanted me to... you know all those years ago," Sarah now referring to the fact she had aborted their baby when only nineteen, which had resulted in John leaving to join the British army which he stilled served as part of the Special Forces division.

"Hey, the past is the past. Your future is now

what you can both make it my friend and no one deserves happiness more than you do."

"Thanks Harry. Oh my word but I'm going to have a baby!" as the two friends hugged each other tightly, looking forward to a future hopefully filled with love and new life.

*

Meanwhile Imogen was bone tired and really didn't want to go to her mum's for supper. She'd had a difficult Governors meeting , mainly because the Chair of Governors was an ill-informed total 'know-all' and just wanted to go home to her apartment, have a bath and a very large glass of red. Arlette had insisted she feed her and also to introduce Imogen to her new neighbour. A single man. Sighing heavily Imogen knew her mother had her best interests at heart but since finding love with Terry, Beth's widowed father, she seemed hell-bent of finding a life partner for Imogen too. She just wasn't in the mood for another excruciating evening with no doubt, a pleasant enough person whom Imogen would not have the slightest interest in. Walking through the back door into the warmth of her mother's kitchen, Imogen was relieved to find just the two of them there.

"Hello Imogen," said Terry, "but you look knackered love. Come and sit here near the fire."

"Thanks Terry. Hello you," as she kissed her mother, "glad it's just the two of you. No mood for your match making if that's ok?"

"I've told your mum love. Interfering in anyone's business never ends well."

"Really Mr Fletcher, because I can remember a certain someone making sure a certain bullying coward kept his fists to himself!" Arlette now smiling and invoking the memory of that night decades earlier when Terry had confronted Arlette's brutal husband after seeing bruises on a seven-year old Imogen.

Blushing now Terry responded, "Well that was different."

"It was Terry and I'll never stop being grateful to you but as for my love life mum? Back off ok?"

Sighing heavily Arlette shrugged as only the French can, saying, "Ok if you both insist in ganging up on me. Just worry about you that's all. You've been without your Neil how long now Pet?"

"Coming up to seven years in December and I know you mean well mum but you can't keep presenting me with men you deem suitable! Most of the time all they need to have is a pulse!" This said with humour and affection as all now smiled at each other.

"Ok. I promise! No more matchmaking."

After a pleasant few hours Imogen got up to take her leave. "Would you just pop this plate of food next door as you pass please love?"

"Mum!"

"No, I'm just being a good neighbour. The poor boy works all hours, just like you and it feels

wrong to waste good food. That's all. Promise!"
"Ok but honestly mum I'm not interested..."
"I'm only being neighbourly so I'll take it..."
"No I'll do it," as she kissed both of them goodnight. Walking down the ginnel onto the newly restored Weaver's cottages, Imogen walked up and knocked on the door of the designated house, balancing the covered plate as she did so.
Nothing could have prepared her for the sight of a shirtless, jeans cladded, shoeless Max opening the door to her. With her mouth falling open, Imogen just stared and it was Max who spoke first. "Hi and I take it that's for me?" pointing to the plate Imogen was now clutching like a life line.
"What are you doing here?"
"I'm living here."
"You're living next door to my mother?!"
"Would appear so although I had no idea until I'd moved in and she's a pretty great neighbour too. I can see where you get your looks from although she doesn't go around with your permanent scowl. You should try that some time and I really would like that plate of food before you drop it?" as he retrieved the plate from her grasp.
Floundering for words Imogen now close to being furious said, "You have no business living here Max!"
Raising his eyebrows, the wry smile now leaving his face he replied, "Excuse me? I have no

business?! You'll find I have every right to live where I please and I've felt at home here for a long time," saying this as he deposited the meal to one side adding, "despite some of the locals not being particularly friendly it would appear."
Imogen was at a complete loss. "But this is my home Max. You're not being fair to either of us."
"Us? I've been told on very good authority that there IS no us," as he now walked towards her, standing more closely to her still poleaxed figure. She could so easily touch him. She could smell that clean soaped male smell of his, that scent that she could never get enough of. He saw it. He saw it in her eyes that she was wavering, remembering what they had had with each other, as he tentatively put his hand to place a strand of her hair behind her ear, a gesture he used to do often. She felt her mouth go dry, he saw her lick her lips but as he moved closer her eyes fell to his chest and to the ugly scar where one of the bullets had lodged leaving its potentially deadly mark. The bullet that had nearly killed him. Suddenly the spell was broken with Imogen backing off as if suddenly coming to her senses.
Turning to leave she looked at him now from a safer distance. "If you ever cared one iota for me you'd leave and live elsewhere. This is my home. How could you?!" Max was no longer smiling and Imogen could see he was also struggling to keep hold of his temper.

"You walked, no ran, away from here and for all I knew you hadn't any intention to return. For all I knew you'd made a life with..." then silence.

Nodding her understanding at his unspoken words she now replied, "Malcolm Speight? Is that what you were about to say?"

Max stood in complete silence and stillness, neither confirming or denying what she was suggesting he had thought before muttering, "Why wouldn't you? You've turned to him before despite never admitting it."

Shaking her head and laughing without humour, Imogen glared hard at him saying, "And there it is Max! The past doesn't have to be our future? Yeah right!"

Max shook his head, ignoring her inference before continuing, "So I've made a life here without you and I strongly suggest you get used to the idea. Perhaps you should also consider that not everything's about you where I'm concerned anymore. So if you're leaving go. If you're planning on staying, then I ..."

He heard the echo of the slammed door long after she'd left.

*

Imogen sat in her car completely stunned. The idea of Max living in Penton was something she had never considered and she was now completely at a loss. Her phone rang and she saw it was Harry. "Hi Harry."

"Hello love, can you come over to Sarah's?"

“Bad news?”

“The worse and she needs us.” Without thinking Imogen disconnected and proceeded to drive the short distance towards the home of her friend.

CHAPTER 9

Sarah was looking unseeingly out of her large kitchen window, unhearing of what was being said. Trey, a fellow soldier who served with her fiancé John was now relating the news to her friends; the news that had left her numb with grief.

"We came under attack, which came out of nowhere because we'd been told the area had been cleared. We'd been sent to extract someone, someone important, you know I can't say more." He now glanced at Bud and Daz who nodded that he should continue. "Sarge did his usual, making sure the squad got back to safety whilst he was the last man holding the line before he began his own retreat. Then out of the blue came mortar fire which dislodged the precipice we were on. He just... just... disappeared into this ravine that just...appeared." Shaking his head, looking at Sarah's back, Trey could say no more.

"But don't think we just left him," this from Daz, "we bloody searched as much as we could but... the conditions were impossible by this time and we were ordered to get the extraction back..."

Sarah now had returned to the group, fists at her side with angry tears streaming down her face. "Because the 'extraction' was more important than my John!" said Sarah in a cold flat tone which voiced her unsaid unfairness that the man she loved had been left behind whilst another had been saved.

All three men just looked at her with silent pity, shaking their heads looking down at the floor. Harry walked over to Sarah and put her arms around her grief stricken friend saying, "I think its best if we get you some bed rest now honey. We've got the baby to consider and this has been a massive shock for you."

Trey's head shot up. "A baby? You're having the Sarge's little 'un?"

Unable to speak Sarah merely nodded. "Sarge never said," said Daz.

"Didn't get the chance to tell him."

Beth now took control saying, "So lads if it's all the same to you I think it's best you leave us to it. I know this hasn't been easy for any of you. I've had to deliver enough bad news myself to unsuspecting families but I also know how much John meant to you all too. So thank you for giving Sarah this courtesy."

The three young men now stood as one as soldiers often do as they made their exit. Outside Trey lagged behind before turning to Beth. "You've got to tell her that we haven't given up. We never have and we never will. If there's any chance he's alive we will find him and if he is alive, no one will work harder to come back to Sarah than the Sarge." Emotions threatening to overtake him Trey now stopped, taking a huge breath before continuing. "I've never in my life seen two people more in love, more devoted to each other. Now a little 'un on its way…do we know if it's a boy?"

"I think it's too early to say. She's just found out."

"I hope it is, a gutsy little bugger like the Sarge."

Smiling at this little more than a boy himself in reality, Beth merely nodded.

"Take care of her won't you."

"Of that you can be sure of. You take care too, you and the rest of you, ok?" Nodding, Trey went to the waiting vehicle to join his friends.

Back in the lounge, Beth found Imogen was alone. "She in bed now?"

"Yes Harry's up there with her. Bloody hell fire! After everything she's suffered and John has to bloody well go MIA!"

"He was on his last sortie too wasn't he?"

"From what Sarah said last time we spoke of him. How unlucky can she get though? Him too? After all what's happened? The way she survived that monster she was married too and to finally have the love of her life back and… now this!"

Shaking her head, Beth reached for her friend's hand saying, "I think we'll both agree that the last thing bloody life is my friend, is fair!" They both turned to see Harry emerging from the hallway.

"How's she doing?" asked Imogen.

"She's exhausted. Sleep is the best medicine. I've just texted Alan and told him I'm sleeping here tonight."

"I'll stay tomorrow night," said Imogen.

"I can the night after. It will be a chance of an uninterrupted sleep for a change," smiled Beth whose twenty month old daughter Lola had not only found her legs but had recently discovered where her parents slept, currently joining them whenever she felt like it.

Now the three friends were looking at each other and each one knew what the others were thinking. All were brought back to past events, when as one they activated to support whoever amongst the four were in need. Imogen after the car accident that had taken her husband and unborn son, Sarah after Grant Downs' murder and now poor sweet, innocent Sarah again. Life truly didn't seem to play fair at all.

*

Sarah now began to live her new reality with the support of her friends who were there for her every need in those first few days until Sarah made it clear that she felt strong enough to carry on alone. "I'm not really alone though am I? I will always have a part of my John now so my friends, let's all just get on with it, ok?"

Not having the ritual of a funeral also made Sarah still have hope, but she didn't share this with anyone else as in reality there wasn't any. She knew her friends would consider this unhealthy so she kept that little flicker to herself. Yet...why didn't she sense he was gone?

*

It was a particularly pleasant morning, the sun was shining and the usually unforgiving Penton wind was being unusually kind for a change, as Sarah with her Pug named Cyril and her Staffordshire Bull Terrier named Scooby-Doo, approached the Kennels where she housed several rescue dogs. Sarah had had hopes of being a vet years earlier but life had again intervened and she now did her bit by billeting some of those poor, badly treated loveable creatures, that were plentiful these day, until a decent home, which was thoroughly vetted, could be found.

As she entered her Kennels she was greeted with the usual barks of welcome as her furry charges rushed to the front of their cages to greet her. Suddenly, Sarah sensed she was not alone. Scooby's wagging tail had now ceased and he began to growl. "Who's there? Show yourself or I'll set the dogs on you?"

Suddenly, with a yelp of delight Scooby dashed forward, followed by an equally exuberant Cyril as both dogs ran into an empty stall at the end of the purpose built facility. Sarah was now astonished to see a very tousled haired Trey emerge with both dogs jumping up at him with yelps of pure joy.

"Sorry Sarah, didn't mean to scare you."

Dumbfounded Sarah replied, "My God Trey? What are you doing here?"

"Well I couldn't think of a place I'd rather be if I'm honest. We're on leave for a while and I thought I'd just come and keep an eye on things like. Sorry if I've overstepped. I'll leave..."

"No you haven't and you don't have to go anywhere. Tell me you haven't slept in here all night?"

Grinning now he replied, "I've slept in far worse believe me."

"Come on young man, you need feeding." As they walked back into the large comfortable converted barn that had been Sarah's home for years now, Trey surveyed the panoramic views of the South Yorkshire countryside saying, "John loved this place and I can see why."

"This place loved him right back too," replied Sarah, "but it will be good to have you here Trey, that is if you really have nowhere better to go."

"I promise you, there's no place I'd rather be."

CHAPTER 10

Imogen always made a point of patrolling the corridors at different times of the day, often popping into classrooms unannounced. It's how the 'hidden curriculum', and the 'hidden agendas' could be scrutinised and it kept her staff on their toes and her pupils aware of her presence, as much as it kept her informed. Behaviour needed careful monitoring so since her return she had insisted that her Leadership colleagues also patrol the corridors and classrooms constantly, not returning to their offices until the pupils had left the premises.

Smelling the unmistakable odour of tobacco, she rounded a corner of the Technology block only to encounter Assistant Premises Manager Damien Bale slouching against the wall smoking a cigarette, with her Deputy Peter Rogers having a very animated one-way conversation with him. Nearing the pair, Damien was the first to spot her. Deliberately meeting her eye, he smirked before taking his time finishing his cigarette, only then extinguishing it on the ground. Peter looked flustered, embarrassed and guilty.

Imogen began, "There's been a ban on smoking in public buildings since 1st July 2007!"
Damien looked at her with the smirk still in place and replied, "Yeah sorry but been busy and needed a fag. I'll go where kids smoke next time. Promise…Miss," the word signifying respect said as a deliberate afterthought, as he moved from his position from the wall, looked at Peter, winked, then walked casually away as if he didn't have a care in the world.
Turning to her Deputy who was now looking like he wanted the floor to swallow him whole she asked, "Ok Peter. Is there anything you need to tell me?" Without a word, he shook his head and walked in the opposite direction.

*

Later that day, Imogen was staggered at the spreadsheet she was looking at. After her encounter earlier she had called a meeting with her Campus Manager Bill Mears and Finance Officer Lisa Holden, who were now bringing to her attention certain discrepancies. Huge amounts of stock were missing, invoices didn't add up and both colleagues were clearly worried and relieved Imogen was now back to try and make sense of it. Peter Rogers had been promoted to Acting Head in her absence and had basically ignored the situation.
"I mean no disrespect but Mr Rogers got really bolshie whenever I brought these discrepancies

to his attention. I mean it's blatantly obvious something isn't right!"

"Tell her the rest Bill," said Lisa who was looking at her colleague urging him on, "she needs to know everything if she's to sort it."

Now clearly uncomfortable Bill began. "He appointed his cousin's lad to Assistant Campus Manager without any input from me or going through the usual procedures. He just turned up one day and I was told he was my new assistant. I mean, when Andy left, I thought he wasn't being replaced due to cost cuts."

"And you'd have been right!" bristled Lisa who had also clearly been side-lined.

"This is Damien Bale, right? And…?"

"Well, I'm not saying it's connected but a couple of weeks after he came here to work, although I have to say 'work' is a concept quite alien to him, I began to notice certain discrepancies."

"So," Imogen questioned, "if you're not happy with his work and you feel there are certain 'discrepancies', why wasn't this indicated on his Performance Review and steps taken to remove him?"

"I bloody did! Sorry, excuse my French Ms Holt," Bill now clearly embarrassed by his outburst but revealing his obvious frustration as he continued. "Mr Rogers read it and basically said we had no grounds for dismissal."

"Where's the paper work now?" queried Imogen.

"My guess", said Lisa, "would be the paper

shredder!"
Imogen was now understanding why the Trust had recalled her back. "Okay. Thank you both for bringing this to my attention. Rest assured it will be sorted but I need to speak to Mr Rogers first ok? So let's keep this between us for now."
Rising from their seats the three walked to the door where Bill turned to Imogen saying, "You have no idea how good it is to have you back, I mean he's been letting the kids do what they want too."
"Thanks Bill. It's good to be back."
Agnes Mane approached Imogen as the others left and said, "There's someone here who'd like an audience with you Ms Holt," then dropping her voice added, "her words not mine."
"Really? Well how can I refuse such a request."
Agnes now smiling broadly ushered a rather shy, almost scared Katie Cowdell into Imogen's office. Smiling broadly at the child, Imogen indicated that Katie join her at the comfortable less formal chairs beside a coffee table that was also part of her office furniture and designed to put, whoever she was seeing, at ease. Agnes Mane returned with a tray that had orange squash, a cup of coffee and a plate of biscuits. Putting the tray down Agnes addressed Katie in a conspiratorial tone saying, "I hope you enjoy the biscuits Katie but try and encourage Ms Holt to eat one too. I swear she's on a permanent diet and really doesn't need to be!"

"My mam's the same Miss, always saying what she should or shouldn't eat, although to be fair she is a bit on the fat side," this being said with all the wide-eyed innocence of those who have yet to learn social politics.

Trying not to laugh, Agnes left as Imogen turned to the child sitting across from her offering her the plate, whilst asking, "So Katie, what can I do for you today?"

Swallowing her half eaten biscuit Katie began. "First can I apologise for my dad coming into school and making a show of himself and of me Miss? My mam's been proper fed up with him."

"You don't have to apolgise for the actions of the adults in your life Katie. That's not your responsibility."

"But he used really bad swear words Miss!"

"He was angry Katie and I'm sure now he has had time to calm down he wishes he'd done things differently."

Shaking her head, "I don't think so Miss. Dad finds it hard ever admitting he's wrong because he thinks he never is," as she picked up the squash drinking noisily.

Imogen felt so sad for this sweet little girl, knowing all too well what it was like to grow up in a household that contained a bully for a father.

"So Katie is that it?"

"No Miss. I'm actually here because I'm worried. Miles hasn't come to school today?"

"Miles?"

"Miles Dunn. He hasn't come to school today and he's never late."
"Perhaps he's under the weather and absent due to illness?"
"He's never ill!"
"I'm sure there's an explanation..."
"We were going to have our own chess tournament today. Just him and me. We've been looking forward to it for ages and he's never let me down. We're special friends, not boyfriend or girlfriend friends, nothing like that," her expression now suggesting, "As if?" but I'm worried Miss."
"Why?"
Sitting back, Katie now tried to find the words which would explain what she was beginning to be afraid of. "Do you ever have really bad thoughts Miss?"
"I'm not sure I understand Katie?"
"Like someone is whispering to you, but no one's there?"
Imogen now looked into Katie's worried expression and something at the back of her skull began to throb. "Does Miles hear the whispers?"
Laughing now Katie responded, "He'd called me daft Miss," then sobering she added, "I wouldn't tell anyone but you Miss or Mrs Downing."
"What's Mrs Downing said?"
"I haven't bothered her Miss. She's been too upset since Ollie did what he did. We all have been."

Nodding Imogen now smiled at this anxious, caring child saying, "Ok Katie, I'll ask Miles' Form Tutor to check for us, just to put your mind at rest but I'm sure there's nothing for you to worry about."
Smiling happily Katie stood up saying, "Thanks Miss," as she took her leave.
Imogen now spoke into her internal phone, "Agnes. Find out who Miles Dunn's Form Tutor is please and tell them to ring regarding his absence. Just routine okay?"

*

Hours later that day, Imogen found herself sitting in the comfortable lounge of Miles Dunn's home, drinking coffee from china cups with matching saucer, listening to the cries of horror and despair that seemed to permeate every nook and cranny of the small space. Miles's parents were huddled together, he holding his grief stricken, inconsolable wife.
"We had no idea. He always seemed so happy, I mean he coped well with his condition, had friends and he loved school. Why would he do something so...so..." as Miles' broken hearted father Geoffrey Dunn tried to make sense of what he had discovered that morning, a morning that had started like so many mornings but would never be the same again.
"I was telling him he was going to be late, that he wouldn't get his hundred percent punctuality certificate. He loves getting his certificates, never

has a day off either because he's so proud when," now turning to Imogen, "when you shout out his name and everyone claps him," as he now put his head in his hands momentarily unable to carry on. "So I went up to his room and tried opening the door but I couldn't, it felt like something was heavy in the way. So I pushed really hard. I couldn't see him at first, I mean he wasn't in his bed. Then I realised he was behind me... swinging on the back of the door. He looked ... he looked..."

Imogen, Janet Downing and Fayre Burrows, the deceased child's Form Tutor, sat cramped together on the small sofa shocked to the core at what they were hearing. After what seemed like the longest time but would have been mere minutes Imogen eventually asked, "Can I call someone to come and be with you both?"

Shaking his head Geoff Dunn replied, "My brother's on his way from Snaith."

Nodding to the others, the three women got up. "There are no words Mr Dunn, Mrs Dunn, but if the school can be of any help, don't hesitate to call."

The two devastated parents appeared not to hear her words, frozen in their uncomprehending grief and horror as the three women took their leave.

Outside Imogen told her colleagues to go home whilst she got into her own vehicle. There she sat for quite a while before picking up her phone.

"Beth, it's Imogen. Can you call in to the school? I'm worried something odd is happening and I'm not sure...I could be completely wrong but... I think I may need to involve the police. Can you come over?" Listening to her friend's response Imogen grimaced, saying, "I'd rather not come to the station Beth, but nice try...again! You will, great, see you later."

*

"It's the third death from the same unit of students in a few months, all deaths very sudden and in two of the cases violent."

"I remember you mentioning it," said Beth, "so another then? Same group?" Imogen nodded.

Lydia who had accompanied Beth had her notebook open asking, "So may I have the names and causes of death?"

"The first was Samuel Fraser and he died in his sleep. Cause unknown, almost like a SID. Can SID be teenagers?" Imogen queried at the term Sudden Infant Death.

"Or SAD – Sudden Adult Death?" questioned Lydia.

"Then we had the horrific death of Ollie Manderson who committed something called 'hara-kiri', and please don't ask me to go into the details but it was very gruesome and now today Miles Dunn. Found hanging from his bedroom door by his father." Imogen now leaned back, as she spread her arms, indicating that a reasonable explanation seemed beyond her reach.

"All three regarded as Special Needs in some way?" asked Beth.

"Yes but all were functioning really well, often attending mainstream classes. Ollie had a mild form of Asperger's Syndrome, Miles had a form of Cerebral Palsy but was doing well and Samuel had epilepsy which presented life threatening seizures if not sufficiently regulated. Am I over thinking this?"

Lydia and Beth both shrugged their shoulders as Lydia replied, "It does seem like too much of a coincidence. What do you think Beth?"

"Wasn't there a cluster of kids in Wales somewhere that had some sort of suicide pact? Wasn't there a particular website or Social Media page encouraging it?"

"I remember that," answered Lydia, "worth looking into the Social Media outlets they may have had access to. Could be where the child thinks the 'whispering' is from?"

"Yes," agreed Beth, "like a form of auto-suggestion. I've read about it and teenagers can be very susceptible to it. It's often how radicalisation works in some respects."

"So you'll look into it?" asked Imogen.

Nodding Beth replied, "Yep. I think it needs a closer look. Glad you brought it to our attention," as both police colleagues got up to leave.

Standing at her door Imogen turned to Lydia. "I hear congratulations are in order."

Blushing Lydia now held up the third finger

of her left hand revealing the diamond cluster sparkling there saying, "Yes, I'm making an honest man out of Dan."

"When is the wedding?"

"In five weeks and three days, not that I'm counting," laughed Lydia.

"She's turned into a right bloody 'Bridezilla'," quipped Beth.

"No," replied Lydia, not taking the least offence, "but things have to be done right. God willing this will be my one and only trip down the aisle."

"That's if Dan doesn't murder you first!" laughed Beth.

"Actually Imogen, I'd love you and the others to come to the Hens Party if you're free? I don't trust Beth not to do something I will regret. I need someone with sense there so will you?"

"I would love to and thanks and you really should be worried too as I still have the nightmares and scars," grinned Imogen.

"Well thanks a bunch you two. Actually Lyds I need a private word with Imogen so see you at the car?"

Watching her colleague's retreating back Beth turned her attention to Imogen and in a lowered voice said, "So I hear Arlette and my dad have a new neighbour then?"

"Don't you bloody start…"

Holding her hands in mock surrender Beth spluttered, "Just saying, Penton has a new resident that's all."

"Can't believe he'd do this to me but I don't expect any sympathy from you."

"Good," replied a grinning Beth, "because you're not getting any!" Then more seriously, "Have you seen Sarah?"

"Going later why? What's happened?"

"No, nothing really just..."

Nodding her understanding of her friend's unspoken concerns Imogen added, "This guy Trey being there?"

"I'm sure he's just looking out for her but..."

Imogen, touching Beth's arm replied, "I think it may be mutual grief playing out nothing more, I mean he seems like a really good lad. They all do."

"I guess after everything she's been through, or should I say what I put her through..."

"Enough Beth! We've got to all move on..."

"Oh yeah," mocked Beth, "just like you are with the Chief?"

Now not meeting her friend's eye Imogen merely muttered, "That's different."

"Well according to dad there's an orderly queue forming at the butcher's whenever he attempts to buy his meat so I'd get a move on if I were you mate," as Beth moved towards the door adding, "but he's back for you Gen and he's going nowhere."

CHAPTER 11

The 'Frog & Parrot' pub was situated directly opposite Sheffield Central and was the natural water hole for the station's personnel. Isiah, Dan and Richard were now seated with their bottled lagers, reflecting on their day.

"So what do you think of us? First impressions?" asked Dan to Richard.

Sitting back after taking a long swig from his bottle Richard replied, "The Chief doesn't take any prisoners does he? Feels like I'm on bloody probation again."

"That's because you are!" clipped back Isiah subtly raising his eyebrows in Dan's direction before asking, "So what exactly did you balls up in Manchester then?"

Smile now gone, Richard looked petulantly at Isiah before flatly replying, "Misplaced a search warrant when evidence gathering."

"As in lost or didn't bother?" asked Dan. When Richard remained silent Dan sighed adding, "Same old 'Dickhead' Braxton then eh? Didn't that stunt you tried pulling when training teach you anything?"

"Oh for Christ's sake mate! How long ago was that and who doesn't occasionally take their eye off the ball?"

Shaking his head, Dan now was clearly angry. "You failed to appropriately search a suspect who went on to stab another prisoner whilst in our custody! Then blamed Debbie Atkins for it who subsequently left! Had had enough, allegedly, of working with you!"

Leaning into his chair Richard had the good grace to look shamefaced. "I know I behaved like a turd back then, but you know she'd have left sooner or later because...well she just wasn't cut out for the job. We all thought so, even you Dan and I aim to go by the book from now on. In fact, I hope not to be here that long to, to quote Isiah here, to 'balls' anything up."

"How come?" asked Isiah.

"Applied to the Met. I mean that's where the action is, where you can get ahead if you know how to box cleverly. So same again lads?" as he got up and sauntered towards the bar, smiling and nodding affably to all assembled.

"And there goes a future Chief Constable if I ever saw one," said Isiah shaking his head, "but how did he not get kicked out of training after pulling a stunt like that?"

Sighing and shrugging his shoulders Dan was pragmatic. "It appeared our Supervisors hadn't been fully aware of all the facts until Debbie resigned and they would have had questions to answer themselves so to save face they let the whole matter just go away. Gave him the usual warning, not that it seems to have made much difference."

"Well I can see why the boss wants us to keep eyes on him."

"Yes mate, Dickie 'dickhead' hasn't registered that he's in the lions' den now, and will get eaten alive if he's not careful."

At this point they were joined by uniformed Constable Sharon Summers. "Mind if I join you lads?" Shuffling up to make room Richard reappeared with the drinks, saw Sharon and did his usual routine when in the vicinity of female company.

"And who do we have here?"

Putting forward her hand to be shaken, Sharon answered for herself, not waiting on any formality. "Constable Sharon Summers, at your service. And you are?"

"DC Richard Braxton who always needs a bit of service from the right company," a response which brought groans from both Dan and Isiah.

"And on that note, I shall leave you to it. Coming Dan?"

Downing his drink, he nodded, "Yeah, see you tomorrow and be early right?" this now being pointedly said to Richard.

"Course mate, I need the 'brownie' points."

After watching his colleagues leave, Richard now turned his full attention towards Sharon who

was looking at him with obvious interest.
"Are they always so serious?"
"Who? Serious Crimes?" as he nodded she laughed, "well yeah they take what they do very seriously. The clue's in the name."
"I get that but they all seem to be … well hero worshipping the Chief."
"Well that's because they don't come any better. They're a good lot and you should think yourself lucky to be given the chance to work with them. I've got some good friends in that team. You'll have met Beth Fairchild?"
"The blonde bombshell?" as Sharon nodded, "yeah and her seriously scary looking husband too."
"Trust me when I say Beth doesn't need Brad to scare anyone off if you had any ideas of trying your luck there."
"Thought never crossed my mind," the lie being so obvious it made Sharon guffaw out loud.
"So new to Sheffield yeah?" as he nodded whilst drinking, "then you'll need showing around then. Perhaps I can be of service after all."
Placing his arms on the table Richard leant forward, flashed his perfect smile, then with his customised, well-practiced smoulder replied, "Perhaps we can be of mutual service to each other."
Leaning forward herself, Sharon lifted her glass and replied, "I'll drink to that."

CHAPTER 12

Karen Raithes gratefully received the cup of tea which her old friend Philip Read placed on the Formica topped table they were seated at. Philip settled into the chair opposite then took her hand in his saying, "Whatever it is Karen, we can sort it. He might have lost his way but Finn is saveable, a good lad deep down. I've always thought so, even when I had no choice but to 'nick' him."

Shaking her head, a tearful Karen replied, "Oh Phil, I wish I could say the same. He's always been easily led but lately he seems... so lost and so quick to take offence, always shouting at me. There are times I daren't bloody open my mouth!"

"How long has he been out?"

"Just a few months. I mean you'd hope prison would make a lad know when he's done wrong and be better for it but instead he's worse than when he went in! How can that be right?"

Shaking his head Philip looked out of the cafe window, not seeing the passing traffic, but the image of his own dead son who had made very

poor choices and who then paid the ultimate price. "At least you've still got him Karen. I'd give all I have to have my lad back."
Placing both her hands on Philip's Karen's stress and regret were evident. "Oh bloody hell Phil. I'm so sorry. Me and my bloody mouth running off, when you and those poor bairns have..."
Squeezing her hands Philip shook his head saying, "It's okay love. My lad made some very bad decisions, got involved with some very bad people and he paid the price. Thing is, so have his wife and kids."
"And you Phil, and you." Nodding former Police Constable Philip Read acknowledged to his old friend how hard it had been to know his only son had not only been executed by members of Organised Crime but who himself had also tried to kill one of their own which had resulted in Philip leaving the job he had loved and lived for.
"I've asked myself time and time again where me and his mother went wrong. At the end of the day Karen, we have to come to the conclusion that each of us have to make our own decisions, take responsibility for our actions. I know we parents and grandparents have this built in guilt but love, you couldn't have done more for that lad of yours. I mean your lass Linda, his bloody mother, just buggered off didn't she? Did you ever find out who his dad is?"
"I'd be surprised if she knew if we're being brutality honest," this now being said with deep

sadness and regret. They stayed quiet now, both lost in their own thoughts, both wondering where it had all begun to go wrong and for Karen, where it would all eventually end.

"So love. What is it you think I can do?"

"Would you try talking to him?"

"Would he listen? I'm the copper that got him banged up last time. How long did he do in the end? It was for Aggravated Burglary wasn't it?"

Nodding Karen replied, "Three years. Got out on good behaviour," as she now struggled to find the words that would explain why she was so worried and also so frightened.

"He's out at all hours and when he's home it's straight to his room. He can't sleep when he's in either unless he's smoking you know what! I hear him mooching about and when he does sleep, he screams out as if having really bad nightmares."

"Who's he hanging out with?"

"Mark Frith, you know him? That daft lad he went to school with. Always getting my Finn into some bloody scape ... oh and that nasty piece of work, Cowden's lad. Have you seen how he bloody struts around as if he owns the bloody streets. I mean, what's that about?"

"I know how some lads and lasses for that matter, do seem to have an edge about them but that Cowden lad is trouble. I can spot it a mile off," remarked Philip, sadly shaking his head.

"So will you have a word please Phil? With Finn? See if you can get to the bottom of why he's so

unhappy and on edge all the time?"
Smiling, Phil now shrugged saying, "I can give it a try, but I honestly don't know how much good it will do."

*

"What the fuck is he doing here?"
"Finn language! I've asked him to come and have a word because you won't bloody well talk to me except to shout and swear and..." Karen stopped as her grandson attempted to barge past her only for him to abruptly halt as Philip stepped in front of him. Seeing the grizzled, granite features of the man he had fled from more times than he cared to remember, Finn now opted for bravado.
"Get out of way old man if you know what's good for you!"
"Or what Finn? Karen love, make me and your lad a nice cuppa eh? We're going to have a chat."
Shaking his head Finn snarled, "I've nothing to say to you so..." but failed to finish his sentence as Philip caught his arm as he attempted to barge pass, easily twisting it so that the boy had no choice but to sit where Philip put him."
Rubbing his arm, he now resorted to threats. "You're not a cop anymore and I could bloody have you for assault!"
"Yep. Go ahead. I've already got my pension." Silence now as the two stared each other down, but Finn was the first to blink. Karen now bustled in with a tray of hot beverages, took one look at the two protagonists and abruptly left the room.

As the silence lengthened, Finn was again the first to break it. “Alright. What’s the old bag been complaining about then?”

Shaking his head Philip replied, “I haven’t spoken to any ‘old bag’ but I have been speaking with your grandmother, the same grandmother who has cared for you since before you were out of nappies. The same grandmother who has stood by you and defended you when everyone else turned their backs. The same grandmother who is beside herself with worry about you.”

Sighing dramatically Finn responded, “She’s always worrying. I’ve told her I’m alright!”

“So being half undressed in the middle of the day, stinking of ‘weed’, having nightmares, being constantly angry. Is that your idea of alright then?” When Finn didn’t respond Philip continued. “Being banged up must have been…”

“And whose fault was that then?”

“Must have been tough. Armley Prison isn’t a picnic for anyone.” Finn now shrugged as Philip continued, “So I imagine to survive, you made some friends, friends that would protect you or you would stick with. Doesn’t mean you have to stick with those same friends now. The world’s a big place Finn.”

“Yeah right, with my record?”

“It’s been done.” Philip now could see what his friend Karen was so worried about. Finn was angry but he was also very unhappy and Philip also sensed that the boy was truly terrified too.

"Look lad, I might not be a copper anymore, but I still have some influence so here's my card. Sad eh, that I still carry my cop details but it has my mobile and also a number to call Sheffield Central."

"Stuff it. Don't want it."

Placing the card next to the tray of now cold beverage Philip got up. "I'll leave it just in case Ok Finn?"

Finn's response was to nod only the once, not looking at Philip but merely staring at the floor.

"Tell your Nan bye for me lad," as Philip left to take his leave.

CHAPTER 13

Peter Rogers looked uncomfortable, very shifty and also unreasonably annoyed. He had always wanted the main job as Head of Grove South and actually had believed once upon a time, that he should have been appointed long before Imogen had been. When the Trust had sent her elsewhere he really believed this was his chance to outshine her not realising how hard he would be expected to work or the hours required to do the job properly. He would never admit it, not even to himself, but he was relieved when she had returned. Worried, but relieved all the same.
Summoning up his usual arrogance he began, "So prey tell why I've been summoned? I do have a mountain of work to get through before the end of day."
In no mood to play games Imogen went straight for the kill. "You need to explain why Damien Bale, your relative, was given a job deemed unnecessary without following the usual employment procedures and why you have ignored obvious discrepancies in terms of a significant amount of missing stock, not to

mention some really creative invoicing, which had been reported to you but which you dismissed without investigation. Explain! Now!"
Momentarily taken aback Peter just stared before he began his usual bluster. "I will not sit here and have you make…"
Interrupting him Imogen continued, "Oh but you will Peter. This has already been reported to the Trust's Head Office and the police, who will be with us shortly but before they arrive Peter, make me understand how you could have been so stupid!"
Imogen saw her colleague deflate before her very eyes, as Deputy Head Peter Rogers, all time 'bull-shitter extraordinaire', now slumped forward with his head in his hands. Minutes of silence passed before he raised his head revealing a grey, haggard face which seemed to have aged a decade in the minutes that had just passed.
Finally finding his voice he began. "I suppose I played the big 'I am' giving Damien a job. Looked big in front of the family, I mean they convinced me he was just having a tough time finding his way," as he rubbed his hands over his face adding, "I had no idea what a little shit he was." Imogen remained silent, just listening, just waiting. She knew more was to come.
"Bill had already said he wasn't impressed with his work ethic and I did have a word. He did promise to try harder, so I gave him another chance and another until…"

"Until?"

Head now back in his hands Imogen waited. Finally, he looked up and revealed all. "Until he found me and Ellie… in the store room." Ellie being Head of Personnel and an appointment of the previous Head.

"In the store room?" Imogen was now dreading the rest. This was not what she was expecting at all.

Shaking his head Peter's belligerence momentarily returned as he was now almost shouting, "Do you want the sordid details Imogen? Shall I paint you a bloody picture?"

Shaking her head Imogen now for the first time ever felt something akin to pity for Peter.

"He found you having sex in one of the school store rooms and he's been blackmailing you to keep quiet?"

"Oh it's worse than that. The little shit videoed us on his iPhone and threatened to send it to the world and he would have too! I mean I couldn't do that to Jane and my kids."

"You have three, right?"

Nodding Peter replied, "And one on the way."

"Your wife is pregnant?"

Shaking his head and wryly smiling he replied, "No. Ellie is."

Now it was Imogen's turn to put her head in her hands. "Oh my God Peter! How could you be so… so…"

"I think the term you're looking for is such a

stupid pillock! Or perhaps daft prick?!"
Shaking her head in surprised disbelief Imogen could only say, "I'm sorry Peter but I wish you'd turned to someone for help before this whole thing got out of hand. We're talking thousands here, not just a few quid and as for the mess you've made of your personal life, well, I have no words."
Nodding his understanding Peter's next words stunned her. "You know the one person I wished I could have turned to was you! After all these years of me resenting you, hating you even and it's you I felt could have sorted this shit show out before I ended up ... well, where I've ended up I suppose, but it would have all come out in the end wouldn't it? Secrets never stay secret forever do they?"
At that point, Imogen was grateful when the knock on the day came with Agnes informing them that the police had arrived, ready to begin their questioning which would Imogen knew, lead to at least one arrest.
"Ready to face the music?"
"Yep. Let's get it done.

*

Peter would later reflect how much better the worse he felt could happen to him, actually was. The Police were surprisingly sympathetic and he was relieved when they immediately confiscated Damien's phone as evidence, before he could carry out his threat.

Imogen had greeted the three detectives waiting for her in Reception but paying particular attention to Isiah. "Good to see you again Detective or can I just call you Isiah? After all you did safe my life not that long ago," as she made reference to the night Isiah had foiled a murder attempt on both Max and herself.
"Good to see you too Miss…" then smiling continued, "Imogen. So where is the man we need to interview?"
At this point Damien Bale was walking nonchalantly into the Reception area, still believing he had protection; that he was untouchable. When he saw the three men, he instinctively knew they were law enforcement but then seeing Peter with them, found his customary smirk and swagger.
Looking at Imogen with his customary insolence he said, "Told I was wanted in Reception."
Stepping forward Dan ordered, "Your phone. Now!"
Eyes widening, he shook his head stating, "That's my property and I don't have to give you owt!"
Producing the paper warrant that allowed such a confiscation Isiah now said, "You'll find this does or do we have to frisk you? I mean what else would we find?" as he purposely sniffed the air around the belligerent man.
Reluctantly handing the device over then turning his attention to Peter he hissed, "Don't think this is over! I can still…"

"Do what you want with it. I'm just relieved I don't have to ever look at your shit-face again." He knew the video could appear and probably would one day and he'd face that too when the time came.

Damien now turned his anger and vitriol onto Imogen, "He said you were a sanctimonious holier than thou bloody cow but I know people, important people and you will bloody get yours!" as Isiah and Dan unceremoniously handcuffed him.

"I think you've said enough," said Isiah as they led him to their waiting vehicle in full view of the school's student population then adding, "looks like you're going to have your own fifteen minutes of fame too on Social Media. Let's see how you like it!"

"Sorry you had to endure that Ms Holt," this from Richard Braxton, as he openly admired Imogen, not bothering to hide his personal interest in what he was looking at.

"Just another day at the office Detective and I thank you and your colleagues for your quick response."

"We aim to serve as well as protect, but here's my card and please let me know if there is any other service I can help you with," as he held Imogen's gaze, the double entendre not lost on either of them, as he allowed his fingers to briefly brush hers.

Squashing her eye roll and grimace, Imogen

merely nodded, binning the card on her way as she returned to her office.

Watching her retreating back, Richard whistled softly under his breath muttering, “Nice. Very nice indeed.”

CHAPTER 14

"Explain to me what you were thinking when you decided this place would make a good hen night?" asked a bewildered Imogen as she, Harry and Beth attempted to thaw out.
"Well look at Lyds. She's positively flying! Never seen her so relaxed and chilled!" declared Beth trying hard not to laugh as a very inebriated Lydia was busy telling a very bemused bar man that he looked just like a drug dealer she had recently arrested, "I'm telling you," she slurred, "you two could be twins. Are you sure your surname isn't Mason?"
"Chilled being the operative word!" stated Harry who was stamping her feet attempting to get her blood flow going again.
The newest club to be opened in nearby Barnsley was an Ice Bar, based on the one to be found in Barcelona whereby you entered a chamber of ice with temperatures between minus five and minus ten degrees Celsius. Imogen, Beth and Harry had lasted the whole of five minutes before retreating into the main bar.
"I mean Beth," said Harry, "we live in Penton

where it's always freezing, even in August!"
"Well with all the conditions I've been given, I was actually left with very little to work with," declared Beth.
Laughing Imogen remarked, "Yes I imagine you wouldn't get a strip-o-gram to venture into this place that's for sure."
"Remember yours Gen?" Harry asked nudging her knowingly.
"Please Harry, it's taken me years to bloody forget it. I mean, Beth, what were you thinking even then?"
"Actually I can't remember much about that night love, all a bit of a blur," as she continued watching Lydia, still interrogating the bar man who was now looking quietly terrified, "except in my defence, I thought he would be wearing some item of clothing underneath that wetsuit!"
"Where did he hide that disgusting kipper?" asked Harry, "I've always wondered."
"It's what he tried to with it, that still haunts me," grimaced Imogen then turning back to Beth added, "and I'm glad you've managed to forget because I still break out in a cold sweat when I remember and do you think we need to rescue that poor boy any time soon?"
"Yes," smiled Beth, "but she's having such a good time bless her." At this point they were joined by Sharon Summers who Beth knew well from her days in uniform.
"Hi ladies, enjoying yourselves?"

"Now we're thawing out we are," laughed Harry.
"I don't think you've met my old friends from Penton, Sharon," as Beth proceeded to do the honours. Settling into the curved banquette where they were seated Sharon smiled at the group saying, "So been friends long?" and smiled when all three as one replied, "Forever."
"So how's it going with our latest edition to the squad then Sharon?" asked Beth.
Smiling Sharon shrugged replying, "Okay I think, I mean he's got some serious moves and he's very pretty to look at so…"
"Good conversationalist then?" asked Beth, laughing now.
"Wouldn't know mate," grinned back Sharon.
At this point they were joined by a very inebriated Lydia, who plonked herself in to the centre of the group after much manoeuvring of bodies and drinks.
"I am having the best time ever!" she declared, "and thank you for coming," this now being said to both Imogen and Harry.
"I hated it when you hated me but I hated me too so I understood," she slurred.
"All a long time ago mate," said Beth, as Lydia placed her head on Beth's shoulder.
"And I'm getting married Beth," slurred Lydia, "to my Dan and we're going to have lots of babies."
"Yes you are mate," smiled Beth.
Then turning to Imogen Lydia declared, "And

you're so, so beautiful Imogen, and the Chief is so, so handsome that you need to get back together because you would have THE most beautiful babies ever, wouldn't they Beth?"

Harry and Beth both tried not to wince at the faux pas that a non- drunken Lydia wouldn't ever normally make and looked at Imogen to make sure the hurt hadn't hit its mark.

Imogen merely smiled and said, "Thank you Lydia, but perhaps some things aren't meant to be."

"Oh but you must never say never must you Beth and have I told you how much I love you? You're the sister I never had. In fact," as she now stood up, climbed onto the velour banquette and declared to the whole bar, "I love you all," to shrieks of support as her precarious swaying made the women now catch her before she fell.

"I think it's time someone called it a night," murmured Harry, only to hear Lydia demand of Beth, "We need to go and dance. Where can we dance? Can we dance here? And Tequila! I've never had Tequila. I need Tequila!"

Laughing, Imogen and Harry nodded their goodbyes to Beth and Sharon as Lydia began to dance, encouraging others to join her.

"Oh but that hangover is going to be legendary," smiled Imogen.

"Will last for days if we're anything to go by. You ok? Lydia wouldn't have realised she was saying something that would sting."

"I'm actually used to it. I mean people assume stuff don't they. They see someone without children and just assume it's a choice made or you haven't found the right partner...and its better than the pity too I guess."

Although autumn had arrived, it was a pleasant evening as they walked to Imogen's car to make their short drive back to Penton. Barnsley's Town Hall lights were shining bright with the fountains in the adjacent square, giving off an almost European ambience. The town had recently risen like 'a phoenix from the ashes' having endured years of hardship but was now enjoying a revival in its new found café culture and amenities. It had in fact become the jewel and pride of South Yorkshire.

Harry now glanced side-ways at Imogen saying, "Went to the hairdressers yesterday and I have to say, Max is the main topic of conversation in there, I mean Barry and a very recently married Lester were positively purring with lust."

"He probably is wherever he goes," replied Imogen with a heavy sigh.

"So no reconciliation for you two on the cards?"

Imogen merely shook her head then smiling at her friend whose life she envied more than anyone else's said, "We can't all be as lucky as you and Alan my friend."

Wincing Harry replied with her customary honesty saying, "How smug must we appear? Eh?"

"No, not at all," placated Imogen, "in fact I'm grateful to have you guys in our lives and see you enjoy such a 'normal' happy life. It means there's hope for the world."

"We never take it for granted Gen and when I think of poor Sarah... it just makes me feel so sad... and scared too. I mean, why are we so lucky?"

"I know Harry, but from what I can see nearly every day, is that luck isn't evenly distributed and life does not play fair my friend. So let's all enjoy yours eh?" Linking her arm through Harry's, Imogen smiled sadly as they continued their walk through Barnsley's town centre to begin their short journey home.

CHAPTER 15

The small, petrified boy couldn't stop shaking although he was trying to be as still as possible because he knew he could explode at any time. He just didn't understand why they had done this to him. He was only walking to school, a bit late admittedly, but they came out of nowhere and now he was here all alone in the school yard. As soon as they'd bundled him out of the black van he had tried to get help, but everyone was screaming and running away from him. Now the scary man in the space suit was coming towards him telling him to stay still and to stay calm but he just couldn't. He knew he was being a cry baby but he wanted his mum. He promised he would be good. He's do his homework, tidy his room, be nicer to his younger brother, not eat too many sweets, not cheek his teachers but please take it off me was all he wanted to scream. He'd also wet himself but he didn't care. Now the scary man was backing away saying something he couldn't understand. Now another man was here, without the suit but a helmet and a bullet proof vest. He looked kind, he was smiling.

Max looked at the terrified boy and smilingly said, "Hi. My name is Max and I believe you are Faisel but your mates call you Fiz. Is it ok if I call you Fiz?" The boy just looked back at him with a tear streaked face that was now in total shock.
Max continued as if he had been answered. "Well Fiz we're going to sort this but it might take longer than we thought but you're not to worry because I'm staying right here with you mate if that's ok?"
Imogen with Eddie, Isiah and a man she didn't recognise were now observing the scene from the designated safe zone. Since Faisel's appearance in the school yard before morning registration, complete chaos had ensued, activating the school's evacuation policy at record speed. Now with pupils and staff safely away from the perceived danger zone, the priority now was to deactivate the suicide vest that was strapped onto the terrified child's torso. It was his screams of "Take if off me. It's going to blow me up!" that had first drawn attention to him, then terrified screams and mayhem had followed. Within what seemed like seconds all had fled leaving the child alone, frozen to the spot in nothing less than abject terror.
Max and his team had been alerted and the police and bomb disposal had appeared in record time but that had still been a very long wait for all those in the school now waiting for the nightmare to end. Benny Reynolds had turned to

Max at one point saying, "Well it looks I might be of some use after all", as they made their way to the waiting emergency vehicles. Max had been unable to speak, dreading what may be happening and hoping upon hope they got there in time.

Arriving at the school in record time they were greeted by Imogen and her Senior Team. Straight to the point Max began, "Where exactly is the boy?"

Imogen responded as professionally frosty as necessary, giving none of her emotions away, her being terrified for the boy involved in this madness and also being confronted by Max so soon after their last encounter. "In the main entrance quad area which is very close to the school's Reception. We've cleared all personnel as far away as possible onto to the top field in case... in case the worse happens."

"What do we know about the boy?"

"Year Eight. Good kid, never been in trouble," was Imogen's clipped reply. Nodding Max moved away to speak to the Bomb Disposal Team who were also assessing the situation.

After what seemed like an interminable age, Imogen with the rest of the police whom had arrived were moved to an area deemed far enough away from the danger zone as they now watched the experts begin the process of restoring order and calm without danger to life.

Sergeant Ray Boyle of Bomb Disposal, whose

ironic nickname was 'Sunshine' was now approaching the terrified boy, examining the device, speaking quietly to him. Watching him speaking into his intercom Imogen was now alarmed to see Max, a hard helmet on his head and now wearing a Flak jacket, approach the two solitary figures.

"What's he doing? Eddie? What's Max doing? He's going to get himself killed!"

Eddie as dumbfounded as Imogen just looked on.

"Well someone's got to stop him!" as Imogen now began to move from the designated area, only to be confronted by armed police barring her way.

"Eddie please," she now begged.

Eddie now put his arms around her saying with a confidence he didn't feel, "He knows what he's doing."

Ray 'Sunshine' had informed Max, that the boy was too volatile in his movements to allow him to deactivate the device. He had rightly identified that his bomb suit was scaring the boy to such a degree that he was being counterproductive so Max felt he had no choice but to go to the boy to calm him enough so Ray could do what he did best. So here he was.

Max was now kneeling before the small boy making sure they had eye to eye contact. Smiling Max began. "So when I was a lad I use to watch these really old movies with my Grandad, Laurel and Hardy they were. Heard of them?"

No response but Faisel was now looking at Max

and listening intently. "They were really funny, well we both thought they were. One of them use to say, "Well this is another fine mess you've got me into." I bet that's what they're all saying about us eh?"

"Mister... you won't leave me will you? I'm scared."

"No Fiz, I'm here and I promise you we will be out of this situation as soon as my friend Sunshine here deactivates what's strapped to you."

"Sunshine? That's a funny name." Fiz now visibly relaxing as Ray 'Sunshine' gave Max a discreet thumb's up as he began the slow process of prolonging life and cheating death.

"It is if you knew him. So which team do you support?" asked Max.

"Don't like football. I like cricket."

"Well you are a Yorkshire lad I guess. So who's your favourite cricketer? Joe Root?"

"Ben Stokes, I think he's great." Then looking at Max with eyes that had aged years he whispered, "I want to go home. I want mi mum mister. I promise I'll be good forever."

Nodding, "We'll get you home son and your mum will be very proud when I tell her how brave you've been." Suddenly Ray made a sudden movement, indicating that both he and Max should leave the boy at once. It took Max a few seconds to register what Ray was indicating, then shaking his head Max simply said, "Thanks Ray. See you later mate."

Clearly alarmed Ray tried again, more forcefully stating, "It's programmed to detonate when the deactivation button is tampered with which means we now have only thirty seconds to clear so move it. Now!"

Shaking his head, Max lowered his body to fully sit as he now took the young, terrified sobbing boy into his arms, holding him tightly, as if he was his own child, saying into his hair, "It's ok Faisel. You're not alone, I'm not leaving you behind buddy."

Imogen, Eddie and the rest watching from their vantage point saw the Bomb Disposal Officer begin to run to safety. Imogen saw Max take the terrified boy into his arms and she knew. She just knew instinctively that it wasn't in her Max, to leave a young defenceless boy to die alone. Closing her eyes, she couldn't believe what she was being made to live through again. Watching another good man die pointlessly at the hands of those intent on doing harm to others, was more than she could physically bear.

All were now waiting for the inevitable, some of the officers looked to be fighting back tears, with many turning away, unable to look. Then it happened.

*

A Sky News helicopter was hovering capturing every moment sending out a 'live feed' which was being watched everywhere. Malcolm, Albert and Ed were watching the events play out on the sixty-inch television on the wall of Malcolm's city centre office.

"I hope our little lady isn't anywhere near this boss," said Albert shaking his head.

"That copper's got some ball though, don't you think?" asked Ed.

"Aye lads, balls of steel," muttered Malcolm then, "oh my Christ! No!" as they all watched the bomb disposal officer running away, leaving Max alone with the boy.

*

In Penton at Sarah's home, Sarah and Harry were besides themselves as they too watched. "She'll never recover if she sees another man she cares for die before her very eyes. At least I've been spared that," whispered Sarah as Harry squeezed her hand.

"Surely they know what they're doing," replied Harry, then, "oh no! What's happening? Why isn't Max moving?"

"Oh please God no," whispered Sarah, "not again."

*

Back at Sheffield Central Dan, Lydia and Beth were scrolling through CCTV looking to see who had done this to the small boy who was now the latest albeit reluctant main focus of the day's news, whilst keeping one eye on the news screen as the events played out.

"Right, Sharrow Vale Road at 8.23 am this morning. Five of them," said Dan as the others crowded round the screen. What they saw were five black balaclava clad faces, a black transit van with no registration plates and a terrified small boy.

"Poor little bugger," said Beth, then looked up sharply as she heard Lydia's cry of distress. "What's happening? Oh my God. What's the boss think he's doing. Move for Christ's sake," were her impotent yells as they stood silently, watching the man they all owed so much to, a man they would follow anywhere, put his arms around the young victim. Lydia turned into Dan's arms, burying her head in his chest as she began to quietly weep.

They now waited for the inevitable.

CHAPTER 16

Imogen had her back to her office door, staring out through the window, unseeing the streams of students making their way out of the school building to go home to their waiting albeit terrified but relieved parents. The city had ground to a halt and it was taking hours to rectify the grid lock that would allow the required vehicles through.

All Imogen was seeing was Max, his arms tightly around the young Faisel, never letting him go, but facing together what was to come. However, instead of the expected explosion came a loud cacophony of 'joker' type laughter and the release of a large phallic shaped balloon.

Imogen was now remembering how she had collapsed into Eddie's arms when they all realised that this had been no more than a cruel elaborate joke, designed to bring terror and chaos. It had succeeded in spades.

Max walked into her office and was now standing behind her. Clearing his throat, he began. "So my team will be doing a forensic sweep of the area and..."

Turning to face him Imogen shook her head, her face deathly white, her voice shaking, her finger pointing. "How dare you! How dare you stand there as if you haven't just… just," then she was in his arms and the tears now came, a deluge representing the fear, the terror, the loss she had felt in those few moments.

"I'm ok. I'm alive. Today was not my turn to die," soothed Max, stroking her hair as he gently held her.

Now angry, she thrust herself from him saying, "More from sheer luck than any bloody judgement you showed. If that had been a real explosive device, you were going to let me see you die! Again!"

Mrs Mane at this moment appeared at the doorway. "Err sorry to interrupt Ms Holt but the Year tutors want to know if some of the older students could cut through the staff car park to help with a potential crush at the main gates."

Standing tall, pushing back her shoulder, wiping her eyes and smoothing down her hair, Imogen responded with, "Thank you Agnes. I'll be right there," then turning to Max said, "and I haven't finished with you yet!" as she stalked out.

Smiling, Max said more to himself as well as her retreating back, "I certainly hope not."

Sitting down in her office chair, he was now beginning to feel the effects of his adrenalin wearing off. That really had been a close call and he hadn't intended to risk life and limb but then... something else just took over. Christ but he could actually hear his heart beating now. Without warning the noise of the unexpected explosion reached him seconds later, shattering the window inches away from the desk, shards of glass showering everywhere as he leapt to his feet and raced towards the noise in fear and dread of what he was about to find.

*

Carnage.
That's the word many used days, weeks, months, years later.
The school car park now represented a typical war zone, a newsreel filmed in a far distant land. Smoke billowed from what was left of the burning car, its metal shards now scattered across the burning asphalt.
A cacophony of screams and distress echoed as if on a stereophonic sound system, its volume seemingly at full pelt.
Chaos. People running in all directions.
Bodies lying unmoving on the ground.
He was now searching for her.
He couldn't see her.
People were shouting words at him, asking him questions he was not able to understand or compute.
Where was she?
Christ, but if anything's happened to her...was all he could think...
Suddenly Isiah was at his side with Imogen in his

huge strong arms. "She's here boss and as far as I can tell she's unhurt. I saw the blast throw her backwards and she seems out of it."
Imogen at this point opened her eyes as Isiah gingerly put her down. Swaying Max now held her. "What's happening?" was all she was able to say.

CHAPTER 17

"This is the early evening News with Carl Mason. Terror came to Sheffield today. Grove School in the city's Hillsborough area has been the subject of a car bombing on the school's premises. Tim Jackson is live at the scene. Tim what can you tell us about today's shocking events?"

"Thanks Carl. It was at approximately 8.50 this morning when a young boy wearing what looked like a suicide vest device appeared on school premises (pans to Sky credited footage shown earlier). *It was hours later that it became evident that this had been nothing more than a cruel hoax, which had been designed to create both terror and chaos. However, worse was still to come. The authorities, assuming the incident had passed had been unaware that an explosive device had been placed under the Head teacher's car, a Ms Imogen Holt, which would have ignited as soon as she had attempted to drive her vehicle. It was by sheer luck Carl, that the device was activated when a stray football hit her car and the explosion then ensued. Several have been taken to hospital although as far as we can ascertain there have been no*

fatalities but make no mistake, today was designed to maim and kill and create as much chaos and terror as possible. Put this in direct contrast with the actions of Detective Chief Superintendent Max Stainmore's act of selfless courage witnessed earlier, which has been heralded as nothing short of heroic."

"It does indeed. Thanks Tim. The Prime Minister has called today's attack as "A cowardly act of terror which will not go unpunished." (Pans to Westminster House of Commons, the Prime Minister at the Dispatch Box) ***"Myself and the rest of this House sends its deepest sympathies to all those in Sheffield caught up in this cruel madness and our pride of the heroism displayed by one of Sheffield's finest means that these evil perpetrators will never defeat us..."*** (pans back to newsreader). ***So to the rest of today's news......................"***

*

Switching off the noise of the television plunged the office into a stony silence. Ed was now the first to speak, "Bloody hell fire boss but Ms Holt's car? What the bloody hell is going on?"

"Lunacy," this from Albert, "bloody lunacy! What has she done to piss somebody off to that degree?"

Malcolm had yet to speak. He had hardly moved from his desk or spoken as he digested the events of the day, events that could so easily have ended Imogen's life. He was now mentally admitting to himself that the thought of some low life trying to hurt her like this was more than he could bear. Sighing heavily, he replied, "Well lads this has just got personal for me and I think it's now time that we convene all forces. I shall call a meeting."

*

Wallace Senior was having a really good day. Despite being incarcerated in Armley Leeds High Security Prison he still managed to know exactly what was happening on the outside due to his acquisition of the latest iPhone, courtesy of a sympathetic to his cause Prison Officer. He was now having a conversation with his first lieutenant Gareth Jackson.

"Well Gareth, been quite a day eh?"

"To be honest I had no idea what was coming and yeah, I love the chaos but how am I supposed to reign the lad in?"

"I get that but you'll think of a way. I mean who knew he had access to explosives and had the wherewithal to use them? As for the fake suicide vest… fucking genius man!"

Gareth was now chuckling as he replied, "Best fucking television for fucking years. Yeah, I know you're probably right mate but I have to say, you certainly know how to turn 'em!"

"I'm telling you straight now. That psychopath needed no turning from me. He's full of hate, probably born hating the whole fucking world. I just steered him in the right direction, that's all but he's going to be very useful. Ramp up the attacks so Mirza's lot are too busy protecting their own, leaving their drug outposts vulnerable. Should be easy pickings after today."

"Yeah," agreed Gareth, "Cowden can up his supplies to us immediately and I'll also find out who supplies the explosives. Can think of one or two uses for that sort of mischief, but you're too modest me old mate. You've moulded our favourite head case in your own image I'd say."

Gareth could hear his old mate chuckling down the phone at this. "As long as you keep one step ahead of him because if he goes rogue on us, he could bring the whole house of cards down with him, so watch him. Remember no one is indispensable. No one is irreplaceable!"

"I'll keep you posted and Wallace? Enjoy the tele reruns mate."

*

Max was standing in Imogen's apartment, looking out at the view of the Pennines, with brandy in hand, wondering if he had ever lived and survived such a day as the one currently coming to an end. Thank God it's Friday didn't come close.

Imogen emerged from her shower, having earlier discharged herself from the hospital where they had worried she would have delayed concussion. He turned to face her, handing her a glass of the soothing amber liquid, as she curled up onto her sofa. Imogen now gestured Max to join her which he did asking, "So? You doing okay?"

"Probably about as good as you I imagine." They

were both silent now, watching the flickering flames of the fire as they sipped brandy, reflecting on what could have been.

Max was the first to speak. "There's no easy way to look at this but that bomb under your car was designed to kill you or at least badly injure you."

"I know."

"I need to know who to start looking at. Who may have a grudge against you?"

"Apart from you and George Cowden you mean?" as Imogen attempted at humour, hating what he was making her think about.

"I'm serious Imogen. Have you any idea how I... how ..." as he struggled to find the words as well as keeping his emotions in check.

Imogen placed their drinks onto the nearby table as she turned herself onto Max's lap and into his arms, putting her own arms around him as she said, "I can't put into words either, how I felt when I thought you had sacrificed yourself to be with that very frightened poor little boy."

Now they were holding each other tightly, both with eyes closed, both grateful they were in this moment.

Max was the first to speak as he whispered, "So does this mean we're now back to where we should be?" Imogen now disentangled herself from his embrace and standing up, walked to look out of her vast windows.

"I want us to be Max. When I thought you were...when I thought you weren't going to walk away from what was happening... but...there are certain things... I have to tell you which may change your mind. Change how you feel."

Max now too was on his feet stating, "The Downs' case has been closed for nearly two years and I don't want to know..." but Imogen shaking her head interrupted him.

Taking a deep breath Imogen spoke the words which could destroy her, in more ways than one. Words she had only ever uttered once before. "Max, when I was fourteen years old I killed my father!"

Max was suddenly very still, the silence between them now almost deafening. Then very quietly Max said, "Ok. Tell me the rest."

Looking unbearably sad, Imogen began the sorry tale of the night she had no choice but to finally stop her father hurting her mother. "It was the usual, him coming home drunk and using mum as his personal punching bag. I was upstairs and heard it, the slaps, the pleading, her cries of pain. His screaming at her, the names he was calling her, the usual bile coming out of his mouth. I walked downstairs and saw the poker and without really thinking, picked it up. When I walked into the kitchen, I saw he was standing over her, kicking her so hard I thought he'd killed her this time. So I hit him as hard as I could. Couldn't stop. Mum had to grab the poker off me." Imogen had walked towards the huge windows overlooking the panoramic scene she was so familiar with, as Max came to stand behind her.

"When we realised he was dead," she continued, "we dragged his body out onto Dark Lane. It was knee deep in snow. We used to have so much snow in those days and we just…left him there. We waited for hours for the police to come and arrest us. When they did come it was to tell us it that he had been killed in a 'hit and run' and they were very sorry for our loss." She now waited for his verdict as she turned to face him.

Without saying a word, Max simply took her into his arms, holding her tightly, swaying with her, consoling her and when she looked into his eyes, she saw no judgement but understanding. "You've lived with this all these years? You and Arlette?" Imogen merely nodded, now unable to speak.

Finally moving away from him Imogen now asked, "So what now Max? I assume you will have to report what I've…"

"Excuse me?" he interrupted, "Report what?" Max now looking somewhat scandalised at her as he questioned, "Are you seriously expecting me to arrest you? For you saving the life of your mother from a piece of garbage that used you both as punch bags? Is that who you think I am? The sort of copper I am?"

Shaking her head, she now tried to make him understand. "No but blood begets blood Max. My husband and baby died and I've watched you nearly die three times now. Surely that must be telling you something?"

"Oh my God, but you actually think you're being punished don't you?" Max running his fingers through his hair as he looked at her in consternated surprise. "Sweetheart but that just isn't how the world works and I should know."

Taking her back into his arms, looking into her eyes he now asked, "Is that why you ran away from me? From your home, your friends?"

"I had to try and keep you safe," she murmured into his chest.

Laughing quietly, he asked, "How can someone as clever and as accomplished as you be so full of superstition? So full of misplaced guilt?"

"I've always believed wickedness has to be paid for?"

"What did your husband say when you told him?"

"I didn't. He knew he had died but I could never pluck up the courage to tell him, to disappoint him. To be judged by him I guess."

Holding her face in his hands, Max now whispered, "Then thank you. Thank you for trusting me with this and as for you owing the Devil? You paid that debt a long time ago."

Now choosing his words carefully Max continued. "You've kept this bottled up a long time and you would have needed counselling and probably treatment for PTSD when it happened and it will have indirectly affected your choices, your decisions, ever since. Trust me, I've seen this too many times."

As Imogen began to protest he continued speaking over her, "Not only for the abuse you both endured for years but also..." He stopped, not sure how his next words would be greeted.

"Go on."

"He was your father and I suspect you've never truly grieved his loss despite the monster he was. Never grieved for the father he should have been, the father you deserved to have."

Looking bewildered Imogen moved away from him to look out of her huge window, unseeing the mountainous view that never failed to take your breath away.

Moving behind her but careful not to touch her, they stood together in silence, until she turned into his arms where they held each other for the longest time. As Imogen looked up into Max's eyes she saw no judgement, but only compassion and understanding reflected in them and she now felt, as if for the first time in years, she could fully breathe. As if for years she had been holding her breath, waiting for a metaphorical axe to fall which would reveal what she had done, revealing to the world, who she truly was.

Now all she could think to say was, "I love you Max Stainmore. I think I always have."

Nodding, Max whispered, "I love you too Imogen, have done for a long time now," as he slowly untied the belt of her gown, allowing it to fall to the floor, looking at her body with all of its scars highlighting what she had already endured and survived. Tenderly lifting her naked form up into his arms, he proceeded to take her to her bed, kissing her soundly the whole way there.

CHAPTER 18

The quiet, gentle, rippling sounds of water that constituted the Victorian Quays at Waterside, felt soothing, calm and at one with nature. A far cry from the burning smoke and mayhem Eddie had witnessed hours earlier. Sitting on a bench at the water's edge Eddie didn't think his legs would carry him home. He'd phoned his near hysterical wife to assure her and his children that he was safe but he felt he couldn't as yet go home; not wanting to contaminate the place where he was his happiest with the stench of fear and hate that had seemed all pervading this day.
Deep in his thoughts Eddie was startled to see his old friend and former colleague Philip Read join him. "Sorry mate, didn't mean to startle you."
"No worries Phil."
"Been a bit of a day eh?"
"Aye, just a bit."
Silence now except for the sound of water and distant revellers from nearby drinking and dining places until Phil said, "Max Stainmore eh!? Bloody hell fire! I've witnessed all sorts of bravery in my time but that was... well

something else entirely."

Nodding his agreement Eddie added, "You're not wrong mate. You're not wrong. I couldn't believe my eyes when I saw 'Sunshine' leave the active site. I honestly thought that one of the best men, best coppers I have ever known was going to... to be..." Eddie's voice broke momentarily as Philip gently squeezed his shoulder in silent comfort.

"I knew there was something about him the first time I met him during the Covid madness. Not bad for a soft London lad eh?"

Smiling now Eddie agreed, "Aye Phil, not bad for a soft London lad."

"Not ready for home yet?"

Shaking his head Eddie now struggled to convey the mass of different emotions he felt almost consumed by. "It was madness Phil. Sheer bloody madness that someone would not only terrify a small child but to then plant a car bomb in a school car park! A bomb that would injure children, innocents... beyond belief mate. I mean what sort of head cases are we dealing with here?"

"I know Eddie, just when you think you've seen it all eh? Any suspects?"

"Some CCTV footage but it's giving us little to go on, but I swear to all that is holy, we will find these bastards, if it's the last thing I ever do!"

Nodding his agreement Philip got to his feet saying, "And that can wait until tomorrow but for now me old mate, let's get you back to that

lovely wife of yours ok?"
Smiling, Eddie got to his feet and began to make his way home, to the comfort of a loving wife and almost grown children, thanking the stars that at least for tonight, all he loved were safe.

*

Max, seeing Imogen's half hidden silhouette against the light of the open fridge, felt at that moment, he'd never seen anything more beautiful. Looking up she smiled at him, giving him a look that suggested she knew exactly what he was thinking. It was in the early hours, dawn was beginning to break and they had yet to really sleep. Imogen had slipped away, had donned Max's discarded shirt and was now searching her fridge for sustenance.
"Hungry?"
"Starving," as he now placed his arms around her waist, drawing her back towards him as she continued her surveillance of her fridge. "but not for food," as he now began to kiss her neck. The rumbling sounds of hunger from him made her smile.
"Even super heroes need food Chief Superintendent and you will have burned a good many calories these last few hours."
"Complaining?" he murmured as he continued his exploration of her neck with his mouth.
"Mmmm," she murmured back because his nibbling of her neck was seriously distracting, "not in the least but we need food. So how does

bacon and eggs sound?"

"Only if the eggs are from the guy who sells them on Penton Market because the yokes are seriously orange and the bacon is from the Farm shop, not the butcher?"

"Oh my word," laughed Imogen as she turned into his arms, her hands full with produce from the fridge, "who are you and what have you done with that soft southern London lad we all know and love?"

"He found his tribe, that's all."

"Is that why you stayed here? To be with your 'people'?"

"No, I knew you'd return eventually, I mean how could you not as he indicated the view from her window."

"You make me sound like a homing pigeon!"

Chuckling he responded, "I wouldn't dream or dare call you a bird of any description and I imagine those poor deluded men who may have tried, lived to regret it. I just needed to bide my time that's all."

"Glad you did," was her whisper, as she moved to kiss him then allowed their kiss to deepen further such was the connection between them now. Pulling away Imogen began to retrieve pans and cutlery, smilingly saying, "Can we eat first before we resume...?"

Grinning Max nodded, "If you insist."

As they now busied themselves with the simple act of making and eating food, Imogen was suddenly struck how bizarre life was. Hours earlier they had been so estranged then Max had literally put his life on the line and her life too, could have so easily been obliterated. It was by sheer luck she hadn't been.

"Penny for them?" asked Max as he poured their coffee.

"This. How normal 'this' is,", indicating where they were and what they were doing.

"Missing the mayhem already?"

Smiling Imogen shook her head, "No, give me normal any time although I don't think I really know what normal is."

Giving this some thought Max now assessed, "I guess there's no such thing. Routine, yes. Boredom definitely. Living on the edge, occasionally. Perhaps a combination of the three is 'normal'."

"Wow a philosopher as well as a super hero," smiled Imogen.

"I have my moments," grinned Max then added, "and this 'normal' right now is about as perfect as it gets for me."

"For me too Max," as she now looked at him, still not quite believing what they had survived, and what they had finally become, literally overnight.

Max continued eating but Imogen was seeing how he had started to think about the day ahead, its impact and worries they would both share and what the final outcomes would reveal.

She began, "I hope I never have to live through another day like yesterday again but you will won't you? That's what you've signed up for isn't it? To run towards danger in order to serve and protect."

"Will that be a problem for us?"

"No," was her reply, without a moment's hesitation. "Life is a lottery Max, something I learnt a long time ago and if it had to happen at all, I'm glad it was Friday. I guess I will have a great deal to sort out won't I? No doubt the police will need a statement, have questions, the insurers will need notifying, the press no doubt not to mention making sure the school structure is safe. I'll have to make alternative provision for the students, particularly those in their exam year and so soon after bloody Covid as well..."

Imogen's last words were cut off when Max's mouth firmly took away all forthcoming words as he reached for her.

"We've got hours yet before the world comes calling."

Moving to straddle his lap as he sat, Imogen nodded saying against his lips, "You're right. So what have you got in mind Chief?"

CHAPTER 19

Turning his car to park in his designated spot was proving difficult as Max was
confronted with a sea of photographers, news readers and television crew. "What the...?"
Finally finding his spot, Max was now trying to make his way through and was relieved when Isiah's considerable bulk appeared as a barrier between Max and the throng shouting their questions and asking him to smile.
"What going on?" asked a bewildered Max as he entered the station's Reception area which was equally as full of the press but also of colleagues from every part of the station who were now applauding as he walked through the revolving doors.
"Would appear you are hot news Chief," grinned Isiah," and rightly so."
"There he is!" boomed Chief Constable Jim Haggerty who was standing closely next to the Police Crime Commissioner, Paul Sanders and Sheffield City's Mayor Clive Butterworth. Max noted how they all seemed very suited and very booted unlike himself, who had finally

torn himself away from Imogen, dashing home to find the nearest clean shirt and suit before arriving at work. He may have even forgotten to comb his hair.

“Max, my boy but you have made this city, this force very proud indeed. Have you met our esteemed guests?” as without waiting for a response Jim proceeded to make introductions before ushering the four of them into the lift to his office on the station’s top floor.

Sitting comfortably in his office, Jim and his guests began to strategise in how they would make the most of the previous day’s events.

“This is priceless publicity gentlemen,” began Paul Sanders the Police Commissioner.

“Couldn’t have come at a better time too,” agreed Jim.

“Although as Mayor, chaps I want the public to feel safe, so let’s not overplay the bomb incident in the car park if that’s ok?”

Max felt at this point he did have to interject. “Every public building in the city needs to be on high alert and undergo rigorous checks. This may have been a random target so could happen anywhere else only next time, someone could be killed.”

The three men glancing at each other, looked uncomfortable and suitably chastised. Jim was the first to speak.

“Fair point Max, and safety measures in every public building are being cranked up as we speak but today we also want to celebrate your heroism because there's no other word to describe it, no Max, let me finish," as Max began to interrupt. "My heart was in my mouth yesterday when you refused to leave that lad and have you any idea how far and wide those images have gone? I got a phone call from the New York Police Commissioner telling me that it's the bravest thing he's ever seen. I mean New York 1PP calling here! Asking to speak to me!"

"That bloke off the television? 'Blue Bloods'?" asked the Mayor.

"Not the actor Clive, the actual Police Commissioner!"

"Oh right."

"Which is why Sir," Max continued, "I need to be with my team. I'm meeting Counter Terrorism personnel in the next hour as time is of the essence."

"Assistant Chief Constable Yale is dealing with that until you've finished here. So Clive, are you clear in what you're going to say out there?"

Sidling up to Max, the station's Press Officer Leanne Wright whispered, "Don't worry Chief Superintendent, hopefully this won't take too much longer."

Whispering back Max replied, "With respect, it's been too long already."

"So Leanne, what's happening?" asked Jim.

Smiling sympathetically at Max, Leanne began to lay out the day's itinerary that would propel Max onto the nation's television screens and radio systems.

Max just wanted to put his head into his hands and howl.

He now found himself outside on the steps of Sheffield Central facing a sea of faces some with phone cameras, some with microphones, whilst the police personnel who were these days, more politician than law enforcement made their proverbial hay whilst their proverbial sun this day shone. Max had never seen the Chief Constable so happy.

Jim Haggerty, looking suitably solemn began his well-rehearsed speech.

"I cannot put into words the immense pride I feel regarding the actions of Detective Chief Superintendent Max Stainmore which was witnessed not only by the good people of this city, but by our nation and indeed, the whole world because it is rare to see such a selfless act of heroism. This man you see here today," pointing at Max now, "was not leaving that poor, terrified, defenceless child to face that unimaginable horror alone, giving a whole new meaning to the term, 'No Child Left Behind'.

Policing today is not an easy business but this man I'm proud to be standing next to, makes me believe we have honour and courage amongst us and we should all be very proud indeed."

As more applause ensued, Max was more than uncomfortable to see the Mayor now step up towards the microphone and realised with that sinking feeling, that today was going to be a very long day indeed.

*

It was after five in the afternoon when Max was finally at his desk, the one place he had been itching to get to since he'd arrived at work. Today had been like being part of a three ring circus and he had hated every single second.

Appearing at his door, Eddie grinned at him saying, "So what time are you on then?" referring to the televised news interviews he'd been busy giving all day."

"Don't know and I don't care," he replied, as he rubbed his eyes, leaning back and looking thoroughly exhausted. The fact he'd had very little rest the night before wasn't helping now either, not that he was regretting a single second spent losing sleep with Imogen. He wasn't enjoying the publicity though and hadn't in all honesty expected the fuss, although he should have realised his superiors would use his actions as good publicity for the Force as a whole.

It was a sad fact that confidence in the police was at an all-time low and for good reasons too, so he should have known, but still he was hoping it would soon become old news because finding those responsible for yesterday was all he could think about.

Eddie looking at him more closely said, "You do know you've still got some make up on? There, just under your cheek."

Rubbing at the mark pointed out and muttering, "Bloody hell," Max now turned to the matter most on his mind asking, "so what have we got so far? Anything?"

Eddie now all police business sat. "CCTV of four wearing balaclavas presumably all males, picking up young Faisel and placing him in a black transit where we assume they strapped their device onto the poor little sod."

"And CCTV of the school car park?" asked Max.

"Ah and that's where it gets interesting," answered Eddie, "because that has been wiped clean."

Sitting back Max asked, "Any suspects?"

"Yes, a Damien Bale, recently sacked by the school and charged with theft, fraud and extortion. Out on bail as it's his first offence, allegedly, but should have been remanded and he's a little charmer who made some very personal threats to Ms Holt in front of our officers," grinning without humour adding, "and you're just going to love him."

*

(Voice over) ***"You're watching Channel Five early evening news with Emilia Sanderson and Don Medley,"*** (pans to newsreaders sitting behind a large desk. A picture of Max in the school yard sat holding Faisel largely displayed on the backdrop behind the desk).

"Very few of us will easily forget the images that

came out of Sheffield yesterday. However out of the senseless carnage came a shining light of hope in the shape of the heroic selfless actions of Detective Chief Superintendent Max Stainmore.
Our reporter, Rufus Langley met with the Chief Superintendent earlier today."
(Pans to out of studio with Max and one other seated facing each other).
"Chief Superintendent, first of all may I thank you for agreeing to this interview as I'm aware you are a very busy man. First of all, could you tell our viewers what was going through your head when first faced with what to all intents and purposes, looked like a suicide vest strapped onto a child?"
(Camera pans to Max only with a close up of his face as he speaks).
"We'd been notified by the school of the situation and by the time we and the bomb disposal team arrived, the young boy was extremely distressed making his movements so volatile that it was felt he was in danger of indirectly activating the device before it was made safe. As Senior Officer in Charge I elected to approach the boy to try and calm him and keep him steady."
"But when told to leave the boy, you elected to stay and face what was to come with him?"
(Max merely nods at the question).
"So yesterday you were prepared to die Chief Superintendent?"
(Max remains silent for several seconds). ***"I didn't think about dying. My only thought in all honesty***

was that I couldn't leave him to face what was to come on his own. That's all."

"It's in sharp contrast to the actions of the Bomb Disposal Expert Sergeant Ray Boyle, who did indeed leave the scene and who in fact implored you to also leave."

(Max now leans forward voice stern). ***"Let me be very clear here. Sergeant Ray Boyle and his team put their lives on the line every single day. He followed the protocol he is trained to follow because he will be needed again and again and again. Also... he is one of the finest men I know and for all those pointless Social Media Trolls out there who believe they have the right to say differently, ought to instead, be grateful for his training and service."***

"And what have you to say to those who did this, not to mention the car bombing that took place later?"

(Zoom close up of Max's face who looks and speaks directly to the camera). ***"You are cowards and misguided. Only the worse kind of scum would terrify a small boy and activate a bomb on school premises. We will find you, no matter how long it takes, make no mistake and you will be brought to face the consequences of your actions."***

"Strong words Chief Superintendent. Do you believe the two are connected?"

"Possibly but our investigations have only just begun."

"And finally, Detective Chief Inspector, do you

think you're a hero?"
"Absolutely not!"
"Well Chief Superintendent, you will find many will be disagreeing with you on that point. A pleasure to meet you Sir."
(Rufus Langley leans forward with his outstretched hand for Max to shake which he does.
Pans back to the Channel 5 studio).
"Well Emilia, he's a hero in my book. My word, but such courage, such modesty."
"Absolutely Don and am I right in thinking that the Chief Superintendent was behind the investigation that brought down a human trafficking network not that long ago?"
"I believe so Emilia. You know, we talk a lot about the 'bad apples' in our police and its absolutely right as investigative journalists that we do so, but it's truly uplifting to be able to celebrate such selfless courage and dedication to the public."
"Couldn't agree more. Well after the break we will discussing the issue of the lack of National Health dentists. Back after this." (Music signifying advert break).

*

Sarah and Trey watched the news report in silence. "Well," said Sarah, "I knew he was a good police officer and a decent man but wow!"
"Wow indeed," replied Trey, "and a handsome sod with it."
Nodding her agreement Sarah added, "Yes he is.

Had a thing with Imogen for a while but…"

"Didn't work out?"

"I think it got complicated. Sad really."

"Well if she now changes her mind, she might get killed in the crush after that interview. Bloody hell and I'm straight. Handsome and brave eh? What a combination."

"One that fits you also," smiled Sarah. "So when are you off?"

"Before Dawn. You'll not hear me leave."

"It's been good to have you here these past few weeks Trey. John would have approved my having one of you here for a while and I don't know how these two will cope without you," as she pointed to her Pug, Cyril and Staffordshire Bull Terrier, Scooby-Doo who were besotted with their guest, following him everywhere.

Looking at her with such tenderness, Sarah now had to turn away. Truth was, she hated the idea of living here alone again, with no prospect of the love of her life returning to her and her unborn little one.

"So, I don't know when I'll get leave again but… well… I was wondering…"

"There's always a place here for you, in fact, I insist on it. Just promise me you'll stay safe."

Nodding he stood up and looked out at the view he had come to appreciate and love. Then said, "I also promise you Sarah, that we've, no, I haven't given up on the Sarge and I won't. Not ever."

"I know Trey, I know."

*

Arlette and Terry had also watched Max's interview. "Well, a bloody hero living right next door. Who'd have thought it Arlette."
Sighing Arlette merely nodded. "What's up love? Still in shock over the bomb at the school?"
"I don't think I'll ever recover from Imogen being so close to danger but... oh Terry, it's just that I had high hopes for him and our Imogen that's all."
"Well they still could happen."
Sadly, now shaking her head, she replied, "No love. Saw him dash home first thing, then dash out in different clothes so he's obviously spent the night elsewhere."
Smiling, Terry began to tease, "Well who's the resident watch-dog eh? Don't need Neighbourhood Watch with you around my love but it might have been innocent enough. Doesn't mean the lad's got himself a girlfriend."
Scoffing at Terry's obvious naivety, Arlette replied, "No Terry. There's some very lucky young woman out there and I just wish it could be my Imogen, that's all."
"Let's just be grateful she's unhurt after yesterday and who knows? They could still happen?"
Sighing with resignation Arlette looked at Terry and replied, "If you say so Terry, if you say so."

*

Damien Bale looked insolently at Max across the

interview table and Eddie had been right. Max's first instinct was to get the young man by the scruff of his neck and nail him against the wall.

"So it would appear you like to threaten women Damien?" was Max's opening question.

The shrug was all the response he got as a reply.

"Well," Max continued, "you're looking at some real time here thanks to Ms Holt."

"That bitch," muttered Damien under his breath.

Keeping hold of his temper Max continued. "You actually told her," looking at a file on the desk, "you'll get yours, I know people." So who are the people you know? Who are the ones who would put a bomb under a car that went on to injure children? It means you're not only looking at attempted murder now, but if terrorist charges are also attached, well, they'll throw away the key. Right Eddie?"

"Spot on Chief."

"What? You can't pin that on me!" Damien's permanent smirk had disappeared and was currently replaced with a look of incredulity and fear. "I had nowt to do with that. Got witnesses that I was nowhere near."

"Ah you see Damien your witnesses can't help you here. You know where the CCTV cameras are and someone who knows how they would work, wiped them clean. That must be you," stated Eddie, "and you made threats, so slam dunk Chief. We've got our man."

Playing along, Max nodded, as he leant back in

his chair, looking at the young man across the table, really enjoying his obvious discomfort.

"No, no. I don't know any bloody terrorists," shaking his head now close to tears, Damien was trying to make the detectives understand.

"I do know people, dangerous people, but they only break your legs, not plant bombs, for God's sake!"

"So you were going to have Ms Holt's legs broken then?" asked Max, his voice dangerously low and full of menace.

Swallowing Damien shook his head. "No. I was just … angry. Wanted to lash out… I mean I was onto a good thing before she bloody turned up!"

Max got up to leave as Eddie said for the purpose of the tape which had recorded every word, "Interview terminated at 6.25pm."

Damien pleading now asked, "You do believe me don't you?"

Turning to him but looking defeated, Max replied, "Yes, unfortunately!"

Walking back to the Serious Crime squad room, Max noticed a lack of activity asking, "Where is everyone?"

Grinning, Eddie replied, "Watching the news."

"Oh for Christ's sake," muttered Max as he walked into his office, closing the door behind him.

CHAPTER 20

They sat silently across Malcolm Speight's conference table in the large dimly lit room, eyes focused, faces closed. The four main men assembled knew each other, respected each other, distrusted each other and despised each other in equal measure.

Joseph O' Malley ran the Irish sector which provided 'Protection' whether a business wanted it or not and supplied weapons to whoever had the money to pay. Jack Smith, the undisputed Leader of the city's Travelling Community was currently riding high on the lucrative benefits of illegal dog and bare knuckle fights. Finally, Omar Miraz, Head of the City's main drug trafficking and money laundering outlet via his taxi business and the man feared the most. Behind each chair stood a designated lieutenant, behind them another foot soldier. Also present, an atmosphere of menace and violence without warning, only a moment away.

Malcolm sat solemnly alone at the head of the table, his face serious. "Thanks for agreeing to meet at such short notice gents," began Malcolm, "but I believe we may have a growing situation here in Sheffield which may suggest that it could be in all our interests if we pool our intelligence and our resources."

Silence.

Shaking his head Malcolm continued, "That is of course if we all agree that waging war on innocent kids is breaking any code real men albeit villains follow?"

Jack Smith was the first to speak. "The city is facing some disruption and it's bad for business, I agree, but we all know who the target is and quite frankly I couldn't give a toss!" Omar's son Mohammad stepped forward, as Malcolm silently shook his head with Omar placing his hand on his son's clenched fist.

"So you're saying that this isn't your problem Jack?" then continued as Jack Smith merely shrugged, adding, "so your little 'uns don't go to school then?"

"Not if they can help it and I'm saying that we all know who's the target and it isn't my lot for a bloody change."

Silence.

Then, from a corner of the dimly lit room came a voice, a soft, well-spoken voice uttering the famous words, "Then they came for the Jews and I did not speak out because I was not a Jew etcetera… then they came for me and there was no one left etcetera," as out of the shadows came Jakob Abrahms flanked by Malcolm's main men,

Ed and Albert whose collective enormous bulks greatly dwarfed the man in the middle, whom all eyes were now focussed on.

"Who the fuck is this?" growled Joseph O' Malley as all as one, were now on high alert.

"Easy gents," murmured Malcolm, "this is a client of mine who has a vested interest in the city's recent events."

Jakob Abrahms now joined the rest of the group seating himself directly opposite Malcolm at the other end of the table. The expensive Armani suit, gold cufflinks, Hugo Boss shirt, hand-made Italian leather shoes, along with that unmistakable smell of wealth, were all noted and assessed as the man began to speak. "Apologies for the theatrics gentlemen but I do like to make an entrance."

"But we don't like surprises," growled Jack, "so who are you and what the fuck is going on Speight?"

Leaning forward Malcolm began. "Gentlemen, Mr Abrahms has a vested interest in helping us find out who's behind what's happening here. Jakob you have the floor and everyone's attention."

Leaning back in his chair, he took his time crossing his legs as he surveyed the room, enjoying the effect and impact he was having. Finally, he said, "I want the scum who kicked to death my great aunt and..." as Jakob now turned his attention to Omar, "your son."

Omar appeared to be transfixed by the man speaking but remained silent.

Jakob continued, "And it does give me some degree of comfort that she died in the arms of a good man trying to protect her. A Moslem trying to protect a Jew eh? Perhaps an example for the whole world don't you think? A tiny glimmer of hope and harmony that such a thing could occur in a world that seems intent on destroying what is good."

All were clearly registering these well-chosen words but it was Joseph O'Malley who was the first to break the silence. "What has the murders to do with what happened at the school?"

"I'm not sure they're linked but it smacks of the same thinking. Look who's being targeted? I mean Omar, it must be affecting trade too?" Malcolm now deftly bringing the subject round to what he knew was their basic interest and concerns.

"Actually Speight, the 'Protection' business has never been better thanks to these head cases," laughed Joseph, then sobered as he added, "but I have kids who go to Grove South so yesterday was bloody terrifying. I came here as a kid myself because my parents wanted to leave this sort of lunacy behind in Belfast. So what is it you want Speight and whoever you are?" as he turned his attention back to Jakob.

Nodding his understanding at the man's subtext Malcolm began his offensive.

"We pool our intelligence. Find out what the word on the street is because nowt can remain a secret if you know where to look and listen. You will of course be paid for the use of your resources."

This brought about smiles and guffaws. "You're forking out coin Speight?" laughed Jack Smith.

"I assume the word 'coin' in this context means money?" asked Jakob before continuing, "but no. I will be paying for your time and information and gentlemen... I have more money than God!"

This brought looks of interest and a renewed respect for the stranger in their midst, the pound signs now evident in their eyes as their collective interest in Jakob Abrahms took on added meaning.

"But Speight? Does nowt for nowt?!" queried Jack.

Shaking his head Malcolm replied, "This just got personal for me gents so I'm not taking a penny. The Head of Grove South is under my personal protection and yesterday she was targeted." He allowed the men to digest this new information then added, "So I'm sensing that we may have an agreement?" The discrete nods indicated what Malcolm needed to see as he now began the real business of the meeting. "Right then lads, bring in the beers and now gents, let's get down to logistics."

*

The meeting had gone well into the night and

Jakob had been both surprised and impressed at the military precision in which these men, who lived on the outskirts of law and order, operated. He also acknowledged how Omar Mraz had barely spoken, merely nodding his agreement or shaking his head in disapproval, whispering to the man behind him who was clearly his son, judging by the shared features.

"Right," said Malcolm, "we know where to begin. The Stag's Head is known for a certain type to frequent it so Omar, I think your lad there could do with paying them a visit."

Omar merely nodded his agreement. Malcolm then looking at the collective gathered brought the meeting to its end. "Thanks for coming over and for agreeing to end this madness. I know men like us don't find it easy to trust one another."

"Oh fuck off Speight," laughed Jack, "we'll be hearing fucking violins next!"

As the men began to leave Jakob approached Omar. Extending his hand, he asked, "May I shake the hand of the man whose son tried to protect my blood?"

Omar nodded to his son Mohammed to leave them alone as he turned his full attention to Jakob whose hand was still extended.

"He was my son in name only. He rejected me as a father many years ago."

"So I understand but you still feel his loss? Want revenge?" Omar remained silent as Jakob continued. "He and his cousin were regular visitors of my aunt since they were children. She often told me stories of their antics and what good boys they were. Isn't one also a Police Officer now?"

"He's dead to me too."

"Shame that you feel this way. Family is precious Mr Miraz, but perhaps you have to have lost nearly all of your blood line to understand such a concept. Aunt Yara lost her parents, her brother and twin sister in Auschwitz. Do you know what Dr Mengele did to twins in Aushwitz, Mr Miraz? The experiments? The barbarity?"

After several seconds Omar nodded saying with a sadness well meant, "I am a well-educated man Mr Abrahms so yes, I know something of the horror of Auschwitz and what your dead relatives suffered there and I too am truly sorry for your loss," as he now extended his own hand to clasp Jakob's.

"Thank you," as he now held onto to Omar's handshake, "but there is one more favour I must ask of you.

*

"So not enjoying the Media attention then?" smiled Imogen, as she looked across the table at Max who had walked into her apartment, clearly not a happy man.

"If the Chief Constable could bear my children I think he'd try!"

Handing him a glass of wine Imogen

acknowledged the obvious. "I know you don't see it, but what you did was... well extraordinary, and you know, it's good to celebrate bravery and honour for once Max so ... go with the flow and enjoy it."

"I've had a whole wasted day of wearing make-up and repeating myself, when the ones that did this, the ones who tried to hurt you, are still out there!"

"I know Max and I also know you will get them... eventually. Do you know you got a round of applause at the football today? At Oakwell as well as Hillsborough?"

"So I've heard. Anyway," as he placed his drink down so that he could fully embrace her, "I'm more interested in how you're going to 'honour me'."

"Oh I have a few ideas Chief Superintendent, don't you worry."

At that moment Max's phone rang. "Oh for the love of..." then seeing who the call was from, Max winced, saying, "I have to take this," then taking a deep breath answered the call. "Sorry mum, I did mean to call you back but... yes I know... well I'm fine really and... I'm sorry I scared you...but... well I wasn't really thinking..."

As she now looked at Max, all Imogen saw was the best of men, not the tough cop or hero, just a very good man telling his mum that he was sorry he had worried her and promising her he wouldn't do it again. At that moment, Imogen felt she had never loved anyone more.

CHAPTER 21

Olivia was quietly beside herself as she made ready to meet Riz. They had been friends since they'd been babies but now she was beginning to see Riz in a completely different light. It was since her friend Daisy commented how 'hot' Riz was and how she fancied him that made Olivia reassess him and the fact she felt irrationally jealous that Daisy fancied him, made her rethink their whole relationship status. Perhaps it was time to suggest to Riz that maybe they become something more. She thought he would agree because she had caught him giving her 'the look', the one that suggests he was a bit interested in her too and not as just friends who'd grown up together. Looking at her reflection though she was now doubting herself. What would she do if he laughed at her? What if he told her that it was Daisy he fancied and not her? Had she actually imagined 'the look'? Gosh but her tummy was doing somersaults.
The ringing of their doorbell made her jump to her feet, as she took a deep breath and steadied herself, trying not to race to her door. "Play it

cool," she was now telling herself as she walked as casually as possible down the stairs and into the large family room cum kitchen area of the large converted vicarage that was their very comfortable middle class home.

"So where is it you're off to?" her mum Harry was asking.

"Thought we'd take in the Art exhibition at the Botanical Gardens in Sheffield," answered Riz as Olivia entered the room adding, "hi Liv."

Olivia smiled her welcome then turned to her mother, "Okay Mum, see you later."

"I've heard the exhibition is beautiful and full of local artists work too. It's too easy to forget the local talent in our midst isn't it? So what time will you be back because I'm doing lasagne for dinner, a meat one and a veggie one and Riz you're more than welcome to join us."

"Thanks Mrs W, love your lasagne," grinned Riz as just at that moment Alan, Olivia's father and Harry's husband entered the kitchen. Olivia now inwardly groaned because her dad had started to become seriously embarrassing of late and if he mentioned what she was wearing in front of Riz she was going to die on the spot.

"Did I hear the words lasagne for dinner just now?"

"You did indeed husband of mine. Surgery finished early?"

"Had to make a couple of house calls so thought I'd call in on my way back to the grind." Alan was head of Penton's main General Practitioners, a dedicated doctor who was well liked and respected by the community he served tirelessly. Turning to Riz, the son of one of his partners in the practice he enquired, "So off out again you two?" as he emphasised the word 'again', adding "anywhere nice?"

"Botanical Gardens Dr Wood, the art exhibition there."

Nodding his approval Alan added, "Well be careful you two. There are some real nutters out there these days."

"Oh dad," murmured Olivia, rolling her eyes as only a sixteen-year old girl can.

"Look what happened at Grove School, not to mention..."

"Enough Alan, don't scare the kids and they aren't daft," laughed Harry.

"I know, I just want them both to be careful, that's all."

Grinning Riz replied, "We will be Sir have no worries," as they took their leave.

Looking at the two young people through the large bay window as they walked down their winding drive, Alan turned to Harry, shaking his head saying, "He's just called me Sir. How bloody old does that make me feel? It's like how I used to address your dad. Bugger me, but I've become our dads!"

Smiling Harry took her husband into her arms saying, "It was always going to happen my love."

"But so soon? She's still very young Harry and I'm not sure she should be wearing…"

"What every other young teenage girl is currently wearing? Yes, you've definitely become our dads," saying this as she laughed.

Alan was now deadly serious as he sat at their kitchen table accepting the coffee Harry had poured for him. "So, what do you think Riz is up to?"

"I'm not following love?"

"Well… I mean… you know…"

"Are you asking what Riz's intentions are towards our daughter Dr Wood?" Harry now openly laughing at Alan's obvious discomfort. Shrugging Alan merely looked embarrassed.

"I think," continued Harry, "that he's a really good lad from a good family. From all accounts he's wanting to follow in his dad's footsteps and become a doctor one day. I also think our rather beautiful daughter will want to kiss a lot of frogs before she settles on her prince. Stop worrying. They're just mates."

"You forget that I used to be a sixeen-year old boy myself. I know what hormones are like at that age and they are definitely more than mates. I'm telling you Harry."

"Our daughter has a good deal of self-respect and good sense."

Nodding his agreement Alan replied, "I know and I suppose she could do worse, you know, marrying the local GP and having great kids," as

he gathered Harry closer for another embrace.
"Well personally, I'd highly recommend it but that will be years away, if ever."
Sighing Alan nodded his understanding before asking. "Have you heard from Imogen today?"
"I text her and she told me she was ok, shaken a little but ok and she promised me she had been checked thoroughly at the hospital but my God Alan? How close was that?"
"I know love," as he now held her tighter, "makes me want to lock the doors and keep the world out and all of us safe."
"We're so lucky my darling," whispered Harry.
"Yes we are." Alan now disentangled himself from Harry's arms, picked up his brief case and mentally shrugging off his anxieties, headed to the door saying, "I know and I also know I worry too much. So lasagne for dinner?"
"Yep and try not to be late... again!" Grinning Alan left to do what he did best.

*

Darren Cowden's crew were high on the success of their suicide bomber hoax and its aftermath. They'd brought the city to its knees, they'd even been the main news item on all channels. It had been brilliant but the only problem being, they couldn't brag about it. Darren had told them to lay low, not draw attention to themselves whilst he took care of some business so Mark, Luke, Finn and Carl found themselves mooching around one of the city's parks.

"The thing is," Luke was saying, "I would have really loved to see their faces. I mean that cop who everyone is calling a hero must have been shitting himself and we did that! Bloody fantastic!"

"Brave though," this from Finn, as the others now turned to stare at him, "you know, to have stayed like. Just saying."

"Well don't!" snarled Carl who was emulating Darren more every day, "the only good copper is a dead un and don't you bloody forget it." Shrugging Finn merely nodded.

"Didn't know he knew how to plant a real bomb either. Bloody brilliant?"

"But when did he do that?" asked Mark, "before we grabbed the kid?"

"Who cares," this from Luke, "but it was fucking genius!"

*

Riz and Olivia had left the art exhibition and were now strolling through an adjacent park.

"I shouldn't be telling you this," ventured Olivia, "but my friend Daisy really likes you."

"Really?"

"Yes, she actually thinks you're 'hot'."

Riz now threw his head back laughing. "Well that's nice of her, but I'm not interested," as he casually took her hand in his as they walked. Olivia felt that her heart would burst at that very moment. "You know your dad looks at me a bit differently these days."

"Oh he's so embarrassing!" declared Olivia.

"It's because he senses that I think you're 'hot'. My dad's the same with our Layla when any lad calls round." Blushing Olivia squeezed his hand revealing how pleased she was with how the afternoon was panning out.

So lost in each other's company and new found relationship neither Riz nor Olivia had realised that they were now being followed. Mark, Luke, Finn and Carl had spotted the pair as they entered the park. Mark had whistled, saying, "Look at that! I'd like to feel those legs around my neck anytime."

"In your dreams," muttered Finn.

Carl snarled at Finn, making him shrink even further into himself. "Why his dreams? Look who she's with? Perhaps she need to know what white cock feels like!"

"Darren told us to lie low, not draw attention to ourselves," this from Luke.

"Who's here? Look around? It's just them and us and I for one am bored. So who's for a bit of fun eh? Let's show that piece of fluff a good time, show her what she's missing."

"Not me, I'm off," said Finn who was now genuinely horrified at what he thought Carl was suggesting.

"You're off when I say you are," snarled Carl.

"Piss off," screamed Finn, "I'm fucking fed up with you. I'm off ok!"

"Whoa finally, our Finley showing some balls,"

laughed Luke.
"Leave him alone," this from Mark, "if he wants to bugger off let him."
"Piss off then," laughed Carl, "more for us. He probably wouldn't have a clue where to put his pecker anyway."

*

Two calls had come into Sheffield Central, one an anonymous caller saying something bad was going to happen and the second being from a very distressed Mr Cooper whom had been taking his dog for a walk. Both had indicated that police assistance was needed immediately in a remote part of Endcliffe Park close to the city centre.
Sergeant Brad Fairchild with his partner Constable Will Davies were the first to arrive on the scene. Mr Brian Cooper, a man in his mid-seventies, was standing almost to attention, as he guarded a clump of bushes, with his sheep dog Toby by his side. On the floor next to the dog was a pair of knickers. "Thank God you're here. I've made sure no one else has touched anything and I'm sorry about the dog picking that up but to be fair that's how I found her..."
Holding up his hands Brad said gently, "Okay Mr?"
"Cooper but call me Brian. There's a young lass just through there. She needs help but that lad over there is in a far worse state if you ask me. Thought he was dead at first, I mean he might

not be far off!"
Sending Will to the second crime scene indicated by Brian Cooper, Brad now made his way to where the first victim lay. What he discovered first chilled him to the bone, then broke his heart. Reaching for his phone he rang his wife, Detective Constable Beth Fairchild. Without preamble he said, "Get to Endcliffe Park Beth asap. It's Olivia … yes our Olivia. It's bad love. Really bad and she'll need you. She'll need us all."
Will emerged from the second crime scene shaking his head. "Two ambulances are only two minutes away thanks to Mr Cooper here who rang for them straight after calling us. Bloody hell Brad, someone really worked this kid over."
"The bastards have done a job here too." They were interrupted by the sirens of the ambulances and paramedics arriving closely followed by Beth and Lydia in an unmarked police vehicle. As luck would have it they had been in the vicinity when Brad had called.
"Where is she? What's…?" asked Beth approaching Brad, her face as white as a sheet.
"Paramedics are with her and the lad she was with."
"What's actually happened Brad?" asked Lydia.
Shaking his head, he simply said, "The worse Lydia, the absolute bloody worse." Beth instinctively knew at once what Brad was inferring. It was written in his eyes, his face a mask of anger and disgust at what had been

perpetrated onto a child who meant so much to them.

"Jesus Christ," muttered Beth then, "has Harry been told?"

Shaking his head, "Not yet. We've just arrived on scene but I'll do that. You and Lydia need to be with Olivia. You know what's got to be done now if we have any chance of catching these bastards."

Nodding Beth and Lydia moved towards where Beth's Goddaughter lay. What Beth now looked at, simply broke her heart. Kneeling down beside Olivia, Beth found herself saying the words she used to use to soothe her when she had fallen or had trapped her finger as a small child, "I'm here now darling and you're going to be fine but we will have to get you to the hospital okay?"

Nodding, a terrified, traumatised Olivia whispered, "Is Riz ok Aunty Beth? I couldn't stop them hurting him and I tried, I honestly did." Eyes now filling with remembered terror she continued, "I couldn't stop them when they... when they..." as the torrent of horror and predictable shame now overcame her as she lay sobbing in Beth's arms.

"He's being cared for and is in excellent hands," answered Lydia, realising Beth was finding it difficult not to cry with the sheer horror of the situation, with barely concealed fury only a layer away.

Gently, the traumatised child was led towards

the waiting ambulance where on seeing the badly beaten prone body of Riz, she screamed out as if in actual pain.

Brad looked on, feeling impotent in his anger and rage as he was joined by his partner Will.

"Bloody hell mate, I didn't realise she was your Goddaughter. What a bloody God awful business."

"Bag the garment and anything else you can find until forensics deign to arrive," barked out Brad, as he looked at the retreating vehicles dreading what he knew he had to do next. This was going to destroy Harry and the rest of the friends. After the Downs business, he thought they'd had their share, and now this. Shaking his head, he indicated to Will to return to their vehicle when he was done. "Be as quick as you can. We've got a house call to make and it's going to be a very tough one indeed."

CHAPTER 22

Max's attention was drawn towards the squad room where there was a sudden hive of excited activity. Walking to his door, he saw huge platters of food being served by several visitors with the unmistakable delicious aroma of spiced cuisine. Then he heard a small voice saying, "He's there, dad. Look!"

Faisel appeared with his father in tow as he now raced towards Max, stopping just short of him before jumping into Max's arms to the spontaneous applause of all assembled.

Faisel's father and mother, with tears in their eyes looked on as their son and the brave man who had stayed with him in the darkest of hours, remained locked in their mutual hug.

Habib and Fatima Hussein approached the pair as Max lowered their son to the floor. Clasping Max's hand in both of his Habib began to choke out the words he needed to say. "We have no words Chief Superintendent for the courage and compassion you showed our son. We believed we were about to lose him in the worse... worse possible way, but we also saw he would not have died alone...and," as he became overcome with emotion, unable to finish.

Faisel's mother Fatima, gently touched her husband's arm saying, "We do not have words Chief Superintendent, but we do have food. It isn't much but please, we needed to show our gratitude in some small way."

Eddie saw how lost for words Max was and came to his rescue saying, "And, it's very much appreciated Mrs Hussein, I'm right, aren't Isaiah?"

"The police canteen will never be the same again. Thank you very much."

At this point Max was truly appalled to see the Chief Constable Jim Haggerty, along with his Press detail appear. Always the politician and never one to miss positive press coverage, he proceeded to do what he did best as Max groaned quietly to the others, "Not again."

"Thank you so much Mr and Mrs Hussein and where is Faisel? Where is that brave little soldier? Come lad, let's both stand next to the Chief Superintendent for a photograph. Max over here, Mr Hussein, let me shake your hand Sir," as he positioned himself then, facing the police press photographer with his customary beaming smile added, "got it Jake? Splendid."

What seemed like a hundred photographs and an age later, Max and Faisel finally found a quiet corner away from the considerable hubbub of interest. Faisel looking at Max, swallowed then said, "Thank you for not leaving me Sir."

"Thanks aren't necessary and I think you've earned the right to call me Max, like I can call you Fiz, right?"

"Yeah I like Fiz better. It makes me sound more English which I am, was born here."

Frowning Max asked, "Is that important to you Fiz?"

Shrugging the boy answered honestly saying, "It's just better to fit in that's all."

Nodding his understanding they both now enjoyed a comfortable silence broken when Fiz declared, "I'm going to be a policeman when I grow up, but one like you not like him," as he pointed to the Chief Constable who was having a really good time, holding court and eating the food brought in by the Husseins.

Smiling Max said, "No I don't want to be a policeman like him either mate."

"Are we mates Max?"

Looking into Faisel's earnest face Max replied, "Of course we are because we have an unbreakable bond Fiz. We faced down danger together, like soldiers and lived to tell the tale and not many can say that so yes we are true mates. Always will be."

At this point, they were joined by Hussein. "Faisel, we must leave now as they are very busy people," then turning to Max said, "Chief Superintendent, I again can't find the words."

"No words are necessary Mr Hussein," then

looking at Faisel added, "I made a friend for life that day too and that's thanks enough."
Faisel aka Fiz was still beaming broadly and waving happily as he and his family left.
Eddie joining Max smiled saying, "It's almost worth the heart attack you nearly gave us all when we get moments like this eh Chief?"
Grinning Max replied, "Almost, although I hope to not find myself in that situation again any time soon if that's ok with you Eddie."
At that same moment, Police Constable Sharon Summers appeared looking grim. Handing Max, the note she was carrying, her tone was clipped, her face a mask of concern. "A double incident in Endcliffe Park Sir, involving two sixteen year olds, a male boy identified as Rizawan Sharma and a female girl identified as Olivia Wood."
Max's frown deepened, something was telling him he knew one of the names, but couldn't place it.
"Who's dealing?"
"Sergeant Fairchild is informing the families and Detectives Constables Fairchild and Smith are at the hospital overseeing the rape kit procedures."
Dropping the formality for a second, she added, "Apparently the female victim is known to Beth and Brad Sir." The penny now dropping for Max, he nodded curtly, effectively dismissing the uniformed officer as he turned to Eddie.
"What are you thinking?" asked Eddie.
"Not sure but I can't help thinking the last few

weeks are connected in some way."

CHAPTER 23

Harry and Alan were silently staring at the four walls of the visitors' room they had been taken to. Harry had begged to see Olivia only to be told she hadn't been ready to see either of her parents. Her friend Claire, the Charge Nurse on duty explained.

"It's really common love, but she will feel differently as soon as the rape kit collecting the evidence is done. I think it's this process that victims don't want their family's to witness."

Wincing at the term 'victim' Harry remained silent as Claire continued to explain. "We've taken bloods to check for HIV and also she's been given the necessary drugs in case... well it's the Morning After pill as you'll both know."

As Harry still remained silent, Claire got up to leave, at a loss on how to comfort them, but squeezed Harry's shoulder to convey her silent support. Alan merely nodded his thanks, he too remaining silent as their well-meaning colleague and friend left them alone.

Beth and Lydia entered the silent room and sat down. Reaching for Harry's hand, Beth began.

"The evidence has been collected and we're about to take Liv's statement. She's asked that her mum be present love, ok Harry?" Nodding Harry got up, still holding onto Beth's hand.

Alan stood also. "I'm sorry Dr Wood," said Lydia, "but Olivia just wants her mum at this moment."

"But I'm her father."

Nodding sympathetically, eyes full of understanding Lydia simply said, "It's what Olivia wants Dr Wood."

"But..."

"And it's important, at this point, that we allow her to make these decisions as I'm sure you understand."

Looking like he was going to argue, Alan's face was now a mask of confused pain as he nodded and sat down, looking at the floor with his hands clasped in front of him.

"Is there anyone we can call for you Alan? Someone who could sit with you?" asked Beth.

Shaking his head Alan remained silently staring at the tiled floor.

"Okay", said Beth as the three women left him to his solitary vigil.

*

Olivia was on her side, facing the window, with her knees drawn to her chest. Walking towards her daughter, Harry now summoned up her nursing professionalism as well as her maternal instinct as she put her hand on her daughter's shoulder whispering, "I'm here now darling and it's going to be alright."

Turning to look at her mother, Olivia responded. "It will never be alright again mum. I'm so sorry," as the tears came. Holding her close, Harry was now rocking her as she had always done from the day she came into the world, whispering those soothing words mothers have used since millennia when comforting their young.

"You've nothing to be sorry about my love and you've done nothing wrong."

"Dad will hate me now though won't he mum? He told us to be careful and he's said for ages that my skirt's too short and ..."

"No of course he won't and you can stop blaming yourself this minute Liv, do you hear me? You and Riz did nothing wrong. Those animals did this to you and no one else is to blame."

Olivia was now openly sobbing in her mother's arms, her pain almost a live presence in the small examination room.

As her sobs subsided, Beth approached them. "I hate this Liv, but Lydia and I need to ask you about what happened. The more details you can give us the better because we really want to catch these scum. Ok love? I'm going to record what you say on my phone and we'll probably make a few notes too if that's ok?"

Nodding but still remaining in her mother's embrace Olivia began. "We'd been to the Botanical Gardens in the city centre but got a bit bored so we decided to go for a walk in

Endcliffe Park. We didn't notice anyone else at first although I do remember glancing back and seeing these four lads, but thought nothing of it."

"Can you remember anything about their appearance?" asked Lydia.

"Really short hair, black hoodies. No trainers, big boots."

"That's brilliant love, you're doing so well," urged Beth, "so what happened next?"

"They started shouting things, really nasty vile, things, to Riz. They were really racist Aunty Beth."

"Can you remember what they said love?"

Violently shaking her head, "I won't repeat the words Aunty Beth. I won't."

"Okay love, okay, we understand and I hate to ask you to relive this and I know this won't be easy for you but... what happened next?"

Staring down at the sheet covering her, Olivia was clenching and unclenching her fists, a reaction the Detectives had seen too many times as she began to recall her trauma.

"Riz said we were to ignore them and to make our way out of the park as quickly as we could without drawing attention. Then suddenly Riz was hit from behind and he fell to the floor. Then they were all over him, kicking him everywhere. I screamed for them to stop but they wouldn't. Then Riz told me to run so I did, but they caught me."

"You said there were four of them?" asked Lydia.

"Three attacked us."
"Not four?"
"No." At this the Detectives looked at each other then looked back at Olivia who was staring at some unseen spot on the wall in front of her.
Her voice breaking, tears streaming down her face, she continued, her voice now merely a monotone. "I tried telling them I hadn't done it before and I didn't want to do it with them. I thought they might leave me alone if they knew I…that I wouldn't know what to do, that I…they just laughed and I remember one saying he'd never had a virgin before."
"Bastard," murmured Beth under her breath.
"Two held me down whilst they took turns and it hurt so much. I tried to fight them mum, I really did but… it hurt so much, it still does," now unable to carry on, the memories opening the hurt and horror further, like picking an open wound." Composing herself, the child continued, saying, "Then the dog came at us and they ran away," as the tears came again.
"Ok darling, you're doing great," this from Lydia, "but can you remember anything about their appearance, like hair colour, tattoos? Any other distinguishing marks that you'd be able to identify if you saw them again?"
Shaking her head, she turned herself into her mother's arms again, then calming herself and taking a deep breath, sat back up and turned back to look at the waiting Detectives. "They called

one Carl and he had terrible acne and he said he should be first because it was his idea. He was the one who said he's never done a virgin before," as her wracking sobs began anew.

Harry now intervened saying, "Surely that's enough for now Beth?"

Nodding Beth switched off her phone's recording device as Lydia closed her notebook. "Can I just say Olivia how amazing you are," this from Lydia, "as you've given us a real chance of finding these scum."

"Absolutely bloody brilliant my darling. So proud of you," echoed Beth before adding, "your dad is waiting love and really wants to see you. Can he come in now?"

Shaking her head, she cried, "He'll blame me Aunty Beth. He's been telling me for ages that my skirts are too short."

"No he won't love," said Harry, "trust me, you are the last person he blames." Looking at the three women, Olivia eventually nodded, as she turned back into her mother's embrace, hiding her face, as Lydia went out to get Alan.

As he entered the room, Olivia, his little girl, looked up at her dad as he walked over to the bed with his arms outstretched. She then reached out to him, fresh silent tears rolling down her cheeks, as he took her into his arms.

Lydia and Beth saw from the doorway the time honoured tableau of loving parents wrapping their arms around each other and their damaged

child. Closing the door, they left them alone for now. Both Detectives knew that the hard part was yet to come.
"They've got a long and painful road ahead of them," said Lydia. Nodding her head, Beth found she couldn't speak.

*

Riz was on a different floor of the hospital. As Beth and Lydia approached the room they had been told he was in, they were met by the man they assumed was the boy's father. Dr Ishaan Sharma was a tall, imposing figure who possessed that indefinable air of trust and authority. Showing them their identification he began, "I don't think he's in any fit state to be interviewed Detectives. He can barely speak... he's lost most of his teeth and he's being sent for a CT scan as he most likely has a serious concussion. Initial examination has suggested his spleen has been ruptured, not to mention the fractured ribs..." as his professional veneer began to crumble, he now found the nearest chair, where he slumped with his head in his hands.
"We can't tell you how sorry we are Dr Sharma and rest assured we will do our upmost to find those who have done this."
Nodding, he looked at Beth, the light of recognition in his eyes. "It's Beth isn't it? Harry's friend?"
Smiling Beth replied, "Yes, we've enjoyed many a barbecue at Alan's haven't we?"

"Yes, when the world felt safe and sane. I can't believe it. I can't believe what's happening in this city. I mean I was born here, have never lived anywhere else. Even got my medical degree at the University here. This is our home and we're being attacked!"

"By a mindless minority Dr Sharma. Don't let their view of the world make you feel this is no longer where you belong," this from Lydia, "because it is they who don't belong."

Looking at the two young officers he now nodded. "My son will help all he can, but not yet. He simply isn't able to but tell me, how's Olivia? Is it as bad as I fear?" At the look on their faces, he didn't need the words.

"He'll blame himself. He'll blame himself for not being able to protect her. Oh God," as he placed his head in his hands once again.

Lydia and Beth looked on feeling helpless, just as a woman joined them saying, "Ish? They're taking him to be scanned."

"Here's our contact number, so please let us know when it will be a suitable for us to interview Riz and we can't tell you how sorry we are but rest assured we will find them," said Beth.

Nodding, Ishaan stood to join his wife. "Thank you and I'm sure you will make every effort to find these animals. And when you do, then what eh?"

Watching them return to their son as he began his long journey to recovery, Lydia was the first to speak. “Why is it the innocent who constantly blame themselves, their actions, their choices eh Beth?”

“I know mate, bloody senseless.”

“But it’s the aftermath isn’t it? Those who have done this will not suffer like these two will for… well God knows how long. Sometimes real justice feels…”

“What?”

Thinking hard and looking for the words, Lydia simply answered, “Out of reach.”

*

“That bleeding dog bit me! Look at it? Will I catch owt? I could get Rabies!” screeched Mark, as he looked in horror at the dog’s teeth marks forming on his buttocks, through the mirrored wardrobe door.

“Hasn’t even broken the skin, you soft pillock,” muttered Luke, adding “people shouldn’t have bloody dogs if they can’t be kept on a lead.”

Grinning, still high on the adrenalin of this last vicious act Carl now boasted, “But it was bloody good weren’t it!? Despite you getting bitten on your arse.”

“Didn’t even have time to finish, thanks to that bloody dog,” moaned Mark.

At the sound of the door banging shut downstairs all turned to see Brandon making his way up the stairs through the opened bedroom door. The look on his face wiped away all smiles as he approached the three, with Mark now pulling up his jeans saying, “Hey up mate, weren’t expecting thee?”

“Hear you’ve all been busy.”

Carl spoke first. “Just a bit of fun in park that’s all.”

Smiling, Brandon walked up to Carl saying as he crossed the room, “So what didn’t you get when I said we needed to lay low for a while?”

“Well I thought...” but his words were lost when Brandon unleashed his pent up rage; showering blows on the unsuspecting Carl until he lay on the floor covering his head with his hands. Mark and Luke now feared they were next.

Breathing hard Brandon now asked them, “So did you use owt?”

Mark shook his head in obvious confusion asking, “What you mean?”

Shaking his head Brandon muttered, “I thought not, bloody idiots. So you’ve had your bit of fun and left your DNA as evidence. What’s more, you’re all in the system so it’s only a matter of time before the Rozzers come knocking!”

This new development of the day’s occurrence seemed to settle around them like a sudden shard of clarity. “Never thought,” said Mark.

“So now we have to get you away from here fast. Where’s Finn?”

“Buggered off,” said Luke, then added, “the prat didn’t want to get involved as usual.”

Narrowing his eyes, Brandon nodded but this information again did not sit well with him.

"Where are we going?" asked Mark.
"Safe house in Huddersfield," was Brandon's clipped response.
Getting up from the floor Carl wincing with pain asked, "When?"
"Now!"

CHAPTER 24

Max turned to face his teams of Detectives as they all scrutinised the board behind him. Photographs of Yara Abrahms and Noor Acharya were at the centre of the board with arrows of the other events, pointing towards them which suggested a connection. At the top of the board were the hate crimes recently reported, the racist literature found in the city's schools, the hoax suicide vest scenario, the bomb at Grove South Car park and the recent rape in Endcliffe Park.

Max began. "This past month we have seen a real escalation of incidents that when put together, would suggest a theme. The reported 'hate' crimes on our Asian community we first thought were drug related, other groups moving in on the Mirza monopoly of drug running[u8] in the city although we've never been able to pin that on them. Since then I would say, other incidents have looked to maim, harm, even kill but still targeting the same group."

Turning to a man standing on his right, Max now made his introductions. "So may I welcome Counter Terrorist Operative Matt Turner, who I believe is well versed in these sort of activities and who is here to advise us on our next steps. Matt?"

Stepping forward was a very nondescript man who would blend in well anywhere. Of medium height, with medium brown hair and of medium build. He was basically, the perfect undercover surveillance team member, as no one would notice him.

"Morning. From what I've seen and heard I think you're thinking on the right lines Chief Superintendent."

"So are we looking at some far-right numpties then?" asked Eddie.

Smiling at Eddie's derogatory remark Matt replied, "Possibly, but we're not aware of any organised White Supremacists groups operating in this area and we do have our people being vigilant. On-line chatter isn't suggesting this is a political group at work either but the car bombing has raised the ante somewhat. We still think you may be looking at some sort of organised crime unit, pretending to have political ideology and looking at a certain recruit to do their dirty work for them. You know, those lads mainly, who have had little education, no decent male role model or parental guidance and who've been in trouble with law enforcement since they could walk," this now being said, with a certain jaded acceptance from Matt.

"Where do you suggest we start looking?" asked

Isiah.

"I'd suggest you look at anyone who may have a history of race related 'hate' crimes speech to start with then look at his or her associates. For instance, if we were looking at Islamic groups I'd be visiting the local mosques and listening to what the Mullahs were preaching."

Murmurs and the shaking of heads amongst the teams were now evident. Where to start looking seemed like an impossible task.

"You know my grandad heard Mosley and his black shirts speak in Barnsley, way back in the 1930s. Punched one of them too, got himself arrested and in trouble with our Nan by all accounts but felt vindicated when the war broke out." Looking at the bemused looks of his much younger colleagues he added, "Just that these numpties have been round for decades that's all and the only one I can think of who fits the bill here would be Wallace Senior, but he's been banged up for years," said Eddie.

"Then look at who he's been banged up with and who's been released recently. That's a start and they're hardly 'numpties' Sergeant. If they're organised and militarised, they're a problem like all extremist groups of all types."

"But he was put in segregation, for his own protection," countered Eddie.

"How long ago was he banged up?"

"Well over ten years now."

"Then the chances are he will now be in the

general population, to give room to another worse offender most likely, particularly if he's getting on a bit."

Relieved that they at least had one avenue to investigate Max issued his orders. "Isiah and Dan, start looking at who in the area has spent time in the same 'nick' as Senior and who has been released in the last six months."

Richard Braxton now put up his hand to ask a question. Nodding at him to speak Richard asked, "What about the bomb under the car Sir?"

"What about it?"

"Well could it be that Ms Holt was an actual target, so possibly could need to have a Protection detail attached to her? I'm just saying that I would very much like to volunteer for such a detail," now addressing the rest of the squad, grinning lasciviously, "I mean have you seen her? Who wouldn't want to get up close and personal with that?"

The 'tumble weed' moments that ensued seemed to last a while. Eddie merely shook his head, whilst Beth and Lydia looked daggers at Richard. Isiah muttered, "Pillock", under his breath whilst Dan had put his head in his hands.

Looking confused at the assembled officers' reactions, Richard asked, "What?"

A very stony faced Max now asked, "Are there any other questions which may help us in these enquiries?" scanning the room, "no? Then go over statements already taken and see if we've missed anything."

Isiah put his hand up and asked, "What about Benny Sir? Did he have a 'take' on anything?"

"Benny?" asked Matt.

"Yes Benny Reynolds, old mate of mine came up on a flying visit. Witnessed what happened at the school, but was called back to London on urgent business. That right Isiah?"

"Yes Sir. I was standing next to him when he got the call."

Nodding his understanding Matt said, "Thanks, I'll catch up with him."

As all began to move, Max then ordered, "Braxton! My office! Now!"

Out in the corridor Matt Turner took out his phone and keyed in a number then said, "I'm afraid it's what we thought."

*

Lake Park was a popular beauty spot situated very close to Barnsley town centre, often full of an army of doting grandparents lovingly looking after their grandchildren whose both parents had to work, in order to survive the cost of living. Brad and Will had been dispatched there in order to help with the search of a missing child as Barnsley and Sheffield both came under the umbrella of South Yorkshire Police and forces combined when issues of child safety were at stake and if more manpower was needed.

Brad was now attempting to calm a hysterical grandmother who had momentarily taken her eyes off her five-year old granddaughter, who had now been missing for over sixty minutes. The grandfather was sitting silently with his arms around his hysterically sobbing wife.

"Can you tell us where you last saw Luna?" asked Brad.

"Just near the static train. Luna loves it and often hides there when we play 'hide and seek'. I'd just gone to the kiosk to get coffee and she ran off to play. We thought she's be safe enough, then when we looked we couldn't see her," explained Arthur Clifton, the missing child's grandfather, "and we thought she'd be hiding in the train as usual."

"If anything's happened to her Arthur, if someone's taken her I'll..."

"Shush Lilly, the police are here now lass. They'll find her."

The park was now awash with officers who had been joined by members of the public, those walking their dogs, others who had been with their own children and feeling their horror, had joined in the search.

"How long's it been?" asked Will, as they joined the teams searching the area.

"Well over an hour," said Brad adding, "I bloody hate it when it's kids."

Suddenly shouts from the area nearest the main road, the dense shrubbery providing real camouflage from the main park area.

Brad and Will sprinted over in record time to find two men, members of the public search party holding onto a man who was desperately trying to get away. "You're going nowhere you filthy bastard," one of the men was screaming.

"I've not done owt. Ger off me!" screamed the captured man.

"Where's Luna?" shouted Will.

"Over here," came a voice as both Will and Brad were relieved to see the missing child in the arms of a woman who was holding her close.

"We caught that dirty pervert trying to get her to go with him. He'd given sweets," as she pointed at the sweet wrappers on the floor, "but she was clinging onto the railings crying for her mummy, poor little bugger, but you're safe now darling."

"I'll bet any money that's his car," said one of the rescuers, as he pointed to a parked white van, just outside the wall of the park.

Brad and Will were joined by several other police officers as they now allowed the local officers to take over control of the scene. As Luna was put in the arms of one of the local female officers, the child's protector a Kylie Smithson, approached the struggling perpetrator saying to the officers restraining him, "Just a minute chaps," as she kneed the struggling man hard in his groin, making him double up, howling in pain. He was still howling when they put him in the waiting police vehicle.

Luna was now back in the arms of her grateful grandparents who were swearing never to let her out of their sights again.

*

Meanwhile, across the city, the hyperventilating man was gasping for breath and the words that would somehow allow the release of the knife which was pinning his hand to his much polished bar.

"I swear on my life I know nowt about it. For Christ's sake..." howled Ted Abbott, landlord of the 'Stag's Head' as he watched the blood begin to seep on to the bar then pool at his feet.

"Everyone thinks the main radial blood artery is at the wrist but it's a network of blood supply vessels in the whole hand so you're doing some serious bleeding mate," informed Mohammed Mirza to the impaled man before him. "Dad wanted me to go into medicine and I did give it a try but... you know I don't like people enough to work the hours if I'm honest. And the pay is seriously crap."

"Please," sobbed Ted, "please. Take it out and I'll tell you anything."

Mohammed leaned in closely now, almost like a lover, "The name of the piece of racist scum who kicked to death my blood?"

"Don't know the name!"

"Get his other hand!"

"No! No! Don't! He's new, not long out of 'nick'. That's all I know, I swear to God, I'd bloody tell you if I knew owt!"

Mohammed looked at the howling man, saw the beer belly, the sallow sagging skin, the terrified look in his eyes and knew he'd got all he could get from him. Wrenching the knife free from the hand, his victim fell sobbing to the floor. Yanking him up by his hair Mohammed whispered in his ear, "Tell that scum we're coming for them and we're taking no prisoners old man!"

*

Gareth looked at Ted's hand wound, shaking his head as he listened to the shaken man who was trying unsuccessfully to stop the wound bleeding further.

"I've been happy for your lot to use the upstairs Gareth but it's all getting out of hand mate! I mean, I'm getting too old for this. Doctor's said I need..." his words cut short as Gareth now grabbed hold of his injured hand, squeezing it hard, inflicting further pain and causing more blood loss."

Practically on his knees, Ted began to plead for the second time in the space of the last hour.

"Christ Almighty... stop..."

"Now, let me make something very clear Ted me old mate. This is our headquarters as long as we need it to be. Do you understand?"

Nodding Ted looked defeated and more than that, looked like a man who suddenly understood what he had unwittingly allowed himself to be part of. Just then, his wife of thirty years, Anne, walked into the bar area where the men were. She had clearly been out shopping and had no idea what her husband had faced that

morning, from both warring factions.
Looking at the blood on the bar and the floor, she stopped suddenly before exclaiming "What on earth is happening Ted? My God, you're bleeding all over the bloody place!"
Nodding with fake sympathy Gareth addressed the shocked woman saying, "Yeah, looks nasty that. Would say it needs a couple of stitches," then turning back to Ted added, "let's hope it's not your throat next time eh mate?" Giving them both a mock salute he walked out.
Trembling Anne walked to her husband and examined the injury saying, "He's not wrong about the stitches, but tell me Ted, how the bloody hell have you got us involved with people who would do this to you...and next time probably me, as well? How come we have a bloody target on our backs these days?"
Anne, had been uncomfortable for a while with her new regular clientele, who had made sure those who had drunk here for decades, on occasions for generations, were now giving the place a wide berth.
"I don't feel safe here anymore."
"I know love."
"So?"
"We're trapped love."
Hating his weakness, she replied, "Well, I suppose that's the price you pay for getting into bed with the Devil Ted. Right, so I'll get the car and we'll get you to A& E then I'm off."

Staring at her with his jaw dropping, Ted was looking disbelievingly at his wife of thirty years. "Off where?"

"Don't know. You may be trapped but I'm not, so come on as I have things to do and plans to make and they don't involve you and your head case mates."

*

Eddie & Brad were sitting across the table in an interview room in Barnsley Police Station. Facing them was the man Brad had help arrest that afternoon, a Craig Jones, a known re-offender, who was out on license and now looking at doing serious time in prison. He was attempting to broker a deal, in exchange for information he was willing to give about the recent attacks in Sheffield.

Eddie began. "Well as it's on my way home, I thought I'd pop in to see if you have anything worse listening to but to be honest, I'm not expecting much. What about you Brad?"

"No Sarge, I mean what would a waste of space like him know?"

Craig had not yet looked at either men, but just sat there at the table, hearing their derogatory tone as he now lifted his head to see the utter disgust and contempt in their faces.

"I have information."

"So we've been told," replied Eddie, "and I'm giving you another thirty seconds to start telling us what this so called information is, before I walk!"

"I need to strike a deal though because they're threatening to put me in general population. You know what will happen to me there?"

"What you deserve," replied Brad.

Shaking his head with eyes full of self-pity Craig said, "You let that woman attack me and did nothing."

Leaning forward, Brad snarled, "Be grateful it wasn't you and me for five minutes in a cell, you snivelling piece of human waste," then added, "I have a daughter, a baby girl!"

"And I need help. Do you think I like being like this? Do you think I don't know what I am!"

Sighing audibly Eddie said, "What is it you want?"

"I just want to be put in segregation, on a VPU," as he referred to the Vulnerable Prisoners Unit, "to be with my kind, that's all."

Nodding his understanding, Eddie now asked, "Well that all depends on what you've got for us?"

Looking up, Craig was now trying to decide if Eddie would keep his word.

As if reading his thoughts Eddie said, "I'll keep my word, no worries on that score."

Realising he had nothing to lose Craig began to tell them what he knew, much of it hearsay, but better than nothing.

"There's a pub just off Attercliffe Road, near the old Firth Vickers steel works. It's called The Stag's

Head. Heard there's some real nutters who go there now, old regulars won't go near the place anymore."

"And?" asked Brad.

"There's a regular who goes there, a Gareth Jackson. Heard he's trying to be a big time drug dealer. Trying to turf the Pa..." then choosing his words carefully, "the other lot out so he can take over. Told he's behind the recent troubles."

Nodding Eddie said, "Right Craig, we'll look into that."

Looking hopefully at the men Craig said, "And we have a deal?"

Shrugging his shoulders Eddie replied, "Who knows?"

CHAPTER 25

Lydia's favourite time of the year was Autumn as she loved the colours and it was a very beautiful Autumnal day that announced the day of her wedding.

Lydia and Dan had chosen to be married at Cubridge Hall Hotel, placed just on the outskirts of Penton itself and also the place where Beth and Brad had married years before. Situated in beautiful grounds with spectacular views, both Lydia and Dan had fallen instantly in love with the place which was steeped in history, dating back to the 1700s.

Lydia had overseen everything, leaving no detail, no matter how minor, unattended. She had been delighted at what they had done with the beautifully converted barn area, which was where the wedding breakfast was to take place along with the later celebrations. Checking everything with military precision, Lydia had quietly terrified Susan, the hall's wedding planner.

"So you're happy?" asked a very nervous Susan. She had worked with many brides in her time, but Lydia had taken it to another level.

Smiling Lydia responded with, "Yes Susan, very happy indeed. I mean thank you so much particularly for moving the chairs, I mean those three inches have made such a difference."

Susan just smiled, remembering the conversation she had had with her team, who had found the request, both time consuming and bizarre with mutterings of "Bloody Bridezilla" in abundance.

Lydia thought she had never seen a wedding venue look so beautiful and she was not wrong. Wreaths of autumn leaves interspersed with tiny fairy lights were hanging everywhere, including the large wooden beams overhead. The whole place looked ethereal and other worldly and she couldn't quite believe they had actually pulled it off, despite Dan threatening to murder her on more than one occasion.

Now sitting in the Bridal Suite where she was sipping champagne with her Bridesmaids, Lydia felt no one had the right to be this happy.

Beth, as Maid of Honour was scrutinising the bride. "Right. Hair perfect, check! Make- up, subtly done and perfect, check! Lip gloss after champagne will need touching up though. Right. Now for the dress." Taking it from its hanger, Beth and Lydia's youngest cousin, Leah, helped the bride step into it. After fastening the zip and tiny buttons, Beth stepped back and blinked hard.

"Oh my word Lydia, but you're completely beautiful," as to her horror Beth found herself tearing up.
"Don't start or I'll start," laughed Lydia.
Her other three bridesmaids, all beautifully gowned in olive green Grecian Goddess style dresses looked on and sighed. Her friend Connie smiled saying, "She's right lovey, you're gorgeous and that cop of yours is a very lucky man."
"Talking of cops," said another cousin, this one called Jennifer, "is THE cop going to be at the wedding? You know the drop dead gorgeous hero one?"
Lydia nodded as she arranged her head dress, making sure her earrings weren't catching the veil. "And please, please tell me he isn't coming with a plus one?" continued Jennifer.
Smiling at Beth, Lydia replied, "I couldn't possibly say."

*

Watching Imogen walk towards his car, Max wondered how she could manage to pole axe him so unexpectedly. Since the car bombing they had barely been apart, except for when both at work. Yet here she was completely taking his breath away once again.
Imogen had been surprised when Max had asked her to be his plus one at Dan and Lydia's wedding as they had yet to go public. Part of her still worried that it was too soon, that the speed of how they were developing into... who knew

what, was too fast.

She and Beth, however had had a really enjoyable 'girlie' afternoon choosing her outfit at Penton's high end designer clothes shop, which was situated on Penton's High Street and had been for over thirty years. The shop owned by sisters Tanya and Zelda were known for their different, unique styles, instinctively knowing what suited their customers. Imogen's floaty emerald green, tiny pleated gown made her look even more stunning than she naturally was and as soon as she had put it on, all in the shop, including complete strangers, had told her that it could not be bettered. Tanya had taken a photograph saying, "I have to post this on FB Imogen if that's ok. You look perfect."

Straight talking Zelda had agreed saying, "I know you would look great in a bin bag, but bloody hell Imogen. That outfit was made for you."

Even after so many compliments, climbing into Max's car and turning to greet him she was momentarily surprised at the expression on his face asking, "Are you ok?"

Shaking his head, he replied, "You know I believe it's bad form to outshine the bride. You look... well I haven't the words."

Moving to kiss him lightly on the lips she said, "As long as you think so, that's all that matters."

"Trust me," he grinned, "I will be one of many."

The drive to the Hall was very short and to be fair they could have walked, particularly from

Imogen's but Max was also on a self-inflicted twenty-four hour call out, until the men they were after were caught so needed his car. Parked up now, they got out of the vehicle and that's when Max held out his hand saying, "Our first outing in public."

Taking his hand Imogen nodded replying, "And hand holding too."

"Isn't that what couples do?"

Smiling, Imogen replied, "I guess. Ready?"

As they walked towards the milling crowd of guests, they were both aware of the amount of phone cameras turning to take their picture, how people were nudging each other indicating who they were and that they were here. It was a relief when Eddie and his wife Pat waved them over to join them.

"Well causing a stir I see, hello Imogen and how lovely do you look and isn't this much nicer than the last time we were in each other's company eh?"

"Much Eddie but I don't think I've had chance to thank you for your support that day. I really..."

Holding up his hand Eddie modestly stated, "No thanks necessary, all part of the service but let me introduce to my good lady. This is my wife Pat. Pat this is the Chief Superintendent and this is his lovely lady, Imogen."

Pat smiled her welcome saying, "Lovely to meet you and oh my word, but that dress is exquisite." Then turning her attention to Max said, "Finally

I get to meet you Chief Superintendent because I've heard so much about you."

"As I have you and please, it's Max."

From across the court yard Richard Braxton had observed Max and Imogen's arrival. He had been chuffed to have been invited and had asked Sharon to join him which she had happily done. Now watching Max and Imogen, he felt like a prize prat. Turning to Isiah, he quietly said, "So that's why I got the biggest bollocking the other day?"

Isiah seeing what he was referring to shook his head. "Nothing to do with the Chief and Ms Holt being an item. You were being disrespectful because where women are concerned you are constantly and in this day and age mate, it's just not on," said as he quietly moved away to join Dan, as his best man and to make their way, with the other guests to where the wedding ceremony was taking place.

Sharon had returned with their drinks and seeing his expression asked, "What's wrong."

"Nothing," replied Richard shaking his head in quiet disgust, "just, the sooner I get to the Met, the bloody better!"

*

The service had been beautiful with the bride and grooms' mothers both suitably in tears as they took their vows. As Lydia said the words, "All that I am I give to you," Imogen felt Max reach for her hand as if he knew, that she was remembering the time she too had spoken those words, seemingly another lifetime ago, the pain of her loss never truly leaving her. As they now looked at each other though, something else passed between them, suggesting something unspoken.

As the speeches unfolded, Lydia's father suitably moved them all, when he told of his and her mother's immense pride for Lydia and how he knew she had found the best man in her Dan.

"We knew, from when she was very tiny, that Lydia had a strong sense of what was right and wrong. The fact that her Barbie dolls were constantly under arrest should have given us a clue and whilst other little girls wanted to dress up as princesses, our Lydia wanted to dress up as a police officer, or a sheriff, so it came as no surprise when she decided to join the Force and I must be honest, her mother and I were worried as we didn't want her mixing with undesirables."

"Plenty of those can be found in the police canteen, not to mention how criminal the food is," shouted one joker at this point, much to the laughter and agreement of all those there.

"I also never thought there would be someone out there worthy of her, but then we met Daniel and as her father, I can't think of a better partner for our daughter. I know she prides herself as being a strong and independent woman, but you will always be our little girl and I see in Dan, a man who will honour and protect you too. So please stand and raise your glass to my beautiful daughter, our lovely Lydia and my son-in-law Daniel."

Clearly moved by Lydia's father's words Dan now got up to speak.

"First may I thank my now father-in-law for those kinds words and Sir, I will always do my upmost to keep your daughter safe and as happy as is humanly possible. To our mothers, thank you for all of your hard and support in making today our special day, and to my beautiful wife Lydia, thank you for agreeing to marry me and for making me the happiest man alive."

As best man, Isiah had done his homework regarding Dan's antics as a boy and had the audience in stitches when revealing some of the situations Dan had been involved in as a police officer ending with, "He did eventually retrieve his trousers so his modesty was protected but for that reason alone, he will be forever known, with great affection I might add, as Desperate Daredevil Dan the Man. To the bride and groom."

For Imogen it was good to be with Max in a social setting where he felt comfortable, to be surrounded by colleagues who were also his friends too. This normality was definitely something she could get used to.

"So, enjoying yourself?" asked Beth as she came to sit with her. Max was at the bar and was having difficulty getting back to her as relatives of both bride and groom wanted his attention albeit briefly, as they all had their phones out asking for selfies.

"Yes, a lovely occasion and you look beautiful by the way."

"Well you turning up on Max's arm definitely disappointed a few," grinned Beth, "especially the bridesmaids although they're making do hitting on poor old Isiah at the moment but I'm sure he'll cope," as they both turned to look at a well inebriated Isiah resembling a human mug tree, with a variety of females hanging on to his arms."

"Looks to be coping fine," laughed Imogen.

"You do know pictures of you and Max will be all over Social Media at this very moment?"

Laughing at Imogen's horrified face Beth continued saying, "For someone in your position, you can be a touch naïve at times love."

Max, finally having extricated himself from the throngs at the bar, picked up on the conversation. "Naïve about what?"

"Your picture together being all over Social Media," adding at the look of surprise on Max's face, "you two definitely don't spoil a pair. Honestly!" as she left them to find Brad.

"Really?" asked Imogen.

Shrugging Max replied, "Hadn't thought but... no matter. It's been a good occasion, though, don't you think? Away from the madness, just focusing on something good."

Nodding her agreement, she said, "There's

nothing like a good wedding. It signifies a hopeful future doesn't it? Having children and growing old together, that is if you're lucky."

"You do know the latest divorce stats?"

"Now don't spoil the moment, but they do seem a good lot you work with."

"Yes good people," agreed Max, "well mostly," as he spied Richard and Sharon making their way over to where they were siting.

"Mind if we join you?" asked Richard. Max nodded but remained silent.

"I believe we've already met," said a smiling Richard to Imogen.

"Yes I remember. Hello Sharon, nice to see you again."

"Hi Imogen, love the dress."

"You two know each other?" asked Richard.

"Yes," replied Sharon, "at Lydia's Hen do in the Ice Bar in Barnsley. I mean an Ice Bar in Yorkshire where it's freezing most of the bloody time anyway!"

"How long did it take her to recover," laughed Imogen.

"Just in time for today I think," replied Sharon, "but a good time was had after we'd manage to thaw out. By the way, so sorry to hear about your friend's daughter. Harry isn't it? She was at the Hen do too wasn't she?"

Nodding, all smiles gone now. "Yes it's a bad business."

Realising her comment had spoilt the happy

vibe, Sharon now attempted to bring the atmosphere back saying to Max, “So Chief, enjoying having a few hours off?”

“Yes Sharon thanks, very much.”

“Well you two caused a bit of a stir when you arrived,” said Richard, wanting to get in on the conversation, “but it’s to be expected I suppose.”

“Why?” asked Max.

Looking at Max somewhat surprised he laughed saying, “You’re the man of the moment Chief, I mean how many marriage proposals have you had since it happened?”

“Really?” this from Imogen.

“We’re running a sweepstake to see who can guess the number up to a certain date,” informed Sharon.

“Oh for pity’s sake,” groaned Max then to Imogen asked, “so, how about a dance?”

Taking his hand, they made their way on to the dance floor where Max held her close, ignoring the looks from others as they enjoyed the music, finding they had a steady, natural rhythm together. Looking at him Imogen observed, “You don’t like him do you?”

Knowing it was Richard she was referring to he nodded, replying, “I don’t like him and I trust him even less.”

“Why?”

Thinking before answering Max answered honestly. “He doesn’t get why we do what we do. He’s in the job for all the wrong reasons.”

"Well then he's where he should be". Raising his eyebrows, he looked at her quizzically as she added, "Because you will put him straight and make him the police officer he has the potential to be."

Holding her closer Max whispered, "You have a lot of faith in me haven't you?"

"I do."

Grinning he murmured in her ear, "You do know you've just said 'I do' to me at a wedding?"

Before she had chance to respond, Eddie and Pat appeared with Eddie saying, "May I cut in?"

Laughing Imogen replied, "But of course," as she left Max's arms to be swept up by Eddie, with Max holding his hand out to Pat asking, "Shall we?"

"Yes please Max and how jealous will my friends be, so you don't mind a selfie as well do you? As proof?"

Inwardly groaning, Max smilingly replied, "It would be my pleasure Pat."

CHAPTER 26

As she looked out onto her large, pristine garden, Harry was asking herself why everything looked the same. That old song, the one her mum loved, sung by someone long dead, asking why the sun kept on shining? Didn't it know it was the end of the world?

The world they all knew, the world they smugly took for granted, had certainly died a tragic, painful death, leaving in its wake an abyss of... what? A large black hole of something vile, which would swallow her whole, if she allowed it to. It had been less than a week, but Harry couldn't remember how life had once been, only what life was like now.

The twins Will and Jasper, barely twelve years old, usually so loud and demanding, were unnaturally quiet, but not understanding why they felt they should be. All they knew was that Olivia was not herself and needed to be left alone.

Alan and Harry now spoke only in monosyllabic tones, only using words that were necessary, both lost, living in their own hells and for the first time since they had met, not sharing, not supporting each other.

Olivia had taken to staying in her room, barely venturing out unless absolutely necessary. Today, Beth and Brad's visit on official police duties, necessitated that she be sitting in their normally comfortable living space, as they did what their job now demanded of them. Both Brad and Beth were shocked at how she looked.

Beth began. "How are you doing my lovely?"

Olivia merely shrugged her shoulders in response to the question.

"We just wanted you to know that we are doing everything we can to find them Olivia and we won't stop until we do," said Brad. "The DNA retrieved has identified them as they are known offenders and in the system. It's now only a matter of time."

Looking at the huge man she'd known all of her life, whom she called Uncle Brad, sometimes Uncle Bear, Olivia now asked, "And when you do, what then?"

Looking puzzled, Beth said, "We arrest and prosecute them love."

"And when they deny it or say I wanted it, what then?"

"Well they can try," began Brad, "but..."

Olivia didn't allow him to finish, "They will try and they will opt to go to court because they have that right don't they?" When no one answered her she carried on. "Then I'll be there, facing them, facing reporters, who will write down all the vile things they did so they can sell their newspapers."

"Hang on a minute now Sweetie," said Beth, "you won't have to face them but can give evidence behind a screen and the court would be a closed one, whereby only those needed to be there would be. That is if it came to that."

Shaking her head, Olivia was angry now. "I've read the stats, I know how many go to court but walk free to do it again to somebody else."

"Livia, honey..." said Brad.

"No, no Uncle Brad," with her hands over ears, Olivia was now in tears, "I don't want to hear it," as she got up leaving the room.

Looking at Harry and Alan Beth shook her head saying, "We know how awful this is..."

"Do you Beth?" snapped Harry.

"Yes mate, course we do. We deal with..."

"Yes, you deal with strangers on a daily basis, I'm sure, as we have as medics. So trust me when I tell you, that you do not know how awful this is."

Silence now. No one speaking. No one daring to.

Getting to his feet Brad said to Beth, "Come on love. We'll see ourselves out and don't forget, we're just a couple of streets away, any time, night or day. Ok?"

Rising with them Alan spoke for the first time since they arrived. "She's right isn't she? About the conviction rate for sexual assault, for rape?"

Taking a deep breath Beth now tried to

make their friends understand. "We don't underestimate for a single second, the impact this crime has not just on the victim but for the whole family and yes too many go to court and don't secure a conviction, but I promise you this would not be the case here. This is not a 'he said, she said' situation. This is something else altogether, so trust us guys. We will get the bastards and they will pay!"

"But not enough," said Harry, "not nearly enough."

"Any ideas where they are?" asked Alan.

"No not yet mate, but we'll find them."

Nodding their goodbyes to a now silent Harry, Alan showed their friends out then returned to join Harry as she sat staring at nothing.

"Looks like they're no nearer finding them."

Nodding Harry said, "What if I told you I know someone who could find them, what would you say?"

Alan was silent. Then, looking at Harry he nodded saying, "Get it done."

*

A day had passed since Beth and Brad's difficult visit to Harry's home. Now Beth, Imogen and Harry were sitting in Imogen's apartment, staring at each other.

"I don't understand Harry," said Imogen.

"Yes you do. I want his number. The contact number for the man who 'fixes' things when paid to or when you click your fingers and ask him to.

The man who got rid of Grant's body and set up Sheldon to take the fall for your murder," now pointing to Beth, "that one!"

Both Beth and Imogen just stared numbly at Harry, barely believing what they were hearing and seeing.

Beth began, "We will find them Harry just give us the time…"

"No! I, no we, want this sorting properly, so give me his number Imogen."

Shaking her head Imogen answered with an emphatic, "No Harry."

Harry leaned back now thinking, nodding her head as if having a conversation with someone else. Finally, she began to speak. "Well Beth, it will be a shame for Lola having a police officer for a mother who is banged up for murder, not to mention what it will do to Brad and Sarah. Yes, and let's talk about poor, sweet, innocent Sarah, the one who tortures herself daily for a murder her best friend committed, not to mention who Lola's dad is. That will come as a real shock, the fact you shagged her gangster husband before knifing him won't it?!"

Staring at their friend who was barely recognisable, Imogen said, "You wouldn't Harry."

"Wouldn't I? Will you keep your job after the world knows you killed your father and then years later perverted the course of justice to protect the real killer, which was, oh let me think?" turning to look at Beth again her lip curled in anger, "oh yes you again Beth, a serving police officer!"

Beth had walked to the window with her back to her friends, with Imogen trying to reason with Harry. "We kept you out of what happened Harry, we protected you. How can you even think of turning on us like this?"

Harry had now walked to the fireplace, looking at the flames that now flicked their orange hue onto her face. Sighing she turned to her friends, two women she loved as if they were sisters as she said, "So who do you think gave Sheldon the lethal dose which killed him? Who do you think the 'angel of death' was then?" Looking at their astonished faces she continued. "I found a burner phone in my locker at work with the instructions on what to do and do you know what? I was happy to oblige because the man was a monster. So yes, me Harry, with the perfect life was there for her friends no matter what. Now, not one but three monsters are out there and they have hurt my little girl, my baby and I fear she will never recover. How would you feel if it was Lola?"

Beth replied with weary honesty, "I'd want to tear each one limb from limb."

Imogen had been very silent, watching her friends, feeling Beth's fear which she shared and seeing Harry's anguish which she felt was bordering on temporary insanity. She had a decision to make, one which would again take them all down another 'Rabbit hole' of criminality. She also knew if she wanted to stay with Max, she could not allow Malcolm Speight in her life again. Thinking of a life without Max in it was now almost unbearable as well as surprisingly alarming. When did her need for him in her life become so important?

Coming to a decision, she handed her phone over to Harry. "Beth will give you his name but you must do the rest. If that's not enough then go and do your worse."

Harry took the phone as Imogen left her lounge to retreat to her kitchen. Beth joined her, leaving Harry to do what she intended as they both stood, shell shocked at what was happening. Pouring two large brandies, they heard Harry's voice then the slamming of Imogen's apartment door minutes later.

Downing the drink in one Beth asked, "Will the madness never end? Do we pay forever?"

Downing her drink in one also, Imogen replied, "It's a hell of our own making my friend and it would seem that the Devil is still owed and pulling hard on our strings, making us dance his dance once again."

CHAPTER 27

Gareth was still feeling the euphoria of the mayhem that had occurred at Grove South and was now wanting to ramp things up whilst they had momentum. Brandon's lads had been a disappointment but all was not lost.

"I can't believe they'd disobey me," voiced Brandon who, thanks to Gareth, was now believing in his own sense of importance.

"We've other lads."

"But they were mine, I'd trained 'em."

"And you can train others because," voice now laced with menace, "no one is indispensable."

Moving closer, squaring up, so that they were practically nose to nose, adding, "and I mean no one."

Brandon was suddenly still, realising he had somehow stepped over a line, that he had inadvertently gone too far. Recovering, he attempted to appease without losing face. "I'm just saying that's all. It takes time to train others up dunt it?"

Moving away shaking his head Gareth asked the burning question. "Who's the explosive expert?"

Swallowing before answering Brandon replied, "Me. Why?"
"Then we don't need them, so they can permanently disappear."
Not liking the direction of this conversation Brandon was temporarily shocked and looked it. Gareth laughed at his expression saying, "I mean they can stay in Huddersfield, permanently that's all mate."
Trying not to show his relief Brandon now asked a question that had been bothering him for a while. "How did you know the Feds would be onto them?"
Grinning, Gareth replied, "How do you think? Got a copper in our pocket haven't we and they are very well placed mate. Very well placed indeed but now we need to get cracking. Tell your dad we need more product because eyes will be off the drug ball when their cars go up in flames and that's what you'll be dealing with. Get it sorted, then we'll strategise where and when to strike. Got it? But first of all, you've got a snitch to deal with and when I say he needs to disappear permanently, I'm not talking Huddersfield, I'm really talking permanently. Got it?"
Brandon merely nodded. He had never been more terrified, more out of his depth, in his life.

*

The terror was coming off the three frightened young men like waves washing ashore. As Malcolm looked at them with mouths duct taped shut and their hands and feet tied together, he felt they looked more like frightened children than grown men as they laid shaking on the cold concrete floor.

Finding them had been easy for Malcolm's network and their abduction even easier from the unguarded fleapit they had been staying, in the nearby town of Huddersfield. He knew what was planned for them and it was making his stomach churn.

Nodding to his men, they hauled the three men and hooked each one of them onto a former butcher's rail, stringing them up like cattle had been. Tearing the duct tape away Malcolm stood in front of them, knowing the intense well defined, well placed light beam of the ellipsoidal reflector shining behind him and his men, would make their identification impossible. He also knew it made their presence even more terrifying.

"You know why you're here don't you?"

"We haven't done owt! You've got the wrong'uns!" screamed Luke.

"Let us go," blubbered Mark, "my arms. It hurts."

"Well I think you all hurt that young lass in Endcliffe Park quite a lot too lads, so I think a bit of pain is warranted here don't you think?" replied Malcolm, his voice quiet, almost kind.

The three strung up young men went silent and almost stilled, suddenly realising how much trouble they were in.

Carl now screamed, “It weren’t us!”
“Your acne lad and your name says different as does that dump we found you in, not to mention the bite mark on your mate’s arse. You’re the ones alright.”
Suddenly out of the darkness another figure appeared, this time dressed head to toe like a surgeon about to enter an operating theatre, with them a trolley of surgical instruments.
Terror really was present in the room now. The strung up young men began screaming their innocence, trying to move their legs, abject terror in their every movement.
Malcolm looked to his left and asked, “Are you absolutely sure this is how you want to proceed? Including the videoing?”
The cladded figure merely nodded as Malcolm, sighing heavily, signalled for his men to approach the struggling men. Carl was the first as one held his legs as the trousers and underpants were removed by the other. Whilst he was held still, the ghostly surgical figure approached him with a surgical saw in hand.
Malcolm and his hardened lieutenants, men who operated on the side-lines of society would not really remember the stench of urine and defecation, the screams that were like no other or the blood; they had seen all of this before many times. It was the clinical, emotionless precision in which the revenge was executed that would remain with them for the longest time.

CHAPTER 28

It had been five days since the video of the young men, who had been strung up like cattle and summarily dealt with, had found itself on all Social Media outlets. Five days since they had been thrown out of the blacked out, no number plate van onto the steps of Barnsley's A & E department, bleeding, unconscious but each clutching their dismembered penises in their hands.

It had taken a matter of hours for the authorities to have the footage removed but not before it had been seen by literally hundreds of thousands, if not millions with the social media frenzy being relentless in its vicious rhetoric with many applauding what they had seen.

Max standing in front of the Incident Board looked grim as he faced his teams of detectives.

"I know. Just when we think we've seen it all. I don't have to tell anyone in this room that this sort of organised vigilante justice is the last thing we need and no doubt we will have the 'usual suspects' in mind when we see the professionalism of this assault. Proving who is responsible will be a problem, but it doesn't mean we won't try. Dan and Isiah are already at the hospital to see if the victims are in any state to be interviewed. Lydia, you need to meet with the Sharmas. Eddie you're with me. Any intelligence from anywhere is now a priority. The Mirzas are key suspects too. Right get to it. Beth, my office." Covert looks passed between the officers present. This was not the Chief Superintendent they were used to seeing.

Beth, walking into Max's office looked worried and confused. "Sir?"

"You and Brad are now off this case. Also, it would be in both your interests if you have no contact whatsoever with the Woods until we've put this case to bed."

"But Sir..."

"No Beth. You're both too close to this. I've assigned you to DI Sheridan for the foreseeable. You're dismissed." Beth stood stock still, just looking at him. Max looking up stared, then slumping back into his chair sighed and said, "Beth you know I'm right. You know what the procedure is and you're too close to the Wood family."

"I know," nodding her understanding, "but it's still tough. I held Olivia in my arms the day she was born but I would never..."

"No one is accusing you of anything Detective Constable."

"So why does it feel that you are Sir?" was Beth's

parting question as she left the office, passing Eddie as he made his way in.
Now staring hard at Max, Eddie began, "I know where your mind is heading and I suggest you don't go there again."
"Speight's name is written all over this…again!"
"And where's the proof," countered his Sergeant before adding, "don't go there, Max. Don't go and ruin one of the best thing's that's ever happened to you…again!"

*

Dan, having recently returned from honeymoon, was with Isiah and Richard with the medics. The young men in question were in no fit state to be interviewed but the Head of A & E made his thoughts very clear. "My God, but are we now back to the middle ages? What on earth is going on out there?"
"We really need to speak to the victims," replied Isiah, "if we are to have any chance of finding out who's done this."
"Well good luck with that," replied the doctor, as he stalked off to deal with the next perceived emergency society had placed at his door.
Now walking into the room where Mark lay, all three detectives only saw a shell of a man who was staring vacantly at the wall.
Dan began with, "So Mark we've come to ask you a few questions in the hope we can find who's done this to you mate."
Nothing.

Isiah now tried. "If you can think of anything that might help us..."

The sobbing began then. Huge body wracking sobs that shook the whole of his body that made him scream out in pain, fetching nurses into the room from all directions.

"Right out you lot, he's in no fit state. Go on move yourselves," was the order from one particularly scary looking Senior Nurse.

As they made their way out, Dan looked back at the man in the bed. "I know he was a bastard, but bloody hell."

"Aye, bloody hell indeed mate," agreed Isiah.

*

After having gone through every second of the video footage of the attack, Max and Eddie were now sitting at Alan and Harry's large dining table. Coffee had been offered and declined as the four faced each other.

Max began, "So you need to be aware that the three men answering your daughter's description were found mutilated and left at Barnsley A & E."

Alan nodded saying, "Yes. We've seen the Social Media footage."

Max continued, "So we must ask you your whereabouts on the night in question which was the Wednesday of last week."

"Easy," shrugged Alan, "my weekly Quiz night at The Red Lion. I was actually with Brad Fairchild," qualifying with, "we're on the same team."

Turning his ice blue probing gaze towards Harry, he noted how she wouldn't look at him but seemed to be looking intently at something on her hands. "And you Harry?"

Looking up, she seemed momentarily surprised to see where she was and whom she was with. "Sorry?" she asked.

"Your whereabouts last Wednesday?"

"Here."

"Here?" reiterated Max.

"Yes here with us," came a voice from the open doorway, where Olivia had just entered. Alan got up and moved towards her saying, "It's okay Liv, we've got this."

"No dad, the police need to do their job so I must help. I've seen the footage," sarcasm dripping from her every word, "they are the ones who did rape me, not that you've bothered to ask but they weren't crying or screaming that day. They did a lot of laughing though, a lot of telling me how much better 'white cock' is. Told me how much I was really enjoying what they were doing. They did plenty of that."

Max and Eddie both took in the clenched fists, the haunted look, the wobble of the voice so close to breaking point. Nodding they got up to leave, as Max said to Alan and Harry, "We had to ask, I'm sure you understand..."

"Because finding the ones who did that to them is more important than what they did to me isn't it?"

"Oh now no Pet, don't think that for one moment," said Eddie.

"I am not your pet! I am not an animal to be stroked or touched without permission."

Eddie, now clearly upset and embarrassed by his inept faux pas replied, "I'm so sorry Olivia. That was thoughtless of me."

As if Eddie hadn't spoken Olivia turned to Max. "When you find who did this to them, will you thank them for me? Will you tell them I'm really grateful that they took something precious from them, something irreplaceable, because that's what they did to me. They took something I can never have back and I despise them for it."

Nodding Max said, "If that's what you want Olivia but... revenge can often destroy instead of solving anything. What happened to you and your friend was unforgiveable but it needn't and shouldn't define you either. One day you and all you love will find some way of coming to terms, to make your peace."

Shaking her head, Olivia replied with venom in her voice, her usually pretty, delicate facial features contorted into something unrecognisable. "The day you feel powerless, Mr Super Hero Cop, completely vulnerable and afraid, that is the day you can lecture me on revenge but until then..."

Harry stepped forward, "Okay Olivia, that's enough now..."

Again, as if her mother hadn't spoken Olivia

continued. “Also tell whoever, what they did was right. Did you know during Antiquity in places such as China, Egypt, even in parts of Northern Europe, captured enemies were often castrated, their penises cut off and exposed. I’ve read about it, looked it up.”

“We’re not at war with anyone Olivia,” said Alan, “what has happened is…”

“Oh but we are dad,” now turning her wrath onto her father, “war is being waged against any woman who dares walk home alone in the dark, or who wears certain clothes because we’re then asking for it aren’t we? You’ve told me yourself!”

“Olivia, please… for God’s sake…” her father now beseeched, his head in his hands.

Harry now took control saying, “That really is enough from everyone. Gentlemen, let me show you out.”

At the door Max said, “We’re truly sorry for what’s happened Harry and you do understand why we’re here don’t you?”

Nodding, Harry just stood looking at the two law enforcement men before replying, “Anything else gentlemen?”

“Only that Olivia will need a great deal of professional help, but we don’t have to tell you that do we?”

“No, you do not.”

Seeing the closed down demeanour and sensing they were wasting their time, Max and Eddie left the home of the Wood family, a once happy home

of optimism and love, now trying to adapt to a dark new reality.
Alan looked up at Harry as she re-entered their kitchen. “Bloody hell Harry but what have you done? What have you brought to our door?”
“What was necessary and how could you not?” was her honest, simple reply as she looked at the man she thought she loved more than her life. Now all she saw was self-pity and weakness and Harry, in that briefest of moments, realised that she loathed him for it.

*

Sitting in the popular ‘Micro Brewery’ on Penton’s High Street Max and Eddie now quietly deliberated. “They’re medics, they would have access to the equipment, they would know where and how to cut without actually causing death,” argued Max.
“Dr Wood’s alibi is iron clad, which leaves us with Mrs Wood.”
“Yep,” replied Max, “helped no doubt by Speight.”
Shaking his head, “Do not go there again Max. Do not let your obsession with Speight get into your head to the detriment of what’s important and let’s not forget that poor bairn, Olivia. My God but she’s... well, mentally scarred doesn’t even come close.”
Nodding his agreement Max leant back in his chair. “I know and seeing what’s happened to that bright, beautiful kid is seriously sickening. Yet he’s a constant presence isn’t he Eddie? If we

can't get instant results, abide by the code of law, then let's get good old Malcolm Speight involved. Give him enough money and he'll get the job done properly."
Eddie now leaned forward and his next words surprised Max to the point of being shocked. "And I have to say Chief, I've never really understood why the bloody hell we don't use him too."

*

Beth and Imogen meanwhile, were trying to make sense of what they knew. They had decided it was time to inform Sarah as keeping her out of the loop seemed to be somehow treacherous even though for some of the details, very necessary.
"You think Harry has done what?! You can't be serious. We're talking about our Harry here, the nurse, the carer. She wouldn't even think about being involved in cutting off... well she just wouldn't. She couldn't!"
"I know love, it's beyond anything any one of us could have ever predicted would happen but she is involved in this somehow," as Imogen began to explain how Harry had demanded Malcolm Speight's contact details. Sarah's response was as they had both predicted.
"Oh God, but this is all my fault!"
Beth began, "No Sarah, you can't..."
"If I hadn't killed Grant, Malcolm Speight would never have been in our lives. I, no, we should have

come clean and told the truth. Pay for... for...my sins."

Gently taking her weeping friend into her arms Imogen began to do what she did best, soothe and calm, taking control. "No Sarah, we had no choice. We had to do what we did because Grant was a monster, who had friends who were monsters. The outcome was just Sarah."

"But... poor Olivia... perhaps if I..."

"No," said Beth, emphatic in her tone. "Bad things happen to good people all the time. I see it every day and what has happened does not come back to you."

Suddenly a crash was heard, as if something very heavy had fallen somewhere in the upper part of the dwelling.

"Is Trey back?" asked Imogen.

Visibly pulling herself together, Sarah shook her head. "No, unfortunately. It will be Scooby or Cyril up to mischief no doubt." Rising to investigate the noise, Sarah left the room, leaving her friends quietly anxious.

Eventually Beth spoke. "She has a right to know the truth Gen. To be fair, we should have told her straight away."

"She does, but not yet. Eventually... but not yet. Let's get this hurdle cleared first, that is if we can." Sinking back into Sarah's comfortable sofa, Imogen closed her eyes, worry etched across her face.

"So... Max?" ventured Beth.

Opening her eyes, Imogen looked at her friend, seeing the worry, the guilt. “Radio silence since the video appeared, so you tell me?”

“Brad and I are no longer part of the investigation due to the proximity of our relationship with Harry and Alan. To be honest, he’s made me feel like a bloody leper.”

Smiling sadly Imogen looked at her friend, acknowledging her worry, her guilt and her shame which she constantly lived with. Stretching to touch Beth’s hand Imogen simply said, “Where Max Stainmore is concerned, well… welcome to my world my friend.”

*

Max watched as the two friends walked to the point on the High Street where they would go their separate ways. He saw their heads together, their arms linked, their embrace of true sisterhood as they waved their goodnights. They’d come from the direction of Sarah’s and as he had predicted, the friends were now casting their invisible shield of love and protection around themselves, as he knew with an unspoken certainty, they had done years before.

Looking up, she saw him watching her before he crossed the road to meet her. Neither spoke or smiled but stood stock still, just looking, each trying to read the other.

Finally, Imogen spoke. “What do you want to ask me?”

Silence.

"Ask me?" she challenged, "go on?"
Nailing her with the look he used in the interrogation rooms he asked, "Have you been in contact?"
"Say his name!"
Shaking his head, he looked down at the pavement, then mutinously back at her. "Okay, we'll have it your way. Have you been in any contact or been in the physical presence of Malcolm Speight?"
Shortening the distance between them, head held high, eyes defiant, she replied, "No I have not! Next question."
Feeling now her righteous anger, he moved to touch her but she backed away. "No more questions? So my turn. You've obviously seen the footage, probably segment by segment" as he nodded, now looking worried, "so explain to me how you could possibly believe or think, even for a nanosecond, that I would be involved in anything so barbaric, so dehumanising? Despite what they may or may not have done, how could you possibly believe I would have any part in that happening to someone's son, brother, child?"
Looking scandalised Max was now emphatic. "Hey! I did not think for an instant you would, but he would, Speight would and he'd enjoy doing it too!" Running his hands through his short military style hair, Max now searched for the words; words that would explain. Words that would draw them back together like the

jigsaw they were; a perfect fit when the right pieces were put in the right place. “You know how I feel about you Imogen. I wouldn’t have turned my back on London or the NCA if not for you.”

“Then go back to London Max. Go back to the NCA!”

Practically yelling Max replied, “How can you say that? After everything we’ve shared? Been through?”

Imogen’s next words made him feel bereft, like he was in real danger of losing something precious, something irreplaceable. “All that we’ve shared and all that we have become is pointless without trust, without honesty, without truth. We’ve barely been apart since the car bomb attack but then you saw the footage and immediately assumed I was somehow involved without even asking me. Where’s the trust? Where’s our future when you can so easily doubt me, suspect me, shun me?”

Max now walked to a nearby bench and sat down. Lifting his eyes to meet hers, he began to speak his honest truth. “One of you has been badly hurt, damaged by …animals, brutes. Again! I know many believe they got what they deserve, had it coming! That all rapists should be treated as such and believe me I get it. Part of me gets why you would turn to Speight too, but it crucifies me to think you may have and I daren’t confront you because part of me doesn’t want to

know!"
Spreading his arms, to emphasise his point he continued, "I just hate what he stands for, hate how he operates outside of the law, dispensing his brand of justice without following due process but taking his thirty pieces of silver along the way," shaking his head adding, "hate that he can still drive a wedge between us."
"He can't. Only we can do that or in this case, only you," as she turned to walk away.
"Let me walk you home?" The silence now stretched as the metaphorical crossroads they had come to, stretched in front of them.
Finally, Imogen answered, "No thank you, I'd rather walk alone," then turning back to face him added, "it appears for some us, walking through life alone is the easiest, most reliable, less painful option." With that and without looking back, she turned and walked away with Max watching her until she was out of sight.

CHAPTER 29

The hanging dead body of Finn Raithes was still in situ when Constable Asif Khan and Eddie Sinclair arrived at the scene. The body had been found by a rough sleeper, a boy of seventeen named Dean Stevens, who had been looking for somewhere safe and away from the cold for a few hours. He had stumbled across the disused warehouse just off the Rotherham\Sheffield canal bank, had been delighted when the door had given way, then freaked out when he saw what was in there. He had then run full pelt, smack into the arms of Philip Read, one of those freak coincidences life sometimes throws up. Philip had gone with the poor shaken boy to the place the body was still hanging. He immediately recognised it was Finn and had immediately phoned Eddie Sinclair.

Turning to his old friend, Philip began. "I know the lad, in fact I was the one who got him banged up the last time. Know his grandmother, known her since school and she asked me only the other day to have a word with him. She was worried, worried who he was mixing with, what he might have got mixed up in. I have to say he looked bloody scared when I did talk to him."

"Any ideas who he was afraid of or what?"

"No, only..."

"Yeah, go on?"

"Only that he seemed out of his depth and worse, out of options. Like he had nowhere to turn."

Nodding Eddie asked, "So, fancy coming with me and Asif to break the news? She'll need a friend?"

Sighing Philip replied, "Aye Eddie. She'll need a friend and a lot more besides as well."

*

Karen Raithes, Finn's long suffering grandmother had taken one look at Philip's face when she had opened her front door, before collapsing into his arms.

Now she was trying to make sense of what she was hearing. "But why? I knew he was unhappy but to do this?"

Eddie began, "We're very sorry for your loss Mrs Raithes. Phil here has agreed to do the formal identification so you'll be spared that at least."

"I tried ringing him then I realised his phone was still here, could hear it ringing so I knew in my heart something terrible was going to happen. I mean, he couldn't move without the bloody thing, constantly looking at it, texting. Then looking even more worried after he'd read summat," said as she went to a cupboard, retrieving the phone which had a piece of paper sellotaped to it.

"May I?" asked Asif as he took the phone from her. "Have you looked at his phone Mrs Raithes?"
"No. It's locked isn't it and I didn't want to pry. I suppose I didn't want to know if I'm honest."
Looking at the note Asif confirmed it was a number saying, "My guess is that this is the number which will unlock the phone. May I?"
Nodding her agreement Karen now appeared to hold her breath, wondering what the phone would reveal about her grandson, the child she had looked after since he was just three years old, after his mother had literally abandoned him. As the phone pinged to life, Asif said to Eddie, "It looks like he's deleted all Apps including Social Media. His text messages are deleted too from the looks of it but there is this. It's a video left in his photos section."
"Permission to play it Karen?" asked Philip.
Karen merely nodded, quietly terrified at what may now be revealed. Finn's face now appeared on the screen his voice following:
"When you find this you'll already know I'm dead. I'm hoping I'll find the guts to do it mi sen, because I dread to think what they'll do if they find me first. I suppose at end of day I'm just a coward. Nan, I want you to know I never meant for that old lady or that shopkeeper to die. I know what people will say, what the papers will write but I want to think that it wasn't my boot that killed 'em. I mean I held back and hoped the others din't notice (pause, swallowing, tears welling then falling)

and I wouldn't hurt that lass the other day either. I'm not a bloody rapist. I phoned the police but they got there too late as per. The lads deserved what they got too, particularly that bastard Carl, who just wants to impress... (Silence)... ***well no matter now. Nan. Thank you for everything you've done for me and I'm right sorry for how I've turned out, for all the trouble I've been because I know you'll cry for me even though I don't deserve your tears. Tell mi mum, if you ever see her again... tell her I'm sorry that I wasn't nice enough for her to love me, for her to want to stay with me won't you. And Nan... I love you Nan...I love you with all my heart. God bless. That's what you used to say to me when I was little...when you tucked me in after reading me a story. God bless."*** (Image now frozen, sound done).

"Oh my Christ," muttered Eddie as he looked at the pale ashen face of Asif as he stared at the image on the phone. At this point the young Constable got up and left the room.

Tears streaming down her face Karen now said, "No not my Finn, not my little boy. Not a murderer. He couldn't, didn't have it in him. Oh Eddie, my poor little lad," as her grief of loss and shame took over.

"It's a dying confession love," said Philip as he put his arms around her, then to Eddie, "is your officer ok?"

Sighing heavily, Eddie candidly replied, "No mate. The other victim was his cousin, his kin, so no he won't be."

Standing up to leave Eddie was now all police business. "We will need this as crucial evidence in a murder enquiry. Also Mrs Raithes we will need to interview you at some point. You may have information that will help us further although you may think you don't but who knows."

Nodding Karen Raithes now looked like she had aged a hundred years as she stared numbly at the phone which Eddie was now placing in a plastic evidence bag. "We will be in touch," as he nodded his goodbyes.

Philip holding Karen's shaking hands in his said, "I'll put the kettle on love."

Looking bewildered and heartbroken in equal measure Karen asked her friend, "How do I get through this? What will people say Phil?"

"You'll get through this one day at a time love and folk will say what they think is the truth or what they think they have the right to say and you won't be able to stop them. So let me make you that cuppa eh?"

Outside Asif was leaning against the unmarked police car, breathing deeply and trying to control the tidal of emotions he was feeling. Eddie having closed Karen's door, came to stand next to him. "You alright lad?"

Shaking his head Asif was honest in his reply. "To be honest Sarge, I don't know if I'll ever be alright again."

"It's a bad business that's for sure."
"I mean, this lad we found today! He's saying he hoped his mates didn't see he wasn't kicking them to kill them and hoped they didn't notice. I mean how bloody hopeless is that?! Like he was just going along with it. Hoped he hadn't upset his sodding mates because he really didn't want to do it! Where were his balls to stop them in the first place eh?"
"I think this poor bugger is another victim if I'm honest lad."
Turning his anger full force onto Eddie, Asif's voice was now raised. "Don't you dare Sarge! Don't you bloody dare make excuses for this scum."
"Now lad I..."
"Save it Sarge. I don't want to hear it."
"Well perhaps you need to Asif, if you're going to be any of use to this investigation."
Breathing deeply, Asif was physically trying to calm himself before eventually saying, "With respect Sarge, it's not your blood who's getting buried tomorrow."
Nodding his understanding, he took the young officer by the shoulders. "No it isn't lad and I hate what they've done to you and your family, hate what they've done to this city I love and am proud to serve, but you heard that lad's last words to his nan. He was lost and scared enough to take himself out. I'm not making excuses for him Asif. I'm just sad at the hopelessness and

waste of it all."

Looking into the eyes of this wise old stalwart, Asif nodded. "Sorry if I spoke out of turn Sarge."

"No apologies necessary lad. Come on, you've got a big day ahead of you tomorrow."

*

Max and the rest of the Serious and Organised Crime Division listened intently to Finn Raithes last message.

"Well, it now looks like we can identify four out of the five we believe murdered Noor Acharya and Yara Abrahms. Forensics came up with five different boot prints so that leaves one perpetrator and I suspect the ring leader, still to be identified but from what Armley Prison tells us, Brandon Cowden was part if not the leader of their group and was released about the same time. The name Cowden has cropped up more than once so we need to pick him up. Eddie, take Richard and do the honours. Isiah, take Dan and go and formally arrest and charge the three in hospital for murder and try to get the last piece of information out of them."

"The medics wouldn't let us near them last time we were there Chief."

"Then arrest the bloody medics as well if they won't let us do our job!" snapped back Max.

"Chief," muttered Isiah, raising his eyebrows to Dan in a silent question.

Max continued, "Right I'm sure you all remember what today is and how vigilant we must all be. It's all hands on deck, with most here in plainclothes blending in with the crowd to see if there's chance of something kicking off whilst uniform will be as visible as possible. Counter Terrorism have also infiltrated various groups of interest so with luck, today will go well. Questions anyone?" With Max's present mood in evidence no one dared ask anything. "Ok stay safe and stay vigilant."

Max then returned to his office, closing the door behind him, something he rarely did.

Max's whole demeanour had been difficult to read for several days with all walking on eggshells around him. This current Detective Chief Superintendent Stainmore was not going down well as the teams returned to their desks, shaking their heads making muttering comments of their own.

"When do we get the old Chief back Sarge?" asked Lydia.

"Not soon enough," grumbled Eddie, "not bloody soon enough."

CHAPTER 30

The streets of Sheffield were lined as the funeral corteges of both Noor Acharya and Yara Abrahms passed together side by side.

It had been the favour Jakob Abrahms had asked of Omar Mirza, the night they had met via Malcolm Speight, when Jakob explained what had been his aunt's wishes on the event of her death; the main one being that 'her boys' as she had come to think of Noor and Asif, would be invited to be part of her funeral. Noor's murder had obviously made this request a sad impossibility so Jakob had suggested what was now arranged and Omar had surprisingly agreed.

Both funeral corteges combining of hearses and those who would walk behind, had convened at the appropriately named Peace Gardens in order for Yara and Noor to begin their final journey as together as possible. The journey would take the vast collection of mourners down Pinstone Street, then onto The Moor, cutting off onto Charter Road, Moor Street then Hanover Street and the roundabout at the end which would then allow the corteges to veer onto their designated places of worship where the ritual for the departed would take place. For Yara, the Psalter Lane Synagogue; for Noor the London Road Mosque.

The route was long and would take time so the required Traffic Regulation Orders with support from the Traffic Division of the police had been faced with a logistical nightmare but the cordoned off roads were now in place, with traffic diversions running smoothly.

Max and his colleagues were out in force, with uniformed police from many of the north's forces, walking beside the corteges as well as lining the route. Plainclothes officers were also in abundance, from Serious Crimes, Major Crimes and Counter Terrorism. Alert was on high and for many in the higher ranks of the police, breaths were also being held until this was done.

Religious leaders Salim Shah and Soloman Kaufman had approached the local schools and asked that children, old enough to understand, would join them. Now children of all nationalities and religions were in line behind the coffins, each holding the recognised symbols of peace in the form of daisies or an olive branch. As the two long lines of mourners began to make their journey a child held out her hand to the child next to her across the short space that divided the two sets of mourners, which the child took without hesitation. Like a ripple effect the rest of the children did the same bringing the two corteges together as one. That simple gesture of connection was not lost on those who were there that day or on the various news outlets present who captured it on film.

Max, in full dress uniform had been asked to walk behind the coffins, along with the Chief

and Assistant Constables. Imogen had also been asked to be part of the procession too along with Faisel. So they began their walk, a silent, solemn occasion with all praying it would also be incident free.

Isiah and Dan, both in plainclothes has spotted unlikely looking sympathisers and were moving closer. "Don't like the look at that bunch," said Isiah.

"I've clocked them too," replied Dan, "let's stand closer, just in case."

Gareth Jackson, along with Brandon Cowden and a few others from The Stag were enjoying what they perceived they had achieved, that being bringing the city to a standstill. Brandon was just sorry he couldn't brag about it from the rooftops, saying to Gareth, "We did this. I fucking did this!"

"And the coppers are looking for you so make sure you keep blending in."

Gareth, spotting the detectives as they moved closer whispered to Brandon, "Watch yourself. Pig alert!" Brandon clocked the detectives immediately and shrunk further back into the crowds along with Gareth and the others. Today was a day to show patience.

The hearses eventually reached the point where the two old friends would go their separate ways. Asif at this point, got out of the car he was in and approached the hearse where Yara's coffin lay. The funeral director opened the back doors which allowed Asif to place a single white Peace Rose on her coffin. Resting his forehead on the wood, his eyes closed, he whispered his final goodbye. "Rest in peace Yara and look after Noor for me until we meet again and share stories."

Then he returned to his own cortege, as both dearly loved victims of such pointless violence went on their separate designated routes. Now only family and close friends, with their police detail would continue their journeys.

The children still holding hands now seemed at a loss what to do. Faisel aka Fiz looking at the girl whose hand he was holding, smiled and gave her his olive branch. Smiling back, she gave him her daisy. The rest of the children followed suit.

"Just when I thought I couldn't love that kid more," muttered Max as he came to stand behind Imogen.

Wiping a stray tear, she looked up at him and merely nodded as Fiz, having spotted Max came over. "Hello Max, I really like your uniform."

"Thanks mate."

"And I think I might have a girlfriend now."

Smiling and ruffling his hair Max pointedly

replied, "Well take care not to lose her Fiz, if she's what you're looking for."
"I won't Max but is it true girls like a man in uniform?"
"I think you should ask Ms Holt that one mate."
"Miss?"
Looking into Fiz's earnest face Imogen smiled and said, "I've heard that some girls find uniforms attractive although I think the man or boy who wears one must be worthy of wearing what it stands for."
"Like Max, Miss?"
Nodding, "Yes like the Chief Superintendent Fiz, now say your goodbyes. We have to get back to school."
Watching him bound back to his new found friends Max whispered, "Thanks for that."
Moving closer Imogen began, "Max I…
"Ah Chief Superintendent," said a voice belonging to Police Press Officer Leanne Wright, "really sorry to interrupt but I really need you to…"
"I'm unavailable …" snapped Max, loudly enough to turn heads.
"I'll leave you to it," said Imogen, collecting Fiz, and making her way to the buses that had been made available.
Max now watched her as she made her way wondering what might have been said, if they'd been allowed just a couple of minutes more.
Leanne now looked anxiously at him saying,

"Sorry Chief Superintendent but the Chief Constable..."
"I know," sighed Max, "duty calls...again as always."

*

Later at Sheffield's City Hall, the mourners from both funerals, with members of the general public and the usual civic dignitaries had been invited to come together and demonstrate to the world that many in Sheffield still believed, as in the words of murdered MP Jo Cox, another victim of senseless hate, that people were more united than divided, despite the circumstances of the occasion.
Max was standing with the Chief Constable when he spied his nemesis. Malcolm Speight was standing with whom Max had understood to be Yara Abrahms only family member, a very well-heeled individual who reeked of money. The fact that Speight was with him and an invited guest at that, set off a load of alarm bells for him. At that very moment Malcolm turned his gaze and locked eyes on Max. Both men now stared each other down for several seconds with Malcolm being the first to blink. Eddie having witnessed the 'Mexican stand-off' sidled up to Max saying, "I can practically smell Clint Eastwood's cigar. So you're clearly the good and Speight is obviously the bad, so I assume I'm the bloody ugly one again eh?"
Shaking his head Max replied, "He's in this up to

his neck and he's making it bloody obvious."

"And he's handed us on a plate three perpetrators of the worse kind of 'hate' crime. Certainly the worse we've seen in this city."

"For money and possibly involved in grievous bodily harm too which last time I looked was a crime."

Nodding his agreement Eddie simply said, "And good luck in proving that one too Chief."

*

In a quiet corner across the room another conversation was taking place. Glass in hand Omar Miraz had subtly acknowledged Assistant Chief Constable Zoe Yale, who moved to where he was standing alone. "Have you any idea how much I loathe seeing you in that get up?" murmured Omar.

"About as much as you love getting me out of it," was her reply, "and are you staying the night this time or do you have to play the dutiful husband?"

"I shall be staying because only God knows how much I need you today." Nodding she moved away but not before Omar briefly allowed his fingers to brush hers with Zoe registering the power that small contact still had on her, something that had been part of them for nearly thirty years.

"I'll be waiting. I'll always be waiting." Then she was gone.

CHAPTER 31

Sarah quietly knocked on Olivia's closed bedroom door. Getting no response, she now opened the door and asked, "Hi Liv. Is it ok for me to come in?"

The girl whom she'd known since she'd held her in her arms on the day of her birth, merely shrugged her shoulders, not looking up but continuing looking at her laptop on her desk. Sarah walked into the room and sat down on the bed opposite her.

Looking around the room Sarah smiled as she saw many of the childhood gifts she and the others had bought over the years and the array of photographs of happier times, still displayed around the room.

Sarah began. "Sorry I haven't been sooner love."

No answer.

Sarah remained silent thinking. Olivia looked up then and asked, "So Aunty Sarah, I'm sure you have words of wisdom about you knowing how I feel so let's hear it?"

Startled and surprised at the tone of bitterness Sarah shook her head saying, "Why would I

know Liv?"
Shrugging Olivia replied, "I know your husband was a gangster and... well I overheard mum and dad saying he wasn't nice to you. That's all."
"He wasn't nice to many people from what the police have told me Olivia and it's been hard to know I married such an evil, cruel man. Even his mother thought so."
Olivia had now turned away from her desk to look at Sarah, someone she had known as Aunty all of her life, who'd always been there, been kind and truthful so she asked, "What did he do to you?"
Without missing a beat, Sarah told her. "He raped me Olivia. He raped and drugged me and hoped I'd die. And there was a point I wanted to and possibly would have if not for my friends and their love and support."
Stunned by the honesty of Sarah's reply, Olivia joined Sarah on the bed, sitting next to her as Sarah reaching for her hand continued. "I remember the day I realised what he had done to me, waking up, my body covered in bruises, bites, even cigarette burns and... no I won't go into the rest my love. It's too awful and what was one of the worse things is that I felt I had done something wrong, because that's what monsters like Grant and those low lives who did what they did to you make us think and feel." Tearing up Olivia now merely nodded. "But Grant hasn't defined me love and what they did won't define

you either because we won't allow it. By we I'm talking about the strong women in your life who are standing by your side and you Liv. You are strong and you are resilient and this will not define you either."

Olivia looked at Sarah's abdomen and touched the small baby bump that was becoming evident. "You've had sex since you were raped Aunty Sarah."

"There's no denying that," smiled Sarah as she stroked her small baby bump, "here's the evidence."

Seeing Olivia's bewildered face Sarah immediately understood. "I never thought I'd be able to again too my love but you will meet someone who is good, kind, patient, understanding, who will earn your trust and your love. Someone who will deserve your trust and your love."

Shaking her head Olivia remained silent, then whispered, "I hadn't done it before Aunty Sarah and I don't think I could do it ever again."

Gathering her into her arms Sarah silently hugged her close, then taking Olivia's face into her hands said, "You've not had sex with someone you feel deeply for or just merely fancy. What happened was ugly, vile and brutal and it wasn't sex. It was a brutal assault born out of disrespect and misogyny. Someone will come into your life and he or she will show you tenderness and make you feel pleasure and joy that will be special. I promise you this and you will recover because we are warriors Olivia. We will not allow the low life's who came into our lives uninvited, to win! Not for a second! Okay?"

Nodding Olivia actually smiled, "Okay Aunty Sarah." The smile suddenly disappeared as quickly as it came as Olivia now moved to look unseeingly out of the window.

"I think mum and dad might have paid someone to hurt them and I was really glad at first but now..."

"Now what love?"

Looking back at Sarah, Olivia spread her arms out, the gesture indicating her feelings being difficult to express. Finally, she said, "I think I feel sorry that it was done to them because of me. Guilty even."

Going over to join her at the window Sarah looked out, saying, "Don't you just love Autumn, the colours and everything, with all the leaves falling so that new shoots can appear in the Spring. It's like nature's spring cleaning, getting rid of the old in readiness for a new beginning don't you think?" Then taking her by the shoulders and turning her so that they faced each other Sarah continued. "Because this too shall pass Olivia. You will wake up one morning and what happened won't be the first thing you think about. I won't pretend that you will completely forget, but I can tell you that this will in time heal and you will be stronger, more aware and more ready to face what else life will have in store for you because it will have plenty and much of which will be wonderful. You've faced the worse my love and you've survived and in that survival you're actually showing compassion for those who have done this to you. I hope you know how very special that makes you."

*

Harry, Beth and Imogen were listening for Sarah's return, wondering how her chat with Olivia was going and hoping it didn't bring back too many bad memories for either of them.

Harry was very quiet, not instigating conversation, except to say how both Olivia and she were going away for a while but now, merely listening to her friends talk of the funeral both had attended but in very different capacities.

"I think the marriage proposals for the Chief have broken Twitter and Tiktok from all accounts," said Beth, "but I suspect one of the techies is deliberately posting 'hot' photos about him so he can win the sweepstake. Did you clock him in his uniform Gen?"

Scowling at her friend Imogen replied, "I did."

"And?"

"No Comment!"

Shaking her head Beth began, "Have you any idea what it's like working with the Chief when you two are fighting? Purgatory. Even the Sarge is ready to kill him and as for..."

"Enough Beth," said Imogen, "it is what it is."

"Thanks to me," Harry quietly added.

No one spoke because it was the truth. Sarah came into the room then at this point, and sensed the atmosphere at once. "So playing happy families are we?"

"No," replied Beth, "Harry was just happily taking the blame for Imogen and Max being estranged that's all, as she should."

"There's nothing happy about any of this!" snapped Harry.

Holding up her hands Imogen intervened saying, "Enough. Okay?!"

Silence. Then from Sarah, "So you and Olivia off to St Paul de Vence for a few days?"

"Yes, it's one of her favourite places, mine too. She needs to get away and Alan can't bear to be around me. Mum is coming over to look after the twins so..."

"You and Alan are one of the strongest couples around. He's just having a tough time..." began Imogen.

"He's having a tough time! Oh silly me and here I thought it was our daughter being the one who's suffering and having a tough time!"

"Don't take it out on Gen Harry alright? Because thanks to you we're all having a bloody tough time," exploded Beth.

"Well that's rich coming from you," snarled Harry.

"Right," intervened Sarah, "let's all take a breath

shall we?"

Shaking with anger and if she was honest, with regret, Harry got up and retrieved wine, pouring everyone apart from Sarah a generous quantity. Everyone was silent, no one daring to speak as all were afraid of words being said that would damage so much, that there would be no turning back.

"The fact is," began Sarah, "if I had to choose between my friends and having John back, I would choose John and I suspect it's the same for both Beth and Harry. You need to finally understand Gen, that we can take care of ourselves; that if it comes to a choice, you need to choose your own happiness. If that is Max, then you need to make him understand. You need to make him understand that you would you choose him, even over us. Do you agree Harry? Beth?"

"Spot on mate!" said Beth as Harry sadly nodded in agreement. Whilst speaking, Sarah had retrieved Imogen's coat and was now holding it up for her to put on.

"You mean now?" spluttered Imogen, "but it's not as simple as..."

"No time like the present and it really is as simple as that," said Beth who was now helping Sarah get Imogen into her coat, adding, "just march up to his front door, grab hold of him and proceed to fuck his brains out! Then all will be as it should be. Simples!"

CHAPTER 32

"Hi. I can take that for you," said Imogen to the pizza delivery youth as she approached Max's front door. "How much?"

"£14 please love."

Imogen produced a £20 note adding, "Keep the change."

"Ah thanks love, sound," grinned the young man who happily went on his way.

Seeing Imogen standing on his doorstep holding the take-out pizza he had ordered earlier, made Max first think he was finally losing it. With her never being out of his head, particularly after their encounter at the funeral earlier, his initial thought was that he was now hallucinating, acknowledging how bone tired he was.

"So I hope this is the thin and crispy version and not the stuffed crust 'heart attack in waiting' one you love so much?"

Shaking his head, he came straight to the point. "What are you doing here?"

Walking past him to place the box on the table, Imogen turned to face him. He was unreadable and she was now wondering if she had left it too late. If perhaps he had come to the conclusion that they were better off staying apart.

Taking a deep breath, she began, “I’m here because you need to ask me something?”

“About what? Why we’re fighting? About Speight?”

Shrugging, she replied, “It’s connected I guess.”

Looking defeated, Max shook his head saying, “No, I don’t think there’s anything left to say Imogen, you’ve made it very clear…”

Interrupting him she continued, “You need to ask me to choose.”

“Choose?”

“Yes choose.”

Puzzled, Max replied, “I don’t understand.”

“You need to ask me to choose between you or my friends.”

Looking completely at a loss, Max asked, “Are you being remotely serious?”

“I am Max. Ask me to choose, for once and for all.”

Shaking his head, he replied, “I would never in a million years ask you to choose between your friends or me,” now laughing without humour he added, “I wouldn’t give much for my chances if I even tried.”

“Well I’m asking that you do,” as she stared at him, now devoid of emotion, an enigma he couldn’t read as she continued staring at him. He also knew that after tonight, he could easily find himself missing her for the rest of his life, with no hope of a reconciliation which until now he had held on to.

Sighing, rubbing his hands over his face, he asked, already dreading what she might so easily reply, "Okay Imogen, make your choice. Who do you choose? The three friends whom you love as if they were your own flesh, who you've known since you were five years old and would literally do anything for or me? The man you've already run away from once because you couldn't trust him enough. A man who now realises how much he's let you down and hurt you... again. A man you've walked away from...again!"

"I choose you Max, I choose you."

Scarcely daring to believe what she was saying, Max walked towards her. "What's changed?"

Looking up at him, desperate to touch him but knowing she needed to bridge the gap with words that would make him understand, she began. "Nothing because I'm still hurt you initially thought the worse of me..."

"And I feel like a jealous fool for doing that and if you'd let me walk you home that night I'd have..."

"What?" she whispered, moving closer to him.

Pulling her into his arms, looking into her eyes and seeing nothing other than trust and hope, he whispered back, "I would have then, as I do now, promise you on my life, that I will never doubt us again or make you feel that walking through life without me will ever be an option for you."

"But we still have a long way to go Max. Mutual trust is everything to me and..."

"I do trust you and I know what it's taken for you to come here tonight."

Grimacing she said, "In the spirit of trust and openness you need to know the girls made me. Made me realise that what I need is important too and that I owe it to myself and to you, to... fight for us."

"Tell them I'm grateful."

"And trust me Max," now giving him a look that suggested hurt was still bubbling beneath, but loving their proximity, "when I say it will be the last thing you ever do if you ever make me live through something like this again!"

"And I'd die a happy man," he murmured, "but never again Imogen, I promise," smiling as he drew her deeper into his arms, finding her mouth to seal their future.

As their kiss deepened, their mutual passion growing, Imogen pulled away, saying against his mouth, "So isn't your pizza getting cold?"

"Have I ever old you," he murmured as he unbuttoned her coat, sliding it off her shoulders, before finding the zip of her dress, "how much I love very cold pizza?" as the zip of her dress opened to reveal what was beneath as it fell to the floor.

"Well I do have my orders" as she stepped out of her dress finding his mouth again, loving the feel of her bare flesh once again encircled in his arms.

"Orders?"

"From Detective Constable Fairchild who has ordered me to fuck your brains out assuring me that by doing so all will be as it should be," said as she finished unbuttoning his shirt, now stripping it from his shoulders to reveal his naked chest, loving the feel and smell of his skin as she caressed his bare flesh.

Grinning Max gathered her closer, huskily saying, "Remind me to recommend her for a promotion."

"I will but can we please stop talking now?"

CHAPTER 33

For the first time in weeks, Harry felt she could finally exhale, as if she'd been holding her breath for the longest time. It felt good to leave the late autumnal gloom and cold of Yorkshire, not to mention Penton's unforgiving wind and the flight from Leeds Bradford airport to Nice had gone without a hitch.

Getting into their taxi, Olivia had observed the weather saying, "Good to see the sun again," as mother and daughter left Nice airport and headed towards the archetypal idyllic medieval hilltop village that was St Paul De Vence. Harry and Alan had discovered it decades earlier and years before their children had arrived. It had become a place Harry always felt at peace in, a respite from the busy daily grind of modern life. Located on a narrow spur between two deep valleys, even the quality of light made the world look brighter, happier, uplifting a person's spirit without really trying. Harry was now praying that this much loved place would work its magic on Olivia and begin the slow process of healing.

The winding roads they knew so well, brought

into view the snow-capped tips of the French Alps, the blue of the sky making their white peaks stand out even more, before revealing the beautiful ancient architecture of St Pauls which never failed to impress. Their taxi could only take them so far as the narrow streets were not built for the age of the car. Walking through the medieval archway, past the old men playing boules, up the steep hill, past the art and gift shops and the ice cream parlour, Harry saw Olivia actually smiling for the first time in weeks and it made her heart sing.

"Okay?" asked Harry.

"Yes mum. It's good to see that nothing ever changes here."

"Shall we call in to see if Camille and Antoine have room for us to eat at theirs later?" referring to their favourite restaurant Le Tilleul which overlooked the valley and the hillside beyond.

"That would be lovely mum and mum? Thanks for this."

And so began the slow process of healing for a mother and daughter who both had their own demons to vanquish. The bleakness and terror of the police questioning, the silent disappointed admonishments of a husband, actions taken with consequences to be lived with and the unspoken horror of the situation they had found themselves in, briefly seemed to fade, left behind for the time being. All of it would still be waiting for them on their return but for this short time, they could both finally breathe again.

*

The windmills of Royds Moor, situated just outside of Penton were busy. Unlike St Paul De Vence, Penton's unforgiving wind still held remnants of the early morning frost as Malcolm turned up the collar of his coat. Turning towards Imogen, sitting beside him, he smiled at her saying, "Beautiful here and very different from Burngreave where I was born and dragged up. Must have been a bit special being brought up around here."

"I imagine you and I had the same sort of childhoods Malcolm. In my case, the scenery was prettier that's all."

Rubbing his hands together to initiate more blood flow against the wind Malcolm now muttered, "Bloody hell but it's cold up here too. No wonder there's no other bugger in sight."

"Thank you for agreeing to meet me here. I know it's a long way off the beaten track and not easy to find."

"Not easy to detect either, that is if our meeting is to remain our secret eh?" Seeing how tense she was, how worried she looked, he realised how much he hated the thought of her being less than happy. Nudging her he asked, "Okay. What is it? What do you need me to do?"

Retrieving her phone, she brought up her contacts and then his number saying, "I need to delete your contact Malcolm as I intend that we are never to be in touch again, not even through a third party. I have no choice," as her fingers now pressed the found delete button.

"But don't think for one moment I'm not grateful… I always will be for what you did for Sarah but now Harry and…"

Holding up his hand, Malcolm silenced her. "But bloody Robocop cop hates me with a vengeance," as he chuckled, "and I don't bloody blame him."

No longer smiling he added, "And for the record, I did try and dissuade your friend but she was very determined and part of me understands it but it even turned my stomach and that's saying summat."

Imogen, now looking relieved said, "I've been dreading this. I owe you so much…"

"No you don't."

"But we both know I do, despite how you look at the world my friend and you are my friend Malcolm and I will always think of you as such."

Silence now stretched companionably around them before Malcolm, suddenly looking up to the sky asked, "Is that a drone? Has Robocop found us? Is he watching our every move, listening to our every word, this very second? No, no it's a bird, a bloody big bird, but a bird nonetheless. It's okay, we're still safe. Phew!"

Imogen looked askance at him then as they looked at each other, they both simultaneously burst out laughing. "You're a bugger Malcolm Speight! You know that?"

"Aye, I do, and the rest." Now being serious he looked at her. "I also know how much Stainmore loathes me. He made it very clear when he came to see me in the middle of the Sheldon affair during Covid and recently at the funeral, we had a bit of a stare off! I bloody hate it that I blinked first as well."

"You're his Achilles heel where I'm concerned and you both behave like, like… well..."

"My old Mam used to say that men grow old but never grow up."

Smiling now, Imogen nodded agreeing, "And she'd be right."

Malcolm's smile faded as he looked at her. "He knows I'd do anything for you and he hates me for it."

"He's jealous of it."

"I would be too if I was in his shoes, not that I ever could be."

"Don't do that Malcolm. Don't put me on a pedestal because I really don't deserve to be."

Looking at her Malcolm began to tell her something he had wanted to say for a very long time and he knew with a certainty that left him hollow, that he would never have this time with her again.

"I remember the first time I ever laid eyes on you. I'd been to see your husband Neil about my case. I was having a fag outside of his office when I saw you across the street. You were wearing this beautiful red coat and you, well you took my breath away. Then you crossed over the road and waved. I remember thinking, she can't possibly be waving at me?!" chuckling now, "then I saw it was for Neil standing just behind me. Your smile, just for him was... well...it was..." shaking his head he concluded, "now I don't have the words. You both looked so happy, so in love, like you were the only ones on the planet."

Looking at the far away horizon but only seeing images of the past Imogen nodded as she remembered saying, "We were going to John Lewis, to look at nursery furniture that day. I couldn't wait to start buying for the baby. Life seemed so simple, so full of promise then."

Squeezing her hand, they both sat there, both lost in thought, both reliving the past, both feeling each other's pain.

"And now," announced Malcolm, "you've got bloody Robocop, or should we call him Super Cop, Superman even? I mean how the bloody hell can us mere mortals compete with the sort of bravery he showed with that young lad eh? And if that's not enough he has to look like he's just walked out of a sodding magazine modelling for Armani or whoever! I mean brave and sodding handsome with it eh?! What a bastard! No wonder I bloody hate him!"

Smiling now Imogen stood up to leave. Malcolm also stood up as they faced each other.

"Sometimes I feel my life would be easier if it were you and not Max I needed. You are a good man Malcolm Speight. Whatever you believe you are, whatever Max believes you are, I know your heart is pure and you will always have a little piece of mine."

Imogen then moved towards the large, physically intimidating man and embraced him goodbye. Malcolm held her tightly, his eyes closed, breathing her in, knowing this one moment in his life, would never happen again.

Without another word, Imogen smiled her sad goodbye as she got into her car and drove away. Malcolm stood watching until she was only a dot on the horizon, before joining his men in the waiting car which would take him back to the life he'd had chosen for him and if truth be told, had never truly wanted.

CHAPTER 34

Olivia, loved sitting in the Chemin de St Paul, the town's pretty cemetery, where the famous Russian born artist Marc Chagall was buried. She found graveyards fascinating, peaceful even, wondering about the lives that had been lived decades, even centuries before.

As she sat she suddenly felt a shadow block out the wintry sun. Startled she looked up to see a tall youth, holding onto the back of the bench she was seated on. He was in obvious pain. "So sorry to startle you but I need to sit down if that's okay?" His voice was soft, his accent American. Olivia got up to bolt immediately. "No please, don't be alarmed. I'm completely harmless, honestly. You've no idea how harmless or should I say legless?" Wincing and in obvious distress he came around the bench to sit as Olivia made room for him.

"Can I help?" asked Olivia suddenly concerned. He was very pale and she wished her mum was with her as Harry the nurse would have jumped into action already. She needed to call her.

"Thanks but I doubt it. It's my own fault. Done

too much and my dad is not going to be happy with me." Leaning back into the bench, the boy closed his eyes for a moment, then sighing heavily, he turned to Olivia and said, "I'm afraid this isn't going to be pretty, so feel free to turn away, run away, or barf away!" He then pulled up his right track suit trouser bottom leg, to reveal a prosthetic limb which he proceeded to take off, revealing a bleeding, postulating stump.

"Oh how awful," exclaimed Olivia who immediately put her hand to her mouth in horror as she attempted to explain her reaction. "I mean that looks so painful!"

"Yeah," grimaced the boy, "trust me it is and gross too."

Just at that moment, Harry turning the corner, saw Olivia with a boy. Heart thumping, she rushed over. "What's happening? Liv are you okay?"

"Oh mum. Thank goodness you're here. Look!"

Tearing her eyes from her daughter Harry saw what Olivia was indicating. At this moment, the young man thrust out his hand to Harry saying, "Hi. I'm Zac."

Shaking the offered hand Harry replied, "Harry which is short for Harriet and this is my daughter, Olivia."

"Cool name," replied Zac before to turning back to Olivia

"Great to meet you both but I really need to get to my dad, who incidentally will be so pissed at, sorry... mad at me."

Harry looking closely at Zac's wound said, "That needs cleaning and dressing before it gets infected if it isn't already so. Where can we find your dad Zac?"

"He has a studio up the hill and thankfully, a car, so he'll be able to get to me except..."

Harry and Olivia looked at him, waiting before he explained somewhat shamefacedly, "But my phone is out of juice."

"You don't know his number?" asked Harry.

Zac turned to Olivia and asked, "Do you know your mum's number?" then smiled when Olivia shook her head, shrugging her shoulders at the same time. "I know Harry. Kids today eh? You got to love 'em!"

Smiling at this most endearing young man, who despite clearly being in pain, was joking with strangers, Harry now became the medical professional she was. "Right then. We're very close so Liv, if you could put Zac's arm around your shoulder taking his weight and let me get the other arm," as they got the boy to precariously stand. "Right. Ready?"

As they began to walk, Zac said, "Er ladies, I think we've forgotten something," as he gestured to the prosthetic limb lying beside the bench. Smiling, Harry bent to retrieve it, as they made their way to the three storey house they had rented in the middle of the village's centre.

Once there, Harry set to work on Zac's injury

whilst Olivia found a phone charger compatible with Zac's device, which after a few minutes allowed him to contact his father.
Taking a deep breath, Zac keyed in the number. "Hi Pops, yeah I know I've been gone a while and ... well if I could explain...yeah I know you worry but I've run into a bit of trouble with the new leg but I've also run into a couple of Good Samaritans too, so all's good. Yeah, I'll need a pick up, walking's out I'm afraid, although I'm pretty good at hopping... I know too soon, I'm sorry. Yeah... the address? Er, Harry would you talk to my very pissed off dad? Tell him where I am please?" as he handed over his phone.
Taking it from him she said, "Hello. Er... you will find us on the Rue de Montague, just past the..."
"I know where it is," said an abrupt voice who immediately disconnected.
Wincing, but smiling apologetically Zac said, "A man of few words is Pops, but you'll grow to love him. Honest."

*

Alan nodded his understanding to his old friend. "It makes sense you take time out to be with Riz. I'm sure he'll be ok...eventually, although we both know he still has a long road ahead."
"It's the psychological damage that's worrying me and his mother," explained Dr Ishaan Sharma, Alan's co-worker who had come to explain to his friend and partner that he was needing to take time away from their General

Practice to support his son Riz's recovery.

"His bones are healing and the plastic surgeon has done an excellent job. His scars will fade and his bones will heal Alan, but I fear what damage lies beneath, I mean, what this will have done to his mental health. He will have to deal with Post Traumatic Stress Disorder eventually and you and I have seen enough fall out from that condition haven't we?" shaking his head. "So how's Liv doing?"

"Not good, as you'd expect really. She's away with her mother for a while."

"Will do her good. How's Harry doing?"

Shaking his head, Alan looked at his old friend and said, "I've no idea Ish. It's like we've become total strangers almost overnight. We don't talk anymore unless we have to and it's really confusing the twins. God knows what all this is doing to them."

Looking sympathetic Ishaan felt compelled to say what he felt his friend needed to hear. "You and Harry have one of the strongest marriages I know Alan. You will get through this."

Shaking his head Alan now looked bereft. "I'm not so sure. I'm even doubting if we've ever been this idyllic family, or ever had this happier than most marriage. We should be helping each other, supporting each other. Instead we're... we're... silent Ish. We're silent. Lost even." Then looking at his oldest friend, he asked, "Did you see the video of the attackers before it was taken down? I know you've been questioned as we have. I mean I suppose we would have been the main suspects as parents of their victims. Police only doing their job I guess." Ishaan nodded but remained silent. "Barbaric wasn't it? Unbelievably cruel." Ishaan still remained silent. Looking scandalous, Alan now had to know what his oldest friend was thinking. "Please tell me you don't agree with what happened to them."

Shaking his head Ishaan said, "As a man of medicine, I took an oath, as did you to "abstain from all intentional wrong-doing and harm, especially from abusing the bodies of man or woman." I, as do you abide by that oath every day. I of course abhor what I witnessed..."

"But?"

"Would I have sanctioned such action? I'd like to think I would not, would have remembered my oath. But our bright, clever, beautiful, innocent children were set upon by animals Alan and I can find no pity in my heart for those who did what they did to them. Not even now as abhorrent as their punishment is."

"But would you have agreed to it?"

Taking a long moment, Ishaan eventually looked up and replied, "No my friend I would not have but I don't know what the answer is either."

Coming round his desk Alan moved to embrace his oldest friend, where they stood locked in a mutual embrace of brotherly love and support for several moments. Patting Alan on his shoulder Ishaan moved to leave. "This too shall pass Alan and life will return as we know it. Older, wiser and sadder but we will get through this."

Lips trembling with emotion, eyes brimming with unshed tears, Alan merely nodded as he couldn't find the words that would express his doubts and silent fears, not even to his oldest friend. Alan now silently acknowledged that there were some things that should never be shared or spoken and that those same things would eventually take away a little bit of your soul, leaving only a shell of your former self behind. How would he and Harry get through this? Now only time would tell.

CHAPTER 35

He was reading it, but he couldn't believe it. Richard Braxton had felt he would be a certain shoe in for the Met. He was under the impression that recruitment was at its lowest, but here it was in black and white: "The Metropolitan Police vetting process has felt fit to reject your request at this stage of your career..."

"What the f..."

"What's the matter?" asked Sharon who was still naked in her bed, having both crashed at hers the night before, after a particularly heavy session at 'The Frog and Parrot'.

"Just got an email about my transfer application to the Met."

"And?"

"Not got in! I've been rejected!"

"You're joking right?"

Shaking his head, eyes blazing with fury, he handed her his phone for her to read, as he proceeded to kick over the waste bin near his feet, feeling impotent in his anger and disappointment.

"Fucking Stainmore's behind this, the bloody

holier than thou shit!" blazed Richard, "and if he thinks he's going to get away with treating me like this, he's got another think coming!"

"Hey now," appeased Sharon, "why would he?"

"Because he hates me, has done from the beginning!"

"I'm sure he doesn't Rich. What reason would he have?"

"Because he's jealous! Jealous of my potential. He knows I would do really well at the Met, would make a real name for myself. I'm better looking too and he knows it! I mean, could you imagine how many marriage proposals I'd get if my picture was splashed around like his is?"

Trying not to roll her eyes at the immature petulance and self- delusion, she attempted reason. "Well then he'd be doing his upmost to get rid of you not block you so come back to bed and let Aunty Shaz make it all better eh?"

Shaking his head, he began to search for his clothes, pulling them on, muttering curses as he did so. "Sorry Shaz, but it's going to take more than a good shag to sort this!"

"Well thanks for that!" she flared, thinking this was not how she had anticipated this morning to go, not after the night they'd enjoyed.

If Sharon was being honest, she did actually think he was rubbish as a detective because he was basically slack. He did not follow through, allowed things to slide and was dismissive of situations if he felt it wasn't worthy of his time.

He was alright in bed though and she really did fancy another round.
"No. Seriously. I know things. I know people. Connected people and I'm going to use them in such a way Stainmore and his bloody lap dogs won't know what's hit them. Devon and Hanson will be bloody loving this! Not to mention Mrs 'Goody-two-shoes'!"
"Lydia?"
"Who else?"
"Well it wouldn't be how I'd describe Beth because Beth is anything but that," laughed Sharon. The look he gave her, abruptly stopped her laughter. She had never seen him so serious. Sitting up, exposing her naked breasts and looking worried, Sharon tried once more. "Be careful Rich. Don't start something that's going to bite you on the bum. There'll be other opportunities, loads and it doesn't have to be the Met. Just keep your head down, do your bit and smile. You've got a gorgeous smile."
Laughing without humour as he headed for the door, Richard stood and looked at her. "You don't get it do you? They, as in Serious Crimes, are bloody lucky to have me here in the first place. A bloody honest to God mistake, which anyone could make and I'm here and all they want to do is stick the knife in! Well I'm sharpening my knives now and they will really feel it when I stick it to them because it will hurt. Big time!"
With that he was out the door, slamming

Sharon's outer door of her apartment in the process.

Lying back in her bed Sharon muttered now only to herself, "I still think a good shag might have helped though."

CHAPTER 36

The attack began with fire. They hadn't seen it coming. They should have known. Should have been on alert. One minute laughs and chat. The next... blood and chaos.

Jakob Abrahms instructions had been clear. "We destroy the head of the snake who killed our blood," as he nodded to Omar, "nothing less."

It began with the obligatory Molotov cocktails, catapulted with force through The Stag Head's windows. Gareth Jackson and his men for once, were unprepared and outnumbered and their injuries would reflect this.

Turning to Brandon he gave his instructions. "Take as many out as you can. Let the bastards know who they're dealing with." Seeing the gleam of fury and lust for blood in Brandon's eyes, he knew he would have a window of opportunity whereby he would make his escape, unseen by those he was sending into the fray, is own self- preservation his only priority.

Now safely at a distance he rang 999. Muffling his voice with a cloth he began to scream, "There's a riot at The Stag's Head on Vickers

Road. They've set the place on fire!" then abruptly ended the call. Taking his Sim card out he then proceeded to smash the phone, making a trace of it impossible. He then found a vantage point to watch from an undetectable distance.

Brandon screaming his war cry, rushed into the full force of the mayhem, making impact on those closest, his fist connecting with flesh and bone. This was who he was. This was him at his best. Mohammed Mirza saw him from across the fighting rolling bodies and perversely recognised a soul mate, a fellow psychopath who thrived on pain, hate and violence too and he was his.

Charging forward, they clashed as if they were the titans they believed themselves to be, fists connecting, blood spurting, then out of nowhere a flick knife. Mohammad and Brandon

were now locked together, as if in a lovers embrace until glassy eyed, Mohammad slumped, enveloped in Brandon's arms, finally falling to the floor, clutching his abdomen.

Brandon's snarl of triumph was cut short as the sound of sirens suddenly broke through the screams and yells with blue flashing lights appearing in the distance. The protagonists now had a mutual enemy which they all intended to escape from including Malcolm and his men, who had played their part, doing what they did best, cracking heads they were paid to crack.

Brad Fairchild and Asif, with their colleagues in blue were first on the scene, as the men from the

pub scattered in all directions, law enforcement officers, chasing down those still in the vicinity.
Entering the pub Asif saw him almost immediately. Rushing to his cousin Asif began to shout, "We need an ambulance here. Knife wound to the abdomen," then to Mohammed, "come on cousin, stay with me. Please. I won't lose another, not today, not again."
Mohammed's eyes flickered open, his expression still that of defiance, then as the pain overtook him, he clutched Asif's arm. "Tell my father I tried and I'm... I'm ... sorry...am I dying?"
"No one is dying here!" Asif shouted then, "where's the bloody paramedics?"
Mohammed eyes flickered closed as Asif began shouting again, "No Mohammed, no! Stay with me cousin! You've got to stay!"
The paramedics now pushed the distraught officer to one side but after only a few seconds, looked at each other and shook their heads. Max and Eddie appeared at the moment Brad took a distraught Asif away from the body of his now dead cousin.
"Jesus Christ but this is sodding madness," muttered Eddie.
"You're not wrong Eddie," muttered Max, "you're not wrong."

*

Malcolm, Ed and Albert had made their escape and were now negotiating the back streets of Attercliffe that would allow them to avoid detection from the numerous police vehicles swarming the area. "Nothing like a good old fashion cracking of heads to get the old heart pumping eh lads?" grinned Malcolm, as he massaged his bruised knuckles, cracking them to ensure they weren't actually damaged.

"Nothing like it boss eh Al?" smiled Ed as he drove.

Albert said nothing but was actually clutching his arm, clearly finding it hard to breath. Ed looked at him in alarm. "Al? What is it?"

"Can't breathe..."

Malcolm knew immediately, suddenly lurching forward. "Jesus Christ but he's having a heart attack. Nearest hospital is Rotherham General. Get your bleeding foot down!" shouted Malcolm as he reached forward, squeezing Albert's shoulder saying, "You'll be alright Al. You'll be alright."

*

Sheffield Central was busy with the fall out of the attack. The ones who had been caught escaping the affray were all singing the same tune, as if they'd met earlier and learnt their lines together.

"Just sitting there having a drink wi' mi mates..."

"Dunt know who started it..."

"Saw nowt..."

"Just hit bloke who hit me first that's all. What do you expect?" And on it went.

All would be officially cautioned with no further action warranted as all arrested proclaimed self-defence and legally could be argued their "actions necessary and proportionate given the circumstances." In other words, the Crime Prosecution Service had better things to worry about. It was the murder of Mohammed Mirza that was the cause for concern.

Although dawn had barely broken, the Serious Crime Unit were at their desks and waiting instructions. Max began, "It would appear war has been declared and the fall out will be immense." Pointing to the Major Incident Board where Mohammed's picture was now added, Max continued, "You will all be familiar with the latest victim, Mohammed Mirza, Omar's son, second in charge within his organisation and Asif's cousin," pausing now as his eyes met Beth's.

"Beth, I think you and Brad should go with Asif to inform his Uncle of his son's death."

An ashen faced Beth nodded then said, "Of course Chief but I honestly don't think Asif should be the one to do the death notification."

"Nor do I Beth but he's insistent. Mohammed died in his arms and gave him a message for his father."

Blowing out her cheeks Beth nodded and left to find Brad and Asif, dreading the pain and anguish to come this day. Max and the others silently watched her leave before he said. "So people, there's a lot to do, so let's crack on."

*

Malcolm had been pacing the corridors of Rotherham General since they had arrived, snarling at anyone who approached him. They had got to the Accident and Emergency department in record time where Albert had been stabilised then taken to the Cardiac Unit where he was being monitored. Ed had refused to leave his side and was with him.

Malcolm was now at a loss. Both Ed and Albert had been by his side for more years than he could remember so why hadn't it occurred to him that they were a couple? He wasn't remotely homophobic so why didn't he know? Why didn't they tell him? But acknowledging to himself, why should they?

His thoughts were interrupted when Ed appeared and sat beside him. "How's he doing?"

"Stable."

"And you Ed? How are you doing?

"I'm alright but by God he scared me."

"You and me both," concurred Malcolm.

Clearing his throat, Ed began. "Look boss I know you must be thinking all sorts but..."

Malcolm held his hand up to stop him. "Your private life is your own Ed. I'm just surprised I never realised that's all."

"Well it's not something you talk about in our line of work is it?" Then smiling he looked at Malcolm as he began to explain. "We met at Lundwood Junior and Infants. I was the biggest, fattest kid in my class, probably the whole school and soft with it an' all. The bullies had a field day until I met Al. He joined the school a year later, then we became a force to be reckoned with."

"Still are," agreed Malcolm.

Smiling as he reminisced Ed continued. "Both glued at the hip, best of mates, like brothers, then all that changed. We realised almost overnight when the teenage years kicked in, why we weren't bothered with lasses. I mean, we both gave it a go like, but finally we admitted lasses weren't for us. We were all we needed."

They both sat in silence for a while, listening to the unique echoes of the hospital. Sounds of trolleys moving, lifts opening, shoes clattering, the occasional voice, all with that distinct smell that only hospitals have. "So, are you two wed then?"

"No. We had a civil partnership in 2010, to protect ourselves legally like, you know with the house and everything, in case one of us... you know."

"So no wedding on the horizon?"

Looking confused at Malcolm, he shook his head. "Why would we need to do that?"

Shrugging his shoulders Malcolm replied, "Always fancied me self as a 'bride's man' or maid that's all."

Ed and Malcolm looked at each other then, both burst out laughing, laughing so much that tears of relief poured down Ed's face which then became sobs as the reality of what he could have lost this night now hit him hard. Malcolm put his arm around the large sobbing man, feeling his anguish and relief saying, "I know, love's a bloody bugger mate. Nothing hurts quite like it does it?"

*

The picturesque village of Dore, situated six miles to the south-west of the city centre, had a reputation of housing the city's elite. Dore Road, where Asif, Beth and Brad were now parked, boasted an average house price of over one million pounds. Looking at the large wrought iron gates of the home of his extended family, Asif had left the squad car and was now talking into the security camera placed at the gate which would allow them access to the home of Omar and his family.

As the gates opened, the three police officers drove their squad car up the vast sweeping drive, past large opulent landscaped gardens as the huge white mansion appeared, looking beautiful and majestic in the breaking dawn light. Beth gasped, Brad whistled but Asif remained silent.

Omar was on the steps of his home before they had alighted their vehicle. He looked solemn, prepared as he waited for the three officers to join him. Asif stared at his father's brother, saw the family resemblance and for a moment, a flicker of a long buried memory came into his head when he Noor were playing tag on these very lawns. Him falling and grazing his knee and the kindness his uncle showed as he lifted him crying onto his shoulders, making him forget the injury and pain, instead making him laugh as only children can.

Omar stepped forward and asked, “Mohammed?”

Asif found he couldn’t at first speak, until a scream of anguish was heard as a woman appeared at the open door. “Where’s Mohammed? What’s happened to my son? Asif! Tell me!” this from Aditi, Omar’s current wife having remarried after the death of Noor’s mother years earlier.

“I’m sorry Aunty Aditi but Mohammed was involved in an affray earlier today.”

“Where is he? Is he hurt? I must go to him, Omar...”

Beth now stepped forward saying, “I think we all need to go inside and sit down.”

Omar still looking at Asif, simply said, “He’s dead isn’t he?” as Asif nodded to confirm his fears, Aditi began to fall, stopped only from hitting the ground by Brad’s quick thinking as he had anticipated her reaction. In the huge sitting room, they assembled with Aditi almost in a trance like state.

Omar now took control. “Tell me what happened?”

“There was an affray at The Stag’s Head in Attercliffe. Mohammed was stabbed and he... he... he...”

“What?” shouted Omar, now in Asif’s face, “what?”

"Died in my arms."

Omar staggered back, turning towards the fireplace, now only seeing the smiling face of his dead son whose picture adorned the mantle.

Aditi, Mohammed's mother was rocking backwards and forwards as she sat on the sofa, a keening sound coming from a place of utter despair. Beth sitting beside her, took her hand asking, "Can we send for someone?" Aditi didn't respond.

Omar asked, "Do you know who did this?"

Brad replied," Not yet, but we will."

"Like my other son Noor you mean?" scoffing at Brad's remark.

"Four out of the five we believe were responsible are accounted for with three in our custody."

"But it wasn't police work that was responsible Constable, was it?"

"You mean Sergeant Mr Mirza," was Brad's quiet but firm reply, not allowing himself and the police presence to be undermined but aware he was dealing with parents who had just learned an awful truth.

The laughter bubbled up from Aditi, a manic sound as she turned to her husband, eyes ablaze with fury, "We all know who's responsible. You may not have held the knife, but you made him what he was. You made him seek out violence and thuggery. You allowed him to leave Medical school," then turning to Brad and Beth said, "did you know he was clever? He had brains and he could have been a Doctor, a Surgeon, someone who did good, but instead," now looking at her husband, her face contorted, making her look like a grotesque parody of herself, "he looked up to you. Wanted to be like you. Someone else may have held the knife, but you're the reason my son," voice now cracking, "my beautiful little boy, my baby... is dead," as she collapsed into Beth's arms.

No one spoke. All that could be heard was the centuries old cries of a mother who had outlived her child, a pain like no other.

The police officers now prepared to leave. As they walked to the door Asif turned and said, "I do have a message from Mohammed, his last words were for you Uncle."

"And?" whispered Omar, his face now full of some kind of hope.

"He told me to, "Tell my father I'm sorry". They were his last words."

Omar remained silent and motionless as they left. Moving toward his wife, he put hand on her shoulder which she violently shook away.

"Don't you touch me!" she hissed, "go to your white whore, let her comfort you, but never touch me or come near me again."

Nodding his agreement, his heart too splintered to care, Omar replied, "I shall. I should never have left her in the first place."

CHAPTER 37

She saw his tall, lean outline as she made her way to her glass frosted door and immediately gasped, as she thought, “He’s home. He’s alive. He’s come back to me.” Throwing the door open, her heart fit to burst, Sarah saw Trey standing there. He saw her expression change and knew immediately Sarah had thought he was John.

“Only me I’m afraid Sarah, only me.”

Tearful but smiling, Sarah moved to embrace him. “So good to see you safe and here where we can look after you eh boys?” as Cyril and Scooby bounded up with tails wagging and yelps of joy. They held each other for the longest moments, both silent and for Trey it was like coming home, a home he had never had, not even as a child.

“How’ve you been?” asked Trey, “how’s the baby?”

“Growing,” smiled Sarah “and you must be hungry?”

Grinning now, which made him look so much younger than his years Trey merely shrugged saying, “Aren’t I always.”

Sitting comfortably at the dining table Sarah

brought Trey up to speed of recent events, such was her trust in him. Trey had listened intently.

"So," concluded Sarah, "it's been full on, not to mention shocking and like something out of a nightmare."

"How's the young lass?" asked Trey.

Shaking her head and sighing, Sarah smiled sadly. "She's traumatised Trey. She's consumed with so much anger and now because of what has happened to those responsible, she perversely feels guilt too." Sarah now cocked her head and asked, "Why do I not sense any sort of shock from you Trey?"

"Are we talking about the rape or the punishment?"

"Both I guess."

Trey was silent for the moment before he replied. "Rape has been a weapon of war since war began and it leaves its mark far longer than a bullet does. As for the punishment? I've seen far worse done by drug cartels, the Taliban and ISIS, to name but a few, believe me."

Sarah looked down and stroked her baby bump. "You make me afraid for the future, for the world my baby will grow up in."

"I imagine many past generations have said the same thing, but babies are still born and lives are still well lived and I know your baby will be one of the lucky ones. Do we know if it's a boy or girl yet?"

"They asked me if I wanted to know."

"But you're waiting to find out with the Sarge, when he gets back eh?"

Looking down at the tablecloth, her lips trembling she nodded as Trey reached over and took her hands in his. "Yeah, the Sarge will want to be here for that."

"I know it sounds mad but I think I'd know if he was really gone. I mean I don't feel like he's never coming home, although I know it's been months now and..."

"We're talking the Sarge here Sarah and no one will try harder to come back to you."

Nodding and smiling through her tears, she allowed Trey to hold her close, only separating when Scooby forced his head between them, making them laugh.

Now wiping her eyes Sarah asked about his friends. "So Daz and Bud? What will they be up to or shouldn't I ask?"

"No doubt causing mayhem and headaches for those trying to keep the peace, of that I can guarantee."

"Didn't feel like blowing off steam too?"

"No, I just wanted to... to..." looking embarrassed he looked away, bending down to stroke Scooby's ears.

"To come home," Sarah finished for him as he nodded, still not looking at her.

"Well, me and my boys," as she nodded to her dogs, "and my Bumpkin here, are so delighted to have you back home too Trey. So glad."

*

Opening the front door that would lead onto to the busy Saturday morning streets, Harry was surprised to see Zac and his father there. Zac grinned his infectious smile as, spreading his hands he announced, “Busted!”

Looking at their feet Harry was surprised to see the biggest hamper, overflowing with cheeses, wine and other French delicacies. Zac's father Christopher looking embarrassed, began to explain. “It's my way of thanking you both for helping Zac here and an apology for my rudeness. I have no excuse but to say...”

“Please” interrupted Harry, “I really do understand and this is very kind but really unnecessary.”

“Oh but it is Harry,” interrupted Zac, “I mean, without you Harry, I could have been on life support... again,” then laughing at their faces continued, “okay so I'm exaggerating, but you were so cool Harry and despite how rude Pops here was, we're both really grateful.” Just then Olivia appeared at the doorway next to her mother. “Hi Olivia. Fancy having a look around the market. They've got some really cool artefacts particularly the vintage stuff.”

Looking at this exuberant young man, Harry found she was stumped for words. Olivia however, had already grabbed her bag, was smiling at Zac before kissing her mum on the cheek saying, “Great. See you later mum.”

"Er Liv?" began Harry as both Zac and Olivia were quickly swallowed by the crowded bustle of a normal Saturday market day at St Paul De Vence. Christopher, turning to face Harry continued from where he had left off, seconds earlier. "I really am very grateful and I was unforgivably rude," as he referred to the previous evening when he had bundled his son into his car, without barely acknowledging or speaking a word to Harry or Olivia.

"I do understand, really. You'd obviously been worried a while and with good reason as left much longer he would have risked serious infection."

Harry was now scrutinising the man standing on the pavement outside of her door. He was quite tall, with the sort of physique that suggested he liked to walk a lot. His hair was what she knew women were currently paying a fortune to achieve the look of; thick and wavy, silvery grey in colour with streaks of black running through. His eyes were brown and had a warmth to them, his tan obviously a permanent one from years in the sun.

Looking at their children as they disappeared into the crowded streets, Christopher was acknowledging, almost apologetically, "Zac is a one off and he does like to push himself, sometimes too much."

"I think he's obviously a very remarkable young man," offered Harry, "and you must be very

proud of him."
As he smiled, Harry noticed how the skin around his eyes crinkled and that he would be described by many, as being handsome. "Thank you, I am. So can I interest you in a coffee?"
"Now?" asked Harry.
"Unless you've already made plans?"
Harry thought for a moment and realised she really had nothing better to do this day than have a coffee with this handsome stranger as she replied, "No. I'd like that. Thank you but...?"
"But?"
"Can we covertly stalk our children too?"
Smiling his understanding, Christopher nodded as he replied, "Oh, that's a given."

CHAPTER 38

Denise Cowden's heart plummeted at the sight of Karen Raithes standing at her front door. She knew Karen by sight and had heard about her grandson's suicide. She also knew that Brandon had known her son, so she was now mentally preparing herself for what Karen had come to her door to say.

"I'd like a word Mrs Cowden."

"What about?"

"What do you think?"

Nodding her understanding, Denise sighed heavily as she replied, "Well you'd better come in then."

As the two women sat across from each other, the silence stretched uncomfortably. Denise recognised the grief etched across the other woman's face and she truly felt her pain, as mother to mother have always done, although her face did not reveal this.

"I heard about your grandson and I'm very sorry for your loss."

Silence. An unblinking silence that said so much.

"What do you want? Why are you here?" the

belligerence in Denise's words returning as she had no other way of dealing with whatever the woman sitting across from her would make her face this day.

Still unblinking, Karen began. "Your son. Your son Brandon. He's responsible for what has happened to my grandson."

"Really? Strung him up did he? So why haven't the police been to have a word then?"

"He as good as strung him up."

Denise standing up said, "Oh for Christ's sake, I haven't got time for this so if..."

"What do you see when you look at him? Brandon? What do you see?" as Denise slowly sat back down. "I can tell you what I see, what anyone who dares look at him sees. I see someone who hates. Hates everything and everyone. I see someone who thrives on others being afraid, loves the fear he makes you feel. My Finn was so afraid and so...lost," as she took out her phone and began to play the last message from her dead grandson.

Denise looked at the image and heard the words in a mesmerised silence, finally saying in response, "I'm sorry but it still doesn't mean my Brandon..." as the hysterical laughter from Karen made her stop speaking. The laughter now had turned into wracking sobs as she now with her head in her hands cried and cried.

Eventually Karen looked up as Denise asked, "What do you want from me? I can't bring your boy back from the dead, I wish to Christ I could. So why are you here?"

Shaking her head Karen replied, "I don't actually know except to warn you I suppose."

"Warn me?"

"Warn you to protect your other children. Your Brandon is like a disease and it will spread unless its stopped. For all I know you might already have other monsters growing in this house as well as him."

Staring at Karen with something akin to horror, Denise was now angry. "Right! Get the bloody hell out of my house before I throw you out. How dare you say..."

Getting up to leave Karen replied with a weary acknowledgement saying, "How dare you not know Mrs Cowden. For the sake of your other children, how dare you not know or act."

Denise had no response as she watched the other woman leave, hearing the door close behind her. She knew deep down that Karen Raithes was right, knew what her first born was, what he had always been thanks to his father George who couldn't have been a worse role model if he had really tried. Brandon had had no real direction, had always felt entitled to having his own way and prison had made him a thousand times worse. Prison had also given him a purpose she had yet to understand, but she had seen the blood on his clothes, on his boots and she was now ashamed to admit if only to herself, that she

was constantly turning a blind eye.
She was also realising that she could no longer do so.

*

Finn's funeral at Greenside Crematorium on the outskirts of Sheffield, was the smallest affair, with only a handful of mourners. Karen's kind elderly neighbours from both sides of her home were there, as was Philip Read who did Karen the courtesy of saying a few words on her behalf. Standing there in his smartest suit he began, his strong baritone echoing in the almost empty cavernous space:
"On behalf of Karen, can I thank you for coming today. Funerals are always difficult, but when it's someone as young as Finn and taking into account the circumstance of his demise, then such events are even more difficult to understand and for those who loved him, to indeed bear. I have known Finn since he was in his teens. Let's be honest, I arrested Finn more than I care to remember, but I always knew that deep down, there was a good lad hiding in there, a decent lad but it would seem, an easily led one too. We all need to belong, to feel part of something and unfortunately Finn made the mistake of belonging to the wrong people. He eventually knew this and could no longer live with the circumstances he found himself in. For me that says a lot about the lad. I only wish I had done more when I had the chance and I

will always regret that I didn't. Let's hope he has found some peace now."

As he returned to sit next to Karen, Philip looked towards the entrance to see Denise Cowden standing there, dressed in funeral black and bowing her head in the time honoured mark of respect. Karen turned to see Denise and as their eyes met, silent words were understood although would never be spoken, the sadness and guilt a tangible presence between them.

CHAPTER 39

Sitting in the La Columbe d'Or restaurant was something Harry hadn't done in a very long time, pre twin boys in fact. Situated at 1, Place de General de Gaulle, Harry and Alan had realised years before that the ambience and expense of this exquisite restaurant was wasted on their children, so when Christopher had asked Olivia and herself to join them there, Harry was happy to do so.

Sitting sipping wine and marvelling at the priceless art works from Picasso, Dufy and Modigliani that adorned the walls, was making Harry actually forget the reasons behind their visit here. "Hard to believe Picasso actually gave the owners that piece in exchange for a meal," said Christopher as he admired the cubist piece from their dining table.

"I think it makes Picasso seem quite human, ordinary even," mused Harry, "and I like that. It's what I love about this place." Christopher nodded in agreement as they were joined by Zac and Olivia.

"Wow, but what a place," said Olivia, "I can't

believe we haven't been here before Mum."

"Actually you have Liv, but you were only about eight months old at the time and the grouchiest of babies that day if my memory serves me."

"So grouchy Harry that you daren't return?" laughed Zac.

"Daren't return with my twin boys more like," laughed Harry who was now realising how easy it was to laugh in the company they were keeping. Easy and non- judgemental, but then again, they had no idea what she had done, what she was capable of. Shoving all such thoughts aside, Harry was now paying attention to what Zac was enthusiastically regaling them with.

"Not just Picasso et al either ladies. Please cast your eye to that piece over there," as he pointed out a piece directly opposite their table. It was a beautiful piece of art, haunting almost. The swirling azure blue colours drew you in as the centre of the painting came into focus, an almost ethereal face appearing as from out of a swirling mist. The face was beautiful, delicately exquisite as it looked to the right, a tear on the cheek, her expression one of sadness and loss with her hair a gold like halo.

"My word," breathed Harry, "but that is just... breath taking."

Christopher was silent, Zac appeared lost, almost mesmerised by the painting he had singled out.

"She was, wasn't she dad? Mom was just that Harry. She could walk into a room and just, well, take your breath away. Not just because she was beautiful, but because she was just so real, right dad? She would be able to sense a mile away if someone needed something and I don't mean material things, but things that matter, like a smile, or a hello or a hug. She was just something else."

Christopher was still silent with Olivia and Harry quietly marvelling at Zac's powerful homage to his dead mother. Harry was now dreading the next bit as she sensed Zac was reliving his own personal tragedy. "Just another ordinary day, Mom taking me to soccer practice and trust me I was a force to be reckoned with when I had two legs wasn't I dad?" Christopher still remained silent.

"What happened?" asked Olivia.

"Drunk driver. I mean it was barely four in the afternoon but from all accounts he lived his life drunk or stoned. He hit us straight on, killed himself, Mom and took my leg."

Olivia squeezed Zac's hand unable to speak. "But, time passes, it was what seven years ago now and life is still to be lived. Mom would insist on it right dad? Dad? Are you ever going to contribute to this conversation?"

Shaking his head, but smiling at his son, Christopher replied, "Well son, you're doing just fine without me."

"So who did the painting? Did you have it commissioned?" asked Harry.

"I was hoping someone would ask," beamed Zac, "go on dad. Tell her!"

Looking pointedly at his son whilst subtly shaking his head, Zac declared with something akin to frustration, "Okay, I'll spill the beans. Dad painted it and the owners saw it and bought it. So here we are, my very own Pops rubbing shoulders with Picasso! I mean, how cool is that?"

Olivia was now completely delighted and as Harry looked at her, she saw her daughter as she was before that fateful day. Here in this beautiful place, she saw Olivia have empathy, compassion and now utter delight. Harry wanted to cry with relief because even if it wasn't to last, her Olivia was still in there, could still be found.

"You're an artist. Why didn't I realise?" asked Harry.

Shrugging, Christopher said, "No reason why you should. I have a studio at the summit of the village. You must come and see my paintings before you go."

"I would love to."

Nudging Olivia, Zac now teased. "Have you seriously asked Harry to come up and see your etchings Pops? And in front of the kids too?"

Seeing the flush creep up Christopher's face and his look of acute embarrassment, made them all laugh out spontaneously, until Christopher said, "Okay. I think we should order before my son gets me into more hot water. Waiter, rescue me."

*

A beautiful, memorable evening was coming to an end. Harry would later reflect how meeting Christopher and Zac had been almost heaven sent, bringing both herself and Olivia back from the brink, in so many ways.

Zac and Olivia had decided to leave the restaurant, to take a stroll before turning in, leaving Harry and Christopher with their brandies. "So you came here after the accident?"

"Eventually. Zac needed a lot of hospitalisation for the first couple of years, then I just needed to be out of the rat race. Zac still lives most of the year in the States with Laura's parents until he finishes College and decides what he intends to do with his life. He comes over to stay with me as much as he can."

"What did you do?"

"Law." Christopher offered no more but the look on his face said a great deal.

"It's hard to recover from something so devastating. One of my oldest friends lost her husband and unborn child about the same time too. We thought she'd never recover, but it's amazing isn't it?"

"What is?"

"The human spirit. How it can somehow find the will to live, to carry on."

Looking into his glass Christopher seemed lost in his past as he began. "The kid who was driving that day, spent his life having one long party.

He was from a rich well known, well connected New York family, the ones with a Brownstone in Manhattan and the place in the Hamptons; rich and entitled. So rich that he was constantly walking away from DUIs, so much, that it was a joke. His 'slime ball' lawyer would find some small legal loophole the cops didn't do right, or pay off some witness or other, so that this kid, this selfish poor excuse for a man thought he was untouchable, the world his personal playground."

"So you blame the lawyer?"

"Oh yes, I killed that sonofabitch as soon as I could. I made sure he never stepped into another court room again."

"My God," muttered Harry, staring at him horrified.

Shaking his head, grimacing as he spoke, "No worries Harry, you're not sitting with a fully confessed murderer here although there are times I feel like one. I was the sonofabitch lawyer. I was the one who played the system because they paid me enough money, blood money. I got my beautiful, talented, patient wife, killed and my only child maimed. That was all on me."

Shaking her head Harry reached for his hand which he placed in hers. "You can't think like that Christopher."

"Oh but I can. I knew, deep down I knew that kid needed serious help, including jail time, but I took the money and it was a hell of a lot of money and it cost me my Laura and Zac... it costs him so much every single day and probably always will. What he has suffered, still suffers despite how he acts...well that's all down to me. Down to me and my choice on how I made money. Don't think he was the only one I got off Harry. You could almost hear the Prosecutors groan when I walked into Court. I became known for it, sought after and boy did I make them pay. I made millions and it was all blood money and I'd give every dime back if it meant I could have my Laura back and my boy in one piece."

"We all make decisions and choices that perhaps on hindsight..." Harry's words trailed away, her head back to where she was trying to escape, to hide from.

"How would you have felt if the driver had lived?"

"I wish he had in some respects."

"Really?"

"But with a daily reminder about his choices, what his sense of entitlement did to others. It should be him maimed for life, him living with his consequences, not my boy."

They sat in silence for long moments, both lost in their own thoughts. Still holding her hand Christopher now squeezed hers as he asked, "So what brought you here? What's your story Harry?"

Shaking her head, Harry found she was unable to reply as the silence lengthened. "Sorry. I didn't mean to pry."

"No. please. It's just too... raw, too recent. Too awful."

They now sat in a companionable silence before Christopher said, "Olivia really came out of her shell tonight."

"Thanks to Zac. He's remarkable."

"He is but it's not what you see that holds the deepest damage, houses the deepest scars. It's what can't be seen that takes the most healing. Particularly for the parents who spend their lives wanting to protect their young, only to realise they can't. Olivia will get there. How can she not with you as her mother?"

"You don't really know me Christopher. We're not always what we seem."

"No one can hide a beautiful soul Harry."

Harry felt her lips tremble as she looked at this kind, handsome stranger who seemed to sense her pain but more than that, understand it. Why wasn't it Alan sitting here, holding her hand and trying to make sense of what life has thrown at them?

"So a toast," offered Christopher, "to our kids. Our brilliant, beautiful, damaged but totally amazing kids!"

Wiping her tears, Harry smiled and raised her glass repeating, "To our kids."

CHAPTER 40

Philip Read looked into the face of the man he had once regarded as his oldest and most trusted friend. The man he had given the honour of Godfather to when his only child, his only son had been born. The same son whom this man sitting here in front of him had corrupted then ordered to be killed. Former and very much disgraced Deputy Chief Constable Ralph Jones, was a shadow of the large bombastic man who had scaled the ranks of the Police Force only to throw it all away when his natural greed, over confidence and love of all things material took over. He had lost a considerable amount of weight, his skin had lost its pallor, now tinged with grey, his fingernails bitten to the quick. More shocking than his physical appearance though was his demeanour, the total loss of confidence, the ever watchfulness, even here in the Visitors Room, forever on alert as if waiting... waiting for the shiv that would finally end it all.

"What do you want Phil?"

"Straight to the point I see. So we're dispensing with the pleasantries are we?"

"You're the bastard who put me in here. Pardon me if I don't feel particularly pleased to see you."

Philip shaking his head and sighing as if too tired to bother replied, "Still blaming me for you being a corrupt murdering bastard I see. The fact you had it all, wife, kids, grandkids, at the top of the work chain and you pissed it all away! For what eh?"

Not meeting Philip's eyes Ralph remained silent. Then said, "So, I've heard all this before. Is this why you're here? To remind me of the poor choices I've made? What an arrogant murdering bastard I've been?"

"No to remind you that once upon a time you were a bloody good copper. I'm here today to give you a chance to be a good copper again."

"In here!? Are you trying to get me killed?"

Choosing his words carefully Philip began. "Stainmore's team need information that Wallace Senior, one of your fellow inmates may be able to give. Like you, he's out of segregation and back in general population. We want you to get that information."

Sitting back in his chair, Ralph's face was a look of complete consternation. Shaking his head, he leaned forward saying, "You want me to risk my life getting information for that sanctimonious shit Stainmore!? Help him do his job?"

"I want you to help the police stop what's happening in our city. The city our grandchildren go to school and live in with their friends. That's all Ralph. Someone is making real mischief and it all comes back to Wallace Senior as its source."

Ralph was clearly thinking now and Philip couldn't help but think his point had gone home.

"I doubt he'd tell me, to be honest very few speak to me in here unless it's to hurl insults. That's the hardest part, the loneliness," then he added, "but I may have a way."

Nodding, Philip got up to leave. "I'll leave my contact number when you're ready to talk, okay?"

As Philip turned to leave the room Ralph called back, "Will you visit again Phil?"

Philip turned back to look at his old friend, the man he hated more and more each and every passing day. He saw his quiet desperation and replied, "Yes. I'll visit again."

*

Brenda Allen had had enough and felt she'd had no choice but to call the police and officially complain. Sharon and Beth were now sitting in her cluttered but immaculately clean living room, nursing their tepid weak teas, as Brenda continued her tirade.

"It was bad enough having that paedophile living next door although I soon got rid of him. I let everyone know what he was so he soon scarpered but then the bloody drug den appears! I mean doesn't the council vet these people?"

"Well," began Sharon, "I suppose it's hard to

know what..."

Brenda was not in the mood to listen to platitudes as she interrupted stating, "But that's not why I'm so bloody angry! Armed police! Armed police with GUNS! GUNS pointing at me! In MY house, breaking down MY door because they can't get the bloody house number right! Beggars belief! And as for an apology?! Well I'm still waiting!"

"Which is why we're here Mrs Allen," began Beth, "it's appalling what happened and the Chief Constable has asked us to tell you..."

"And why isn't he here to tell me himself? Too busy is he or too high and bloody mighty for the likes of me and the rest of us here in Stockdale eh? We barely see a police car these days so it's little wonder paedophiles and drug dealers think they can live here amongst decent folk."

Stockdale being the small industrial town a mere four miles from the outskirts of Penton and the home of one of the few specialist steel outlets left in the country. It had been a once thriving, proud little town but like many areas that relied upon the steel industry, had seen better days.

"Absolutely not Mrs Allen, or can I call you Brenda?" asked Sharon.

Brenda nodded, lips pinched into a straight line, her face a picture of righteous anger. "It's unforgiveable that the police in question got the wrong house and caused damage to your property but more than that caused you to feel fear and anxiety. As for the lack of apology well...I really can't apologise enough," said Sharon.

"I'm also still waiting for my compensation too. I'm told by Mike down at 'The Eagle' that I'm owed."

"We can look into that too," added Beth before trying her own charm offensive to placate this still angry resident. "You clearly take pride in your home Brenda, so we can only imagine the distress this would have caused you, I mean you put my housekeeping skills to shame, I must say."

Brenda now physically relaxed and actually smiled as she looked around her room, a room full of artefacts, photographs and memories of happier days. "My late husband and I bought this when we could, wanted to leave summat for the kids when we've gone but the area has gone to pot. I mean who would buy this now when you've got drug dealers and God knows what living around here. It just doesn't seem right," her anger now dissipated, leaving only a forlorn sense of hopeless acceptance.

Nodding their collective agreement, Beth and Sharon stood up to take their leave. "Please accept out apology Brenda and we promise to look into the compensation for you," urged Sharon. Brenda merely nodded as she showed them out.

Back in their squad car both women took a deep

breath. "Got to feel for her," said Beth.

"Yes, it can't be easy living alone around here," remarked Sharon, eyeing the overflowing dustbins and the discarded bicycles strewn around the various houses.

"So where's the nearest place for a decent coffee that has actually been acquainted with a coffee bean? Sharon?"

Sharon seemed to shake herself out of her reverie saying, "Sorry Beth. Yeah I know a place where we can get a coffee and something edible to eat."

Beth was now concerned. Sharon was normally very bubbly, larger than life, with very little phasing her. She wasn't herself and hadn't been for the couple of days she and Beth had been partnering together.

"So come on mate? Somethings bugging you so spill?"

Sharon looked conflicted as she turned to face Beth, someone she had known for years and whom she did trust implicitly. "It's probably nothing and I'm probably just being a bit anal but..."

"What?"

Taking a deep breath, the words tumble out. "It's Richard. I'm worried he's going to get himself into a lot of trouble."

"What kind of trouble?"

"The worse kind."

"Come on Shaz, you're going to have to give me more than that mate."

Looking more worried and sad than Beth had ever seen her look, Sharon began to recall the conversation she'd had with Richard the morning he had left her flat.

"Well did you know he applied to get transferred to the Met?" as Beth nodded she continued. "Well he didn't get in and he blew his top mate. I mean he was seriously upset and he..."

"Go on?"

"Blamed the Chief, saying that the Chief was jealous of him and that he knew people and that... well that he would get even somehow. Make Serious Crimes pay, would 'stick the knife in' his words not mine. I'm just worried he'll do something he won't be able to walk away from and I..."

"Go on?"

"I really like him Beth. I mean I know how he comes across but I really do like him," then putting her head in her hands added, "Oh I sound like a bloody teenager, mooning over a boy for God's sake!"

A very worried, concerned Beth remained silent before saying, "No you don't but I will have to have a word with one of the team, to make sure Richard doesn't carry out his threats which will probably be hot air in all honesty. He will have just been venting because he was disappointed."

"I hope so but will he know I've said something? I mean I'd really miss the sex if nothing else." Sharon was now desperately trying to laugh the whole business off, now worried that she may have opened a can of worms which would lead back to herself.

“I’ll try and be discrete mate but I can’t promise anything. You did right telling me though.”

Sighing heavily as she started the car’s engine, Sharon’s reply already had undertones of regret, “Well that’s me isn’t it? Good ol’ Shazzer, can always be relied upon to do the right thing.”

*

Ralph eyed Wallace Senior across the prison canteen. As usual Wallace Senior was holding court with some of the younger inmates hanging onto his every word. Wallace to Ralph’s eye looked like a weasel in human form. He had long unkempt hair with a face full of wiry bristles, his body skeletal thin. He wasn’t particularly tall too, but neither were Napoleon or Hitler or Charles Manson come to that, thought Ralph, guessing the man he was observing had that indefinable quality called charisma, something a person had or didn’t have.

Ralph was now joined by one of the few who deigned to give him the time of day, a young man named Graham Young. Graham was an affable chap, his large moon shaped face always set in a smile for everyone. He was also built like the proverbial ‘Brick Shithouse’, which made those who would consider sorting him out, think twice. For some reason, Ralph was yet to understand, Graham had taken a shine to him, often sharing meal times with him, clearly not caring what others thought of this.

"Penny for those Ralphie?" asked Graham as he set his tray on the opposite side of the table, thereby directly facing Ralph.

"Just thinking what an ugly bugger Wallace is that's all."

Chuckling Graham nodded, replying, "You're not wrong there and he's getting wed. Can you believe there is some poor cow, deluded enough to want to marry that. I mean he isn't getting out anytime soon either. I suppose he'll get his conjugal rights though so I suppose it's worth the trouble."

Shaking his head Ralph informed the young man saying, "You don't get any conjugal rights when you're banged up in this county lad. You've been watching too much American tele."

"Really? Another reason I'm going to move over there one day."

"They won't let you do that now my friend, now that you have a record of incarceration. A pity you like stealing other peoples' cars so much but you're right. I've never understood the hundreds of women and men who actually believe they've found the love of their sad pathetic lives whilst the object of their adoration is banged up. So what other garbage is he spouting then? I mean those new lads are hanging onto his every word."

Shovelling in copious amount of mash potato, Graham swallowed before answering, "The usual shite, about 'our' country and the jobs waiting for the lads once outside if they play their cards right. It seems our Wallace's empire is going from strength to strength whilst he's been inside. Coining it in apparently."

"How?"

"Dunno and I'm not that interested any road except it's summat to do with cornering drug market, getting rid of the competition and all that."

Ralph now deliberately scoffed, pretending that the whole idea was ridiculous. "Bloody idiot wouldn't stand a chance. The Mirzas will eat his lot alive."

"No mate you'll find you're out of touch."

"Well if not the Mirza's my former colleagues won't be having any of it."

Smiling benignly, his moon faced jowls actually making his eyes look like tiny slits Graham, simply replied, "Now Ralphie me old mate, you don't seriously think you're the only bent copper in Sheffield?"

"No but the copper would have to have some serious juice?"

"One of the inner sanctum apparently. Someone very close to that hero cop everyone's been swooning over. Wallace's words not mine mate."

Smiling Ralph replied, "Well that lot deserve everything they get."

"Who? Wallace's lot?"

"No Graham lad, the fucking police and

especially Stainmore. Bloody hate his guts!"

CHAPTER 41

Time out from reality is simply that. Time out. Yet reality is always there lurking to take its place centre stage, reminding you that whilst a person may be able to run, hiding from the truth of your life is never a true option. As her car turned into the large sweeping drive of the converted vicarage that was her family home, Harry felt conflicted. She had missed her sons desperately but she was reluctant to return to what both she and Olivia had left behind albeit only briefly.

Both Christopher and Zac had been well needed reprieves from their real lives, a tonic even and Harry was missing their presence already but especially Christopher. It had been so easy talking with him, listening to his views on things. They had developed an easy camaraderie in their brief time together and Harry was realising that he was the last person she should be thinking of on her return to her home. The pressing matter of her marriage should be taking priority as well as her daughter's well-being.

Driving back from Leeds Bradford airport, Olivia had become increasingly quiet and further

withdrawn the nearer they approached Penton.
"Penny for them?" Harry had asked.
Looking out of the car window, at the array of different housing they were passing, some beautifully old, some beautifully brand new, some shabby and unkempt, others obviously well-loved, Olivia shook her head. "Just thinking about all the different worlds each house represents. All the problems, all the worries, all the horror in each one."
"All the love and happiness too Liv," Harry had replied.
"If they're lucky mum, like we used to be."
Turning into their driveway Olivia now observed, "No one would want to believe bad things could happen to someone living here would they? It all looks so perfect doesn't it?"
Before Harry could reply, Will and Jasper came bounding out of their front door as soon as the taxi came to a halt. Will threw himself at his mother with Jasper closely following. "Have you brought us loads of presents?" were Will's first words.
"What do you think?" Harry laughed as her boys, who she thought had grown taller in the two weeks she'd been gone, took their suitcases and began to lug them into the house.
Jasper, always the more sensitive of the two looked at his mother and whispered, "I'm glad you're home mum. I was worried you weren't coming back."

Standing still, she looked at the earnest face of her boy, not yet a teenager and took him in her arms, holding him tight, trying hard not to cry. "I would never leave my boys my darling. Not ever. You're my life and I love all my children like I love no others and I can't begin to tell you how much I've missed you too."

"Is Liv better now mum? Back to normal?" asked Jasper, his eyes huge and all knowing.

"She's getting there. Being away has done her good."

Suddenly Will appeared at the door shouting, "Jas, hurry up will you! Bossy boots Liv won't let me open the presents without you!"

"You'd better do as he says," laughed Harry as Jasper, abandoning the suitcase, raced into the house passing Jeanette, his grandmother and Harry's mother as he did so.

"Welcome home lovey. Good trip?" as mother and daughter embraced.

"It's what we needed thanks mum. Everything alright here?"

"The boys have been like cherubs."

"Yeah right mum. Only a devoted grandmother would describe those two as cherubs but thanks for stepping in at such short notice."

"Just good to see Olivia with some colour in her cheeks. How's the poor love doing?"

"She's doing okay mum. Well as well as she can in the circumstances."

Jeanette was now watching her daughter closely,

wondering how to broach the next subject. Taking a deep breath, she asked, "And Alan? How are things with the two of you? Has being apart helped at all?"

Smiling sadly at her mother, Harry shrugged her shoulders. "Who knows mum, who knows."

*

Riz looked up as Olivia walked into the study of his parents' home. "Your mum said it would be alright for me to come in," said a very nervous Olivia.

"Hi Liv. Good to see you."

"I've been away."

"I heard. So have I in a fashion."

"Dad said. So how have the surgeries gone?" asked as she looked closely at this boy she had known forever but in the most important way, felt she had only just met. The swelling on his face had all but disappeared although he looked different somehow. Perhaps it was the light in his eyes that now seemed dimmed or the diminished air of confidence Riz always seemed to possess.

"They took away my spleen but it's not needed anyway and the ribs are knitting together nicely. Apparently I was lucky one didn't puncture a lung so yay eh?" Riz's attempt at levity was so like him Olivia thought, making light of something so brutal.

"Worse is this pallet thing. Can't wait to get my new teeth implants then I'll get my movie star

smile back so Hollywood can still come calling."
Olivia was horrified that her bottom lip was now trembling as she tried hard not to cry. Riz came over to sit beside her and taking her hand said, "No more tears Liv. It's happened, we've survived, we're recovering and we're moving on."
"You don't blame me do you?"
Looking scandalised Riz's reply was emphatic. "Blame you? Why would I?"
"Perhaps I was wearing my skirt..."
"Stop right there! The only ones to blame are the thugs that attacked us. They had no reason, no excuse except for having warped ideas or something... something we'll never understand."
Riz put his arms around her and drew her closer as they sat together, both remembering, both trying to make sense of what had happened, knowing that they were both changed forever because of it.
"What do you think about the attack on those who did it?" asked Olivia.
Looking at the floor Riz seemed to be searching for the words, then said, "I wish I'd been there to hold his coat, whoever he was." Looking at Olivia's shocked expression, Riz continued. "They'll never be able to hurt another woman like that again, never feel like real men ever again. Every day they will be reminded of what they did and its consequences. Yeah, I want to thank whoever did it and what's more..."
"Go on."

"Perhaps other 'would be' rapists will think twice now, just in case they get a bit of the same."
"But," argued Olivia, "it's so brutal, so barbaric, so ...medieval!"
"Oh yeah," agreed Riz, "just like raping someone or kicking someone half to death because you don't happen to like the way that person looks. Yeah, brutal and barbaric. Don't waste your time or pity on that scum Liv. Just don't."

*

As Harry and Alan faced each other across the dining table, the same table they had been given as a wedding present nearly twenty years earlier, Harry was wondering how they had so easily come to this point in their marriage. The fragility of their perceived perfect relationship, perfect life was making her realise that there really was no such thing, that such an idea was just a manufactured illusion that now lay in tatters around them.
"So shall you tell the children or shall I?" as Harry referred to Alan's decision to leave their family home for the foreseeable future.
"Perhaps it will be better coming from you," offered Alan, not able to meet Harry's eye contact.
"Why?" the challenge in that one word a palpable echo.
"You're just better at explaining things Harry where the kids are concerned, you know you are."

"Jasper is already fretting and Olivia is still… well her recovery hasn't really started in all honesty. Your leaving won't help our children Alan."

Running his hands through his hair Alan now looked at his wife, a wife he had adored for years but who now seemed to be a complete stranger to him. "But it's what I need, I'm sorry but it just is."

"And that's that then isn't it Alan, your needs! So when did you become such a selfish self-absorbed prick eh?" asked as she shook her head, her eyes hard, her smile brittle.

"Probably the same time you became a …" he stopped, unable to voice his anger, his disgust, knowing there would be no going back, no forgiveness if he actually said the words.

"Oh don't stop there Alan. I became a… what?"

Alan stood up, stared hard at his now estranged wife then without another word, walked out of the room, leaving Harry more alone than she'd ever felt in her entire life.

CHAPTER 42

The large school Sports Hall was now full of expectant students ranging from Year Sevens to Sixth Formers, all immaculately turned out in their school uniforms.

Since the explosion, Imogen and her staff had worked hard to keep the teaching and learning as uninterrupted as possible and finally, the structural engineers had deemed the whole school premises once again safe. Imogen now felt it timely to celebrate the stoicism of both staff and pupils so had arranged a celebratory all school assembly with a special guest.

Max had been reluctant but knew that refusing Imogen anything was becoming more and more impossible. Eddie's advice had been pragmatic. "Just do as requested Max and life will be sweet. Take it from me, the key to a happy life is to have a happy wife... or its equivalent."

So here he was in her office waiting to be paraded in front of nearly a thousand young people and in his full dress uniform too, another thing he hated. He was even expected to say a few words and he was really trying hard not to feel nervous.

Looking at Imogen as she was busy at her desk laptop, he was wondering how she managed to do what she did where he was concerned. He had been emphatic in his refusal and that must have lasted a whole ten minutes. Okay five if he was being really honest.

Looking up Imogen smiled at him as if reading his mind. "All the things you face on a daily basis and a few young people are making you nervous. How come Detective Chief Superintendent?"

"I don't do public speaking, or at least I didn't and we're not exactly talking a few are we?"

"I'll make it worth your while," Imogen now grinning and actually enjoying his discomfort.

"Too right you will," he muttered just as Agnes Mane knocked on the door and popped her head around.

"They're all ready and assembled Ms Holt."

"Thanks Agnes. So, come on my reluctant hero, let's get this over and done with so you can go back to consorting with the criminal fraternity of South Yorkshire."

"Who are a lot less frightening," muttered Max.

Max was surprised how quiet the school was as they walked across the quad to the Sports Hall where all staff and pupils were waiting. As they entered the Hall he was amazed to see it silently full. "So this is where everyone is," he whispered, as Imogen nodded, scanning the assembled and being pleased with the result. As they walked to the stage that had been built just for this purpose, all that could be heard were their footsteps.

Turning to face her students, Imogen began. “Thank you pupils and staff of Grove South. Today is a special day because we are celebrating not only your achievements but also the fact that our school is once again safe for us to fully use again. Before we begin though, may I introduce to you someone whom many of us, if not all of us in here, owe a great deal too. Detective Chief Superintendent Stainmore has kindly agreed to not only give out the well-earned certificates some of you will be receiving today but he has also agreed to say a few words,” as she smiled at Max. She then turned back to the pupils who were quietly and eagerly waiting, adding in a conspiratorial tone, “He’s also told me that facing down hardened criminals is much easier than facing you lot so... be gentle with him okay?” The ripples of smiles, nudges and giggles were polite and appropriate as Max, first clearing his throat, began to speak.

“Thank you Ms Holt and yes this is a new experience for me but it’s good to be back here in much happier, less dangerous circumstances. From what I’ve seen and from what your Headteacher Ms Holt has told me, you are all to be congratulated for the way in which you have all got on with what needs to be done. In your teachers’ case, to make sure your learning continues uninterrupted and for you all to try

and always give your best effort. Terrible things happen every day but it's how you deal with the terrible that's important.
This school has faced the worse that can happen, but look at you all now. Look how smart you look, how well you're achieving and how brave some of you were that day," as he now searched the rows of students, looking for Faisel who was grinning from ear to ear as his friends nudged him. Max caught his eye and nodded. "I for one am proud of you and proud to be here." The spontaneous applause and cheers that followed were instantaneous the feel good factor priceless. Max had more though. "I also know that some of you in here have not always made the right choices so let me speak directly to you. I want you to think about the life you want because that can start today and it starts with honesty, respect for others and doing what is right and knowing what is wrong. You've much to look forward to or much to fear because my officers will always serve and protect others from wrong doing, so choose your side." That brought on further applause and a standing ovation from the staff who had been positioned sitting on the side-lines.
Later as they walked back to the school Reception area, Imogen was smilingly smug. "Well that wasn't so bad after all was it Chief? Born for public speaking in my opinion."
"You have no idea yet what this is going to cost

you."
"Can't wait," she grinned back as their hands briefly held a few seconds as Max was about to leave.
"Max!" came a voice, then, "I'm telling you Sir, he's my mate and I..."
Turning they saw Faisel aka Fiz, trying to bypass one of the Campus Supervisors. "It's okay Sam," said Imogen as Fiz made his way over to them, giving Sam the Campus Supervisor an 'I told you so look' as he passed him.
"Thank you Miss. May I have a word Max but in private please?" as he stole a glance at Imogen.
Imogen, looking surprised, smiled at the earnest looking boy saying, "Of course Faisel," then to Max, "so see you later and thanks again. You were great."
"My pleasure and you're cooking by the way and that's just for starters," grinned Max.
"Beans on toast then," she quipped over her shoulder, as she walked back to her office giving the two of them the privacy Fiz had requested.
Still smiling at her retreating back, Max now turned his attention to Fiz. "So, you ok?"
Looking serious, hands on his hips, Fiz began. "So I'm right."
"Right about what?"
"You and Miss."
Completely thrown Max found he had no words for a moment as he looked into the boy's worried face. "Well, I guess Miss and I are friends Fiz.

Why? Is that a problem?"
Shaking his head Fiz replied, "It could be Max, I mean I thought you liked her when I saw you both at the funeral. You were definitely acting shifty."
"Was I? Well I do like her mate, so why is that a problem?"
Sighing heavily Fiz now endeavoured to explain. "Even though Miss is really old Max, everyone and I mean everyone, thinks she's really pretty. I mean, even I do."
Trying not to smile, Max solemnly nodded. "I think so too mate."
"Well then!"
"Well then what?"
Hands still on hips, giving Max a look suggesting he needed serious help, Fiz now explained, "So you're going to have get a move on Max and put a ring on it before someone else does! I'd hate to see you miss out."
Before he could find a reply, Max was saved by the school bell system, indicating that lessons were resuming as Fiz, moved to make his way to where he was meant to be, his parting words being, "As your mate Max, I just had to warn you to get a move on."
"Appreciate it Fiz," as he made his way out of the main doors towards his car thinking, "No, I could not love that kid more."
He was still smiling when he felt his phone buzz in his pocket. Retrieving it, he saw Matt Turner's

name, the Counter Terrorism operative who had recently been advising his team.

"Hi Matt. What!? You must be mistaken... but...you're in no doubt? Okay, I'll get the next fast train down."

Shaking his head, he turned back to look at the building he had just left, now seeing the carnage that had been perpetrated here just a few weeks ago, the fact no one had been killed nothing short of a miracle. He was being called back to the capital and he dreading what he was about to learn.

CHAPTER 43

Eddie hadn't visited the capital for years so was quietly impressed with the cavernous majesty of St Pancras Railway Station whistling his awe. "So this is why my train ticket cost a fortune."

"It's certainly impressive," replied Max as they both navigated the ticket system that allowed them access on to the streets of London, as they made their way to the headquarters of the MI6 cubist style building situated on the Thames Embankment beside Vauxhall Bridge.

Max had been quiet for most of the journey and Eddie had respected his need to think through the latest intelligence they were dealing with. Today was not going to be easy for a variety of reasons, but when it may involve the betrayal by a friend, such days didn't get much harder.

The security checks as they entered the building took a while, as to be expected, before they were shown into the office of Matt Turner. Matt stood as they entered, offering his hand to both men saying, "Thanks for getting here so promptly chaps," then looking at Max offered, "so sorry Max. This must feel like a real kick in the balls."

"It's taking some sinking in I have to say."
"Before we start can I offer you coffee, tea?"
"Will it be Yorkshire tea?" asked Eddie.
"Er... I don't know."
"I'll have coffee then thanks," replied Eddie, his tone implying he was in the company of philistines.
"So," Max began, "how long has he been on your radar?"
Leaning back in his swivel chair, Matt thought hard before answering. "Not sure to be honest. I mean he's always been a character and a loose cannon but he hated being stranded overseas during Covid, then with the Jakarta business... well I think he had a more difficult experience than he's let on. He came back changed but then a lot of operatives are affected by what is asked of them and to be honest, we're all only human at the end of the day."
Eddie, arms folded, face set was clearly unhappy with Matt's pragmatism. "Please tell me you are not making excuses for this poor excuse for a ..."
Holding up his hands as if in surrender Matt jumped in saying, "Of course not Sergeant. I mean, this has gone down like a lead balloon with those upstairs and beyond. Believe me."
Max shook his head as he got up to look out of the large window which overlooked the Thames. He saw the boats full of tourist sightseers, the bustle of the Embankment, the Christmas lights already up, weeks too early and twinkling in the

distance. He loved this city and until Imogen, had felt it would always be his home.

Turning back to Matt he asked, "When can I see him?"

"Let's have that coffee first eh?" said Matt.

*

The grey windowless, airless room with its unforgiving white lighting, resembled a steel cell. Benny Reynolds sat facing his old school friend with his customary smirk, which always suggested he was about to tell you something salacious or politically incorrect but which would make you smile despite its content.

Max remained silent, waiting. Finally, Benny began. "Well me old mate, fancy meeting you here?" Max continued to stare, still remaining silent, still waiting.

"So," continued Benny, "what can I say? Busted, er... fair cop. I did it. I planted it, although it was a fairly small explosive, could hardly call it a bomb, I mean..."

"Cut the crap Benny," Max's voice menacingly low, barely disguising his anger which was ready to detonate.

Benny at this point at the good grace to look away, smirk now gone. "What can I say mate?"

"How about the truth Benny? How about why? How about what you hoped to gain?"

Leaning back in his chair Benny looked up to the ceiling, thinking as the long silent minutes passed. Max knew better than to push his point,

knowing the prolonged silence would do the job. Finally, Benny said, "Well where do I begin?"
Max remained silent, just staring.
"What can I say? I'm just a sucker for a shed load of money and good sex, no, make that fucking great sex, pardon the pun."
"So who paid you and what reason was given? Why was Imogen Holt the target?"
Sitting back and grinning broadly Benny looked to be enjoying himself. "You know I've always been jealous of you, Maxi boy. The way the girls always fell at your feet even when all you were interested in was getting on the football team. Remember Lesley Phips? I really fancied her and you only had to crook your little finger and she was off! And that time you punched me just because I said I fancied your sister!"
"For Christ's sake Benny how many years ago are we talking? We were kids! We were at school! Start talking because I'm not wasting anymore time here."
"Places to be Maxi boy?"
"Too right I have which is more than can be said for you unless we count the high security segregation cell you'll probably die in!"
Silence now as the two childhood friends stared at each other, Benny completely nonchalant, still smirking despite his grim circumstances whilst Max's need for an explanation he could make sense of, simmered between them.
Benny was the first to break the silence. "Okay

even though I was enjoying our trip down memory lane, I'll tell you why. Well I had to make up for the fact that, despite my best efforts you actually survived didn't you? I mean, I bloody hit you squarely in the chest twice, I might add, but you just wouldn't bloody die would you?"

It was as if all the air had been sucked out of the room. For those watching and listening from the control room where all such conversations were watched, monitored and recorded for the obligatory evidence, it was complete and utter consternation at this turn of events.

"You were the one who shot me?" Max barely believing what he was hearing, repeated the words, "You Benny? You shot me in Penton?"

"Yep Maxi boy, guilty as charged but I failed to actually kill you although to be fair I was still paid, but I take pride in my work so I offered to do it properly."

"I don't believe you."

"Why? Because we went to school together a few decades ago? Being up North has made you soft!"

His face now like thunder Max controlled himself before asking, "But why target Imogen? Why not come after me again?"

"I was going to put the explosive under your car to be honest, that was the initial plan. Then fate kind of intervened didn't it when the call came in about the young lad and the vest. I mean what a heaven sent opportunity, or should we say hell sent eh? I got to target someone whose death would hurt you more than your own and for the one paying, that was priceless, perfect even and worth a bonus if I'd managed it. So I changed tack and targeted instead, the reason you turned your back on London and all you knew, even the NCA. I mean, that was the plan but what did I do? Made you a sodding National hero instead. I mean Maxi boy you couldn't write it could you mate? I mean the one paying me is hopping mad! I'm safer in here I can tell you."

Max just stared, barely believing what he was hearing. "So what happened to you Ben?"

"What are you talking about?"

"Tell me. What happened to you that's turned you into...into this?"

Benny for the first time since Max had entered the room, now wouldn't meet Max's eye as the silence stretched between them. "Laying your life on the line for Queen and Country isn't as noble as it sounds although I suppose it's King and Country now isn't it. The things I've been ordered to do... well perhaps it's hard to know who the good guys are anymore and thanks to those who give the orders, I've come to realise that I'm a very bad man indeed. You know, perhaps I've stopped even knowing the difference between good and evil, right or wrong and actually don't give a toss if truth be told. It's easier doing a deal with the devil at the end of the day because we're all going to hell anyway. Some of us have even been there already."

Max now had his head in his hands before looking up at his former friend. “So are you going to tell me who paid you to kill me? When that failed, to go after Imogen? A complete innocent in all this?”

Shaking his head, “Never mate because I intend to live a lot longer, even inside, even in my segregated grey cell where the sun will never shine but think hard enough. Who should you never have turned your back on? I mean I know you’ve still got the scar?”

Max stared at this man he thought he knew well, a man he’d enjoyed a shared childhood history with, a man he thought he could rely on, could trust, now only seeing a stranger and a bitter corrupt one at that. He stood up to leave but Benny hadn’t finished.

“It would seem that some things can never be forgiven, some memories just refusing to do one. They’re not finished with you, far from it. I may be banged up for the next few decades but there will be others itching to take my place, in fact there will be a disorderly queue forming as I speak, particularly now. Your heroics have made you an even bigger target, thanks to me. I won’t be the only one who won’t be able to resist the money and sex on tap but next time you may not be so lucky mate.”

Staring hard Max merely replied, “I’m not your mate. It seems I never have been,” as he walked out of the door leaving Benny alone and finally finished, the smirk now permanently gone.

*

Desperate for her first morning coffee of the day at what she considered the best coffee place in Penton, Imogen gave her order at the counter of her favourite deli cum gift shop whilst checking her phone to see if the email she was waiting for had arrived. Smiling her thanks at her favourite barista cum shop owner Kaz, she retrieved her cup, then nearly collided with the tall man standing in the queue behind her, standing too close she might add. "Nearly," he said, giving her a smile she assumed he would describe as part of a fool proof charm offensive.

"Well perhaps you should be more careful before invading a person's personal space by standing too close in a queue," was Imogen's tart reply.

"So your phone number is out of the question then?"

"In your dreams!"

"Bloody hell but are they at it again?" this from Alice who with Kaz were shaking their heads in a bemused kind of wonderment as Imogen and Max, now smiling at each other made their way to a nearby table.

"Does it never get old you two?" asked Kaz, still shaking her head and laughing as she handed Max his usual double expresso.

"Well to be fair Kaz, in the original scenario Max is still in his leather jacketed, smouldering tough cop phase," laughed Imogen.

"Nah, suit and tie doesn't quite have the same impact," shrugged Alice, "but the leather? Now you're talking."

"Well thanks for the advice ladies," this from Max, as he pretended to be offended as both women, still laughing continued serving their other customers, "I'll resurrect the leather look then shall I?"

"Please. We'll sell tickets and make a killing," laughed Kaz.

Looking closely at him, Imogen saw how tense and tired he was despite his smile and good humour, as she reached over to hold his hand. "So how was London?"

"Still there, still too crowded but definitely warmer," smiled Max as he stirred his coffee, giving nothing away in his expression as he looked at her.

"Not tempted to stay then?"

"No, would miss 'God's Own Country' and its clean air too much and a few other things, a few people," his look and tone now serious.

"Missed you last night," said as she stroked the side of his hand with her thumb.

"Missed you too, couldn't actually sleep if I'm honest."

A silence settled between them as Max still stirring his coffee looked deep in thought. Imogen was worried, instinctively knowing something was wrong. "So how did yesterday go or can't you say?"

Squeezing her hand that was still in his, Max acknowledged her worried expression and realised how much he wanted to protect her from everything and at this point, really didn't want to worry her further. Yet she had a right to know that she may still be in danger, that elements from his far distant past were coming back to haunt the both of them. "We at least have some answers to certain questions but nothing that makes any real sense, well not yet anyway."

"So do you know who planted the car bomb?"

He nodded and he knew how his next words would affect her. "The same person who shot me outside of your home over two years ago."

Imogen's gasp of horror as she put both hands to her mouth spoke volumes. "How can that be possible Max?"

Shaking his head, he searched for the words. "You said it yourself not so long ago, that the past can be a dangerous place. My past has become very dangerous and unfortunately not just for me."

*

Eddie was not a morning person particularly after the day he had experienced in London, still reeling from what he and Max had learned. His old mate Philip Read had left him a text message asking him to meet with him urgently. He was now sitting in the Portakabin converted café which was permanently situated on a lay-by on the Stockdale by-pass, surrounded by tired lorry drivers eating what was undoubtedly, the best bacon sandwiches in the world.

A bleary eyed Eddie peered at his old friend asking, "Why all the cloak and dagger?"

Philip Read shook his head, looking around making sure they would not be overheard. "Couldn't risk being seen talking to you in case I've been spotted visiting Ralph."

"Sounds serious."

"It is Eddie."

"And? Don't keep me hanging mate?"

"You've got someone on your team working for Wallace Senior's people on the outside."

Eddie leaned back in his chair, then shaking his head replied, "No mate that's just not possible. Ralph Jones' got it wrong or more likely is causing mischief in a bid to get even or something."

"No Eddie, I believe him. Apparently it's someone in 'the inner sanctum'. It's why I've met you here. I wanted to be sure we weren't seen by anyone from City Central's patch, even the Traffic cops. Who knows how deep Senior's people have infiltrated your team?"

Rubbing his tired eyes Eddie looked at his old friend and saw how he was feeling, reflected in his eyes also. "Why do we bother eh Phil? Why do we bloody bother?"

Smiling sadly his old friend said what Eddie deep down already knew, "Because we have to Eddie. Because if we don't, who will?"

CHAPTER 44

Max handed Eddie his coffee stating, "Too early for alcohol I guess seeing as it's barely 8.30 in the morning, but I could use a shot of something."

"Yesterday and this morning is enough to drive the best of us to drink Max. Have you seen Imogen yet?"

"Yes, first thing. She's a bit shook up to say the least."

"I'll bet, and you? Get any sleep or is that a stupid question?"

Grinning sadly at this older stalwart whom he regarded more as his friend, Max shrugged in reply, then looking serious began to tell Eddie what his new information from Philip Read had made Max realise. "What Phil Read has told us makes sense if you think about it. We've been playing catch up with recent events all along. We had the men that raped Olivia Wood already in the system but they disappeared before we could arrest them and we now know they were guilty of much more. Cowden too, cannot be found and The Stag's Head, more or less deserted except for a disgruntled Landlady on the point of leaving her Landlord husband. Yes, Eddie it seems someone is alerting those we would like to bring in and question at the very least. It all makes perfect sense."

"But who? I trust those out there with my life and have done on more than one occasion."

"Me too Eddie but stations everywhere have more leaks than the average colander. A careless word spoken at the coffee machine or even in the gents is all it would take."

"But the inner sanctum? That suggests someone close to us Max. Are we seriously suspecting Isiah, or Dan? That's before we get to Lydia or Beth?"

"And Braxton? You've heard he's been rejected by the Met?"

"Yes and according to Beth, he's putting the blame squarely on your shoulders. It would give him motive."

"It would but I don't see it but do a bit of discrete digging over in Manchester. I bet you've got a contact or two?"

Chuckling self-deprecatingly Eddie confirmed, "I have contacts in Timbuktu Chief."

"Of that I can believe. We'll tell the team that all we learned yesterday is that the car bombing is a separate crime and unconnected with what's been happening here. We need to smoke whoever is passing on information out of the woodwork and we need to do it as discretely as possible."

*

Brandon Cowden was bored. He had things to do, plans to make and sitting here in this backwater shithole in the middle of nowhere was making him stir crazy. Gareth had said he had the means to help him leave the country. He fancied Ireland because at least they spoke English over there. Hearing the door slam open, he sat bolt upright but was relieved when Gareth appeared with his two usual minders, huge men with fists like ham hocks, fists he'd seen make literally, mincemeat out of those unfortunate enough to be beaten by them.

"Fuck's sake, you gave me a scare. Thought Feds had found me."

Smiling benignly, Gareth moved to stand over him. "No just us, your mates, I mean that's what we are aren't we Brandon?"

Eyeing him Brandon sensed he was missing something. "Course we are."

Gareth nodded, still smiling. "Mates are honest with each other though aren't they? Wouldn't try to make a fool out of a mate, I mean that would be wrong. Right?"

"Yeah right why..." the fist, connecting with Brandon's jaw was swift in its execution, rendering Brandon unable to speak as both blood and teeth spurted out of his mouth. Gareth pulled him up by his hair out of the chair he had been sitting, throwing the stunned man into the arms of the two men he had brought with him.

As they secured Brandon, Gareth sauntered

towards him. "Bomb expert are you? Needed time to get the equipment did you? Needed time to plan these things did you? You lying piece of scum! Making out you're such an asset, such a big tough guy eh?"

Brandon tried to speak but was unable to, the swelling already making speech impossible, the blood still pouring from his wounded mouth.

Gareth hadn't finished though, far from it. "Well you're going to find out what happens to those who lie to me, who make a fool out of me. Over to you lads and don't stop until I say so."

CHAPTER 45

Finally, after all the endless years of waiting, it had arrived. Her very own wedding day. Today was the day she would be married. Today was the day she would finally marry the man of her dreams and a man who was truly worthy of her. She would become the wife of a visionary, a man of courage, a man ready to make tough necessary decisions, a man ready to make the world a better place. A man, who like herself, had had to make so many personal sacrifices for the greater good. History would eventually acknowledge this and of this she was in no doubt.

Looking at her reflection in the mirror she was quietly pleased. She had spent a small fortune on making her husband-to-be proud of her this day, from her Izzy Miyake dress down to her Jimmy Choo shoes. She'd always wanted a pair of ridiculously expensive, beautiful shoes which other women would envy, would sigh over and tell her how lucky she was. Yes, the dress and shoes were beautiful, her hair perfect, the real pearl jewellery delicate and fitting for the occasion. Such a pity she was so very plain of face but Wallace had reassured her that the beauty of her soul was, “a shining light that would never dim” and when he said, “others will grow old but you will forever remain my very own vision of loveliness because your soul is beauty and will always be so, until death us do part,” she thought her heart would burst with love. She hoped he would repeat those very words in front of the others there today, those there to witness their union. Her only regret was all the secrecy, that she couldn’t let her family, friends and work colleagues know; particularly her work colleagues. She knew, without being told that she was the subject of pity, especially by the young pretty ones but she also knew she would eventually be the envy of all she knew. Still, she would have loved a ‘hens do’ and all of its silliness but she understood the significance of Wallace’s work and how her key role in the continuation of his work was more important than such frippery. Still, he would eventually be released and she would finally experience intimacy... and sex. She’d waited this long, what was a few more years in the scheme of things.

The Prison Governor, Greg Hines, had taken some convincing but eventually had given permission for Wallace Senior to marry the woman who had been visiting him five times per month for the past two years, a woman who was surprisingly non-descript and older than his usual type, to say the least. Due to Wallace’s prison status he would not allow the ceremony to be performed in the local Registry Office but instead in the prison Chapel and was more than slightly amused when Wallace had asked him to be a witness.

"Really Wallace?"

"Why not Greg? I've known you longer than most since I've been banged up?"

Leaning back in his swivel chair, Greg eyed Wallace with suspicion. "What's really going on Wallace? What's the point? You're not getting out any time soon so why? Why her? I mean she's not your usual type."

Shrugging Wallace was pragmatic. "Why not her? I mean the heart wants what the heart wants right? Age is just a number too and perhaps I've realised that the love of a truly good woman is what every man needs. It's also what my fiancé wants and I want her happiness more than anything despite my being locked up."

Guffawing Greg replied, "Am I expected to believe a word that's just come out of your mouth Wallace?"

Wallace had merely smiled, his enigmatic smile acknowledging that Hines was one of the few he could never fully fool. "Well it's also a change of routine too Greg. A change is always as good as a rest isn't it?"

"Now that's more like it although I can't for the life of me think what the lady in question is getting out of it."

Wallace merely smiled his enigmatic smile once again.

*

"I Wallace Oswald Senior take you Janet Deirdre Downing to be my wife. To have and to hold from this day forward for better, for worse, for richer, for poorer, in sickness and in health, to love and to cherish, till death do us part."

Janet gazed into Wallace's eyes, not breaking eye contact once, not even when exchanging the rings, she had purchased for them both. Finally, the moment she had been dreaming of, waiting for, when the Registrar finally said, "You may kiss your bride,"

The kiss was chaste, without any hint of passion as Wallace held Janet's hands in his as he whispered, "Is my wedding gift ready?"

Janet nodded, her eyes shining brightly, brimming with love. "It's all arranged my love."

"Perfect my Janet. As perfect as you."

*

Meanwhile, whilst Wallace Senior and Janet Downing exchanged their wedding vows, Denise Cowden looked at her first born son with both horror and heartbreak in equal measure. Her husband George had found him in their shed, barely conscious and very badly beaten. She had wanted to ring for an ambulance but both husband and son had told her to forget it. Medical assistance meant police involvement and Brandon was still wanted by the police to "assist with their enquiries".

She had done what she could, getting him to bed, giving him painkillers, sitting with him till he finally slept but she knew his injuries both external and internal were serious, possibly life threatening.

"He's probably got broken ribs George and damaged kidneys looking at those bruises."

"They'll mend, doctors would tell you that."

"He probably has head injuries too and they can be serious, life threatening even."

"His head is hardest part of him, he'll be right."

"He'll never be bloody right thanks to you!"

"That's right Denise, bloody well blame me as usual!"

"Because you are to blame, because you are a poor excuse for an arsehole never mind a father!"

At this George had sprang up, towering above Denise as she sat with his fists clenched tightly, his stance threatening.

"Yeah that would be right, Mr bloody big fists. Go on then, do your worse!"

Staring at the woman he had known since they had been at school, George felt he was looking at a stranger as, feeling deflated and defeated he sat back down. "Why do you hate me so much Denise? Why?"

Momentarily stunned by the question Denise now pondered her answer, then for the first time in their lives together, revealed her sadness and disappointment. "You have been no kind of father George. Never once have you shown or set any kind of good example for the kids. You would never tell our Brandon when he was being a little shit which was often, constantly going against me when I tried to make him do as he was told and the other two lads are going the same way. Thank God for our Katie because..."

"Oh here we go, bloody Kate..."

Staring at him, Denise looked scandalised. "What do you mean "bloody Katie" George? She's our daughter for God's sake and the only shining light in my life if I'm honest. Without her my life would have no meaning, do you know that? Do you even bloody care?"

Sitting with his head in his hands George said, "Of course I do lass. I just don't know..."

"Don't know what?"

"What you want from me anymore."

Looking away Denise felt all of her pent up anger slowly disappear. "You know this is the first time you've ever asked me what I wanted. You know that?"

As George sadly shook his head Denise continued. "I never wanted this life George, never for one second."

"Well it is what it is. I'm too old to change."

"And Brandon?"

"What about him?"

"He's done something bad George, something really bad. Karen Raithes has told me..."

"Well that old bag can do one!"

"Really George! Is that the best you've got?"
Shaking his head George now answered his truth. "Whatever he's done we can't change it like we can't change that he's ours. Ours Denise. We look after him and we protect him the best we can. Agreed?"
Nodding her agreement Denise now asked her husband, with a defeated sadness in her voice, "And who's going to protect us George?"
Looking puzzled George asked, "From who? What?"
"From our Brandon George. Who's going to protect us from our own son?"

CHAPTER 46

Katie Cowden knew what she must do. The voice told her, had been telling her for weeks now and today was the day she was to do exactly what the voice said. The voice was kind but firm, insistent even, when it told her that she must leave the world. The world did not have room for her and she would be far happier in a place called Death. Katie had tried to argue with the voice, telling it that she would miss her mum too much but the voice told Katie that her mum would be proud and relieved because her mum knew the world wasn't the right place for Katie too. So here she was at the top of the world and she was terrified.

*

Josh Brigg and Otis Delaney were doing what they did best, skiving a lesson to meet undiscovered, in order to have a crafty fag somewhere yet to be discovered by the Campus Supervisors or on duty teachers.

"When she got 'Macbeth' books out I thought just kill me now," moaned Josh.

"Better than what Diabolical Dybill wanted to do. The Corn Laws? I mean what the... who's that?" as

Otis suddenly pointed upwards, “who’s that on top of the Science Block. They must be mad!”
Stomping out the illicit cigarette Josh now jumped into action. “We need to tell someone quick!”
“We’ll get done!”
“Not as done as they’ll be if they fall. Come on!”

*

Janet Downing was now becoming quite cross. Katie was still on the roof but not actually doing what she had ‘suggested’ she do, what she had been suggesting for a while now. It wouldn’t do thought Janet. This was her wedding gift to her dearly beloved, a special gift. Katie was her favourite pupil but she was willing to sacrifice her as a token of her love for Wallace. She also hadn’t realised what damage she had been doing over the years, until Wallace had pointed it out to her. There was no room for weakness in Wallace’s New Order, so such genetics had to be eradicated. She’d done well so far, with the deaths of Miles, Oliver and Samuel with no one suspecting her of ‘suggesting’ what they should do. Who knew, Janet now mused to herself, the power of what happens when a suggestion is accepted by the subconscious mind. How the more an idea is acted upon, the stronger and more fixed that thinking becomes. In her delusional state, Janet didn’t even consider for one moment that Wallace Senior had played these mind games with her own psyche and had

enjoyed the way she had blindly been sucked him by him.
Suddenly she saw people dashing across the main quad area, pointing upwards and dashing towards the Science block. She must act quickly. This was her wedding gift and Wallace must not be cheated.

*

"How long did the fire response team said they'd be?" snapped Imogen.
"They're close. Five minutes...tops," replied Agnes.
"Not soon enough then, I'm going to her."
"Well Ms Holt, I've tried to open the roof door but it's jammed and I think it might be locked from the outside as my spare key won't work. Wain't budge!" this from Sam the main Campus Supervisor, "and ..."
"And what?" asked Agnes.
Scratching his head Sam now looked confused and very afraid. "Well Miss Downing told me she had everything under control and that some things are best left to nature taking its course and that I was to leave well alone."
Swallowing hard Imogen asked, "And where was Miss Downing when you saw her Sam?"
"She was going up the steps to the roof and ..."
"And?"
"I think she may have a roof key. She asked me for it the other day as she said she was doing some research about... well I can't remember but I can't

remember her returning the key either and now I can't open the door."
"Oh my God," murmured Imogen as all of the pieces began to fall into place. The sirens of rescue could now be heard but Imogen now feared they could all be too late.

*

Paul and Jo Cowden hated their new school and spent a lot of time avoiding it much to the frustration of their mother. Idling their time on the local Recreation ground, they were surprised to hear their phones ding several alerts. As they looked at the pictures being sent to their phones, they looked at each other then, without words raced for home.

*

Chief Fire Officer Nick Benton was looking grim. Having been brought up to speed, he was now directing his firefighters to designated areas, utilising equipment that would reduce the possibility of a fatality if the worse came to the worse. The school population had been evacuated onto the far school field in case the worse possible outcome occurred. It was the last thing any child or member of staff of any age needed to witness.
"So we think this Miss Downing is wanting the child to fall from the roof?"
"Looks like it," replied Imogen, she herself still in shock from what was happening.
"Any chance she could be talked down, once we

break onto the roof?"

"I could try."

Suddenly screams were heard from the roof as Katie was now clearly struggling to free herself from Janet's grip. Imogen and several firefighters now raced to the stairs which led to the roof. Imogen could hear the breaking down of the door and was relieved to see the splintered opening appear before her.

"Now take it steady," ordered Nick, "don't make this Downing woman angry ok?"

Nodding, Imogen stepped onto the roof. "Janet, Katie, it's cold up here, freezing even. Come on, let's get you both back to the warmth eh?"

"Please Miss, I don't want to go to Death, but Miss says I have to."

"I'm sure Miss wants you to be safe and warm isn't that right Janet? Please let Katie go now. She's frightened and she's cold. Please Janet."

Janet turned to look at Imogen and later Imogen would recall how unrecognisable Janet was in that moment. Her normally kind facial expression was distorted into a grim determined parody, her hair standing on end, making her look deranged which she clearly was.

"Oh Imogen! What are you doing here? Go about your business because this for once has nothing to do with you!"

Fighting for calm Imogen just smiled at this woman whom she had thought she knew so well.

"I care about you both. Both you and Katie Janet,

so if it's okay with you I'd like to stay and see if we can make this alright."

Sighing heavily Janet looked at Imogen. "This is my wedding gift to my husband Imogen," then seeing Imogen's surprise, Janet's lip curled with a cruel satisfaction adding, "yes my husband. Me, spinster of the Parish, destined to be a lonely old maid. I have a husband and what a husband he is."

Recovering, Imogen now changed tack. "Well congratulations! You should have said so we can all celebrate with you. That's wonderful news. So... can Katie come over to me now Janet? Please? Then we can concentrate on organising your celebration, okay?"

Shaking her head and looking pityingly at the woman before her. "You really do think I'm stupid don't you Imogen? You really do think you're so superior too don't you? I mean it's just pure luck you were born beautiful and I was born ...so plain. Why does it have to matter so much?"

"It doesn't matter Janet."

"Only the beautiful and pretty ones would utter such rubbish. You've always made me sick do you know that Imogen? The way you glide into a room, all eyes on you, your presence so wanted everywhere you go. Always immaculate, always in control, always the centre of attention. Hate you! Hate you! Hate you!"

Suddenly there was the sound of running feet

as both Denise and George Cowden appeared on the roof with Nick Benton and his firefighters desperately trying to bar their way.

"Katie!" screamed her mother.

"Oh here she is!" snarled Janet, "mother of the year!"

"Mum, I don't want to go to Death but Miss Downing says you want me to though, but I don't want to leave you."

"I don't want you to go either my love. How could you say that to her!? You wicked evil..."

"Please," urged Imogen, "don't upset her..."

"Upset her," growled George. "I'll bloody do more than that. Let my daughter go NOW or I'll..."

Janet now clutched Katie harder, edging ever closer to the edge. "Ah Mr Cowden. We've never met before have we? Parent's Evening not your bag I take it. Then again our Katie here is flawed isn't she? Not worth bothering with, not like your Brandon. Oh now he's one to watch isn't he? What a son to be proud of and my Wallace is well impressed with him. He's already done great work and will go far when the New Order comes and come it will."

As Janet had been speaking, Brad and two other uniformed officers had discretely joined them on the roof, circling around the air conditioning compressors, coming up on Janet's blind side. Suddenly one of the officers tripped over the uneven concrete, causing Janet to turn quickly to face them, slightly loosening her grip on the frightened child. At this point Katie, finding strength from somewhere, shoved Janet away from her as she rushed into the waiting arms of her mother. Brad lurched forward, attempting to grab Janet, who with flailing arms was trying to keep her balance, fear and horror sketched across her face. Then as if without warning, she just disappeared, her screams, as she fell echoing around the vacated school walls. Then silence except for the relieved sobs of a terrified child, now safely in the arms of those who loved her.

CHAPTER 47

Frank Ackroyd, Grove South Chair of Governors was doing his best to show Imogen how important he was. Stretching his legs out, Imogen thought she should be grateful he wasn't actually placing them on her desk such was his sense of his own self-importance. A local councillor, Frank liked to be in the loop of everything but in reality, had little idea of the workings of a school or anything else if truth be told.

"It's publicity we could well do without Imogen. I mean after the car bomb which..."

"Was placed under my car as I recall Frank making me lucky to still be alive."

"Well yes and I'm not saying any different but..."

"And what has happened recently stems from the same source who strapped the joke vest onto Faisel which the police are still pursuing. These last few weeks have been unfortunate but there was nothing I or any of my staff could have done to prevent any of it. Okay Frank? Unless you have evidence of it being otherwise?"

Blustering, Frank now knew he had been wrong

footed. "Don't think for one moment I was casting aspersions. I'm just worried what Ofsted will make of all this?"

"Ofsted will be too concerned with the quality of the teaching and the progress of our pupils Frank, as they should be because that is their job as it is mine." Rising from her seat, Imogen purposely walked round her desk, giving Frank a clear hint he had outstayed his welcome.

"So Frank, thank you for calling in and for your concerns but as you can see, it's business as usual. Now let me show you out."

Watching his unhappily retreating back from her desk, Agnes Mane raised her eyebrows at Imogen asking, "Okay?"

"I think so but who knows where he's concerned."

"Any news regarding Miss Downing, or whatever she's called now?"

"No. No doubt the police will get to the bottom of it now."

Janet had miraculously survived the fall as the Fire Fighters had placed a safety net which had ultimately saved her life, although she had sustained injuries but none that were considered life threatening. It was the state of her mind that was the real concern.

Imogen returned to her office and asked herself for the millionth time, what had she missed? Peter Rogers, her Deputy popped his head around her door and asked, "You okay? Just seen 'Captain

Mainwaring' leave."

Gesturing to come in Imogen replied, "He's worried what Ofsted will make of recent events and to be honest an Emergency Safeguarding visit could well be triggered."

"How could we have known what Janet was up to? I mean it's beyond belief!"

Shaking her head, Imogen merely shrugged before asking, "Have we put the necessary support in place for the pupils and some of the staff?"

"Yes, it's all in hand. Imogen this was no one's fault, well no one except bloody Janet Downing! I mean what could have possessed her?"

"I know Pete. I know." Yet three children had died on her watch and she hadn't seen it coming. It was something she would be finding very hard to live with.

*

Walking into Brandon's bedroom, Denise found her son in a deep asleep. His injuries looked even worse, if that was at all possible, the bruising turning all different shades of purple and she could only imagine his pain particularly as he was coughing blood too, and from the stains on the pillows, a lot of blood. George had given her the fentanyl to help ease Brandon's pain informing her to be careful with the dosage.

"That's stuff's lethal especially mixed with strong spirit, so be careful with it," he had warned.

Denise now mixed the potion of fentanyl with a large measure of whisky then positioned herself on the single bed next to her son, just as she had done when he was a toddler. Waking him she now murmured, "Hello love, I've something to help your pain, I've made it especially for you."

Opening the one eye that was barely like a slit, Brandon nodded, then tried to sit up until he cried out in pain, the effort being too excruciating. Easing his head to drink Denise placed the glass to the swollen lips and kept it there until all had been consumed, wiping the dribbles away that had fallen down his chin, just like she'd done when he was her baby.

Placing the glass on the bedside table, Denise stayed and stroked her eldest son's hair, not seeing the man he had become, the bullying monster whom she feared, just her small son, saying the soothing words spoken by mothers for millenia. "Go to sleep now my love, let sleep take away the pain. I'll be here until you feel better and don't feel the pain or fear anymore. You're my boy, my first born baby and I had so many hopes and dreams for you but that's all done with now. Despite everything I do love you and I will stay with you until it all stops so go to sleep my precious, go to sleep now."

Brandon stirred, murmuring, then felt for her hand and that's how they both remained, hand in hand until Denise could not hear her son's breaths any more.

*

Denise and George sat facing each other across their kitchen table. George was the first to break the silence whispering, “Why?” as tears of bewilderment and anguish streamed down his face,

Denise did not speak for a very long time then, “Brandon was like cancer and cancer spreads and rots everything in its wake unless it’s destroyed first. Paul and Joe hero worship him and are going the same way and I can’t have that and...”

“And?”

“They’re coming for him and would have sent him away for decades, probably never letting him out because... because he was lost George, wicked even. His life would have been bleak and brutal every day until the day he died. He was my boy, my baby and I couldn’t bear the thought of the rest of his life... being like that...” then the deluge of tears came as Denise and George Cowden found themselves in each other’s arms, looking for comfort as they grieved the loss of their first born.

*

Isiah and Dan looked at the very dead, very battered body of Brandon Cowden. Seeing the empty glass, Isiah donned the gloves which would ensure non contamination of evidence, sniffed it and concluded, “Whisky but I imagine it had a sting in its tail too,” as he placed the glass in an evidence bag.

Dan now spoke into his phone. "Chief. Yes, Brandon's here but he's dead. Looks like a drugs overdose or a result from a beating he's received or both. He's had a job done on him either way. Okay Chief, will do," as he disconnected the call, saying to Isiah, "Chief wants the parents brought it for questioning."

"Right, let's get it done," replied Isiah as he took one last look at the dead man, a man they had been searching for and a man they knew had been responsible for so much wrong done since his release. "Wish we'd brought him to justice Dan. I feel like he's got away with it all."

Nodding his agreement Dan concurred. "Yeah, I know what you mean mate."

Back in the kitchen cum living room of the Cowden household Isiah began. "You both need to come to the station...."

"I'm the only one you need. My wife had no idea what I was doing when I gave Brandon pain relief and I realise now that I over did the amount of fentanyl but my Denise knew nothing about it."

"You're admitting you have access to fentanyl?" asked Dan.

"You bloody well know I have so stop pissing about."

"George..." began Denise.

"No love, this is down to me. It's all down to me," as he reached over to squeeze her hand adding, "and we have our Katie to consider. She's got enough to deal with after yesterday and she needs her mum, alright?"

"Come on then George, let's be having you," said Dan, as the two officers led him away leaving Denise alone. She had merely tolerated her husband for the longest time often feeling despair for what he did, for what he'd become. Now she felt only immense gratitude.

CHAPTER 48

Max addressed the teams of detectives gathered in the Incident Room, pointing to the Incident Board. “Just a heads up everyone. Brandon Cowden has been located and is being brought in for questioning so finally, we should be getting some answers and for many some sort of closure. Hopefully now, we will also get whoever’s been pulling the strings. We know Wallace Senior had been operating from inside Armley Leeds ‘nick’ but I want the main man on the outside, he’s the one I want put away. So, let’s carry on doing what we do best.” Max nodded discretely to both Beth and Lydia who had made their way towards the back of the conference room.

“Finally!” enthused Sharon Summers to both detectives as she passed them on her way out of the Major Incident room.

“Oh I don’t know, I’ll miss the overtime,” quipped Beth, smiling at her old friend.

Sharon leaving the others on the pretence of going to the Control Centre, instead stepped into the Ladies toilets. Making sure she was alone, she took out her second phone, the one she only kept when contacting him in emergencies. "Gareth, they've located Cowden. Yes, he's still alive and they're bringing him in under caution. Well he must be... yes...so get gone. I'll meet you when I can, and Gareth... be careful love."

Breathing deeply, she prepared to leave only to be met at the door by both Beth and Lydia.

"Oops ladies," gushed Sharon, "nearly."

"Yep Shaz, you nearly got away with it didn't you?" stated Beth looking hard at her colleague, all smiles gone.

Stuttering Sharon looked behind the women only to see Max, Eddie and Richard standing behind them. Lydia had walked to the hand drier, retrieving her phone from its hiding place where she played back the words Sharon had spoken moments before. To her credit she didn't try to bluff her way out of the situation she was now in.

"So, phone please Shaz," said Beth "and an address of the man you've just been speaking to?"

"In your dreams Beth. I'll never betray him."

"Wow loyalty but none for me. Just wanted to point the finger at me eh Shaz?" said Richard.

"Well why not? You mean nothing to me, just a half decent fuck when you could be bothered."

Max stepped forward. "Get the device to the techs to get a trace asap. Do the honours Beth and Richard? Don't waste your breath. We'll be having quite a chat Sharon, believe you me."

As Sharon was led away, Richard turned to Eddie

in quiet disbelief. "Half bloody decent?"
Eddie merely chuckled, saying to the quietly outraged young detective, "It is what it is lad. Chalk it up to experience...or lack of it."

*

Gareth knew this day would come so had a bag already packed with his passport at the ready. He would eventually meet Sharon at their place just outside of Jerez in Andalusia, a beautiful little place way off the beaten track. Sharon would discretely take her holiday leave and not return, covering her tracks as she did so. They had planned for this, had made enough money which was now earning mega interest in an off-shore account, enough to make their next few years very sweet indeed. They had even planned their escape route, taking a ferry from Hull to Zeebrugge then catch a series of trains across Europe. He was actually looking forward to it now the time had arrived.
Picking up the ring box, he had purchased just days earlier, he opened its contents and admired the ruby and diamond engagement ring he intended to give to Sharon when they were safely away and reunited in their own little piece of paradise. Sharon was the real deal for him and he wanted to make it official and he couldn't wait to see the look on her face when he went down on one knee. Perhaps he's do it in their favourite restaurant where all the locals would cheer and celebrate with them, making her feel so special.

Suddenly Gareth knew he wasn't alone. He sensed a presence. Slowly turning round he felt his blood turn to ice when he saw who was standing behind him, who had entered his home as silent as the predator he was. Omar Miraz just looked at him, unblinkingly still as if made of stone. Gareth then knew. The Devil had caught up with him and it was payment time.

CHAPTER 49

Looking across the interview table Beth felt she was looking at a stranger. She and Sharon Summers had walked the beat together when Beth was still in uniform. Sharon had even had a fling with Brad before Beth and Brad had become an item. Besides Lydia, there was not another colleague in the station Beth felt could be totally relied upon one hundred per cent, yet here they were. Beth could barely believe it. It made so sense.

"I don't get in Sharon. You need to explain your actions and the reasons for those actions."

Sharon remained silent, had actually not uttered a word since her arrest, except to refuse Federation representation, as was her legal right.

Opening the file in front of her Beth began reading. "Well this Gareth Jackson is... well as my dad would say ... a bit of a lad to say the least!"

Sharon still remained silent.

Beth continued. "Started young didn't he? In and out of Youth Offenders then a stint in Strangeways Manchester for Aggravated Burglary and Assault, then onto Armley for GBH.

So that will be where he met Senior and started their latest enterprise I'm assuming. Right Sharon?"

Sharon was still unresponsive as the door to the Interview room opened, with Max entering the small room. Sitting next to Beth, Max merely nodded at Sharon but he too, remained silent.

"So Sharon, you're in as deep a hole as you can get. You need to make us understand what the hell you've been thinking. I mean how long have you been working with Jackson for starters?"

Sharon shook her head. "You wouldn't understand Beth so don't even try, but I'll never betray Gareth. Not ever so you may as well..."

"He's gone Sharon," said Max.

Smiling Sharon leaned back in the hard plastic chair. "Yes, I knew he'd be long gone by now. We'd already planned for this eventuality, I mean, all good things come to an end, right Beth?"

Shaking his head and looking serious, Max now explained. "No Sharon, he's obviously been taken but not by us."

"I don't understand."

"When we got there we found his ready bag, his passport and Euros and there'd clearly been a struggle too. He's disappeared Sharon and we don't know where to start looking so perhaps you can help us find him, for his own sake as well as yours."

Sharon had gone deathly pale. Then said, "You're lying. Gareth's too careful, too clever."

"And for all we know 'too dead'. He's upset a lot of dangerous people in this city Sharon, taking their business away from under their very noses, getting just kids in some cases to do his dirty work. You know this as well as we do."

Sharon remained silent, just staring at the wall behind Max, giving no one eye contact.

Eventually Beth broke the impasse her tone scathing and full of contempt. "So where did you meet such a prince then?"

"Same way you met yours, through the job. Routine traffic stop, down Prince of Wales Road, just off the Manor. Eric my partner couldn't be arsed to do the paperwork so we let Gareth off. He gave me his number and the rest just happened."

"You don't just happen to get into bed with a bloody known villain Sharon. What were you thinking?"

"Oh for God's sake Beth! What would you know eh? I thought Brad and I had a shot of something then the blonde bombshell made a beeline and that was that wasn't it? Good old Shagga Shaz was history wasn't she? Even when you couldn't treat him with any kind of decency he followed you round like a bloody pathetic lap dog!"

"What!?" exploded Beth, "you're laying this on Brad and me? Your collusion with a known criminal, giving information and God knows what else is our fault?"

Sharon now smiling shrugged her shoulders, her voice hard, her eyes brittle revealing no warmth or regret. "You don't know what it's like to be invisible do you Beth. We all know when you enter a room, a bit like your mate Imogen," as she looked at Max, "all eyes on you, your every word hung onto like blood limpets. Not like me, just good for a shag Sharon when there's no better option. Yet here I am, someone who's run rings round you, who actually made your squad look like the clueless bunch of tossers you all are!"

Beth was visibly shaken and upset as she looked across at the woman she had always regarded as a valued work colleague and friend.

"So Sharon," Max began, "are you sure you don't want legal representation? You do know what we're looking at I hope?"

Sighing Sharon leaned back in her chair, arms folded with a suggestion of boredom, as she waited for Max to continue. "Immediate dismissal for starters although I'm sure that comes as no surprise. Perverting the Course of Justice is pretty serious on its own but you're obviously guilty of 'Aiding and Abetting' in criminal activities as well as 'conspiring to obtain and supply information' that would enable suspects to avoid arrest, like the three men who have pleaded guilty to raping Olivia Wood. However, we're looking at a murder conviction there too Sharon, and you made sure they avoided arrest, which now makes you 'an accessory to murder after the fact'. You have also most likely committed offences against data protection too. All in all, you could be going down for life."

"Oh Christ Shaz," muttered Beth, her head in her hands, no longer angry but shocked to her core, as Max stood up to leave.

"I don't care much for Gareth's chances either so I think you're on your own, although perhaps you could plead mitigating circumstances."

"Why would I?"

"You need to start looking at self-preservation former Constable Summers. Your next few years are going to be very tough indeed because we all know what happens to corrupt cops in prison don't we?"

Walking back to his office Max was surprised to see Richard Braxton waiting for him. "Can I have a word Chief?"

"Sure. So?"

"Do you want my resignation?"

Looking completely surprised Max shook his head. "And why would I want that? What have you done?"

Looking uncomfortably embarrassed, Richard looked for the words. "I said stuff, shared bits with Shaz, sorry Sharon that I obviously shouldn't have so under the circumstances I thought you'd... well that..."

"Do you want to resign?"

"Well no but..."

Max gestured to the young officer to sit. "Sharon was a colleague, a cop. Why wouldn't you think you were safe in telling her what you'd been doing or what you'd heard especially if she was subtly probing, but perhaps it's been another lesson for us all. I don't think it has ever been harder to be in the Force as it is right now. Not just because of the criminals, I think they're the easy part, but we've got too many bad apples in the Police and the public know it too and therefore don't trust us like they used to."

"So what's the answer?"

Thinking before replying, Max said, "Those of us who are in the job for the right reasons just have to keep working with honesty and honour Richard; to serve and protect to the best of our efforts and conscience. To be the best we can be."

Looking down Richard asked, "So you want me to stay?"

"Do you want to stay?"

Nodding the young detective was earnest. "I do Sir. I really do."

"And the threats you made? About making the team pay for you not getting in the Met?"

Blushing a deep crimson, Richard looked deeply embarrassed to the point that Max felt sorry for him. "Sir. That was just... just... and also what I implied about Ms Holt Sir. I didn't know you and she were..."

"All women deserve to be treated with respect Richard and not fair game for whatever you may have in mind and you were disappointed about the Met and lashed out. Today's a new day, perhaps a new start? A new perspective on many levels? I'm prepared to give you the opportunity to show me that you're finally now understanding why we're here, doing what we do."

Standing up Richard offered his hand to Max, who standing too, took it. "Thank you Sir. You will not be sorry. I promise you."

Smiling Max replied, "I know Richard. So finally, welcome to the Serious and Organised Crimes Division."

*

"Have you thought this through? You are a shoe in when I retire Zoe, the first female Chief Constable in South Yorkshire and about time too. Why resign now!?"

Zoe Yale nodded acknowledging the enormity of what she had chosen to do. "Perhaps the job is just that Jim. A job and I've decided finally... life is more than just a job." Then smiling at the man she liked and thought of as a friend as well as a colleague she added, "I have a son Jim and I'm finally going to meet him."

Looking at his bewildered expression Zoe continued. "It's a long, sad story Jim, going back nearly twenty-five years. We met at University and I had our son when I was barely eighteen and was made to give him up by both of our families. Back then Jim, we never stood a chance for reasons I won't go into but we've also never really given each other up despite how hard we've both tried, despite our very different worlds."

"So why now?"

"Our son was taken to a place called Wollongong in Australia when he was adopted but I've always held on to the hope he'd one day get in touch and he has because… well Jim it appears I'm also a Granny now too."

"Bloody hell Zoe. Congratulations to you, but I still don't know why you feel you must resign. Christ, what a day. You will have heard about Constable Summers?"

"I have Jim and I know what it feels like when you love someone everyone else hates and basically can't understand why you feel like you do. Unlike Constable Summers though I've been given another chance."

Knowing she couldn't be completely honest Zoe tried to explain. "We want to start a new life together and away from all we've known, if not in Australia, away from here. It holds too many bad memories for us both. My partner has lost two sons already, has endured two unhappy marriages too and he needs this even more than I do. I hope you understand Jim."

Nodding sadly Jim reached into the deep drawer of his desk bringing out his favourite malt whisky and two small glass tumblers. "Well I believe this calls for a celebratory drink," as he poured them both a small measure. "To your future happiness Zoe and to your new family. I hope you find both."

Taking the offered glass Zoe replied, “Thank you Jim,” as she clinked her glass to his, sealing her fate and never being more sure that she was finally making the right decision.

CHAPTER 50

It was a cold bleak day that heralded the funeral of Brandon Cowden, the lack of mourners indicative of the life the dead man had led. Denise with her three children sat silently, stoically looking straight ahead, her husband George currently on remand, being allowed to attend albeit flanked by two prison officers. There was no eulogy, no fond recollections or memories, just a brief acknowledgement that Brandon Cowden had lived and died.

Outside of the Crematorium, Imogen approached Denise, steeling herself, unclear how her presence this day would be greeted.

"And why are you here?" the challenge and belligerence in Denise's tone evident, "making sure he's dead are you?"

"I'm sorry for your loss Mrs Cowden."

"Really?" shaking her head, the familiar sneer in place, "you hated him as much as everyone else. Kicked him out of school as soon as you could."

"He gave me no choice Mrs Cowden as you well know, but he was your son and I know you did the best you could as his mother, so I am offering you my sincerest condolences because I am truly sorry for your loss."

Blinking away her sudden tears, Denise Cowden looked away but now looking mollified whispered, "Well thank you for that because God knows I did try. I really did but... there was... there was so much anger in him. So much hate and George was less than bloody useless, always has been if I'm honest."

Imogen touched the woman's arm. "I grew up with an angry man for a father who also died a sudden and violent death too. My mother tried, I tried but... sometimes there is no reason or answers for the rage of others Mrs Cowden. I also think you've made the right decision, about moving away from here particularly after what Katie has had to deal with. We had no idea what Miss Downing was up to."

"Our Katie thought the world of her. I did to be fair."

"We all did. I still can't believe it."

Nodding Denise Cowden looked at her remaining sons and daughter. "The Cowden name is dirt round here, has been for a long while, but now well we need to start over, for the boys' sakes if no one else."

"So why Birmingham?" asked Imogen.

"My sister Diane and husband live there and we're going to stay with them until we find our feet. Bill is quite important in the Fire Service and I think he'll be good for the lads, you know, a good role model. God knows they need a good influence after... after... and well he intends to sort those two out big time. Actually he remembers you from school," as she waved him over. Imogen was now looking at the burly balding man who was making his way towards her. He looked vaguely familiar but she couldn't quite place him.

"Well Imogen Taylor. It's been a while."

Suddenly it hit her. The stance and the smile hadn't changed since Junior school. "Billy Boyle! Well I never!"

"Yep as I live and breathe. Good to see you again Imogen or should I say Ms Holt."

"Imogen will do thanks Billy. I don't believe it. How many years has it been?"

"Quite a few, but you haven't changed a bit I must say."

"I wish. So a Firefighter, in Birmingham?"

"Well somebody has to be I suppose," as he smiled at her. "I also know these lads of Denise's have been nowt but trouble, so time for some big changes. I don't think Denise could take much more if I'm honest."

Nodding her agreement Imogen smiled as she looked at the man but was now remembering the boy. Bill Boyle smiled back at her and as if reading her mind said, "I remember a little hard case trying to bully a bunch of lasses and getting sorted out good and proper behind the 'tuck' shop big time! Never been so bloody terrified

since and I've faced raging infernos!"
"Stop it!" smiling and shaking her head as she said so.
"Seriously. You had the words but your mate had some serious muscles on her. Do you still see each other?"
"Yes, still a foursome, still a force to be reckoned with, now more than ever. Beth's a police officer actually."
"Christ! I almost feel sorry for South Yorkshire's villains," as his gaze now fell on Denise and George who with their tearful children were saying their goodbyes as he was being led away. "Bad business this, to know you're responsible for your own son's death. I've never liked George, nothing more than bloody lazy chancer, but I wouldn't wish this on him although when you deal with the filth that is drugs, well, you're asking for it aren't you?"
"What do you think will happen to him?"
"Denise tells us that he's pleading guilty to a charge of 'Accidental manslaughter' so he's looking at some serious time, particularly as he's pleading to 'Possession with intent to supply' too."
"It all seems so pointless Billy, or should I call you Bill these days?"
"Naw, I'll always be Billy Boyle to you and your friends Imogen won't I? The lad who made little Sarah Green cry."
"Always Billy," smiled Imogen as she looked

with affection, at this strong good man, a once childhood nemesis, who was preparing to take on the huge task of bringing up another man's flawed and damaged teenage children. "Always and good luck," as she thought how much he was going to need it.

*

Ralph Jones looked up from his bottom bunk bed and smiled. "How do Graham lad. So for what do I owe the pleasure of a visit then?"

Graham Young standing at the open doorway of Ralph's cell smiled his affable smile. "I'm afraid it's not much of a pleasure for me today Ralph mate but a bit of a chore."

Frowning, Ralph looked confused. "What's up lad?"

Entering the room, Graham proceeded to sit on the bed opposite Ralph's. "You see Ralphie mate, you've put me in a bit of a situation."

Ralph had stopped smiling as he looked at the huge man sitting there with that affable smile still on his face. "What situation would that be then?"

"Now come on, let's not play those sorts of games, not when we've been friends of some sort. But Ralph, I can't be made a mug of can I? I have to live here too. So I've told the lads that I'll sort it but I promise you I'll make it quick okay because I have enjoyed your company. I mean we've had some laughs haven't we? Some good 'crack'."

Swallowing hard Ralph nodded. “I take it this is about Wallace Senior being put back in the Segregation Wing then?”

“Aye afraid so mate and there’s only one way, certain information got to your old mates and I do feel a bit let down I have to say.”

Silence crackled around the cell, an atmosphere of dread a live presence as Ralph replied, “Well, once a cop always a cop Graham lad. I just wish I’d thought of that a lot sooner, before I landed myself in here.”

Ralph looking towards the open door, contemplated what he should do in the next few moments, moments that would mean the difference between life and death, survival or oblivion. Ralph made his choice.

Smiling sadly, Ralph looked at the man who would now end his life, a life he had thrown away for all the wrong reasons. “I’m glad it’s you Graham and you know… I’m glad… I’m actually glad it’s all done with now.”

Nodding and still smiling Graham stood and opened his arms, the life ending shiv in his right hand, waiting to be used. Ralph stood and walked towards the deadly embrace as Graham wrapped his arms around him as if they were lovers. They stood for moments like this, giving each other comfort until Graham using his expertise quickly and efficiently ended the life of former Deputy Chief Constable Ralph Jones. As Ralph slid soundlessly to the ground, Graham smiled his final affable smile to the now dead man. “Nice knowing you Ralphie mate. Pity you were such a low-life fucking grass at the end of the day.”

CHAPTER 51

The dogs barking alerted Sarah to the fact she had a visitor and was delighted to see the tall male outline that could only signify that Trey was standing outside, waiting for her to open her front door. Scooby and Cyril were dancing their dance, yelping with excitement as Sarah made her way to let him in.

"I know, I know you two, I'm happy he's back too," as she opened her door, her smile warm, her arms outstretched to greet the young man she now regarded as a dear friend.

"Trey how wonderful..." her words now trailing off into silence as Trey stepped to one side to reveal he wasn't alone.

Sarah now stunned just looked, barely believing what her eyes were telling her to believe. For standing there, flanked by Daz and Bud, using sticks that enabled him to stand unaided was John. Her John. The man she had loved since she'd been a child of seventeen and the father of her unborn child. The man she had lost once but found again and had feared she had lost again, but this time forever.

Her knees began to buckle making Trey lurch forward to hold her up as she looked on at the love of her life, taking in how changed he looked. In just mere seconds she registered how his granite build had been replaced with a gauntness that suggested he had spent months in pain, months without sustenance. Moving towards him she touched his face, tracing the scar on his cheek, as he dropped one stick to hold her as she put her arms round him, tears streaming down her face.

"Hello my Sarah, sorry I've been so long getting back to you, getting back to you both," as his hand touched her ever growing abdomen that was housing their child.

Turning to the three friends Sarah said, "You never gave up. Thank you."

*

The package leaning on Harry's front porch was huge, the postman relaying in detail the difficulty he had endured getting it undamaged into his van, not to mention getting it out again.

"Well it should be in one piece Mrs Wood, but it weighs a ton and it really hasn't done my back much good if I was to be brutally honest. I suppose you want help getting it inside then?"

"If it's not too much trouble but what about your back?"

"Of course it's not too much trouble and I'll just have to be careful," although this was clearly not the case as he looked with concern at the offending package again, then taking a deep breath took up one end as Harry took the other, as they eventually manoeuvred the parcel into the hallway.

"Wow, but I can see what you mean," breathed Harry.

"Well whatever it is enjoy it," as the postman took his leave, his hands massaging his back, his demeanour very grateful to be rid of it.

Harry looked to see who may have sent it and to her surprise found a post mark from Nice, in the South of France. Harry was now desperately trying to still the butterflies now evident in her stomach, chiding herself for reacting like a foolish teenager. Christopher hadn't been far from her thoughts since their initial meeting and now, the idea he was somehow in touch with her via whatever this was, was both thrilling and terrifying.

Ripping the paper from the parcel revealed a cardboard casing, then bubble wrap. What lay beneath the bubble wrap? For Harry, there were no words to describe its significance for her.

*

Sarah was still pinching herself. John was here, home and alive. She'd learned how on the Paraguay, Argentine border, they had been ordered to rescue a captive aid worker who had been snatched by a faction belonging to Hezbollah, who had been active in the area for decades, capitalising on the large Lebanese and Shiite diaspora communities there and who secreted funds raised from that region, back into Lebanon. Such a fact many didn't know or would understand, such was international politics these days. After John had fallen into the precipice he had laid undetected for a long time until he was found by mere accident by local farmers.

"I honestly thought my time was up," explained John, "it seemed forever. I couldn't move and then suddenly, they were there. These farm workers just appeared and took me back to their village and looked after me, nursed me back from the brink. It was risky for them too and they knew it but... well they just kept me hidden until I was strong enough to be moved."

"Thank Christ they did," muttered Daz as they all nodded their agreement.

"I want to get money to them when I can," said John, "ask back at the base how I can do it will you lads?"

"They can have everything we have," stated Sarah, "it's priceless what they've given back to us," as she indicated her growing abdomen.

"You wouldn't believe how little they have or want, but their generosity and kindness have been beyond anything I could have imagined."

"Brave too," interjected Bud, "because the drug cartels in that area would have been very pissed off if they'd found you, a British Army officer and

Special Forces to boot."
"Well it's what I've always believed," offered a tearful Sarah, "that most people are basically good."
"Until they're not!" said Trey.
Bud nudged him hard saying, "Don't go spoiling this beautiful moment, I mean, I'm actually tearing up here!"
"Yeah right!" laughed Daz.
Smiling at their banter Sarah began to organise. "So, I need to get the bedding sorted... "Actually," said Trey, "we're going to stay in the local B&B, to give you two time alone Sarah."
"No... you don't have..."
"Yes we do," said Daz, "but bacon butties for brekkie would be great?"
As the three took their leave John called out, "Trey?"
"Yes Sarge?"
"Thanks Trey. Thanks for looking after my family, for being here."
Trey merely nodded, giving nothing away, as he turned to join his friends with both Sarah and John watched his retreating figure.
"He's been my rock John." John nodded remaining silent.
Finally, alone after months of anguish for Sarah and pain and despair for John, Sarah curled herself up next to him, gently stroking his hair, instinctively knowing how weakened he was, how very much diminished from when they

were last together.

As if reading her mind, John began. "I've still got a long way back to full fitness love but I will get there eventually. I know I won't be what I was and that active duty is now over for me but I still have a living to earn and I..."

"We already have more than enough money and I thank the heavens that your active duty days are behind you. I, no we, couldn't bear it if you went away again...."

John held up his hand as he laughed saying, "Your dad is now turning in his grave! He always suspected I only wanted you for his money!"

"Let him. You're back and you're safe but I always knew you'd return to me."

"Whilst I have breath in my body, nothing would keep me from coming back to you, to you both."

*

The Trans Pennine Trail was bathed in winter sunshine and the frost on the trees shimmered and sparkled making the 'cheesy' term a winter wonderland come to mind. Imogen and Arlette loved the Trail and made time to walk it together as often as Imogen's job allowed which currently had been very little.

Now arm in arm with her daughter, Arlette sighed happily saying, "It really doesn't get much better than this for me. The sun is shining, the birds are singing and I have my girl here spending quality time with her mother. Yes, for me this is what life should be about, family and sunshine."

"In Penton, sunshine is often missing in action," laughed Imogen.

"Which is why it's so special when it arrives unexpectedly," then looking at her daughter added, "and it's good to see you smile my love. You've had a worrying time of it lately, what with one thing or another."

"I know mum and I also know I've neglected you of late too."

"Nonsense, you've had enough to think about without worrying about me and I know how hard you take things. What that awful woman did and was trying to do was... well, beyond anything you could possibly imagine, not even in your worst nightmares. I mean to hurt children, and vulnerable ones at that is just beyond any understanding. I don't know love but the older I get the less I understand where human nature is involved."

Imogen nodded but didn't respond as her mother studied her profile, seeing the worry, the tension. "Is there anything else I need to worry about? I'm your mother and it's my job?"

Smiling and shaking her head Imogen attempted to put her mother's mind at ease. "No mum, honestly, I'm fine. How can I not be with a man like Max in my life?"

Beaming her delight Arlette replied, "I could not be happier. I knew as soon as I met him that he was special enough for you. Just knew it!"

"But I'll never truly forget Neil though mum and the grandchildren I could have given you."

Nodding her understanding Arlette squeezed her arm. "I know that love but I can die a happy woman knowing you have such a man as Max in your life."

"Which will be years from now mum, I mean look at you? You're only just in your prime."

Looking ahead and seeing the beauty that was surrounding them Arlette didn't initially respond. "Mum? You are okay aren't you?"

Batting away her daughter's concern Arlette deftly changed the subject. "Of course I am. How could I not be with Terry and lovely little Lola to keep me young? You know I couldn't love that little one more and this Christmas is going to be a Christmas to remember too, because I have plans my daughter."

"Should I be worried?" laughed Imogen as she now tried to ignore the feeling her mum was keeping something from her.

"No, because we all know you worry far too much about everyone and everything. Let's live and enjoy the here and now Imogen because I intend to do just that from now on. Let's both agree to make every day a day to remember from now on! What do you say?"

*

"Wow mum, but ...well wow," declared Olivia as she stared at the painting which had arrived earlier that day before asking, "when did you sit

for him?"
Her eyes not leaving the painting which was in fact a portrait of someone who looked remarkably like her, Harry shook her head. "I didn't."
"So he must have done this from memory then and I think it's beautiful mum."
"I think if it's supposed to be me then it's very flattering."
"Or how he sees you."
Harry knew she was blushing furiously and couldn't look at her daughter. Instead she busied herself with practicalities. "Well it weighs a ton and it can't stay here in the hall way, not when those two tearaways get home which will be any minute now."
As if on cue, the door flung open announcing the twins' arrival from school with Alan following closely behind.
"Mum, you'll never guess what Josie Denton has said we've done this time! Oh... what's that? Is that you mum?" asked Will, wide eyed with surprise.
"Crikey!" said Jasper, his eyes also wide with wonder.
"A gift for mum, all the way from France actually. Hi dad," said Olivia pointedly at her father, "beautiful isn't it, just like mum. I mean the likeness is fantastic don't you think?"
Alan looking at the portrait, was clearly speechless. Harry feeling exposed and

uncomfortable, was unable to look at her estranged husband but instead turned to her boys. “Right you two, we need help in moving this because it weighs a ton.”

“Where do you want it moving?” asked Alan.

“Well it needs to be out of the way so ...”

“Mum, it’s just too beautiful to be hidden away. I mean Christopher’s art hangs next to Picasso’s so we have to display it where everyone can see it. Don’t you agree dad?”

Olivia was clearly enjoying her parents’ mutual discomfort as only teenage girls can. “Personally, I think over the fireplace in the lounge for all to see and admire!”

Alan turned to his daughter and said, “I believe I have never met this Christopher person Olivia but he’s clearly very talented.”

“Well that’s your loss isn’t it daddy dearest?” Olivia’s tone was disparaging, her anger and resentment at her father leaving them in the circumstances he had, never far from the surface.

“The study, at least for the time being,” said Harry hurriedly, attempting to diffuse what could be an unpleasant scene, particularly if Olivia had her way, “and Alan, thanks for picking up the boys but we’ve got it from here.”

Nodding Alan moved to leave, just as his eyes fell on the note Harry had left on the side board, the note that had arrived with the painting earlier that day:

To a beautiful soul.
Where's there's life there's hope,
Where there's hope, there's love,
Where there's love, there's peace.
C.

Alan picked up the note and read it several times before looking back at Harry.

"I believe that's for me Alan and for me alone." Harry's quietly spoken words were without anger but Alan heard the subtext and understood its message. Nodding, he replaced the note and without another word walked out.

"Is dad ok mum?" asked Jasper, his expression one of worry, one he had worn each day since Alan had left and it broke Harry's heart every time she looked at him.

"Who cares if he isn't," muttered Olivia.

"He'll be fine love. Now come on everyone, let's get this moved and out of the way."

CHAPTER 52

No one at Sheffield Central Police was surprised to learn that Max was to receive The King's Police Medal, the first given by the new King for services to policing and The King's Gallantry Medal, awarded for exemplary acts of bravery. No one except for Max of course. However, it was 'The Pride of Britain' nomination that had given Jim Haggerty the greatest pleasure. "You're actually going to meet that gorgeous Carol Vorderman. You're a lucky bugger!"

"I am more than happy for you to take my place Sir," was Max's reaction, "I'm probably washing my hair that day!"

Shaking his head, his expression one of total bemusement Jim Haggerty asked, "Why can't you enjoy the accolades Max? After what you were prepared to do for that young lad deserves all this attention."

"There are real acts of constant bravery and sacrifice every day and there's always a war somewhere, places that the news stations don't even bother reporting about," as he was remembering John's return and how heroic and

brave total strangers had been, a continent away, to get him back to those who loved him. “I just think it’s time we all moved on that’s all and I’ve got more things to worry about if I’m honest.”
“Any more intelligence on what or who may be coming for you?”
“No. Not yet.”
“We’ll be on alert until the bastards are found and put away, you can be sure of that Max.”
Nodding Max got up to leave as smiling Jim Haggerty asked, “So have you heard about the latest sweepstake that the techies are running?”
Seeing Max’s look of confusion, Jim was now enjoying himself. “They’re taking bets on who will be playing you in the film? I’ve put my money on Brad Pitt.”
Max’s following expletives only made the Chief Constable guffaw out loud adding, “I’ll pretend I didn’t hear that Detective Chief Superintendent and give my regards to the King when you see him tomorrow.”

*

The pomp and circumstance of Buckingham Palace was something Imogen knew she would remember forever and not just because of the main reason they were there.
As they walked towards the ballroom where Max would receive his dual awards, she was very much aware how his every move was watched and followed by those in attendance. It made her both proud and afraid, keenly alerted to the fact

that he was still a marked man. Today was not the day for such thoughts though as he steered her to a quiet corner away from the main hub of activity.

"So before we meet mum and dad..."

"And you meet the King," smiled Imogen.

"Which is the easy part because... because there's something I need to ask you first," as he took the small ring box from out of his pocket. Imogen gasped, as he opened the box to reveal a platinum and diamond trilogy ring.

"I've chosen this ring because we have our past and let's be honest, it's not been an easy time for either of us has it? I sometimes think our getting to this point has been nothing short of miraculous but we're here and living our present and I feel two people couldn't feel closer than how we do and I never thought I'd find that with anyone, doing what I do, seeing what I see." Max now taking a deep breath continued, "And I want us, more than anything, to always share our futures together too, well... until death us do part. So? Will you?"

Imogen saw the pure honesty in his eyes and felt the slight tremble in his hands as he spoke words she would remember until the day she died.

"I will Max, I will," as he slid the ring onto the third finger of her left hand. "It's a perfect fit," she whispered, looking at the diamond ring he had chosen and the significance behind his choice.

"Like us, no matter what or who comes for us," as they now held each other. Smiling, and standing straighter as if pulling himself together Max asked, "So are you ready to meet my parents as my fiancé? Oh and I have to give Fiz a call too and tell him the good news."

"Fiz as in Faisel? My Year Eight Faisel?" asked a bewildered Imogen, thinking could this day get any more wonderfully surreal.

"Yes, well he told me to get a move on, to 'put a ring on it' were his actual words."

Laughing, Imogen acknowledged, "We really couldn't love that kid more could we?"

"No I don't believe we could. Come on, let me introduce you to your new family and remember my mother lives four hundred miles away from us, can't drive and doesn't trust the trains."

*

Sharon's time on remand was obviously taking its toll on her as she sat opposite Beth. She had dark circles under her eyes, her hair was lank, her complexion grey and she had lost weight too. Facing Beth, Sharon silently waited to learn why she was in an interview room as she had made it clear, she had nothing to say.

"Well I don't have to ask how you're doing Shaz because I can see that for myself."

Sharon merely shrugged, still remaining silent, keeping eye contact with her former partner as she waited.

Filling the silence Beth began. "Well I suppose

you're wondering why we're here?"

Sharon still did not respond and at this point Beth was questioning her own intentions in arranging this meeting, but there was no turning back now.

"There's no easy way to tell you this but we've recently found the remains of someone we believe to be Gareth Jackson. I thought you should know."

Sharon now blinked and looked away before saying, "You're sure it's him?"

"Dental records are conclusive as you know, so yes we're sure."

"Unrecognisable then was he?" her face still devoid of any emotion, her voice flat.

"I'm not going into the details and I suggest you don't dwell on them either, that way madness surely lies."

Laughing without humour Sharon almost snarled at Beth. "Don't give me that. Don't pretend you're not enjoying this."

"Why the bloody hell would I? You were my friend and work mate and I trusted you. You would have been the last person I would have suspected Shaz. I have been betrayed before, but this? This takes it to a whole new level."

Suitably chastised Sharon now sat back into the chair. "So is that all? Can I go now?"

Reaching into her pocket Beth produced a ring box which she placed on the table. Sharon just stared at it, wondering and fearing what it would reveal. It could possibly give her answers to questions she would always have but could also indicate what she may have also lost too.

“This was found on his body and I believe it may have been for you.”

“Why?”

“Don’t know. It’s just you wouldn’t have thrown the job away for someone you weren’t serious about would you?”

Sharon remained silently transfixed, staring at the tiny square then asked “Is it a ruby and diamond engagement ring?”

“Yes it is actually, so it is yours.”

Beth would describe the next few moments as if watching someone internally deflate, like one of those blown up Santa balloons when the air is released. Sharon appeared as if all the air had been taken out of her body as she collapsed on to the table, her sobs echoing around the grey square windowless box. Beth let her cry, for long minutes until Sharon eventually looked up, wiped the snot from her nose onto her sleeve and began to speak.

“He asked me ages ago what my favourite gem stone was. I said I loved rubies as it’s my birthstone and diamonds of course because every girl loves a diamond right? I even pointed a ring out in Earnest Jones window. Nothing like dropping hints eh?”

“The ring is from Earnest Jones or at least the box is. Take a look?”

Sharon reached for the box, opened it then crumpled again saying, "I can't believe he actually went back for it, that he remembered that was the one I wanted. The sort of ring I dreamed someone would one day give me because they thought I was good enough, special enough."

Beth stood up to leave, indicating to the prison officer present that the meeting was over.

"I've arranged that you be able to keep it, if not yet, but eventually."

Looking confused Sharon asked, "Why? Why would you do that for me?"

Beth merely shrugged. "Your life is effectively over for a good few years Shaz so why not? And..."

"And what?"

Nailing her former friend and colleague with a look that conveyed, hurt, disappointment and disgust, Beth replied, "Perhaps every time you look at it you'll remember what it cost you Sharon. What it's cost others too who are either maimed or dead because of your greed and corruption and the fact you chose a man who had no moral compass on any level. What it's cost the Force and the people who trusted you. Perhaps you'll remember and perhaps you'll realise what a bloody fool you've been and you know? I want you think and feel that every day for the rest of your sad and sorry life."

*

Jim Haggerty placed his pint on the table and sat down. Philip Read looked up from his reverie and nodded his hello to his former colleague and commander. “How do Jim.”
“Phil. Did you go?”
“Found myself standing outside the Crem but I didn’t go in. Saw his wife and son arrive with the hearse but nobody else attended, none of his daughters or grandkids and certainly no one from the job.”
The two men sat in a companionable silence for a while, drinking their drinks whilst
thinking their thoughts until Jim, breaking the silence said, “You know, but it seems somehow fitting that Ralph’s funeral is the same day Max Stainmore is honoured by the King. I don’t know why but it does.”
Phil shrugged, then asked, “Do we know who did for him?”
Shaking his head Jim replied, “No and we probably never will either but...”
“What?”
“At least he died a copper in the end, don’t you think Phil? He wasn’t always a bad apple.”
Phil drank the remains of his pint as he stood up. “With respect Jim, I’m just glad the bastard is dead and went the same way as my lad did, alone and lying on a dirty prison cell floor. Now that’s what I call fitting.”

CHAPTER 53

Winter had come to Yorkshire with a vengeance. There had been a heavy snow fall across the whole region, bringing with it, it's customary chaos. The Victoria Quayside footpath was as treacherous as sheet ice, the railings so cold it burned if touched. Dusk was falling, Christmas lights evident in the distance and early evening revellers were keeping warm in the Dorothy Pax and other Waterside venues.

Max sensed his presence before his shadow loomed over him, followed by the unmistakable overpowering scent of his aftershave. Malcolm Speight certainly never did anything in half measures. Both men did not acknowledge each other, finding the water below something easier to focus on. Max was the first to break the silence.

"Thanks for agreeing to meet me."

"Let's dispense with the niceties as I'm a very busy man. So what do you want?"

Max began to explain, knowing the effect his next words would have on this hardened man, a man he wished he didn't need, but need he did.

"Someone is coming for me, has been for a while.

They're powerful and organised."
"So do they want someone to hold their coat?" the humour and disdain evident in the other man's response.
"I'm aware that would be something you'd happily be up for but they're coming for Imogen too. Have already got her in their gun sites."
Malcolm was silent, taking in this information.
"So the bomb was meant to harm her then, not just a random attack?"
"Yeah, put there by the same bastard who shot me in Penton. It would appear that harming Imogen will hurt me far more than a couple of bullets and they're not wrong which is the reason I asked to meet."
Malcolm now nodded his understanding as both men fell silent, looking down at the rippling water, both lost in their own worries and thoughts. "They'll have to get through me to get to her, you do know that don't you?"
Max nodded. "And this changes nothing between us. Don't think for one..."
"I'm not doing it for you!" interrupted Malcolm, his voice raising, his anger barely in check.
"Unbeknownst to her, she's been under my protection since her husband stood up to those bastards you work with, who went on to make his life a bloody misery, I might add, and then he went and bloody died on her."
Malcolm shook his head as the memories came flooding back. "I saw her at the sentencing of

those who did for him. She was so frail, so damaged, so dignified, so... I'm rubbish with words... perhaps there aren't words to describe someone so beautiful and not just to look at either because for me her looks are the least of her. I offered to have them sorted whilst they were inside, but she would have none of it. So if anyone is coming for her, then they've got to deal with me and I will die fucking trying, before I let that happen! Right!?"

"She's also agreed to marry me. Thought you should know that too."

Chuckling, Malcolm turned from leaning on the freezing rails to look Max squarely in the eye. "Of course she fucking has, I mean why wouldn't she? And if protecting her means saving your handsome sorry arse as well, then so bloody be it. Give me your phone!"

As Max handed over his device in order for Malcolm to put in his private contact, Max finally understood what Imogen and Eddie had always understood where this man was concerned, despite him being everything he hated. Imogen would be safer with Malcolm and his people on alert and Max actually felt he could breathe easier just knowing this.

Handing back his phone Malcolm merely uttered, "So anything else?"

Max shook his head remaining silent.

"Right then," as both men turned and walked in their opposite directions without another word and without looking back.

*

Alan sat nervously nursing his glass of red wine as he waited for Harry to join him. He'd booked a table at the local Italian, Harry's favourite Penton restaurant. She had been surprised when he'd suggested it but had agreed so as far as he was concerned, that was the first hurdle cleared.

He saw her arrive, with her customary smile as Matteo the owner went over to greet her, kissing her on both cheeks as he took her coat, before leading her to where he was waiting. Alan realised he was sweating, was nervous as he watched her approach. Something had changed in Harry since her return from France and that stunning portrait and cryptic note held the key to that change. The unfamiliar sensation of pure unadulterated jealousy had hit him like a hammer blow and he just couldn't bear the thought of his Harry having another man in her life.

As she approached he stood up and knocked over the wine he had been drinking. "Oh bloody hell. Sorry Matteo, I'm so clumsy."

"Not a problem Dr Wood," gushed Matteo, smiling but swearing silently as his waitresses changed the cloth and cutlery.

Harry sat and smiled her thanks before she turned her attention to her estranged husband.

"So Alan, this is a surprise."

"A nice one I hope?"

"I'll let you know," as she began to scrutinise the menu.

"You know you'll be having the lobster ravioli because you always do and with the scallops to start with."

"I know, I'm just a creature of habit."

"And my creature of habit," he blurted out, before he could stop the words. Harry looked up from the menu, looking both surprised and confused.

"I haven't been your anything since... So what is this about Alan? Why are we here?"

Alan looked down, afraid she'd see his desperation because that was how he felt, desperate and lonely, wanting his life back more than anything else.

"I guess I'm trying to tell you that I want to come home Harry. That I miss our children, our life and most of all, I miss you."

"Even after what I did?"

Alan remained silent, merely looking at her just as Matteo came over to take their orders.

"Could you leave us a minute mate?" asked Alan before turning his attention back to his estranged wife. "I don't know if I'll ever understand what you did but I want to try and I'm asking you, no I'm pleading with you, to let me come home please Harry."

"I never wanted you to leave."

"I know."

"So what's changed?"

Alan remained silent at this, unable to speak

what he felt, knowing how childish and selfish it could sound to her. “Is it the fact another man has shown me attention Alan? Seen something in me you haven’t for the longest time, that is if you ever did?”

Alan ignored her inference, instead saying, “Our life was perfect before... before...”

“On the surface but it wasn’t strong was it? When it mattered, when we should have been there for not only Olivia but for each other, we just weren’t Alan.”

“You mean I wasn’t Harry. I was weak and selfish in your eyes and probably still am aren’t I?”

Shaking her head and looking sadder than he’d ever seen her, Harry answered honestly. “I don’t know Alan. I honestly don’t know anymore but...”

“But?”

“We also can’t just throw away nearly twenty years either so... if you want to come home then I think you should. Jasper is desperately unhappy at the moment but Olivia is furious with you and it will depend on her okay?”

Nodding, then reaching for her hand and with tears in his eyes he said, “I’ll take that Harry and I promise you, we will make us work again. We can have our lives back, but better than ever.”

Squeezing his hand and smiling when he ordered champagne, Harry knew with certainty, that life would never be the same for them again.

The portrait sitting in the study was testament

to that.

*

The four were sitting in their usual spot in their favourite wine bar and were celebrating. Harry and Alan were trying to sort out their marriage, Max had proposed and John had returned to Sarah. Imogen's news that Billy Boyle was now one of the nation's unsung heroes had also caused immense consternation. "Bloody bully boy Billy Boyle is a bloody hero! Actually runs into burning buildings and rescues cats from trees! Who would have thought that was in the stars!" Sarah had declared.

All in all, and for once in the longest time, life felt good, lucky even and with the exception of Sarah, for obvious reasons, the girls felt it was time for tequila shots which were now lined up.

"That must be three carats all day long," declared Harry as she admired Imogen's engagement ring, "platinum too. It's just perfect Gen."

"About bloody time too," laughed Beth, "I mean are we looking at a double wedding very soon?"

"Well we won't be getting married for a while what with John's mobility and I think I'd rather wait until the baby is here too now. You know so he or she could be my flower girl or page boy, that is if we bother with all the fuss, I mean I've had all that once before and look how that turned out! What about you Gen? Another big wedding?"

Smiling at her friends Imogen simply said, "I'm

enjoying living in the moment for once, so my friends let's toast today and let tomorrow take care of itself. Today is a good day!"

"To today," they all echoed before taking their shot, wincing on the lime and salt as they did the required routine.

Imogen looked at her friends and for a moment, couldn't believe how life was turning out although her friends weren't aware of the possible threat hanging over both herself and Max and she really was starting to believe that living in the moment was how she now wanted to live. Life could change in an instant no matter what precautions were taken and the future would be what the future would be and that was all there was to it.

Beth looked slyly at Harry, mischief written all over her face and Harry knew what was coming next. "So Harry, about the portrait?"

"Yes," gushed Sarah, "the stunningly beautiful portrait!"

"And the one I need to return because it's ... it's just too much and I think it makes Alan uneasy."

"Why haven't we heard about this Christopher then?" asked Sarah.

Looking surprised Harry began. "So how? Ah Olivia I take it."

Sarah now reached for her phone, "Yes and I have photographic evidence of this Christopher, artist person. Olivia forwarded it to me," as the other two friends edged closer to have a look.

"Oh but you're a dark horse Harriet Wood!" declared Beth, "Patrick Dempsey eat your heart out."

"I was thinking more Hugh Jackman," added Sarah, "and he's seriously easy on the eye."

"I take it Alan has seen the portrait and hot footed it home big time," laughed Imogen, "I mean Harry, he's seriously handsome as well as talented if that painting is anything to go by. No wonder Alan wants rid of a reminder."

"Did you get to sample any of his other 'talents'?" asked Beth, the glint of mischief still in her eyes.

Shrugging and ignoring Beth's inference, Harry was enigmatic. "I can't think what other 'talents' you could be referring to Bethany, but...he's a special man in many ways and I'm grateful we met him and his son Zac. I honestly think he's what I needed, who I was meant to meet. Does that make sense?"

The atmosphere had changed as the friends looked at each other, smiles now gone, as memories of recent events came back into their collective focus. "I'm also aware he wouldn't have painted me as he did or indeed if at all, if he knew what I'd done, what I was capable of doing, who perhaps I truly am. Looking back, I can't believe I did what I did either. Almost like an 'out of body' experience, although I'm not trying to make excuses."

"Would you do it again?" asked a now very serious Beth.

"Honestly? I don't know Beth. I honestly don't know. I felt such rage that I could barely breathe for wanting to hurt them, for wanting to make them pay. Olivia is forever changed, will never forget the brutality and I'm still angry that it happened to her, that is happens to any young woman. But do I regret it? My actions? Every minute of every single day."

They all sat silently, all lost in their own thoughts, own past actions and for some of them, their own sense of guilt.

Beth was the first to speak. "Well it turns out they were murdering racist bastards too so..."

"It doesn't make it right though does it?" asked Imogen, "and living with it will be hard for a long time Harry. Trust me."

"I live every day waiting for the knock on the door, knowing the police could come to arrest me at any moment Imogen."

"And that's punishment in itself," said Sarah, "got that T-shirt."

"However," declared Beth, "I do see every day, how good people can be driven to do unspeakable actions. It's being human and Harry, you are one of a group of women who are human and flawed, beautiful and brave but whom I wouldn't want to live a single day without each one of you in it."

"And this Christopher person saw the real you Harry," added Imogen, "because you are a beautiful soul despite what happened, what you were driven to do."

"What we've all been driven to do," whispered Sarah, "I mean," looking around the bar, "if only people knew what each one of us has done, with the exception of you Beth of course. I mean if our lives were in a soap opera, viewers would say it was all too farfetched and switch off!"

Beth closed her eyes, the weight of her guilt never far from the surface as she looked at sweet Sarah, the one true innocent amongst them all.

Reading her mind Imogen added, "Well at least we can all plead temporary insanity not that it will come to that. The Devil is no longer owed my friends so our next toast is to...? Any suggestions?"

"To life," said Beth, "to all that life has thrown at us and for telling the Devil to go and get stuffed!"

Downing the tequila shots, the friends looked at each other, each thinking her own thoughts, remembering what they had each endured and what they had collectively overcome.

"So," began Beth, "this Christmas is going to be epic because for once we are all in a really good place, although if I was Alan, I'd not let you near the electric knife to carve the turkey Harry. You know just in case." Looking at the scandalised faces of the others she then added, "What? Too soon?" as they all, as if as one, put their shaking heads in their hands, before throwing the table beer mats at her, their grimaces turning to grins at the sheer audacity of the remark that only true friends would be able to share.

EPILOGUE

The stark, white, clinical room, with its smell of antiseptic and its subtle scent of worry and fear made Beth feel unusually exposed. Scrutinising the medic who was busy looking at a computer screen, she wondered how old he was, not that it mattered. He was very good at his job and was actually called a Mr, not a Dr so that in itself spoke volumes about his acumen and ability. He finally looked at her and smiled. She knew that smile. She'd seen that smile before. The smile said it all.

"Beth..."

"Just tell me and quit with the smile already. I know why I'm here, you know why I'm here so... let's hear it."

Nodding Mr Prendergast looked down, clasped his hands and asked, "Why do the Police have Confidential Informants Beth?"

"To gain intelligence. What the bloody hell does CHIS's have to do with..."

"You never came to be tested for the BRCA gene after your mum, even though you were advised to do so. I wish you had Beth. I truly wish you'd let us gain 'intelligence' about your cancer status because intervention is so much better than the alternative. We're now dealing with the alternative." Beth had stopped listening, could only hear her own heart loudly beating and all she could think of at that moment, was her baby, her little girl, her Lola.

"I'm sorry Beth. I know this is a lot to take in and..." his voice fading as her own thoughts echoed the loudest in the sterile, unforgiving room.

"Beth?"

"You know my Nan had a saying about the ones who go unpunished, the ones who do harm but seem to get away with it. "God does not pay debts with money," she'd say. I suppose we call it Karma don't we?"

"Cancer is a cruel, insidious disease not a punishment Beth and no one deserves it in their lives, least of all someone like you. Someone who spends her life serving and protecting others."

Smiling sadly at the good man before her and knowing that his assumptions about her had not always been the case, Beth got up to leave. As she reached the door she turned to look back to the kind and now unsmiling medic, her parting words being, "So it looks like the bloody Devil still feels owed then doesn't it? And the payment is overdue."

ACKNOWLEDGEMENT

May I first thank each and every one of you who bought my debut novel 'When Evil Walks Amongst Us' and the fantastic reviews and feedback many of you took the time to give me personally or on Amazon. I'm now nervously praying that this sequel has lived up to your expectations and that after reading this, you're looking forward to Book 3 in this Penton series. Again, a review on Amazon would help me greatly.

Of course none of this would be possible without my wonderful publishing friends that constitute WandS. Phil Sokell and Graham Saunders will go down in history as the most generous of chocoholics, with their time, expertise, patience and commitment. Absolute saints particularly putting up with me as they do and without complaint.

I have many to personally thank too. Ian Harding for his police expertise and insights and to my son Tom Yates. I'm amazed how informed you are in terms of International Politics allowing me a plausible explanation within my story's plot line. I had a proud mum moment there. Milly Johnson, for your constant, generous support and 'shout outs' in 'The Barnsley Chronicle', the lovely Karen Close at 'All is Good' for allowing her wonderful shop as a local outlet for sales and book signings and to Andy Pollard of Barnsley Libraries for the opportunity to speak to audiences about this new, exciting and sometimes terrifying journey I'm currently on. Also to the people of Penistone who have shown me so much support, loving the fact I've written loosely about where we live and I love where we live.

However, I want a huge shout out to those wonderful, disparate groups of women I have the privilege of being part of, who have shown me so much love and support in recent months including my daughter-in-law Steph and her friends and to former colleagues and pupils of many yesteryears who have shown up and supported me. It's all been rather wonderful and completely surprising.

Finally, to my Nick, for always being my Super Hero every day, for his love and never ending patience and understanding. Rumour has it, I can be a bit of a Diva sometimes!!!

So on to Book three.

Love, hugs and best wishes to each and everyone one of you,

Chrissie Yates x.

ABOUT THE AUTHOR

Chrissie Yates

Chrissie Yates is a happily retired English teacher/ Assistant Principal living in the beautiful market town of Penistone, South Yorkshire. She is the founder of Penistone Arts Week as she feels passionately about the creative arts and its importance to the well-being of all. When she's not writing or looking after her granddaughters, she likes to travel, tap dance and is world class at shopping.

COMING SOON

'WHEN THE DEVIL IS PAID'.

The third book in the Penton Series.

Find me on Facebook – Chrissie Yates Author

Printed in Great Britain
by Amazon

37061574R00245